TO THE FEARLESS O

NOS NUMQUAM IMM

VOLUNTATEN .

HOPE YOU ENJOY !

MINOLOGY

First Published in Great Britain 2014 by Netherworld Books an imprint of Mirador Publishing

First edition: 2014

Any reference to real names and places are purely fictional and are constructs of the author. Any offence the references produce is unintentional and in no way reflects the reality of any locations or people involved.

A copy of this work is available through the British Library.

ISBN : 978-1-910105-11-5

Netherworld Books
Mirador
Wearne Lane
Langport
Somerset
TA10 9HB

Minology

By

Mark Murphy

Netherworld Books

Chapter One

Introduction to 'The Min'

Have you ever wondered what makes you click? What makes you tick? How do you walk, talk, run or breathe? How do you eat, drink, sleep or think? How do you feel, seem, need or dream? What makes you get up in the morning? You? Your wife? Your mother? Your life? Or is it just your alarm clock?

Ok, let's say it's your alarm clock. You set it before you go to sleep and it goes off the next morning.

'Brriiinnggg!'

7.30 a.m. sharp, you're awake. You reach out, turn it off and get up. You get washed, dressed, have your breakfast and leave. You go about your daily business and that's it. You don't really think about how or why you heard the alarm clock, you just heard it. It's simple biology, right?

Your ear picks up the sound frequency, sends a message to your brain, your brain tells you it is a sound, in this case an alarm clock, and you hear it, right?

Wrong!

Well your ears do hear the sound of the alarm clock, there's no question of that, and the message does get sent to your brain, everyone knows that. Otherwise, how would your brain know? But what actually sends the message, your ears? Those little two inch lumps of flesh stuck to either side of your head? Can an ear actually send anything anywhere? I'm sure if you cut your ear off, gave it a pound and sent it down to the shop for a loaf of bread, then you'd be waiting a long time for your supper tonight!

There are a lot of things in this world today we don't understand but simply put them down to an -ology. When some whiz-kid somewhere invents a super car which doesn't need fuel, doesn't need oil or water but will go from 0-100 mph in less than a second, and comes in every colour as long as it's black, then we just put it down to technology.

When a leading scientist invents a human-like robot that will do all of our housework for us, make a pot of tea every morning and routinely mow the lawn on a Sunday afternoon whilst we lay snoozing in front of the telly, then we put it down to homology. Although some would put it down to being downright lazy.

When a top professor discovers the reasons why a hardworking, loving and dedicated family man turns his back on his life to run off with the neighbour's wife to live the rest of their lives in Tahiti, it's put down to psychology.

Even when a man wakes up for work one morning with a blinding headache and is violently sick all over his wife's new furry slippers, with the fluffy lions faces on the front, at the side of the bed, then it is simply put down to biology. Although his workmates will tell you that it might have had something to do with the twelve pints of lager and the prawn vindaloo that he'd had the night before.

In short, most of us don't even try to understand how things work, especially the human body. But what none of us realise is that the thing which sends the message from the ear to the brain, the thing which makes us hear the alarm clock, the thing which actually drags us kicking and screaming out of bed in the morning is not biology, nor is it psychology. It's not micrology, nor is it mycology. It's not autology and it's not even audiology but it is in fact called minology.

Well it's a min. No, that's not really true; it's more than one min, quite a lot of min actually. In fact, sending a sound signal to the brain is the job of the many min who live and work in the Ear Department, or one of the Ear Departments depending on which side the sound comes from. Very strict about that, the Ear Departments.

'Can't have a left sided sound coming through the Right Ear, It's against union rules!' Snap Potts always says.

Snap Potts works in the Left Ear Department and, in fact, loves to quote union rules and regulations whenever he possibly can. Apparently he'd been voted Senior Shop Steward for the Left Ear Department some years ago, although the rest of the department couldn't quite remember when. Maybe it was that time when the ear got bunged up with wax and they all got emphatically drunk on wax brew, leaving the ear out of order for four days. Oh the stories some of the older folk would tell about The Great Wax Brew episode of '14! Some of them even sing songs about it to this day!

Old Mrs Drum who lives on the canal, well some say she's permanently drunk, and she'll never recover. Not that it seems to bother her in any way, or anybody else for that matter, apart from maybe Snap Potts. He sometimes gets a bit miffed as he's a firm believer that nobody should enter the workplace whilst being remotely under the influence of alcohol. Not that he could ever prove anything of course, as it happened such a long time ago, but if he were ever to catch anyone drinking on duty again then he'd throw the book at them!

Everybody had their doubts if this election actually took place but nobody really had the courage to confront him about it, even though deep down they were all quite happy that they didn't have to do it themselves. Too much responsibility all that union stuff; anything for a quiet life was the overall consensus.

Everybody generally seemed to get on well with one another in the Left Ear though and most min agree it's one of the nicest places to live and work. The general feeling amongst them is that that a happy ear is a healthy ear.

This particular ear belongs to a man. A man who is thirty-four years old and is called Will. And just like everyone else in the human world, he doesn't know that there are thousands of tiny little creatures inside his body, pulling the strings of his routine and ironing out the creases of his everyday life. But there are, and they are called min.

***

The smaller of the two figures was knelt on the ground, sobbing through cupped hands.

'Please don't do it, Sir, please don't do it. My family, they need me! Please, I'm begging you!'

The other stood staring, ignoring the cries of mercy. He snapped his fingers, and then there was silence. He stood for a while, staring at the spot where the sobbing figure had been, thinking about what had just happened and thinking about what he had done. He would never forget the words he had just heard, forever echoing around inside his head, but that was something he was just going to have to live with. After a few minutes, he turned and walked off into the darkness.

Friday 26th October, 7:42 p.m. Left Ear.

Penelope was bored. She was always bored. This is the most boring place in the whole wide world, she thought to herself.

'Bored, bored, bored,' she said out loud, knowing it would probably wake her father up. At least if she had someone to talk to, then it might bring a crumb of excitement into her drab and boring existence. He was still asleep. She tried a bit louder.

'Bored, bored, BORED!' she said.

Her father stirred slightly in his chair but her efforts so far had not paid off. He was still snoozing.

She tried again. She crept up to the chair, leant over the back of it and almost straight into his ear she shouted, 'Bored, bored, bored, bored, BORED!!!'

This time it worked. Her father sat bolt upright and opened his eyes like a startled rabbit.

'Whas-as-aa-what, shop floor, right everybody out!' said Snap as he awoke from his nap.

He always had an evening nap in his favourite chair and hated being woken up. Penelope knew this but was willing to occur his wrath just so she could talk to someone. She quickly ran to the other side of the room so as to avoid blame.

As he looked up, Snap noticed his daughter standing rather awkwardly next to the bookcase with a somewhat guilty look on her face.

'What time is it girl?' he snapped, now recognising he was not dreaming about work any longer but was once again back in the land of the living. He leaned back in his chair again.

'Oh you're awake, Father,' said Penelope, with the innocence of a lamb. 'It's, er, a quarter to eight.'

'Quarter to eight, is it? Where's your mother gone to, girl?' said Snap, in a rather less angry tone than before. He realised that now he was talking to his daughter and not that spotty little good for nothing errand boy from his dream.

'Bingo,' said Penelope. 'Boring, boring bingo.'

'Yoooaarrraaah!' Her father yawned out loud. He always did this for some unknown reason. To anyone hearing this for the first time, it sounded like he was in pain. He wasn't, it was just the way he yawned. His arms stretched out above his head. The union rule book he was reading before his nap slid down from his chest and dropped on to the floor.

'I thought you liked bingo,' he said his rubbing his eyes. 'You liked it the first time you went, didn't you? Your mother said you had a great time, wouldn't stop talking about it for weeks. Said it was the only interesting thing to do around here, in fact.'

'Yeah but that's coz I won the first time I went. I won a brush for my hair, and a whistle,' muttered Penelope.

'Well, there you go then,' said Snap. 'Good prizes them, if you ask me.' He was now sat up in his favourite chair, still rubbing his eyes and wondering where his spectacles were.

'Yeah they were, but I never bloomin' won since, did I? Bingo's boring when you don't bloomin' win innit?' said the girl, as she stood there with her hands cupped behind her back. She was looking down at the floor and swishing her long blond hair from side to side, as if to say to anyone who happened to be watching, that this was the body language of a girl who was very, very bored right now.

'Ah, so that's why you're not going anymore, coz you're not winning all the time. Isn't it?' said her father judgingly. 'You can't always win at everything you know my girl. Folks don't always come out on top in this life. With the greatest will in the world, someone's always gonna turn out second best.'

Penelope thought about this for a second, but couldn't really be bothered to utter an intelligent response, so she just said, 'Phfft.'

Deep down, she knew he was right. There were some people who were so competitive that they wanted to win at everything they ever did and finishing second best was just failure. Henry was like this. Henry Grip was her best friend. He lived over in the Right Ear. They were the same age as each other and they were always together doing something or other, apart from now. Henry wasn't hanging out tonight because he was getting ready for the contest.

Stupid bloomin' contest, thought Penelope. Bloomin' waste of time, if you ask me.

'Where's them ruddy glasses got to?' said Snap to nobody in particular. He had now got up from his chair and begun the hunt for his spectacles. 'Where's Henry tonight, anyway?' he added. 'Like two peas in a pod you two normally. Like Siamese cats, yez are.'

'Twins, Father,' said Penelope.

'Eh?' said Snap, rooting through cupboards and drawers looking for those damn glasses of his.

'Siamese twins, not cats,' corrected Penelope.

'What are you going on about, girl?' muttered Snap. Piles of papers were falling out on to the floor as he rummaged.

'Ah found 'em!' he said, fishing a pair of spectacles out from underneath the chair and placing them towards his rather rounded face. The spectacles he had found had a long thin wire frame, they were green in colour, and had what looked like some sort of floral design on the top of each lens.

'Oohh, no, they must be your mother's, girl, definitely not mine them. Where *are* my damn glasses?!' he said, rather running out of patience with himself.

'On your head, Father,' said Penelope.

'Eh?' Snap reached up to find his spectacles perched on top of his hat. 'Oh so they are, girl,' he said, rather embarrassed. He began to clear away the mess he had just created. 'I really must get my eyes tested one of these days, can't see past the end of me bloomin' nose sometimes. Now what are you going on about cats for anyway?'

'Siamese cats are cats that originate from Siam,' she paused for a moment, and then ventured, 'or whatever it's called now.' She was slightly embarrassed that she couldn't remember a fact. 'And Siamese twins are twins who are conjoined. You said we were like Siamese ca.., oh never mind.' She gave up trying to explain.

She knew about a lot of things did Penelope Potts; she was a very intelligent girl, in fact. When you spend most of your life being bored then you tend to wander around a lot looking for things to do. And it is whilst you're looking for things to do, that you tend to hear things and see things and generally learn things about things. Stuff, she called it. She knew about stuff.

Stuff was something which could get you through life a lot easier than if you didn't really know much about stuff at all. Stuff like never wake your father up when he's having his evening nap because it will put him in a bad mood, or stuff like never try and drink a glass of ale leftover from a party the night before because it doesn't taste very nice, especially with tobacco in it.

She did, however, learn something which many min could not learn. It was an art form only a handful of folk could do. Although she never told anyone about it, her mother knew she could do it, even though her father was oblivious to her talent.

Nerves. You could learn a lot from listening to the nerves. You see, the nervous system seems a very complex system at first, however, when you learn how to use it then it becomes quite a simple one. It carries information. It tells the body what the brain is thinking, and vice-versa.

If the left foot needs to move because some bumbling delivery man is about to drop a ruddy great piano on it, then somehow it needs to get a message from somewhere else to tell it to move. The left foot can't move on its own, can it? And even if it could, it can't see anyway because it hasn't got any eyes. The order of events is thus: Said piano is about to squash said foot, the Eyes Department see the danger and send a warning to The Brain. The Brain sends a message to the Left Foot Department saying 'MOVE FOOT SIX INCHES TO THE LEFT IMMEDIATELY!' and the Left Foot Department duly obeys.

Simple minology.

Sometimes things didn't run quite as smoothly as that, mind you, which is why the odd accident occurred every now and again. Apparently when The Will was ten years old, one of its so called friends told it that it could walk across two high fences on just one thin piece of cardboard. The attempt didn't go quite to plan and it fell eight feet-six inches through the wet cardboard, cracking its head open on the concrete below and had to spend two weeks in hospital.

This was its will however and the min could not do anything about it. Even though everyone had a pretty good idea of what was going to happen, the min could never change The Will. That was the most important rule of all. 'We can never change The Will'. 'Nos Numquam Immutare Voluntaten'. This motto was written on the walls in Central Head for everyone to see. It was the law. The written law, and the unwritten law, but it was the most important thing a min would ever learn. If the silly bugger wanted to throw itself to the floor and crack its head open, then so be it. It was its will. Will was everything to the min, and it could never be tampered with.

Penelope had learned how to listen in. She would often wander over to the Spinal Meadows and just put her ear to the ground and listen. For hours and hours she would just listen and listen. Every second of every day there are thousands of messages travelling up and down the body to and from the brain, relaying information to hundreds of different departments within the body. That's how it works, you see, and Penelope Potts knew how to gather information. That's why she was so smart, that's how she knew about stuff. That's how she knew about The Brain. That's how she knew about Siamese cats, and that's how she knew about Siamese twins.

'Conjo what?' said Snap, retrieving his union book from the floor and sitting back in his chair, happy now he could see who he was talking to.

'Conjoined,' said Penelope. 'Twins that are conjoined. Oh just forget it

8

anyhow, Father. I can't be bothered tonight, anyway. I wish I had gone to bloomin' bingo now.'

She shuffled across the room and sat down on a stool on the corner, not before picking up and opening up the book which was sat on top of it.

'Henry's swatting up for the contest next week. He thinks he's gonna win,' she said, through a disappointed frown.

'The contest, that no good bloody contest! Ha! He thinks he's gonna win does he?' said Snap mockingly. 'He's not even old enough to bloody-well enter it! Not turned sixteen yet, the boy. Opened up a bloody junior gig now, have they, eh? Poisoning the minds of our children now as well, are they?'

'I know it is stupid, isn't it? He knows he's too young to enter but he insists on doing it anyway. He likes to play along with it. He says it'll prepare him for when he enters it for real!' scoffed Penelope. 'Do you know he actually believes that he would've won it last year? He said he was better than that boy who won.'

'Oh yeah, what was his name now?' said Snap. 'Never liked the look of him, shifty looking little so and so, if you ask me. Fit right in up there, he will. Feel right at home amongst that shower. I've told you before, my girl, you'll do well to stay away from anyone who messes around up there. I've seen a lot of good min turn bad on account of that place. Poor old George must be tearing his hair out knowing his only son wants to go and get himself mixed up with that lot. The boy is all he's got now since he lost poor old Mary. God bless her soul.'

Penelope was messing with her hair. She was making ringlets by twirling her fingers round and round. Starting at the bottom of her beautiful blonde locks and working her way up until her finger had wound up her hair, tight to the top of her head.

They heard voices coming from outside the door.

'I'll see you Thursday, Winnie, love. Mind you don't fall in the canal on your way home again, darlin'.'

It was Penelope's mother coming back from the bingo, her pockets laden with sweets.

'What are you going on about now, Eric Potts? Spouting more of your union nonsense to our little girl again, I bet? She's not interested in bloody lone working hours, fire drills, tea breaks and what-not. Ain't healthy for a girl of her age knowing all that stuff. She should be out with her friends enjoying herself, shouldn't you my love?' She kissed her daughter on the cheek. 'Mwahhh!'

Penelope tried to surreptitiously wipe the kiss from her cheek without her mother seeing.

'Excuse me, Maggie Potts. Firstly, I was not filling her head with union nonsense I'll have you know and secondly, it is not bloody nonsense. It's important bloody stuff!' snorted Snap. 'And thirdly, don't call me Eric!'

He hated being called Eric. He was called Snap because he was so good at cards. He was always winning at cards and in fact, he was so good at cards that nobody would ever play him anymore. He wasn't a cheat, he was just good; and he liked the name so much that everyone called him it. It was down to moods, you see. If you called him Eric, it always put him in a bad mood but if you called him Snap, then that would generally put him in a better mood. He was never in a good mood.

'Ah shurrup, you miserable old sod,' said Maggie. 'Look what I won for you my little princess, sweets and bloomin' loads of 'em!' she said, pulling bag after bag out of her apron pockets and loading them on top of the pages of Penelope's open book. 'Well, actually, it was Winnie Drum what won 'em really but she can't eat 'em on the count of her teeth you see, so she gave 'em to me.'

'What's wrong with her teeth, Mother?' said Penelope

'Nothing wrong with 'em, she just hasn't got any, my love,' said Maggie, emptying a full bag straight into her mouth.

Penelope looked confused. 'Cant she suck them?' she offered, somewhat puzzled.

'She'd be sucking 'em if they were bloody wine gums, alright!' said Snap sarcastically from his chair. 'And you for that matter, both as bad as each other you two are.'

Snap was teetotal. 'On account of his responsibilities and all', he would say, 'have to show an example to the workforce.' Maggie, however, was not. She was anything but teetotal, in fact. If she could get her hands on liquor of any sort then she'd be only too willing to try it.

Alcohol for the min was something of a luxury item for a number of reasons. The Will never really drank much alcohol so whatever it consumed would have to be stored and preserved for as long as it could, just like any other liquid, then hopefully it would still be ok for the min to re-drink. Also Central Head didn't really condone the drinking of alcohol amongst its min. It wasn't illegal as such, but it tended to interfere with the day to day running of things.

The general order must not be upset. If something went wrong, and you were drunk on duty, then you better start running, because you would probably have to spend the rest of your life in exile, and it wasn't very nice down there.

Just like in all walks of life, however, there is always somebody that will find a way to get drunk. There were many different concoctions which people had tried over the years, and min have tried to make a brew out of many a different thing, some ideas being more successful than others. Maggie and Winnie Drum had their own recipe, and luckily enough, the main ingredient for their illicit quaff was in abundant supply. It was wax. Living in an ear tended to provide you with a lot of wax, in fact most Lugland folk were surrounded by it at all times.

'Nowt wrong with me, Eric Potts, and nowt wrong with Winnie neither!

You take no notice of him my love, he's just got a bee in his bonnet, always has this time o' year ain't he?' said Maggie, settling down to sit.

'I ain't got a bee in my bonnet about anything, and it's got nothing to do with the time of year neither!' said Snap. 'And there ain't nothing wrong with you and Winnie, eh? Ain't nothing wrong with yez? Both bloody pickled, that's what's wrong with yez, bloody pickled yez are!'

'Alright, keep your hair on,' said Maggie chuckling to herself and Penelope. 'Oh you can't, coz you haven't got any have you?' she continued.

Snap was completely bald, and always wore a hat to cover it up. He even went to sleep with his hat on. He squirmed in his chair, sat back and continued to read his copy of 'Shop Steward Do's and Don'ts Revised Edition '34' this was the latest copy of the regulations. He almost knew it off by heart and he'd only had it for two days.

'Why is Father always grumpy this time of year then, Mother?' said Penelope intrigued by this apparent revelation.

'Your father is always grumpy this time of year because of the contest dear,' said Maggie. She wasn't looking at Penelope while she was talking; she was looking at her husband, trying to wind him up. She was succeeding. 'He doesn't like the contest dear. He thinks that anyone who aspires to better themselves is an idiot, dear. He thinks that Central Head are out to get him, dear, because he's bloomin' well paranoid, isn't he dear?!'

Penelope looked embarrassed. She didn't really know which side she should take. Her father was a bit of a stickler, but her mother was rather making fun of him in front of her, which she didn't think was right. She carried on eating the sweets from the bingo and listened. She always felt comfortable listening to people.

Snap decided to respond to his wife's accusations. He was remarkably calm. 'Look, petal, you know why I don't like Central Head. They're not the same as us folk. I'll never stand in anyone's way if they wanna better themselves, you know that, but that place changes people, they're never the same again. Look what happened to... Well you know how I feel about the place. It's too creepy up there. Too much information confuses things, too much going on. A lot of knowledge is not good for ordinary folk like us, we're not meant to know.'

Penelope twitched nervously on her stool as her mother gave her a knowing look. She knew a lot of information, and she knew stuff. What did he mean we were not meant to know, why are we different than other folk? she thought. Why is too much knowledge a bad thing? Surely if we all knew about stuff we could help people. Organise things a bit more, have some fun! Listening to the nerves can open up a wealth of knowledge for us all. If The Will sees something then through the nerves we should all see it right?

'Cobblers!' replied Maggie, ever the understanding housewife. 'Right, bedtime for you young lady,' she continued. 'We've got a long day ahead of us tomorrow, we've all been summoned to you know where.' She turned to look at her husband. 'Someone's for the chop around here, and I know who my money is on.'

'Why, what's happened?' said Penelope, pretending she'd not heard.

'Well somebody's department didn't do their job properly this morning, did they? The Will never heard the alarm, did it? Missed half the day apparently, caused all sorts of confusion I hear. Going bloody bananas up there by all accounts!' said Maggie.

'Look, it was nothing to do with me, I never...' started Snap.

'Save it for the inquiry tomorrow, my lover,' Maggie interrupted her husband before he could say anymore. 'Time for bed eh, darlin'?'

'Aye, perhaps you're right,' conceded Snap. 'Long day tomorrow, eh? Come on then, petal.' He held out a weary hand as Maggie pulled him up from the chair. 'Nighty night, Penelope, love,' he yawned.

He and his wife walked to their bedroom, hand in hand. Despite all of the talk between them, they loved each other very much, even though they didn't often show it.

'I wish you'd take that bloody hat off though, it falls off anyway when you drop off you silly old sod,' a distant voice said from behind the door.

'Nag, nag, bloody nag!' came the instant reply.

'Night, Mother. Night, Father.' Penelope sat for a moment, thinking. She was thinking about what her father had said about knowledge. A few minutes later she was interrupted by her mother who had come back out from the bedroom in her night gown and cap.

'You still up, love? Ooh I'm busting for a wee, me and Winnie had a drop of ale on the way back, best not mention it to your father though, eh?' she said as she passed Penelope on her way to the lavvy. Penelope looked embarrassed. Why do old people always tell you when they're going to the lavvy? she thought.

A few seconds later Maggie returned. 'Ooh, that's better,' she said. 'If I don't go before I go to bed, I always wake up in the middle of the night, but can never seem to drag myself out to go until morning, plays havoc with my sleep it does.'

'Mother, can I ask you something?' said Penelope.

'You should be getting to bed you know, we've got a lot of travelling to do tomorrow, it's a long way to Central Head from here, my love,' said her mother.

Penelope persisted. 'You know what Father was saying about knowledge, and knowing too much, well what did he mean by that?'

'Oh never mind about that now, love, it's getting late, off to bed now, eh?' she said, trying to avoid the question.

'But it doesn't make any sense. Why would anybody not want to know stuff? Why would anybody not want to learn?' replied Penelope

Maggie walked over and sat down next to her daughter. 'Now you and I both know you're an intelligent girl, don't we, my love? And we both know that you can...' she paused for a moment, '...well, you have a talent for, er, finding things out, let's say. But listen, take it from me, there are some things in this world that are sometimes better left unknown.'

'I don't understand, Mother,' said Penelope.

'When I was a girl about the same age as you are now, in fact, I had a friend. She was very similar to you in many ways, and she, like you, always wanted to know about things, always wanted to learn. And she could also find things out by watching and listening, just like you can. But what she didn't realise was, a little knowledge is a great thing to have if used correctly, but too much knowledge can be dangerous,' said Maggie.

'Who is she, Mother?' asked Penelope.

'Oh we don't see each other anymore now, we sort of lost touch a long time ago. She went down a different road, one which her curiosities lead her to. But it was too much for her, you see, the knowledge took her away from herself. She wanted to know too much. Like your father said, some things we're just not meant to know.'

She threw her arms around Penelope and gave her an enormous hug. 'You're the most precious thing that your father and I have in the world, and we love you so much, you know that don't you?'

'Yes of course I do, Mother, you tell me all the time,' said Penelope.

'Well that's alright then,' said Maggie, releasing Penelope from her grip. 'Now off to bed with you girl, come on. Got to be up early in the morning you know, got to make butties and everything before we leave, loads to do.'

Maggie walked off to her bedroom. 'Might even take a drop of ale for me and Winnie. Yes, a nice drop of ale to take with us, that'd be nice, take some of those sweets I just won and all. Ooh yeah, quite looking forward to it now,' she muttered to herself as she went.

Penelope strode off to her room with a bag of sweets in one hand and her book in the other. She lay in bed thinking, as she so often did. Thinking about what her mother had said. None of it made any sense to her. She couldn't understand why anybody would not want to acquire knowledge. After all it couldn't harm anyone could it?

Penelope wasn't the only one who thought like this, and she wasn't the only one who could listen to the nerves. There were others who thought that they could use the knowledge, there were others who thought that they could harness the information. Somebody else thought they could help people, help The Will. So why did he fall and crack his head open? Why did he have to spend time in the hospital? Why did we let it happen if we could stop it from happening? Wouldn't that make things better? Just like stopping the piano from crushing the foot, right?

Chapter Two

It was morning. Mornings were a good time for the min, everyone looked forward to starting a new day with a fresh approach and an enthusiasm for what The Will would bring. This morning was different. There had been an incident, and someone was to blame.

It was not often that so many different departments were ever seen together in one place, especially during the day. Work never stopped for the min, somebody was always working. They usually did it in shifts. It was generally accepted that three shifts per twenty-four hours was the model everyone should be working towards. Morning shift was 6:00 a.m. -2:00 p.m. afternoon shift was 2:00 p.m. – 10:00 p.m. and the late shift was 10:00 p.m. – 6:00 a.m.

The best shift to get on was the late night shift, because most humans tended to go to bed at around midnight so it meant that you didn't really have to do much after that because humans don't really do much when they're asleep.

The Brain always kept on going during the night shift though, but it never made much sense to anyone. Sometimes it would tell the legs to run as fast as they could to get away from the approaching killer ice cream cones, or jump off the giant cliff and swim to the moon for hors d'oeuvres and pancakes. Whatever horse's dooveries were? Everyone knew it was nonsense though because The Will was actually tucked up in bed fast asleep and wasn't about to be jumping of any cliffs anytime soon. When this happened, the night shift lads tended to give everything a good firm whack with the palm of the hand and go back to playing cards. It generally did the trick.

The morning and afternoon shifts, however, were always very busy. All of the various departments would be bustling away with their various functions and practices, in order to keep their individual parts ticking over, which is why you would hardly ever see them together. That was the time when all of the work happened, that was the time when The Will lived.

There were probably only two reasons why you would see so many different groups of min gathered together in one place during the day, one reason would be for the contest and the other was because someone was in deep doo-doo.

The room was vast. It was bigger than any of them had ever seen before. 'Nos Numquam Immutare Voluntaten' was painted in gigantic letters on every wall. The sheer scale and opulence of the surroundings were overwhelming to the many that had travelled across from the Luglands, nervously awaiting their fate.

Living inside an ear could generally be described as cosy. In fact, most working departments inside the body didn't exactly leave you much room to manoeuvre. Unless you were fortunate enough to be born in an affluent area of Central Head, then you had to create your own home by making use of whatever was around in your particular area, without damaging the body of course. A bit of undigested food was always good and bits of floating bone and gristle were fantastic for furniture, but the vast majority of things inside The Will were made from its food.

Because most folk would have to live and work in the same area, they tended to sort of blend the two together, and never really travelled very far. A kind of community you could say. But like most communities, they tended to have a lack of space.

Central Head was different. Here the walls and ceilings seemed to stretch for miles and miles until they disappeared into a distant dot on the horizon. The furniture was made by the finest craftsmen in the entire body, the best and rarest materials brought in from every corner of The Will. There was no expense spared, everything here was pristine. This was where it all happened. This was where it all stemmed from. This is where decisions were made; this is where the rules were made. This is where the important people lived. This is where the most feared person in the entire body lived; this is where Sananab lived.

In the centre of the room stood a long table. An enormously long table. Longer than nine or ten Lugland dwellings put together. The most ornate decorative features adorned the high backed chairs meticulously placed along its length. Either side of it sat the dozens of min, the representatives of the Left and Right Ear. Almost the entire two departments were here, except for the few who had been left behind to min the pumps.

Even a lot of the children had travelled with them, not because they had been summoned along with the others, but they didn't really go out much so a trip to Central Head was too exciting an opportunity to pass up on. They brought packed lunches with them in case they got hungry on the journey.

Towards the top of the table sat the representatives of Central Head. They somehow looked like a different species to the rest of the min. They were all dressed the same, immaculately turned out in blood red and midnight black. They each had a crest upon their tunic with the motto 'Nos Numquam Immutare Voluntaten' emblazed underneath the embossed head of two crossed keys. They sat in silence with their arms folded and stared judgingly at the lesser citizens further down the table.

Everybody else was whispering amongst themselves, trying to make sure they got their story straight. Trying to make sure their story wasn't going to drop anybody else in it and more importantly that nobody else's story was going to drop them in it!

Penelope was sitting next to her best friend. 'Why do they wear those funny uniforms?' she said

'Funny? They're not funny!' said Henry Grip, with instant disdain. 'It is the proudest moment of a min's life when he or she is awarded the uniform of Central Head. Many years of study, practice and endeavour have gone into the acquisition of such a prestigious award. The uniform itself is achievement for the years of hard work and dedication which the good min and womin of this land have gained by winning the contest!'

'Phfft! Rather you than me, look at the size of those collars. They look like they'd all fly away under a draught. And if it is the proudest moment of a min's life when he or she is awarded the uniform, as you say it is, then why are they all male? There's not a female amongst them. Bloomin' sexist if you ask me!' said Penelope, none too impressed.

'Well maybe girls are not as good as boys when it comes to that stuff? Maybe they just wouldn't cut it? In fact, who ever heard of a girl winning the contest anyway? I've never seen one? And I've seen every contest since '29. How would they pass the physical anyway? I... mean... there... are... You...'

Henry suddenly felt the gaze of Penelope burning into his eyes as he spoke, realising this probably wasn't the best conversation he could be having with her right now. He changed his approach somewhat by adding, 'But I'm sure you could do it, Loppy, if you tried? I'm sure you could.'

Still unimpressed by her friend's chauvinistic approach to the morning she added, 'Yeah, I bet I could, Henry Grip, I bet you I bloomin' well could! Girls can do that stuff just like you can, you know!'

She thought about this for a moment, she thought about what Henry had said. Why couldn't girls enter the contest? Why couldn't girls be as good as boys at it? Why couldn't *she* be as good as boys at it? After all, she had helped Henry with all of his questions every year when the contest had come up, even though he was only playing along with it. There was the matter of training too which would mean she would have to go away to the trials. That would mean she would have to leave home for a while, that would mean she would finally have something to *do*!

Henry was fishing around in his pockets for something.

Penelope looked around. It was beginning to become slightly more appealing to her the more she thought about it, apart from the uniform of course, she would have to do something about that. 'I wonder...'

Henry held out an apologetic grubby hand, 'Wanna sweet, Loppy?'

Penelope reached down to take the olive branch from him. 'Have you noticed how much light there is here? And hardly a lantern lit anywhere,' she said, popping a jelly into her mouth.

'Yeah they say it's the brain what does it, it omits a kind of light source they reckon. It's the same all over I heard,' said Henry eagerly. He loved the fact that he was here. Even if it meant that one of them was gonna get the proverbial kick up the arse at any minute.

'Maybe that's why it's all so clean up here? They can actually see the floor!' said Penelope. 'I would love to live in a place with so much light for a change. I think I could actually read a book without a lantern.'

'Well I'm gonna live here next year when I win the contest, Loppy. You can come and visit me anytime you want, and we can read all the books there are!' said Henry confidently.

'Sshh, you two, will you? You'll get us all shot, you will. You've got to behave yourselves up here, don't you know where you are?' said George Grip, from across the table.

George was Henry's father. He was head of the Right Ear Department. He was very similar to Snap Potts in many ways, only he didn't really go in for all of that union business like Snap did. They had been friends all of their lives and were still very good friends now. He was a kind min, and a good father to Henry.

Henry's mother Mary had disappeared many years ago, nobody knew why. George was devoted to his wife, and desperately missed having her around. The circumstances of her disappearance were even more puzzling to everyone, because that sort of thing just did not happen. Min existed for a purpose; they lived to serve The Will. They did not die. They lived for as long as The Will did, and when The Will eventually dies then the min will die with it. Basic minology, everyone knows that. So what happened to her? It was a mystery that nobody could ever find an answer to.

It wasn't as if she had retired, as many folk believed. Most of the working folk do retire when they reach a certain age, or whenever they get bored, whichever comes first really. Most of them decide to go travelling, while a youngster steps up to take their place. That was how they kept a fresh approach to things and there was plenty of room in The Will for folk to go exploring. To get from one leg to the other would take about six months in itself, not to mention getting from anywhere in Top Country down to the depths of the Lower Foothills which could take years.

'Travelling!' Snap never saw the point of travelling. 'What's the point of going somewhere, without anything to do, when you're only going to have to come back one day? Waste of bloody time, if you ask me,' he always said.

'Sorry, Father.'

'Sorry, Mr Grip.'

The children offered their apologies.

Suddenly the whispering turned to silence as everyone immediately stood to attention. Three figures had emerged from a side door at the end of the room. They took their seats at the head of the table.

In the centre was Sananab. He was extremely tall for a min, taller than anyone else in the room, even sitting down he was taller than anyone else who was standing. He was as thin as a pin, almost skeletal in appearance. He wore a long black cloak which hid his stick like body from view. He had thin, jet black hair which came to a little point at the top of his forehead, and an exquisitely cultivated beard which encircled his mouth. His eyes were piercing and cold. He was in total charge of everything, the Overseer, the Foreperson, the Ruler. He was answerable to nobody but The Will itself. He said nothing. He sat back in his chair, his hands cupped together in front of his mouth. He stared down the table at them intensely.

He was flanked by two others; one older, and one younger than him. The older was Leopold Schmidt. He was Sananab's right hand min. He was the one who was entrusted to carry out the orders. He was the Zamindar, the second in command. He was the one who would collect your taxes, or throw you in jail.

He was an older min, more experienced in life than his leader. He had the appearance of a min who had once worked in a different environment, the wear and tear on his face and hands would seem to back this up. He was now a rather portly figure but in his younger days he'd had the perfect physique, the sort of body which most min could never achieve. He had been a manual worker who was now in a position of authority, making decisions which would affect the lives of everyone else.

A min who had quickly forgotten his roots, and had traded them in for an easier ride. A min who had given up his life for power. The worst kind of min. Some say he was worse than Sananab himself.

The younger min was Cornelius Crail. Cornelius Crail was the winner of last year's contest. He was, 'the shifty little so and so, who would fit right in up there', as Snap had described him. And as descriptions go, it wasn't far from the truth. He was indeed not the biggest of min; in fact he was barely a min at all. He had only just turned seventeen.

He could barely be seen under the red and black uniform which dwarfed him in size, yet the pride of wearing it made him feel like the biggest min in the room. Everyone could see it in his eyes. The youthful ambitions of a boyhood dream written all over his face. He knew that he would one day grow up to control and manipulate the lives of others. He always knew he was a boy who craved the idea of being powerful. And this was his prize, to live and work in Central Head.

All winners of the contest get to live and work in Central Head, but it is very rare that an opening of such importance and magnitude comes along for a trainee Head-worker. Most trainees would become vision workers, brain technicians, or even nerve analysts but a new position had been created for this boy, a special position for a special kind of min. He was The Will's first 'Thought Apprentice'.

Penelope turned and whispered to Henry, 'Is that...?'

Henry answered before she even had a chance to get her question out. 'Yeah that's Sananab. I can't believe we're this close to him. He's so powerful, he can do anything he wants and nobody can stop him.'

'And who is that big min next to him, he looks familiar somehow?' said Penelope to her friend, 'I'm sure I've seen him somewhere before.'

'You couldn't have done, unless it was at the contest of course. That's Leopold Schmidt, he's Sananab's second in command, I've heard some bad stories about him, Loppy, they say he's not to be crossed,' said Henry.

Penelope thought for a moment, and then said, 'Yeah must have been at the contest.'

'I could definitely do a better job than Crappy Crail could do any day!' scoffed Henry.

'Sshh you two, I won't tell you again!' said George.

The three figures at the top of the table whispered amongst themselves for a moment, while the rest of the room stood in silent terror.

The Zamindar looked up and began to speak. 'All min shall bow before his Eminence.'

Everybody duly obeyed.

'Be seated,' he continued.

The workers all sat down in silence.

Cornelius Crail's eyes were skipping from face to face amongst the min, trying to see beyond each terrified stare. This was the Thought Apprentice's first official hearing since he had started in Central Head, and he couldn't wait to start doling out punishment. Penelope's gaze caught his eye but unlike the rest of them, she didn't seem scared.

Sananab too had noticed this, and he watched her with a great deal of interest. She felt his gaze burning into her thoughts. She could sense something different about him. She sensed that he had knowledge. A lot more knowledge than anyone she had ever met before.

'I think we all know why we're here, so let's formalise the preliminaries shall we?' said Leopold Schmidt. 'Do we have representatives from both the Left and Right Ear Departments?'

Penelope and Henry both looked worried as their fathers stood to face the music.

'Er, yes, er, Sir, er, Mr Grip from Right Ear, er, here, Mr Schmidt, Sir,' uttered George Grip, nervously.

'And has any dignified representative from the left graced us with their presence this morning?' said Leopold Schmidt sarcastically.

'Yes, and before....' started Snap Potts, until he was instantly interrupted by the Zamindar.

'Ah, Mr Potts, how lovely to see you again, I do so look forward to our little chats, I do like to keep abreast with how the lesser half live these days.'

Snap gave him a look, the look of a min who knew he had to do as he was told, but hated every minute of it. He didn't say anything, he just stared.

'Cornelius, my dear boy?' the Zamindar continued, as he looked to his right in order to get his young apprentice involved in the proceedings.

'Yes, Leopold?' said the apprentice.

'And who has the honour of speaking on behalf of our fine central institution today?' said Leopold.

'That will be Mr Fourway, Sir,' said the boy.

'Ah, Mr Fourway, what an excellent choice, Cornelius.'

The boy smiled a smug smile as his mentor turned to look at the chosen representative.

'Peter, my dear chap, how are you today?' said Leopold. 'Stand up my good min, don't be shy. There's a good chap.'

Peter Fourway was a Head-worker. He was a very honest and hardworking min, not unlike many of those who plied their trade in Central Head. He happened to be on duty the previous morning when the incident occurred. He looked even more frightened than the Lugland folk at having to be at the hearing but he'd been requested to be there like everybody else.

He stood up gingerly. 'I'm very well thank you, Mr Schmidt, Sir, thank you very kindly for asking, Mr Schmidt, Sir,' he trembled.

'Ah nonsense, my good min. Call me Leopold. After all we're all friends up here, aren't we?'

Peter looked around for a minute as he didn't exactly know what to say to that, but at this moment in time he thought that he would rather be friends with him than not be friends with him, so he eventually answered, 'Er, yes, Leopold, thank you very much, Mr Leopold, Mr Schmidt, Sir.'

Some of the Earside workers were whispering to each other and starting to realise that perhaps they were not going to get the fairest of trials here today, especially George Grip. He looked across at his son and sighed. It was at times like this that he missed his wife so much.

'Jolly good,' said the Zamindar, 'now let's get started. Cornelius my dear boy could you please read out the details of this case?'

The apprentice started to read. 'Ahem... On the morning of Friday 26th October in the year '34, at precisely 7:15 a.m. The Will...'

'Stop, stop, stop, stop...' Leopold Schmidt interrupted him almost as quickly as he had started.

Some of the Lugland folk were becoming increasingly convinced that this trial was indeed not going to go their way and the whispers had gradually got louder and louder, which had eventually turned into noise.

Lugland folk tended to talk quite loudly on account of them living in an ear all day long. It tends to get loud inside because of the constant processing of sound so it is never quiet, even at night. Most people never stopped talking at all, even in their sleep and not just to themselves, they often had full blown conversations with each other, it was quite common there.

And by this time of the morning, most of them had been awake for several hours, and some of the children were starting to get bored, especially the younger ones. They'd started opening up their packed lunches, and were munching away on their jam sandwiches. And like in any situation where the volume increases, people tend to talk louder and louder so as to be heard.

'Mr Potts!' exclaimed the Zamindar. 'Are all of these...' he hesitated for a minute, then continued, '...people, with you?' He used the word 'people' then left a long pause between the words 'people', and 'with', suggesting that it should have been followed by the phrase: 'for want of a better word.'

'Of course they are with him, and me, and every bloody-one else here for that matter, and what do you mean 'people'?!' A voice shouted from the back of the room. It was Maggie Potts, she obviously heard the silent: 'for want of a better word' and was none too impressed with the inference.

'And you are?' said the Zamindar.

'You know bloody-well who I am. I'm Margaret Agnes Potts to you *Mister* Schmidt, and I won't have you calling any of us decent folk with all your fancy words and your 'chap' this and your 'my bloomin'' good min' that and all!' said Maggie.

Snap and Penelope both looked as embarrassed as each other at the outburst but, nevertheless, both agreed with her sentiment entirely.

'Ah, I should have known, another one of the Potts clan,' said the Zamindar sarcastically. 'Well may I remind you Mrs Potts, that this is a formal hearing, and not a blasted crèche!? And as you seem to be the appointed adult for this Lugland playground, may I suggest that you gather up your bunch of degenerate hoodlums and take them outside!'

This seemed to spark off quite an angry reaction amongst the min. One or two of them were finding the courage to speak out as Maggie had done.

'Degenerate? Hoodlum! I'll come over there and give you a piece of my mind!' said one.

'You forget where you bloody-well come from you jumped up little...!' said another.

Cornelius Crail had a worried look on his face as the noise grew. He started to hide inside his overgrown uniform.

It started to get louder and louder as more folk plucked up the courage to speak. The noise built up into a crescendo.

'You bloody-well think you're better than us don't you, Schmidt? Well we'll soon come and see who's better eh?!' shouted an angry Earside worker.

'I'll shove that bloody uniform right up your ar...'

'SILENCE!'

The word came from Sananab. He never shouted, he just whispered it quietly. Nevertheless, it was the loudest voice anyone had ever heard. It echoed louder and louder as the individual letters seemed to visibly flow through the air before gradually disintegrating into a cold mist and gently falling on to the people below. Everyone immediately stopped. They stood still like statues, a petrified look on their faces. The children even stopped chewing on their sandwiches. Henry could hear his own heart beating amongst the deathly silence. Everyone feared Sananab.

'Now, Mrs Potts,' he continued. The tone of his voice had changed. He spoke with eloquence and articulation, his sheer presence commanding the highest respect. His every word seemed to bypass the ear and go straight to the brain.

'Would you be so kind as to accompany all of these wonderful children out into the courtyard where there will be ample facilities for all of you to enjoy your short time here with us here today? Mrs Warnock will see that there is enough food and drink for everyone. Mrs Warnock?' he gestured to a lady who was standing at the side of the room.

'Yes, Your Eminence?' said the lady as she curtseyed to him.

'Please see that Mrs Potts and her party have everything they need, will you? Anything that they desire please, Mrs Warnock?' said Sananab.

'It'll be my pleasure, Your Eminence,' said Mrs Warnock, 'This way please, Mrs Potts.'

Like everybody else in the room, Maggie was speechless. She was stunned, and that didn't happen very often with her. But it's at times like these when instinct takes over and being stunned was not going to stop her from getting all of the free food and drink that was promised her. She looked across to her husband.

For one brief moment he thought she was going to wave this offer of luxury from this evil tyrant and all that he represents.

He thought she would stay and fight the injustices brought against the hardworking folk of the Luglands, alongside her husband and fellow workers.

He thought she would stand up for what was true, what was pure and what was right.

Then she shrugged her shoulders and said, 'See you later, love! I'll save you a sandwich.'

He sighed.

'Come along, kiddies, come with Auntie Maggie and we'll get you some nice free grub then,' she said gleefully.

The children followed in their dozens. A nice day out with free grub was a luxury even the youngest min had quickly learned how to appreciate.

'Might even be an ale or two in this for us, Winnie, love,' she whispered to Winnie Drum, who happened to be thinking exactly the same thing.

'I hopes they got some of those little sausage rolls,' said Winnie, her eyes lighting up with excitement, 'and some of those what d'yer ma'call 'em, volley vents or summat?'

'What with your teeth?' said Maggie slightly puzzled. 'Lawrence, what on earth are you doing down there?' she shouted to a young child under the table.

'I've lost my jam butty, Miss!' muttered the boy.

'Never mind that now, come with me, lad,' said Maggie as she ushered the last of them out of the room. 'If jam's all they got here I'll be bloody-well disappointed, I'll tell you that for nothing!' she added on her way out.

There were only a dozen or so left in the courtroom. There should have been a lot more of them in there but most of them had left with the children to get the free grub. Any min would rather get free grub than stay to watch a trial. Especially food from Central Head; they had food here that most min folk had never heard of. Everybody knew what the outcome of the trial was going to be anyway.

'Now, where were we? Ah yes, please continue, Mr Crail,' said Sananab.

Snap, George and the remaining Lugland workers looked on as Cornelius once again would have his moment in the spotlight.

*   *   *

The main entrance to the courtroom had two enormous wooden doors at its heart. The head of two giant crossed keys was magnificently carved onto each of them. Either side of the doors were two huge arched alcoves. Next to those were two more alcoves, slightly smaller in size, and next to those, two more. The alcoves continued on with perfect symmetry around the vast oval shaped room, getting smaller and smaller in size as they went.

The smaller ones had stairs next to them, leading up to more levels above. They in turn lead to more and more levels eventually culminating in a viewing gallery with hundreds of arch shaped recesses, each with striking views of the colossal room below.

In one of these tiny alcoves, peering through a tiny door which had been wedged slightly ajar was a boy. He was a small boy, yet quite broad in appearance. He was not fat but sort of well built. He wore glasses. They were red in colour and the lenses were round in shape but seemed somehow to be too small for his large, round, red face. He wore a red and black uniform, not unlike those worn by the Head-workers but not identical. He was scribbling frantically. He was watching everything closely, watching the courtroom intensely. He was watching the people. Watching their every move, and then writing it all down in a huge book.

Saturday 27ᵗʰ October, 10:37 a.m. Outside Courtroom No.1, Central Head.

Penelope and Henry had gone outside with the others, much to Henry's annoyance. He wanted to stay and watch the trial and to be near the great Sananab, but his father had told him to go.

Henry was muttering his disappointment under his breath. 'Stupid bloomin' stupid...'

'Did you see that boy in there, Henry? Sort of up in the wall, looking at us?' Penelope said to Henry.

'Eh, what?' said the disappointed boy.

'There was a boy staring down at us all, from up there in the walls. Did you see him?' she said.

'Er, yeah, I think so, he looked like he was dressed in a Head-workers uniform,' replied Henry. 'He looked like he was writing something down, in a book of some kind.' Henry's eyesight was impeccable. In the sometimes dimly lit environment which came with living in an ear, your senses had to be pretty good but Henry's were better than most.

'Yes I saw him earlier on as we went in, he didn't do a very good job of hiding did he? He wouldn't last a minute in a game of 'Hide 'O',' said Penelope.

Hide 'O' was the same as hide and seek but living in such a small place as an ear, it never really took very long to find anyone. The 'O' was short for 'Oh there you are, what a surprise!'

'I wonder what he was writing. I wonder what that big book was all about,' she said to him.

'Well we won't bloomin' well know now, will we!?' moaned Henry. 'Why did they have to make us go outside with the bloomin' kids? I'm not a bloomin' kid, I'm bloomin' well fifteen years of age, I am!' He was still miffed at his father for making him leave. 'Not bloomin' fair, Loppy, not bloomin' fair!'

Penelope turned around to see where her mother was. Maggie Potts and Winnie Drum were having a whale of a time with the children. There was a huge statue of Sananab outside the courtroom and the children were all dancing around it, whilst eating as much grub as they could. Mrs Warnock had never seen such carnage; she was struggling to keep up. Maggie and Winnie were singing a song. It seemed to go along the lines of:

'Oh there ain't no thing like a salty bugger,'
'Earwax pips and a bag of sugar,'
'Cinnamon sticks and a moo cow's udder,'
'And we'll never have a drop this fine, Oi!'

The children all joined in on the last words of each line, much to the enjoyment of Winnie. She was crawling around on all fours pretending to be some sort of farm animal in-between bouts of rolling around on the floor laughing hysterically.

'What are they singing about, Loppy?' said Henry looking confused.

Penelope knew all too well what they were singing about. She'd had it sung to her since she was a baby. This song and many other songs of a similar nature.

'Oh it's how Mother and Winnie make wine. Well, it's one of the recipes they've got anyway. Either wine or ale or beer, or whatever the newest concoction they've dreamed up this time is. They make up songs about them so they don't forget the ingredients. They can't write them down because if Father was ever to see them he'd go nuts,' replied Penelope.

Winnie overheard the word nuts. 'Nuts! Woo hoo, Nuts! Maggie let's do the Nutty Brew! Woo, ha, ha!!' By this time she was doing a handstand, inadvertently giving everyone a great view of her huge pink bloomers and striped stockings as her skirt had fallen down over her head.

'Ah I see,' said Henry. 'I did wonder.'

The two friends sat for a while, and watched as the rest of the Lugland folk enjoyed the biggest party they'd had for years. The fact that one of their own was in for a hiding next door didn't seem to dampen their spirits at all. Some of them had even brought musical instruments with them and were playing along with the festivities.

'Shall we have a look round, Loppy? Father will be in there for ages yet, and we'll never get a better opportunity to have a look round Headquarters than this, I don't reckon? What do you say, eh?' said Henry.

He knew it was a leading question, and he knew very well what the answer would be. To a Lugland girl who had longed to go somewhere further than the beginning of the Auditory Canal, the opportunity to go exploring around Central Head was not one that she was about to pass up lightly.

'Oh I don't know, Henry, we might get into trouble, what if someone sees us? I don't suppose they would take too kindly to us wandering about on our own.' she replied.

'Trouble?' said Henry. 'I thought trouble was something that you always wanted to get into. You're always complaining you've never got anything to do!'

'Oh, ok then, but as long as we stick together. And we mustn't go too far from here either, we don't wanna get lost do we?' she said.

He knew she would break eventually.

'Of course we'll stick together. Always do, don't we? Always have,' said Henry. He pointed to a corridor across the way. 'I wonder what's down there, shall we go that way?'

'Yeah, ok, come on then.' Penelope agreed, and they started to walk. The sound of singing became gradually quieter with every stride.

'Oh you stick your nuts in the air, and you mix 'em with a pear, and the biscuits crumble on your knee...'

'Oh, Lawrence, I told you not to have that jam butty, oh come here sweetheart, we'll get that nice lady to clean it up eh? Mrs Warnock, love...'

***

Henry and Penelope walked down the long corridor. The ceiling rose so high up above them that they could barely see it. Along the walls there were huge painted symbols. Neither of them had ever come across markings of this kind anywhere else.

'What are they do you think, Loppy?' said Henry as they walked along in amazement.

'I dunno. Never seen anything like this before, Henry,' said Penelope. 'Although I think that one was the same as the symbol we saw on those stupid uniforms earlier.' She pointed to the enormous crossed keys on the wall.

Henry gave her a disparaging look as they heard the faintest sound of voices coming from further down the corridor.

'Can you hear that, Loppy?' said Henry.

'Yeah, where's it coming from?' said Penelope.

'Down there, I think,' said Henry. 'Come on, let's find out.'

They followed the voices along the corridor until they reached a set of stone steps. After climbing the steps, they continued along another corridor and eventually up another set of steps. The voices became louder as they walked, until they reached the point where the voices became familiar. It was, in fact, the hearing which they'd stumbled upon. They had found their way up into the gallery area above. They peered through the door of one of the alcoves on to the diminutive figures below.

'It's the trial, Henry. See, look, there's your father down there,' said Penelope, 'and there's Cornelius Crail about to speak again.'

The young Thought Apprentice, for the second time began to read.

'On the morning of Friday 26th October in the year '34, at precisely 7:15 a.m. an incident occurred which resulted in the most wide-ranging of consequences.

The recurring morning alarm of The Will, which had been checked at precisely 11:17 p.m. the previous evening, was due to go off at the aforementioned time of 7:15 a.m. There is evidence to suggest that the alarm did indeed sound at the correct time of 7:15 a.m. However, there is also evidence to suggest that the sound was not detected at Central Headquarters thus preventing the sound to be officially logged and detected as being 'heard'.

This drastic turn of events, as we all know too well by now, led The Will to miss the entire morning due to it not rising until 11:02 a.m. The rather unfortunate events which followed, we believe, caused a great deal of pain and anguish to The Will. Consequently, we believe this led to the exceedingly high alcohol intake which is currently flowing through our system. This is a very serious matter indeed.'

Most of the min were actually quite pleased about the alcohol. There was enough drink in the system at the moment to last them for months. Everyone knew that The Will never usually consumed much of it so it was a very rare treat to get pure liquor to distribute. This amount could be stored up until March. It was like Christmas had come early for them and with another Christmas just around the corner anyway, alcohol would be in abundance. Central Head were very much against this, of course, which is why they needed someone to take the rap for all of this.

'Thank you, Mr Crail,' said Leopold, 'and very well read out, my dear boy.'

Cornelius' smug smile was likely to hang around on his face for some time.

Leopold continued. 'Mr Fourway, have we managed to ascertain the exact sleeping position of The Will at the time of the incident?'

'Er, one moment, Sir,' Peter Fourway looked down at the piece of paper in front of him. 'Er, this is the official logged chart of The Will's activities between 6:00 a.m. and 2:00 p.m. on the 26th October, Year 34, Sir. That was when I started my shift, you see, Sir. I was on earlies that day you see, Sir. I swapped with Mr Trent on account of him not feeling too good after he ate all of those leftover berries from last week you see, Sir. Otherwise, I wouldn't have normally been on duty you see, Sir. Normally, I would've been on afternoons, Sir, normally, Sir.'

'Yes, yes, yes, can we get to the point please?' interrupted Leopold.

'Ah right, sorry, Sir, right.' He began running his finger down the page until he came to the time in question. 'Er, right, ok let me see now. Right, 6:00 a.m. snore, snore, snore, 6:21 a.m. cough loudly. 6:30, scratch left buttock, 6:32, break wind, snore, snore, snore, break wind again, 7:08, turnover on to side, 7:15 snore, snore... Er, it was, er, sleeping on its side, Sir,' he eventually said looking up from the page.

'And which side was The Will sleeping on, Mr Fourway? The left side or the right?' said Leopold.

Peter Fourway looked back down at his notes. 'Er, let me see now, er, that'll be the left, Sir.'

'Are you sure it was sleeping on its left side, Mr Fourway? You're certain of this?' said the Zamindar.

'Er, yes, Sir. Positive, Sir.' said Peter Fourway. He looked back at the log again to confirm his findings. 'Yes, sleeping on its left side. Under a blanket, with its hands cupped together under its chin, Sir.'

George Grip could see what was coming and was beginning to fear the worst.

'The left side of the face, buried in its pillow?' said Leopold.

'Er, yes, I do believe that was the case, Mr Schmidt, Sir,' answered the Head-worker.

'And so the majority of the sound should've been detected by the Right Ear, Mr Fourway? Am I correct?' said Leopold.

'Er.... yeah... I, er, suppose so, Mr Schmidt, Sir,' offered Peter Fourway, reluctantly.

'And no sound was detected at Central Headquarters? Is that correct, Peter?' said Leopold leadingly.

'Er, no, Sir. I mean yes, Sir. I mean the answer to your question is yes, Mr Schmidt, Sir. Meaning no, Sir, we heard nothing at all, Sir,' replied Peter, confusingly.

'Thank you, Mr Fourway, you may sit down,' said the Zamindar. 'You may also sit down, Mr Potts, as it seems that, unfortunately, you are off the hook this time,' he added. 'Mr Grip, you will make your way to the stand.'

Snap Potts sat down but his blood was boiling. He was raging inside. He was sitting with his fists clenched, muttering to himself. He knew his friend was going to be in trouble and it seemed there was nothing he could do about it.

All the time Sananab said nothing. He just stared. He stared intensely at everyone in the room, skimming from one set of eyes to another. If anybody's eyes caught his gaze staring back at them, it was frightening. It was as if at the point of impact, he could see directly into their mind, directly into their thoughts, directly into their soul.

Chapter Three

Henry and Penelope watched the proceedings intensely from their lofty position, the grandeur of the surroundings breathtaking to them both. Penelope was overwhelmed by the sheer scale of everything she saw. It was like another world to her, a world which she hoped would exist outside of her humble homeland, yet a world which she thought she would never see.

She grew up in a place which was small and dark but this place was a million miles from home. She scanned every inch of everything she could see, trying to take in and remember as much information as her brain would allow. Luckily for her, her brain held a lot of information and she remembered a lot of things. Like most people she would forget the odd fact now and again, but that was very rare. She remembered words and sayings, people and places, names and faces. She was exceptional at remembering faces.

She would never forget the face of Sananab, nobody would forget that face in a hurry, but Leopold Schmidt, now he did look very familiar to her but she couldn't remember where she knew him from. She'd been racking her brain all morning trying to remember where she'd seen him before but she couldn't quite place him. It must have been the contest like Henry had said. Yeah, it must have been. One face that she did recognise straight away, however, was a face that she'd seen only a few minutes earlier. It was the boy with the book.

'Hey, Henry, there's that boy again,' whispered Penelope. 'He's just over there, look.'

They were now on the same level as the mysterious onlooker; he was in the opposite alcove to them, still frantically writing in his book.

'Oh yeah,' said Henry, 'I don't think he's seen us.'

Penelope looked closer at him, 'I wonder who he is?'

'He must be from Central Head, coz he's got a uniform on, look,' said Henry.

'He seems quite young though. Not as old as all of the other Head-workers we've seen this morning,' said Penelope. 'He can't be more than fourteen or fifteen at most. What a funny little round face!'

'Yeah, and that book that he is holding is bigger than him!' said Henry.

'We better not let him see us or we could get into big trouble, Henry,' said Penelope cautiously. She was, however, intrigued to know what he was writing in that ledger. 'I do wonder though, what is he *doing* there.'

'Only one way to find out,' said Henry. 'Come on let's see what he's up to. I reckon if we follow that corridor, we can get round there.'

They started down the long oval corridor hoping it would lead them to the other side of the room. After passing dozens of the now familiar alcoves, they reached the other side. They could see the boy clearly, standing a few yards ahead of them. He hadn't noticed them creeping up behind him, all the time he was scribbling frantically. Henry tapped Penelope on the shoulder. He gestured to her to be quiet by putting his finger over his lips, then pointed to the boy and then again to himself.

Penelope was a bright girl, very intelligent in fact, but she wasn't going in for all this Boy Scout code nonsense. She thought it'd be better just to tell him.

'And I'm supposed to know what you mean by all this pointing and fingering am I?' she said out loud.

The boy almost jumped out of his skin with fright. He dropped the giant book and turned around to face the intruders.

'Aaaghh!' he screamed.

Henry and Penelope were not expecting this sort of reaction and quite often in a situation like this, instinct takes over. They did the first thing that popped into their heads, they both screamed. First Henry, then Penelope.

'Aaaghh!'

'Aaaghh!'

The boy, who had absolutely no idea what was happening, took advantage of the sudden confusion and darted between the two of them. He ran off as fast as he could down one of the many corridors which lead away from the alcoves. After a few seconds, he was out of sight.

'What the hell did you do that for?' said Henry.

'Do what for?' replied Penelope.

'Scream like that, of course!' he said.

'You bloomin' well screamed first, Henry Grip!' said Penelope.

'Yeah, only coz he screamed first. It just sort of came out like....' said Henry, embarrassed at what he'd just done. 'Anyway, you shouldn't have spoken out loud like that, that's what spooked him. I was gonna grab him, I had it under control. Did you not understand the..?' he once again re enacted his earlier mime.

Penelope was not impressed. 'No, I bloody never, ok!' she said. 'Anyway, he'll be long gone now but I guess he could come back at any minute, couldn't he?'

It was suddenly dawning on her that this situation could get a lot worse. 'He's probably gone to get help, Henry, we should get out of here before we get caught. Who knows what they'll do to us if they catch us?'

'Yeah, I suppose we should,' said Henry. 'Hey, look there though, he's dropped his book.'

They looked down, and indeed the boy had left his book behind.

'Oh yeah, he must have dropped it in the confusion,' said Penelope.

Henry picked up the book and held it in his hands. It was huge in size, almost too big for Henry to hold. It was dark blue in colour and had magnificent dark leather bindings around its edge, with gold markings running through it. There were four words and a number written on the cover. It said 'Montague Schmidt's Journal. Vol IX'.

'That must be his name, Montague Schmidt,' said Penelope. 'Isn't that the Zamindar's name too, Henry?'

Henry nodded, 'Hmm.'

He flicked through the book until he came to the last page, the ink still wet from only minutes before. The borders and margins adorned with beautiful gold scrollwork. This was definitely the book of someone from Central Head. Most Lugland folk would be happy to live in a book of this size, never mind read one. He began to read it to himself.

'The minutes of the meeting are...... Mr Crail started to speak...Blah, blah, blah....All rise etc, etc... .' He turned to his friend who was busy peering along the corridor, and trying to make sure nobody was coming to capture them.

'Hey, Loppy, I think I know what this is. This Montague Schmidt has been writing everything down as he saw it, absolutely everything. Look, that's where we all came in this morning, see? That's where Sananab came in and that's where we had to go outside. But why would he write everything down if he saw it all anyway? Couldn't he just remember it? Unless he was writing it down for somebody else's benefit? Doesn't make much sense to me, either way.'

'It's his diary, Henry,' said Penelope. 'You know a diary? People keep diaries every day, they write down exactly what they do.'

She looked at her friend for a response, but only got a blank look. 'I used to have one when I was little, but felt there wasn't really much point after a while because I never forget anything. If I want to know what I did four years ago, I just think back four years and I see it quite clearly. I know a lot of people who keep them though, they're quite common.'

She looked more closely at the diary. 'Never seen one this big before though. Got to have a bloomin' big ego to have a diary this size though, and a bloomin' big head to go with it!'

They were interrupted by the sound of voices. They were distant, but they seemed to be getting closer. They looked at each other, both thinking exactly the same thing.

'Quick, someone's coming,' said Henry. 'We need to get out of here!'

They started to run. Henry was slowed down by the sheer weight of the journal. Penelope was yards ahead when she stopped to see where her friend was.

'What are you bringing that thing with us for? Just throw it away, it'll slow us down,' she said.

'No way!' said an out of breath Henry. 'This could tell us everything, this could be priceless!'

'We're going to get caught, just throw it away!' said Penelope desperately.

Two Head-workers in full uniform had reached the alcove. They looked around and saw the quill belonging to Montague Schmidt on the floor near the door, but there was no sign of the diary. They knew the intruders were not far away. They stood and listened. At the end of a corridor, they could hear the faint, distant sound of footsteps. They set off down the corridor after them.

***

Downstairs, George Grip was standing in the dock.

'Now, Mr Grip, could you kindly tell us, who was the Overseer on duty in your department at the time of the incident? At precisely 7.15 a.m. yesterday morning?' said Leopold Schmidt.

'That would be me, Sir,' said George Grip.

Leopold paused for a moment to look at Sananab and then turned back to his questioning. 'And did you have direct eye contact with those responsible for the operation of the middle ear?' he continued.

'Yes I did,' replied George. He knew that no matter what he said, he was going to be in trouble one way or another but the last thing he wanted was for anybody else to get the blame.

'And at no time did they leave their post?' said the Zamindar.

'I was there for the whole time,' replied George.

'And those people are here?' asked Leopold.

'Yes,' said George reluctantly. He turned and looked at his fellow workers behind him and gestured towards the min who were on duty that morning, knowing that there was no way he could avoid them being questioned. There was a pause as the four Lugland workers got to their feet and walked towards him.

'What splendid ambassadors for the Lugland people we have here,' said Leopold sarcastically. He walked over to Sananab and sat down next to his Master. He looked up at the thought apprentice and said, 'Cornelius, would you show these people to the stand, please?'

'Yes, Leopold, it would be my pleasure!' said the boy. He was grinning from ear to ear. He was delighted with his position of authority here. 'This way, come on, as quick as you can, please, we haven't got all day.'

Snap was muttering under his breath to himself, he couldn't believe they had to answer to this cretin.

Leopold sat for a moment, whispering something into his Master's ear. Sananab tilted his head slightly towards the Zamindar. His eyes looked down towards the table and to his left side where Leopold was sitting. Yet at no

32

time did he ever look him in the eye. He listened carefully but did not say anything. When Leopold had finished whispering, Sananab looked up and stared again at the defendants. All the time his left hand cupped around his beard, with his thumb placed under his chin, his right hand placed on the table in front of him.

Leopold stood once again to address the Lugland workers. 'Would you please introduce yourselves to the court? Starting with you, boy!' he said, pointing at the unfortunate chap who happened to be standing nearest to him.

'My name's Ronnie Drum, Sir, I work the drum, Sir!' said the boy, whilst saluting his questioner.

Ronnie Drum was the son of Ronald Drum Snr and grandson of Winnie Drum. He was only eighteen years old and had not been doing the job for very long. He wasn't the brightest of boys but he was an honest lad and worked hard. He loved his job for many different reasons; the main one being that he got to hit things a lot.

He loved to hit things, especially the drum. He loved to hit the drum as often as he could. He couldn't wait to get the call to start off the chain reaction which makes the sound. That meant he could actually 'play' the drum.

He'd made a drum of his own some years back out of some hair stretched over a piece of bone, which he'd found floating around and he played it in the Lugland band. When they had parties, usually organised by his Granny, the band would play along to the traditional songs which they always sang. Ronnie's drum beat was always at the heart of it. But not even that was as good as playing on the real thing to him.

He stood alongside his fellow workers and looked Leopold Schmidt in the eye. He was brave and true to his colleagues and he knew he had done absolutely nothing wrong.

'And we're the Ossicle brothers!' said the other three min, at exactly the same time. Then each in turn, they called out their first names.

'Hammer,' said the first.

'Anvil,' said the second.

'Stirrup,' added the last brother.

'The Ossicle brothers!' they added once again in unison.

The three brothers were identical in appearance. They each wore the same uniform, which consisted of blue overalls, shiny black boots, and a white tunic with a red and white neckerchief. Only with close scrutiny could anyone tell them apart and this was because of the length of their beards. Anvil Ossicle had the largest beard, Stirrup Ossicle had the smallest and Hammer Ossicle had the size in-between.

Very few folk could tell them apart, including their own wives, which is why they all got a tattoo of each of their wives' names on their forearms. This way their beloved spouses could work out who they were, and more importantly, who they were cooking supper for when they got home every evening. Even so, they would still get it wrong on occasion.

Gertie Ossicle always maintained that on a Wednesday evening she would quite often cook for somebody other than her husband, even though she never let him know. Wednesday night was always a soup night in Gertie Ossicle's house and not many people seemed to like her soup very much, she never knew why.

The three brothers were experienced workers and had been doing their job for many years. This was the first incident which had ever taken place on their watch, and like Ronnie Drum, they too were confident in their innocence, and would not be intimidated by Central Head. They each stood firm.

'Now you, Drum. Can you tell the court what happened yesterday morning while the incident was taking place? Please tell us the exact details?' said Leopold.

'Well, Sir, there was definitely the sound of the alarm. I remember it well, Sir. Coz I was playing me drum you see, practicing for the group. Me and the lads well we get together on Thursday nights, you see, to have a jam and that, and I wrote a new tune for me drum. 'Bang bang the bon bons'. Would you like to hear it, Sir? I've got my drum with me, Sir?' said Ronnie enthusiastically.

'I think you can spare us that luxury, boy,' said Leopold. 'Carry on!'

'Oh right ok, Sir,' continued Ronnie. 'Well I was practising away when I heard it. I definitely heard the alarm at 7.15 like I said, and I gave that big old drum a right good pounding, I did. I played it good and loud like I always do, I used my new sticks I made too. A couple of bits of bone all smoothed off at the end they are, make a right good sound they do, Sir, even if I do say so myself!'

Ronnie looked very pleased with himself, not for one moment did he have the look of a boy who was standing trial. 'Now what was the tune I was playing now?' he continued. 'Er, was it 'Fat Belly Blues', or was it 'Ragtime Rhonda', you know I'm not too sure if it was either of...'

'Ok, enough of your incessant babbling, boy,' interrupted Leopold. 'What happened after that?'

'Well you did say the exact details, Sir. I was only doing what you told me to do, Sir,' offered Ronnie.

'Yes, yes, yes, ok, what happened next?' said Leopold impatiently.

'Oh well then it must have passed along to the brothers, I guess then, Sir. Don't rightly know. After I have done my bit, then it's not down to me anymore then is it, Sir? I'm not allowed to leave my post at the drum, Sir. And I never did, not until two 'o clock when I knocked off, Sir,' said Ronnie.

'And your account of the morning's activities?' said Leopold turning to the three brothers.

Once again the three of them spoke in unison. 'We maintain to this court that we did our job in accordance with Earside Right Regulation 614, Paragraph 3, Appendix 12 which clearly states 'Any vibration detected and passed on by the tympanic membrane shall be interpreted as a potential sound, and therefore be filtered through the hammer, anvil and stirrup bones as thus. Sending an amplified signal to the oval window from where this formatted signal can, and must, be processed into sound.

Which we did at 7:15 a.m. yesterday morning and we have written documentation to prove this, signed by our immediate superior at the end of our shift at 13:59 hours and 59 seconds, Standard Will Time, on Friday 26th October, Year '34.

Furthermore, any person who disputes this fact will have to do so in writing, as each Earside worker is entitled to the representation of a Senior Shop Steward throughout any disciplinary talks. They must be given a minimum of thirty days to respond to said allegations, according to Union Rule Number 75 Point 2, as stated in the revised edition of the 'Listeners Code'.

Failure to comply will result in us taking industrial action, forcing a heavy loss in production and have a knock on effect on the general morale of the people, causing widespread anger and unrest amongst the workforce, Sir!'

They each produced a ledger, which they opened on the same page at exactly the same time and held out in front of them for the Zamindar to see.

The remaining Lugland folk all wanted to get up and cheer, but they each sat there trying to take in what they had just heard. In his seat looking on, Snap was seriously impressed by this amount of efficiency, he could only dream of having a workforce as good as this in his department.

Cornelius was aghast. He stood there with his mouth open; he had never seen anything like it before in his life. Even Sananab looked confused.

Leopold was stuck for words. At the back of his mind he knew that the outburst sounded like a threat but somehow he couldn't bring himself to make that accusation.

'Erm. Well, erm, that all seems to be in order, right, er, ok, Mr Grip?' he managed.

'Sir?' said George. Even he was still taking it all in.

***

Henry and Penelope had made their way back over to the other side of the room. They were trying to find their way back outside to the others but had got lost amongst the miles of corridors and alcoves.

'Which way now? It all looks the same,' said Henry.

'I don't know, do I?' said Penelope. 'It all looks the same from here too.'

The two Head-workers were still following them. They were now very close.

'Henry, I can hear them, they're right behind us. What are we going to do?' said a frightened Penelope.

'Just keep running, Loppy, for Will's sake!' said Henry to his friend.

They had reached the end of a winding passageway, which brought them to a set of steps. They ran down the steps to the bottom and they were confronted with a sort of crossroads. In front of the pair was another set of spiral steps leading back up. To the left was a corridor and to the right was another corridor sloping away from them.

'Which way now?' said Henry. As he spoke, the two Head-workers were following them down the steps, they were so close they could nearly touch them.

Penelope grabbed Henry and dragged him off down the corridor to the right. 'It is at times like this, Henry Grip, that you don't ask questions. You just do something!'

With this, she snatched the enormous diary from the grasp of her friend, turned around and hurled it towards the onrushing guards. It slid across the marbled floor like it was made of ice, the guards stood no chance. It slid into their feet knocking them over, like a bowling ball, against the last two remaining nine pins, sending the pair of unsuspecting runners somersaulting up into the air.

The book carried on its path like a rocket, making its way into the alcove towards the side of the corridor, where it almost disappeared out of sight. Instead it gradually slowed down before coming to a gentle stop, precariously balanced on the edge of the marble step. The guards came falling back to earth seconds later, they were knocked out cold.

Henry and Penelope didn't stop to look back. They ran as fast as they could until they eventually had to stop to catch their breath. After they realised that they had reached relative safety, they sat down with their backs against the wall.

'Where did you learn how to shoot like that, Loppy?' said Henry, still out of breath.

'I don't know, but it worked didn't it?' replied Penelope, impressed with her own quick thinking. 'Anyway, never mind that now, we need to get back outside with the others before those guards, or whoever they are, realise what has just happened to them.'

'What about the book? Did you see what happened to the book?' said Henry.

'No, Henry, I was too busy running like the clappers and looking in the opposite direction, remember?' she said sarcastically.

'Yeah, I suppose you're right,' conceded Henry. 'I would have liked to have kept it for a bit longer, mind, and read a bit more of it though, eh? There could have been all sorts of good stuff in it.'

He sat looking around at the vast walls, when suddenly they became familiar to him. 'Hey, isn't this the corridor where we first came in?' he said.

They both now recognised the huge symbols on the walls from the corridor where they had first entered.

Penelope paused for a moment, and listened. 'Yeah I think it is, and what's more, can you hear that?'

There were the distant sounds of a somewhat subdued party coming from down the way.

'I think that's the others outside, it must be that way,' she said pointing towards the huge symbols along the wall. 'Come on, let's get out of here before they come looking for us!'

They hurried down the passageway and quickly made their way outside.

***

Inside, the trial was nearing its conclusion.

'We seem to have established the path up until the, er...,' Leopold looked down at his notes '...the, er, oval window?'

'Oh right, Sir, yes,' said George.

'And can we establish what happened after we reach the oval window?' said Leopold.

This was the part George was dreading; this was the part where he would undoubtedly get the blame. 'Er, that would be where I come in, Sir. You see I was working at the window, you see, I was minning the Cochlear,' he said.

'Ah, I see,' said Leopold happily. He was looking forward to dishing out the blame. 'And how does this tale of woe unfold further, pray tell?'

'Well there's nothing really more to tell you, see. The sound came in like the lads said it did. I took the signal, shook it round like normal, and then sends it up the nerves like always. I did what I've done millions of times every day, just the way I always done it. No different than normal, I remember doing it, like,' said George.

He knew that his was the last physical act of the chain. He knew that after him it was down to the nerves, and once it's gone into the nerves then there's nothing any min in the whole world could do about it, even if they wanted to. Once anything was in the nerves then you couldn't touch it. That was The Will, and nobody could change The Will.

Leopold knew this too, and he knew now was the time that he could move in for the kill and get his min. His face lit up with excitement, toying with his prey.

'But there seems to be an anomaly here, Mr Grip, does there not? I mean we've already heard evidence from your fine Earside workers to suggest that the sound did in fact make its way to your station. Or are you disputing this?' said the Zamindar maliciously, his voice increasing in volume.

'No, Sir, not at all. I stand by everything they've said. Don't you be putting words into my mouth now, those lads are the best in the business and I won't have a word said against them or any of my min for that matter, not

37

any of them!' said George angrily, even though he knew he was playing right into the Zamindar's hands.

'Quite,' said Leopold. 'And we've already heard evidence from Mr Fourway to suggest that indeed the alleged sound was not detected at Central Headquarters. So are you suggesting that Mr Fourway is somehow wrong? Perhaps that he is implicated in this somehow? Deflecting the blame, hmm?'

Peter Fourway was sitting in his chair, trembling with the fear that somehow this might end up being his fault.

'No! I'm bloody-well not!' George was beginning to lose his temper, and was becoming more and more frustrated with his accuser. 'And you bloody-well know it an' all, Mr Schmidt! You're making everyone think things that aren't true. Peter is a good min and I wouldn't accuse anyone of doing anything like that. You're just twisting my words you are, twisting them all up in knots!'

The rest of the Lugland folk were getting annoyed with this line of questioning too, and one or two of them were starting to voice their opinions as the volume in the room started to increase again.

'What was it then, Mr Grip, drunk on duty were we? Wouldn't be the first time would it?' said Leopold.

'No! No way! I never drink on duty, no, this is just not right!!' said George.

Leopold was closing in. The volume was building up to a crescendo again with all of the Lugland folk angrily pointing and shouting towards him. He had to shout louder to be heard above them.

'Then I put it to you, Sir, that you, George Grip, and you alone were to blame for this outrage! You were not at your post; you did not carry out your duty to The Will! You are charged with a dereliction of duty and you, Sir, are found guilty of gross malpractice and you will be punished in accordance with the law of The Will! You will be sentenced!'

George desperately tried to plead his innocence. 'No, Sir, honest, Sir, I never did anything wrong, I did everything I was supposed to, I was there doing my job same as always. I moved it on like I always do, honest, Sir, I swear to you I did everything right. You must believe me, it must be something to do with the nerves.'

'No, no, no!' Sananab stood up from his chair and smashed his fist down on to the table in front of him with such force that the opposite end of the table lifted into the air like a seesaw, taking some of the unexpected Lugland folk for a ride with it. One by one, they returned to earth with an almighty thump and landed on top of one another in a heap. They were closely followed by something that looked like a huge leather bound book, which seemed to come from nowhere and landed square on the head of the unfortunate min that was sat on top of the pile.

Everyone had heard about the mighty Sananab. Indeed everyone was fearful of him and afraid of what he could do, but up until now not many had actually witnessed it. The anger in his voice was terrifying. The words themselves were pure rage, they frenzied around inside everyone's head, injecting instant fear into everyone in the room. Cornelius again tried to hide inside the comfort of his oversized uniform. Even Leopold Schmidt was shocked.

'You lie!' continued Sananab. Everyone else in the room was trembling with abject fear. Nobody would dare do anything.

'How dare you attack the nerves? How dare you disrespect their power? These allegations are preposterous! Nos Numquam Immutare Voluntaten! We can never change The Will! You will abide by these rules, Sir, or you shall be exiled!'

Every word he said seemed to be amplified a thousand times, it was the loudest voice anyone had ever heard.

'And that goes for all of you!' he said pointing at the others. 'We exist for a purpose in this world and you will all do well to remember that! How dare you stand before me with your pathetic lies? The Will is everything, The Will is sacred! The Will is all powerful! Nos Numquam Immutare Voluntaten! Nos Numquam Immutare Voluntaten! We can never change The Will!'

The min froze with terror. The Ossicle brothers were each holding on to their beards trying to generate some inner strength. Snap Potts tried to hide by covering his face with his hat while Ronnie Drum wet himself with fright.

Sananab turned to Leopold Schmidt and said, 'Sentence this min with the maximum punishment allowed, and then send these wretched fools back from whence they came!' With this he swirled his long cloak around his body and walked out through the door at the back of the room. The entire room waited in terrified silence.

Leopold turned to the accused. He had already thrust his knife, now was the time to twist it. 'Mr George Bartholomew Grip, you have been tried by this court and you have been found guilty on all charges put before you. Guilty of dereliction of duty and guilty of leaving your post. Furthermore, you have committed the most despicable crime of all, in trying to deflect the blame from yourself and on to The Will itself.

I have been ordered by this court to sentence you to the maximum punishment allowed for such crimes, in accordance with the law of The Will. As you are well aware, this is a Central Supreme Court, and the maximum sentence which can be passed by this court is indeed a life of exile.'

There was a huge gasp by the min as Leopold paused for a brief second.

'But... but...I never even...' muttered George.

'However,' Leopold continued, 'the law states that you cannot be exiled for this particular crime. Instead you will lose your privileged position as Auditory Manager and you will spend the rest of your working life as a lowly Undermin. As of this moment, your status has been changed. This court is adjourned, you will all leave immediately.'

Leopold gestured towards Cornelius as he started to walk away from the courtroom. The boy quickly followed him. They left using the same door that Sananab had exited from.

George stood in the dock with his head held down in shame. Everyone else had made their way out of the courtroom, everyone except for Snap Potts. He walked over to the desolate figure staring down at the floor.

'What am I going to do, Eric? What am I going to do now?' said George.

'Come on, pal. Let's get you home, away from this place. We'll figure it out somehow,' said Snap.

'I really miss her, you know, Eric. I miss her so much,' said George.

'I know, George, I know you do, pal,' replied Snap.

'She would've known what to do, she always knew what to do,' said George.

Snap put his arm around his friend, the two min walked out together.

Saturday 27th October, 9:51 p.m. The Luglands.

The journey back to the Luglands was a long one, and not a very pleasant one. Normally the journey to get *back* from anywhere seems to go a lot quicker than the corresponding journey did to get there in the first place, as the inevitable conversation tends to pass the time. Today was different, nobody said anything at all.

The outcome of the trial was not really a surprise to any of them, in fact they were all expecting a loss for the Earside workers but it was the way in which it unfolded. That was what had offended most people. The severity of the punishment to George Grip was the most deeply upsetting part of it all.

The Lugland folk were colleagues, neighbours, families and friends, and their community spirit would now be tested. The usual response against something like this would be to stand up and fight back for the people they loved and cared for, and not accept the harsh penalty which Central Head had unfairly given out to one of their own. To come together as one in the face of adversity and possibly even get a couple of more days off work doing it, but this time they couldn't. They couldn't do anything about it, and they knew it.

They lived to serve The Will; this was the only reason that the min existed here after all. Their sole purpose was to serve The Will. This was not a petty incident which could be dealt with in-house, like being late for work, or pilfering muffins from the Earside canteen. This was an offence which affected The Will itself, and it was out of their control. Everybody was crestfallen. They travelled on foot, long into the night, trying to put this day behind them.

One of the min had brought back something from the trip, however, something which just happened to be lying around when nobody was looking. Something which moments earlier had fallen from the sky and whacked him straight on the head, a gift he thought, a gift from someone up high. A huge leather bound book with gold edgings and trim. A diary of some kind maybe? He would have to take it back with him and find out what was in it, providing he could find somebody who could read it to him, of course.

Chapter Four

A new morning had dawned and the Luglands had once again awoken to take in the new day.

George and Henry had gone over to see the Potts family. Snap had given himself the morning off as he was still angry at what had happened. All of the Earside workers had gone back to their daily routine, filtering and processing the sounds which came their way. Whenever there was a setback of any kind, it was always considered the best approach was to carry on as normal, and things would generally take care of themselves.

The excitement and optimism of a day out, and indeed a trip to Central Head, which yesterday's morning had served up, was now a distant memory. Everything was very much business as usual for everyone, that was everyone, except George Grip of course.

'Penelope, love, Henry's here,' said Maggie, as she opened the door. 'Penelope is out the back, love, if you want to go and find her.'

'Ok thanks, Mrs Potts,' said Henry eagerly. 'She can help me with the questions for the contest, I've got my book with me!' He held the book up to show her.

'Yes, I'm sure she will really enjoy that, lovey,' replied Maggie sarcastically. She knew her daughter very well.

She watched as Henry went out the back to find his friend. 'Come here George, love. How are you feeling this morning?' she said to George. She gave him a hug, and he sat down.

'Ah, been better, Maggie. I'm still a bit numb to be honest with you; it all came as a bit of a shock really. I had a feeling I'd get the blame for it somehow, like, but well, you know,' said George.

Maggie sat down in the chair opposite him. She quickly removed a crumpled copy of 'Union Rules and Regulations '34' which she'd inadvertently sat upon, and threw it behind the chair.

'Yes, we were all shocked at the sentence, George. I mean, demoted to Undermin, that's just not fair at all.'

To be classed as an Undermin was indeed an unfair punishment. There were three basic levels of punishment which could be administered to the min. The worst one of all was to be exiled. This meant that the perpetrator would have to give up contact with all min, and be sent away to roam the depths of The Will. Anyone in exile was branded with the motto 'Nos Numquam Immutare Voluntaten' across their forehead so all could see it, and he or she was not allowed to speak to, or be in direct contact with any other min. More importantly, no other min was allowed to speak to, or be in direct contact with the exiled or risk punishment themselves. This part of the edict tended to work very well, and therefore would police itself.

The exiled were also not allowed to settle anywhere either, the conditions of exile meant that they had to continually roam as long as they lived. It was a desperate life.

Another basic punishment was to be thrown in prison. This was Leopold Schmidt's territory, and the most common crime of anyone in prison was non-payment of taxes.

The prison was on the shores of the Stomachic Sea, and anyone who was sent there would be put to work. Most people would stay there for months having to work for their freedom. They would have to work constantly without rest for days on end; it was exhausting and intensive hard labour. Some say that the Stomachic Sea contained acids which would burn the skin of any min that touched it; others say the scars came from being beaten by Leopold Schmidt and his prison guards. Either way, the people who came back from the prison were always scarred, and everyone knew where they had been.

An Undermin was one step away from exile. An Undermin was not allowed to work for money, he was not allowed to gain any position higher than his own, and he would have to do whatever he was told by anybody with status higher than him, in accordance with the law of The Will.

The only min that had a status lower than that of an Undermin, were the exiled. This included children too which meant that in effect, George Grip would have to take orders from his own son if it came to it, not that Henry would ever take advantage of such a rule.

Henry loved his father very much, and this love was the only thing keeping the family together right now. But Maggie was right, to a min who had been in charge of a whole department, a min of status that had an exemplary service record for many years, this indeed was a desperately harsh and unfair punishment.

'I thought it would just be a suspension for a few days or something like that maybe,' said George. 'Ah, I don't know,' he added.

Snap came in from the bedroom, he hadn't heard the others coming in. 'Anyone seen my union book anywhere? I'm sure I left it round here somewhere. Had it this morning, I'm sure I did, I was sitting in that there chair.'

Maggie nervously looked over her shoulder. 'No, love, can't say I have. Er, George and Henry are here, love,' she said, conveniently changing the subject.

'Hello, George, how are you this morning, old pal? I still can't get my head around this business at all, you know, been up all night thinking about it,' he said as he sat down next to George.

'We were just talking about it before you came in, love, it's just so unfair, isn't it?' said Maggie.

'I've been thinking all night too,' said George. 'Thinking about all sorts of things. Thinking about what happened, thinking about me, about Henry. Thinking about my Mary. Trying to figure out what to do for the best.'

I know what I'd like to do,' said Maggie. 'I'd like to go back up there, get hold of the three of them jumped up little Herberts and smash their bloody heads together!'

'That's not gonna help much now is it, Maggie?' said Snap to his wife.

'No but it'd bloomin' well make me feel better though,' she replied.

'Yes, and me come to think of it,' conceded Snap. He turned to George. 'There's definitely something fishy going on about all of this though, and I don't mean one of Maggie's fishy drinks neither.'

'I don't know what you mean,' said Maggie innocently. Damn it, she thought, I didn't know he knew about that one, we'll have to hide those in Winnie's from now on.

'Did you see how angry he got? Sananab did, when you were talking?' continued Snap. 'The reaction and all, it was like you hit a raw nerve or something, I mean he just exploded.'

'Yes, I did wonder about that. It was when I mentioned the nerves, he went ape. He hardly said a word all morning and then all that happened, strange. But I did what I told 'em, Snap, you know me, I just sent it up as normal,' said George.

'Yes, he's up to something I bet you, up to no good again. The three of them in cahoots with each other, I shouldn't wonder. They make me so angry they do, and that Schmidt, I'd love to see him fall of his bloody high chair one day. I really would,' said Snap. 'And don't get me started on that Crail neither, his father was the same, always crawling,' he added.

'Needs a smacked arse him, if you ask me!' said Maggie, never one to mince her words. 'He's got a face like a smacked arse and all, come to think of it,' she added.

'Well it's no use us getting upset with each other over it now, is there? What's done is done. Can't change it now, can we?' said George.

'It's not right George, it's just not right though, is it?' said Snap.

The three of them knew that George was right, they couldn't change a thing. Maggie was furtively trying to push the crumpled union book under the chair with her foot.

'She sometimes talks to me in my sleep, you know, when I'm dreaming of her. She talks to me, she really does,' said George. 'We have proper conversations and all. We talk about the old days, when we had good times together; you two remember those times, don't you?'

'Yes pal, how could we forget? They were the best days those were, the very best. We were inseparable back then, the five of us did everything together, went everywhere together,' said Snap.

'Yeah, before you swallowed the union book and became a miserable old sod,' said Maggie from her chair, the offending article now out of sight.

Snap turned and looked at his wife in disgust.

'But I still love you, my little day off in lieu!' said his wife apologetically.

'Do you remember the times when we used to go away together camping?' said George, ignoring the Potts' insults to each other. 'We used to go down to the Adam's Apple Campsite, and climb the trees, sit on the hill and watch the waterfall. Do you remember? It was beautiful down there. We had some great laughs there, didn't we?'

'Ah, the old Adam's Apple, now that does bring back a few fond memories,' said Maggie. 'Mary and I had been going down there ever since we was little nippers, did a lot of growing up down there we did.'

'We all did a lot of growing up down there, yeah good times, George. Very good times indeed,' said Snap.

'That waterfall must be one of the most beautiful places in the entire Will. I can still picture it now. There we all are sitting on the hill, holding hands, looking over the edge and watching the river flow into the gorge. Well, the four of us holding hands of course, me and Snap, and you and Mary, of course George. Leo was always there with us, but he was always the one, who sat by himself,' said Maggie.

'Yeah, we should've known then why he always sat by himself an' all shouldn't we?' said Snap.

'Well, he was different back then, wasn't he?' said Maggie. 'He was kind and honest, and a good friend to all of us. Anyway, Mary always said we had to look after him. She had a lot of time for him, didn't she?'

'She always saw the best in people, did my Mary,' said George. 'Never had a bad word to say about anyone, that's why I fell in love with her.'

'Yeah, that's why *he* fell in love with her an' all. Always sniffing around he was, pestering the poor girl, wasn't right all that if you ask me, wasn't right at all,' said Snap.

'Oh I didn't believe any of that stuff for one minute. We were all friends together back then, all looked out for each other. There was always a helping hand to share. Do you remember the time when Leo fell out of the tree, and got caught up in his braces?' said George.

'Yeah he was bouncing up and down for ages, ha, ha!' said Maggie.

'And there was that time when Mary nearly lost her shoe in the gorge, she was leaning over to grab it and nearly bloody fell in! We all had to form a chain to pull her back up again. Mind you, it was Leo that pulled us all up again like. He was very strong in them days, after all,' said Snap.

George had a hint of a smile on his face as the three friends reminisced. 'Yeah, she was always getting us into scrapes was my Mary. She was the best thing that ever happened to me, she was my rock. I'll never forget what she said to me when Henry was born. 'George,' she said, 'our child will do all of the great things that we've always wanted to, through him, we can live our dreams'. She always had the perfect thing to say, she always knew what to do, that's why I miss her so much.'

'We all miss her George. Never a day goes by that we don't think about her, she was my best friend, always was,' said Maggie. 'But you've got to be strong for Henry's sake. He needs you to be there for him now.'

'Maggie is right, George. You've got to do it for Henry,' said Snap.

'But I'm not strong, am I? I'm not strong at all.' George paused for a moment, and then continued. 'I've been up all night thinking about it and I've come to a conclusion, but I'm going to need your help.'

Maggie and Snap both looked worriedly at each other as George continued. 'I've decided I'm going to go away for a while. I'm not sure how long I'm going to be away but I'm leaving tonight.'

Maggie and Snap were completely shocked.

'Away? What do you mean you're going away? Away where?' said Snap.

'To be honest with you, I don't really know,' said George. 'But I need you two to look after Henry for me. Will you do that for me? I wouldn't trust anyone else with him, only you two.'

'Well of course we'll look after Henry for you, George, that goes without saying but do you think that's the best thing to do right now? I mean he's already lost his mother, and if you go as well, then that might too much for the boy. He's only fifteen years old, remember?' said Maggie.

'Yes I know that, Maggie, but I may only be gone for a little while, and he's going off to study for the contest trials next week anyway if he gets picked so we would've had to be separated sooner rather than later. Besides, if he does manage to get into Central Head then he'll be gone for good, so I think it's the best thing for both of us right now. Plus, I hear Penelope is thinking of studying for the trials too, so they'd be able to keep each other company,' said George.

Snap immediately jumped up from his seat, he was furious at hearing such a revelation. 'What? Over my dead body!' he shouted. 'No daughter of mine is gonna get mixed up with that shower of snakes and vipers! Where did you hear this anyway?' he turned to his wife. 'Did you know about this too?'

'No, I bloody-well didn't, Eric Potts. First I've heard of it. But thinking about it, might not be such a bad idea. They could keep each other company, as George says. After all they are best friends, and you know how bored she gets here. It'll give the girl something to do for a change,' said Maggie to her angry husband.

'Sorry, Henry sort of let it slip this morning on the way over but like Maggie says, Snap, Penelope has got adventure in her. It won't be long before she wants to go somewhere, this way they can go together,' said George, trying to appeal to his friend's better nature.

'After all they've done to you, George. You of all people! I can't believe you want to let him go up there again. I thought yesterday had proved to you they're all corrupt? Nothing but greedy vultures, the lot of 'em!' said Snap.

'I couldn't stop him if I tried, Snap. It was all he ever wanted to do. It's all he ever thinks about. As soon as he could walk and talk, it was always about winning the contest, you know that. He comes here often enough. It's his dream, and how could any father stop their child from fulfilling their dream? I accepted it a long time ago, one way or another, he will get there somehow,' said George.

'George is right, love. Sooner or later she'll want to go travelling or whatever they calls it. At least this way they can look out for each other, makes perfect sense, doesn't it?' said Maggie.

Snap sat down again, he put his head in his hands. 'Ah I dunno, you two have always had a habit of ganging up on me and making me do things I never wanted to do. I suppose you've always managed to get your way. I reckon if I was to let her go with anyone, I'd prefer it to be Henry. I'm not happy about it though. Anyway, they might not even get chosen for the trials, yet, might they?'

'Yeah that's right, love. They've still got to be chosen yet, might not get picked,' said Maggie.

'Yeah, perhaps they won't. They could stay here and work with me then,' said Snap hopefully.

Maggie and George looked at each other; they were both thinking the same thing. A life working in an ear was a fine job for most min, but not for Henry and Penelope.

'So when are you going to tell Henry that you're going then, George?' said Maggie.

'I reckon there's no time like the present, eh?' said George. 'I'll tell him now.'

He got up from the chair and walked out into the back where Henry and Penelope were sitting opposite each other on the floor. They were studiously going through the questions from Henry's official 'Contest and Trials Book of General Things '34'.

'Now let me see, that would have to be the tibial nerve, or is it the femoral? Er, no, the tibial nerve. Yes the tibial, am I right?' said Henry.

'Penelope?' interrupted George.

Penelope looked up from the page. The sight of George was a welcome relief from the endless questions she had been instructed to ask. 'Yes, Mr Grip?' she replied.

'A little bird tells me that you might be thinking about applying for the trials this year?' said George.

Penelope immediately looked at Henry. He'd seen that look before. It was a look which contained his full name, including both of his middle names.

'Er, sorry, Loppy, it just sort of, er, slipped out,' he said. Henry closed his eyes expecting a whack on the head, but nothing came. After a second or two he dared to open them again, just as he did the book came down hard on his head. 'Ouch!' he began rubbing his head.

George ignored the violence inflicted on his son. 'It's ok, Penelope, I've mentioned it to your mother and father, and they say it is ok for you to put in your application. In fact, your mother seemed to think it was quite a good idea.'

Penelope had a look of bewilderment upon her face.

'I'd go in and speak to them about it now, if I were you. Strike while the iron is hot, before they change their minds. You know what they're like. Also, I need to have a quick word with Henry, here,' said George.

'Er, ok, then. Right I'll just, er, go in then, shall I?' said Penelope rather puzzled. She gave Henry his book and made her way inside to go and speak to her parents. She had a feeling that her father would not be very pleased about it, no matter what Mr Grip had said.

But if it were true, and her parents had indeed agreed for her to apply, then it would mean that she could finally get away from here. She could finally go somewhere and have something to *do*, even if it was only for the trials. The training. Well that would just be the start of it, to go away for a year and study with all of the other hopefuls, meet hundreds of interesting people, from different parts of The Will.

There would be people from different cultures and backgrounds. She could find out about where they were from, and what things they did there, what it was like to live anywhere other than the Luglands. It would be fantastic.

But wait, she might not get chosen, she might not make the final one hundred? What if she didn't make the cut? That'd be disastrous. She would have to spend the rest of her life living and working in an ear! To her knowledge no other female had ever won the contest before. In fact not very many girls ever really entered into the trials and so what was so special about her? Why would they choose her?

No, hang on, let's be positive she thought. It will be ok. Everything is going to be ok. Think positive thoughts, and positive things will happen. Yes, positivity, that is the key. Be confident, like Henry. Right, now it's time to speak to Father.

George sat down next to his son. He wasn't really sure how he was going to break the news to him. He wasn't even a hundred percent certain that he'd made the right decision. Nevertheless, he knew it wasn't going to be easy telling him.

'How's the studying going, son?'

'Very well, Father!' said Henry. 'I know I'll have no problem passing the knowledge tests, it's the physical that I need to practise on.'

'Why is that?' said his father. 'You're such a fit and healthy boy. You'll pass the physical with flying colours, I'll guarantee you!'

'I just need to get a bit faster, that's all, Father. A bit more speed on my running is all,' said Henry.

'Don't worry; you'll be fine I've told you. You've got your mother's spirit in you, son, and you work hard. That's what'll get you through. One day you'll be in charge of everyone up there, you will, you know?' said George.

Henry smiled a beaming smile, 'I just want to make you proud, Father.'

'I know, son, and you already do make me proud,' said George, 'which makes what I've got to tell you all the more difficult, so I guess I'll have to just come out and say it.'

Henry's smile soon faded into a look of surprise.

I'm going away for a while, Henry, away from here. Away from the Luglands altogether. I'm not sure how long for and I'm not sure when I'll be coming back, but I'm going tonight. I've packed my things, and I'll be gone before nightshift ends.'

It was the most difficult thing George had ever had to say.

Henry stared at his father in disbelief. 'What? Going away? Why? Where to Father? Where are you going?'

George hadn't really thought about where he was going. 'To tell you the truth, son, I'm not really sure. All I know is that after what happened yesterday, I don't really have any choice. They've stripped me of any dignity I had, everything I have ever worked for has been taken away from me. Everything I have built up has gone. I have to go.'

'But why? What will happen to me? What will I do Father? I haven't got anybody else, there's only ever been me and you,' said Henry.

Don't worry, son, Maggie and Eric will look after you while I'm gone, you're going to stay here with them, and Penelope too. They will treat you as if you were their own son. I wouldn't just leave you with anyone now, would I? Besides you spend much more time here than you ever do at home anyway. You practically live here as it is,' said George.

'But I don't understand?' said Henry.

'I don't really understand it either, Henry, I don't really understand any of it.' George looked down and put his arm around his son.

'But I don't want you to go, Father. Why do you have to go? Why can't you just stay here with me?' said Henry, his voice filled with sadness.

'You will always be with me.' George put his hand upon his chest. 'Here in my heart, and I will always be there, with you, wherever you are in the world. Always remember that, you only have to close your eyes to see.'

Henry couldn't believe the bombshell which had been dropped upon him. He sat for a moment in the safe hold of his father's arms.

'What was she like, Father? What was Mother really like? I wish I would have known her. Why did she leave us?'

'She was the finest womin ever to have graced The Will. She was always happy and smiling, she would light up the room wherever she went. She was kind and honest, and true to her friends. She was the most popular girl in the Luglands, everyone wanted to be friends with Mary. She loved you very much you know, Henry. You were her little diamond, her little treasure.'

'So why did she go, Father, why?' said Henry.

George sighed. He knew this question would come someday. 'Nobody knows, Henry, nobody really knows for sure. All I know is that she would never have walked out on us willingly, not your mother, no chance of that. She's out there somewhere I know it.'

He paused for a moment. 'Anyway, that was a long time ago, all in the past now, things were different then, no use in dragging all that up again now, is there?

Now if I know Henry Grip, I know he'll be wanting to carry on with his studying. The contest trials start soon, don't they? You'll definitely get chosen this year, I know it. This is gonna be your year to shine, son, I can feel it in my bones!'

'Yes, Father,' said Henry.

George reached into his tunic pocket and pulled out a purse of money. 'Now, ever since you were born, I've been putting a little bit away each week for a rainy day and well, I think I can spot a few clouds heading our way so this seems like a good a day as any to give you it.

Now there's enough there to keep you going for quite a few years to come yet, son. I want you to go inside and give this to Mrs Potts and tell her that she is to use this money for your keep. And she's not to argue with you, neither, tell her I said to keep it and give it you, as and when you need it. You're going to need a load of books for starters, and I suppose you all have to wear that silly uniform.'

'The uniform of Central Head is the....' Henry started to speak.

'I know son, I know,' interrupted his father. 'Now run along and give that money to Mrs Potts before you lose it.'

'Ok, Father.' Henry turned to run.

'´Ere, come and give your father a hug before you go,' said George.

Henry turned back as his father knelt down to give him a hug. George was struggling to hold back the tears, not knowing how long it would be before he would see his son again. He tried not to let Henry see his emotion. 'Now go on, son, in you go.'

He watched his son as he ran back inside. 'And tell Maggie not to be buying any booze with that neither!' he shouted after him.

Henry went back inside, leaving his father alone. He gave the money to Mrs Potts as instructed and told her what his father had said, even about the booze. 'Cheeky bugger' was a phrase he'd heard many times before so it didn't shock him at all. He knew he would get well looked after with the Potts, but he would desperately miss his father.

He would miss the late night chats he used to have with him, he would miss all of his stories about the inner workings of The Will, how sound was produced, and how food was generated from the mines of the Stomachic Sea. How the Kushnick Tribe worshipped the offerings from The Will itself, and how they thought that in some way everything had to be returned. How the skilled craftsmen from all parts of the land could form and create the tools which they needed to build cities and empires throughout The Will.

Together they had survived for fifteen years, just the two of them, and now he was on his own. Henry was an intelligent boy, however, and he knew that his father couldn't carry on living as an Undermin in the Luglands. It was humiliating for a min of such honesty and integrity, and he knew that he had to accept things the way they were.

George Grip began the long walk back to his home. It was a familiar journey to him. One which he had walked a thousand times before, passing many of the Earside workers along the way. He never told anyone else that he was leaving. He thought it would be easier that way.

When he got back, he picked up the old worn out tunic which he had earlier tied into the shape of a pouch. He jammed what few belongings he could fit into it, tied it with a piece of string and threw it over his shoulder. He stood for a moment, looking around at his home, at the memories which flooded his head. Who knows, perhaps I'll bump into her one day, he thought to himself. He started to whistle a tune, a tune they used to whistle in the old days, a happy tune with happy memories. He closed the door behind him and walked away.

Sunday 28th October, 12:18 p.m. The Luglands.

Not too far from the Grip house, in a small clearing at the foot of the Eustachian Hills, there were three figures trying desperately not to be seen; although they were not doing a very good job of it. They were all male, in their early twenties, and anybody observing from afar would definitely get the distinct impression that they were up to no good.

One of the three seemed to be in charge. He led the other two to the edge of the clearing. 'Right, this'll do I reckon, we'll stop here. Ollie, make sure you keep Dixie,' he said.

His name was Stony Pickles. He lived and worked in the Right Ear Department, although he hated every minute of it. He was the type of min who would do a day's work if he really had to but would do everything he possibly could to get out of it. Sometimes the scheming and pretending which went into getting *out* of work was actually much harder than going to work itself.

Today was one of those days where he had found an excuse not to be in work. In fact, he hadn't really been at work for some time now, on account of his sore ears. Sore ears were his latest excuse not to go in. Working in an ear tended to require pretty good hearing so he thought he had a good excuse this time, even though he was lying through his teeth.

Yesterday was different, however, because yesterday his ears were miraculously back to normal and yesterday he was ok to go back to work. No coincidence then that yesterday was the day that everybody had been summoned to Central Head. So for everyone apart from the skeleton crew who stayed behind, work had been suspended for the day. He wasn't going to miss that for anything. Today, unfortunately his ears were sore again so he didn't go in.

'Right, ok, Stony, leave it to me,' said Ollie.

Ollie Gimble was also an Earside worker and a friend of Stony. He was a huge figure of a min, who many described as a gentle giant. He attended work regularly, and had never taken a day off sick in his life. He didn't believe in missing work for any reason whatsoever and had an immaculate attendance record to prove it.

Unfortunately, as most of his colleagues put it, he was as thick as two short planks. Whenever he got to work, everything he touched went wrong so they tended to give him jobs which didn't require any thought, which there weren't a lot of. Most of the time he just sat there and waited for people to give him things to do; he was good at that, especially as nobody ever did. He pretty much just sat there all day long.

Every now and again someone would come along and pat him on the back and say things like, 'Well done, Ollie, keep it up, you're doing a grand job!' This would make him smile and feel a part of things. Today however, Stony had given him an *actual* job to do and he was suddenly very excited about it.

The final member of the trio was called Raymond Curley, also an Earside Right worker. He had not long turned twenty years of age, and was about eighteen months or so younger than the other two. He had been brought along by Stony because he was supposed to be clever. Well, cleverer than the other two anyway but considering who he was up against, this wasn't hard. The three of them sat down behind a small bush.

'Right then, boys, are you ready for this? Here we have....' Stony Pickles reached into his tunic and began to pull something out from underneath, before he was interrupted by Ollie Gimble.

'Er, Stony?'

'What is it? Is someone coming?' said Stony, getting ready to run.

'No I don't think so,' said Ollie looking confused.

'Well, what is it then?' said Stony.

'Er, what's a Dixie?' said Ollie.

'What's a what?' said Stony, the confusion was catching.

'A Dixie,' said Ollie.

'Eh?' said Stony.

'Well, you said as to keep Dixie. Well I don't think I've got a Dixie to keep, you see. But I'd be more than happy to keep it for you, if you were to lend us one, like?' said Ollie.

'No I don't mean, oh...' Stony Pickles sighed and looked at the other two. 'Curley, will you tell him what I mean? He doesn't even know what Dixie is,' he said.

Curley started to laugh. 'Ha, ha, what a dummy! He doesn't even know what a Dixie is ha, ha!' He looked at Stony who was also joining in ridiculing their friend.

'Everyone knows what a Dixie is,' continued Curley. 'A Dixie is, ha, I can't believe he don't know. A Dixie is...., ha, ha. Well, a Dixie is a...., er, I don't know. What is a Dixie, Stony?'

'Give me strength!' said Stony. 'Look, to keep Dixie just means to keep an eye out, doesn't it? Make sure nobody's coming, like, ok?'

'Oh, right you are, Stony. Yeah, I'll keep Dixie,' said Ollie, happy now that he knew what to do.

'Oh, that type of Dixie,' said Curley. 'Oh I thought you meant the other type of... yeah, I know now, yeah, tut.' He stopped talking before the hole he was digging for himself got any deeper.

Stony once again reached into his tunic and started to pull out what was inside. 'Right, fellas feast your eyes on this little beauty!'

He pulled out Montague Schmidt's diary and placed it down on to the grass in the middle of the three min. The other two gasped in amazement, they'd never seen anything like this before in their lives.

'Wow, Stony, what's that?' said an amazed Ollie.

'What do you mean what's that? What do you think it is? It's a book, isn't it?' said Stony. 'And a bloody big one and all.'

'Jeez, the size of that! My mamma's kitchen table at home isn't as big as that!' said Curley.

'My mamma's not as bloomin' big as that!' said Ollie.

Stony and Curley had both met Ollie's mamma before; she was a mountain of a womin. Each of them wanted to say something sarcastic at this point but they both thought equally better of it.

'It's a beauty though, isn't it?' said Stony. 'See that there? That's gold edging if I'm not mistaken and it's all over the pages too, look.' He turned over page after page to reveal the gold margins which adorned every single one.

'Where did you get it from, Stony? Is it stolen?' asked Curley.

'No, it's bloody-well not stolen, Curley. But if it's all the same I don't want anybody else finding out about it, right? That goes for you too, Ollie, keep it zipped.'

Stony thought about what he's just said, and to whom. 'Er, that just means keep it quiet, Ollie. It doesn't mean you have to get a zip and, oh never mind, this is just between us three, you got that?' he added.

'Right you are, Stony. I can keep a secret and you can count on me. Where did you get it from anyway?' said Ollie.

Stony looked around again to make sure nobody else was about and then huddled back over the book. 'Well, remember yesterday when we went up to Central Head, well when...'

'Stony,' interrupted Ollie.

'Yes what is it now, Ollie?' said Stony.

'Well I remember yesterday alright. Very clear, in fact. I remember it as if it was only yesterday,' said Ollie.

Stony and Curley both gave each other a confused look.

'Well of course you do. That's because it was yesterday, wasn't it, you big oaf?' said Curley, rather regretting calling Ollie a big oaf. He was stupid but he was also certainly big, and Curley didn't want a slap from him.

'Yeah, I remember it because I weren't there, you see,' said Ollie.

'Eh?' said Curley.

'What are you going on about now? You weren't where?' said Stony. He was beginning to lose his patience.

'Central Head, I never went you see coz I had to go to work. There wasn't much to do, like, but I had to stay behind and do an important job, Mr Grip said. He said he had special duties for me. He said I could be in charge of waiting around,' replied Ollie with a beaming smile.

'Oh right, well ok, when the rest of us went up to Central Head yesterday,' continued Stony, 'well that big pointy fella, what's his name? Anyway, well he went mad, didn't he Curley? He smashed his fists down on the table so hard, that we all flew up in the air and fell on top of each other, didn't we Curley? And anyway, as soon as I could work out which way up I was facing, this ruddy great thing came down from the ceiling and whacked me on the bloody head! Damn nearly knocked me out. Gave me a right big lump and all it did. Might have to have a week off work with that, I reckon.' He started rubbing his head as if to prove he had a genuine injury.

'So who's do you think it is then, Stony?' said Curley.

'Well it's mine now, innit, Curley? I got the bump to prove it and all!' replied Stony.

'Oh yeah, I suppose so. What you gonna do with it then?' asked Curley.

'Well, my old mucker, that's where you come in, see,' said Stony.

Curley looked confused again. 'How d'you mean, Stony?'

'Well everyone knows that I can't read, like. I mean I was doing ok with it and all, but the circumstances made it, er, difficult for me to carry on like,' said Stony.

'You mean you got thrown out of school for stealing all the teachers' money when they were having their dinner, Stony,' said Ollie.

'I'll whack you one in a minute, Ollie!' said Stony. 'Besides, that was never proven. It was their word against mine and there was ten of them, they all ganged up on me. Never did like me, that lot. Especially that old bag who taught us sums, she was always accusing me of things she was.'

'That was your mamma, Stony,' said Ollie.

'Er, yes ok, can we please stop changing the subject? I'm trying to tell you that we've got something here. This thing could be valuable, could be worth a lot of cash to us, this could,' said Stony.

'Sorry, Stony,' said Ollie.

'So where exactly do I come in then?' said Curley.

Stony rolled his eyes. 'Well you're the only one out of the three of us what can read.'

'Yeah?' said Curley.

'So we need you to read it to us. Tell us what it says like, don't we?' said Stony.

'Oh yeah, tell you what it says, like,' said Curley rather uncomfortably.

'Yeah, that's it.' Stony opened the book at the first page, gestured eagerly towards it and waited expectantly for his friend to start reading. 'Well go on then, read.'

Curley put his finger on the first page. His tongue was sticking out of his mouth, the concentration on his face was apparent for all to see. 'Er...'

'Well, what does it say then?' said Stony.

An expectant silence filled the air, after a minute or so Curley said, 'I don't know.'

Stony looked at his friend. 'What do you mean you don't know?'

'I mean, I don't know what it says,' said Curley.

'Well why not, you can read, can't you?' said Stony.

'Yes, of course I can read,' replied Curley, 'I just can't read this.'

'Well why not? It's not a foreign language or anything is it? It's just words that you say one after another, can't be that hard can it?' said Stony, becoming increasingly frustrated.

'Well when I said I could read, I meant I can only read certain things,' said Curley sheepishly.

'Certain things like what?' said Stony.

'My name,' said Curley.

'Your name? Your bloody name!' shouted Stony.

Ollie started to laugh. 'Ha, ha, you thought he could read but he can only read his own name and even I can read my own name! Ha, ha, what a dummy!' For once in his life, he felt a lot less stupid than someone else. He would savour this moment for as long as he could remember it.

'You let me drag you all the way out here believing that you could read, and all the time you could only read your own bloody name! Even I can read my own bloody name!' said Stony, none too impressed with Curley. 'Come on, Ollie, let's go and find someone who can really read, not like this bonehead, and to think I thought he was cleverer than us.'

Stony picked up the book. He and Ollie started to walk back towards the other side of the clearing, closely followed by a rather embarrassed Raymond Curley, shouting after them as they went.

'I'm sorry, Stony, I know someone who can read properly though, honest I do. I'll take you to them, it's not that far from here. Really, it's not.'

The three of them disappeared beyond the trees, with Montague Schmidt's diary closely tucked away for safety.

Chapter Five

The magnificent splendour of Central Head was apparent around every corner. The deep winding corridors flowed into a circinate-like maze, the vast walls and ceilings stretching on for miles. Anyone walking these floors for the first time would need a map or a guide, or even both, and would still probably stand a pretty good chance of getting lost.

Cornelius Crail had neither. He'd studied the geography of The Will during the trials, and indeed had specialised in this particular subject for the contest. He passed with distinction. He would know his way around here with his eyes closed.

Each small door he passed would lead into another vast room beyond containing hundreds of min, all immaculately dressed in the uniform of Central Head and working arduously at their stations. He walked swiftly towards his destination, barely even acknowledging the dozens of min who had stopped to say Good Morning to him. He was on his way to a meeting. The applications for the trials were in and it was his job to collect them and take them to be processed. He didn't want to be late.

He was heading towards the most intense and important part of The Will; the epicentre of the whole operation. The place where only a handful of people had ever set foot in, the only restricted part of the entire Will, the Neocortex.

The door to Sananab's office was different to any of the others. It was bigger, stronger and tougher. It looked as though it had been made to withstand an army; the crossed keys symbol and the motto Nos Numquam Immutare Voluntaten embossed on to its centre. All of the other doors in Central Head were various shades of brown in colour but this door was a deep shade of black. It had the look of importance and prominence about it, the look of a door which had secrets lurking beyond it, almost as if it had a memory.

Cornelius knocked twice. His tiny fist barely making a sound due to the sheer density of the door.

'Cornelius, please come in,' said Sananab from the other side.

Cornelius turned the gleaming brass doorknob and pushed the door. It was a struggle, but he just about managed to open it and scurry into the room before it slammed shut behind him.

Sananab looked at Leopold and then back to the boy. 'Perhaps we ought to fatten you up, my boy. Get some strength in those bones, Leopold?'

'Yes, Sir, I think that would be a good idea,' said Leopold.

'I have the applications for the trials here, Sir, as you requested. They've just come in this morning, Sir,' said Cornelius, still standing near the door and completely ignoring the jibes at his physique.

'How many do we have this year?' said Sananab.

Cornelius sat down. He emptied the bag of applications on the small round table. 'Around seven hundred or so I think, Sir, give or take a few.'

'There seems to be more and more each year. Gone are the days when we could barely make the one hundred required,' said Leopold. 'Now let's see who we have here, three piles as usual, yes, no's and maybe's. Master the yeses; I'll take the no's and Cornelius, the maybe's.'

'There will be no maybe's, Leopold. Anybody other than an emphatic yes does not deserve to work in my presence, is that clear?' said Sananab.

'Yes, Master, of course,' said the Zamindar. 'Cornelius, will you start by reading out who you have, dear boy?'

'Yes, Sir, actually the first name I have here is Montague Schmidt, Sir, your son,' said Cornelius.

'Well hand it to the Master then, boy. This is obviously an emphatic yes,' said Leopold.

'Ah, the boy finally comes of age, my Zamindar. He reaches the age of achievement, and do you think he has what it takes? Does he possess the necessary desire to succeed?' said Sananab.

'Yes, Master, there's no doubt. He won't let you down, I promise,' said Leopold, grovelling before his Master.

'Oh, you will make sure of that, Leopold. You will see to it that he never lets me down,' said Sananab.

'Of course, Sir,' said Leopold, feeling the pressure, 'and, er, Cornelius, would you please continue?'

Cornelius handed the application to Sananab and carried on reading. 'Johnny Thorns, Red Skym, Daniel Porter, Amy Poles, Catherine Worms....'

'No, no, no, no, no, no....' Leopold dismissed each name in turn after they were read out.

'Henry Grip,' Cornelius continued.

'Most definitely not! After the disgrace his father has caused to The Will? He should be hanging his head in shame, he's got some gall, I tell you!' said Leopold angrily.

There was a moment of silence as Cornelius looked up from the application forms where he was caught by the piercing stare of Sananab from across the table.

Cornelius knew Henry Grip very well, and he hated him. He hated everything about him. He would like nothing more than to destroy him, to twist his knife into his pathetic little delusions. It would give him no greater pleasure than to see him take the trials, to watch him go through all of the pain and mental anguish that they brought to him, and then to watch him break down before his very eyes. To see a boy's hopes and dreams shattered amongst the misery of failure. Yes, this was what he hoped for Henry Grip; this was what he deserved.

But could he dare speak out against what the Zamindar had said? He would have to say something quick; he would have to be brave, very brave. He would have to convince Sananab that Leopold was wrong about him, and how could he do that? He would have to take his chance, and for his wicked plan to work, this opportunity was too good to be true.

He cleared his throat, 'Well he is very good, Sir. I mean he's certainly a cut above the rest.'

Leopold looked angrily at the boy. 'How dare you speak out against your superior, boy? You are in the presence of your Master! You give me one good reason why I shouldn't make an example of you? Why you ought to be....'

Sananab interrupted him. 'Now, now, let's not get excited, Leopold. Please let the boy speak, he clearly has something to say about this Grip boy.' He then turned to his Thought Apprentice. 'Cornelius, are you vouching for this boy? Are you saying that the Zamindar is wrong about him?'

Cornelius looked worried. 'Well, sir, I don't particularly like him. I mean, we were never ever friends by any stretch of the imagination but I do think he is brilliant in many ways. And I think that if you are looking for a certain 'something' in the winner, then I suppose he could be the person to step up, Sir,' he said.

'You do?' said Sananab, interested in the boy's response.

'Yes, Sir, and his father, well I'm sure Henry wouldn't want a decision which could affect the rest of his life based on those unfortunate events, Sir. I'm sure that he would have had nothing to do with what happened,' said Cornelius.

Sananab was impressed at the boy's answer, and even more impressed that he had the audacity to speak out against Leopold Schmidt. He held out his hand for the application form. 'Very well, the boy will attend, and well done Cornelius, I can see that you've learned a lot from your time here so far. Carry on.'

'But, Sir, he's a Grip sir, I mean....' Leopold tried to make his protest, before he was instantly dismissed by Sananab.

'I have made my decision. The boy will attend the trials, Leopold,' he said smartly. 'Now Cornelius, you will continue.'

Cornelius was overjoyed at the praise bestowed upon him by the great Sananab, even if it did go against the wishes of his immediate superior. But it was worth it, his plan could work, he would watch Henry Grip squirm beneath his feet. He had even managed to fool the Zamindar and the great Sananab himself, and what was more, it was easy.

He continued to read from the rest of the list as Leopold gave each name his judgement.

'Knotty Pine, Henry Gold, Owen Smallhaven, Diggy Johnston....'

'No, yes, yes, yes....' said Leopold.

'Penelope Potts, Jackie Proudfoot, Tom Sticks....' the boy continued.

'Definitely not, no, yes....' answered Leopold.

'Danny Cow, Robinson Sneed....' said Cornelius.

Sananab interrupted once more. 'The Potts girl, this is the girl with the long yellow hair, is that right?' he said.

'Er, yes, I believe so Master,' said Leopold, worriedly.

'From the hearing?' said his Master.

'Yes, Sir, she was at the hearing but the Potts family spells trouble, Sir. We'll get nothing but problems from them, I'll guarantee you,' said Leopold.

'No, Leopold, I have a feeling about this girl, there is something...' The Master paused to think of the right word, '...different about her, something I haven't seen for a while, not in anyone. She has thought and she has knowledge. There is something intriguing about her, something unique. Yes, she will attend the trials, she shall have her wish. I will watch her progress with some interest.'

At the back of his mind, Leopold had his doubts. He had a feeling that this was going to be a mistake. If this was his decision, then the girl would be rejected without a second thought. The decision however was not his to make.

'Well, if you're sure, Sir?' he said.

'Yes, I'm sure Zamindar. I'm certain of it,' said Sananab. 'And there won't be any problems, you'll see to that. No trouble.'

'Of course, Sir,' said Leopold.

The meeting went on long into the morning. The one hundred trialists were decided and the applications that didn't make it were discarded. There would be no letter of explanation as to why they had not been successful, in the same way as there would not be any reasons given to those who were accepted. The decision had been made and that was final. There was no room for sentiment amongst the leaders of Central Head.

'I believe that was the one hundredth, Sir, the last one,' said Cornelius.

'Fine, that's settled then,' said Leopold. 'I shall process these applications immediately and the new trialists shall be notified at the contest tomorrow. Is there any other business, Master?'

'Yes, Leopold, I'm afraid there is,' said Sananab.

Leopold detected a slight change in the atmosphere. 'Sir?' he said.

'I hear from Cornelius, here, that there is some unrest at the prison. A protest of some kind. Is there any truth in this?' said Sananab.

Leopold looked accusingly at the Thought Apprentice and then turned back to his Master.

'Nothing out of the ordinary, Sir. I'm sure my min have the necessary means to deal with any trouble, Sir. They are quite capable,' he said, having been taken somewhat off guard by this.

'Perhaps a stricter hand may be required this time, Leopold. Quash the unrest for good, yes?' said the Master.

'Sir?' said Leopold again.

'Maybe you should go there and see to it yourself, you are more capable than most after all?' said Sananab.

Leopold looked surprised. 'Do you think that is wise at this time, Sir? I mean what about the contest? A lot of things are already in place, yes, but there are plenty of things still to be organised. Then there are also the trials to consider, we still have so much to do before tomorrow.'

'Perhaps it would be for the best, Leopold, and I am confident you will have everything in order for the start of tomorrow's proceedings. You have never let us down before,' said Sananab.

'I think a good time for you to leave would be after the winner is announced at the end of contest tomorrow night. The trials will take care of themselves. Cornelius can help us look after them, he has trained well.'

'Well if you're sure, Master?' said Leopold. The last thing he needed to do right now was to travel half way around The Will.

Sananab looked him straight in the eyes. 'Yes, I am certain, and my Zamindar will fulfil his duty to The Will.'

'As you wish, Master,' said Leopold reluctantly.

He knew he had to do exactly as his Master commanded, but was not happy about it at all. Cornelius glanced across at him with a look that said, 'This was nothing to do with me'; while Leopold returned a look which said, 'I don't believe you for one second.'

'Now, Leopold, you may go, thank you,' said Sananab.

'Thank you, Your Eminence.' Leopold bowed before his Master and turned towards the door. 'Cornelius, come with me boy,' he snapped. He would certainly be having a few strong words with his young protégé the second that they were outside of this office, that was for sure.

'Er, no,' said Sananab. 'I have some things to speak to my young Thought Apprentice about. He will catch up with you later, Leopold.'

'Oh,' said Leopold, a little surprised by this. 'Of course, as you wish.' He bowed to his Master once more and then walked out of the huge door, leaving Sananab and Cornelius alone in the office.

Cornelius was extremely relieved that he didn't have to walk alongside an angry Leopold Schmidt right at this moment. He had seen the Zamindar's temper at first hand and he wasn't a min to be crossed. He also hated doing anything which was forced upon him, as this was.

The Will's first Thought Apprentice, however, had never expected to be given a job with a level of importance as the one he'd just been awarded, and this early in his Central Head career. No more carrying pointless messages and sending memos for Cornelius Crail, oh no. This was a real position. The thought of it was already making his head swell. He had only ever dreamed of having such power and it would soon be a reality. To become the Overseer of the trials was indeed a powerful position, even if it was only as an assistant, but he would be there and that was what mattered. And it was at only this time last year that he was a hopeful trialist, himself.

Sananab turned to Cornelius again. 'Cornelius, do you believe in loyalty?'

'Yes, Sir, of course I do, Sir,' replied the boy.

'Do you know what it takes to be completely loyal to someone?' said Sananab.

'Yes, Sir. I think so, Sir,' said the boy again. This conversation was becoming more interesting to him by the sentence.

'Loyalty can bring great benefits Cornelius. To be loyal to someone can be a great privilege to a min. Indeed, to be trusted with loyalty is a considerable honour. I need people who I can trust, people who I can rely upon to do as I ask, without question.'

Sananab leaned across the table, until his face was so close to his Thought Apprentice that they were almost touching. 'Are you loyal to me, Cornelius Crail?' he said.

Cornelius knew that this moment could be pivotal in his career in Central Head. Indeed an important moment which would affect the rest of his life. For a boy who had dreams of pure power, this was the type of question that didn't come along very often. His answer was eminently predictable. 'Of course, Sir, completely.'

'Good, very good, Cornelius, I'm glad.' Sananab put his arm on Cornelius' shoulder. 'I knew I could trust you. There are qualities in you that will take you a long way.'

'Thank you, Sir. It is indeed a huge honour to be considered by someone as great as yourself,' said the boy, laying it on thick.

Sananab slowly leaned back in his chair. He was gently massaging his beard with the thumb and forefinger of his left hand. 'I need you to do something for me, Cornelius, something of great importance, something which requires loyalty,' he said.

'Yes, Sir, anything, Sir,' said the boy eagerly.

'I have...,' Sananab paused for a moment, '...a task which I need you to carry out. An extremely important task. Can you do that for me, Cornelius?'

'Yes, Sir, of course I can,' said Cornelius. 'I will do whatever is required of me. What is this task, Sir?'

'As I have just said, I need you to help us oversee the trials this year. For you have worked well Cornelius, very well, it will be your reward,' said Sananab.

'Of course, Sir. Thank you, Sir,' said Cornelius as he was still taking it all in.

'But I want you to do slightly more than just help, Cornelius. I want you to oversee the trials completely. I want you to be in total charge, complete control, everyone shall answer to you. Do you understand?' said Sananab.

Cornelius' mouth dropped open as wide as a tunnel; his chin was almost

'Sandwiches, what sandwiches? Oh Will's teeth, they were for the journey those were,' said Maggie rolling her eyes. 'I made them specially last night. I'll have to go and make some more now, won't I? I've got to get dressed and all, I hope this is not going to make us late now.'

She walked off muttering to herself. 'I hope they never drank that flask of brew, mind, they'll be high as a bloody kite before dinner time if they did.'

'Sorry, Mrs Potts.' Henry offered his apology as Penelope just sat there rather embarrassed.

'Right, you two, have a good time at the contest today, won't you?' said Snap. 'I'm off to work. I'll see you when you get back tonight. But before I go, I want you to listen here to what I've got to say.'

Henry and Penelope gave him their full attention.

'Now, don't be too disappointed if you don't get accepted for the trials now do you hear? It's not the end of the world if you don't get in. There's always something else around the corner; plenty of opportunities in this world. And remember, there's always a job for you both with me on the shop floor whenever you need it, ok?'

'Thank you, Father.'

'Thank you, Mr Potts.'

The children offered their thanks. Although the sudden threat and quite realistic possibility of having to work in an ear for the rest of their lives had now put even more pressure on them being accepted for the trials.

'Look after each other up there today and make sure Winnie and you're mother don't get sloshed, eh?' Snap gave Penelope a kiss on the cheek, and patted Henry affectionately on the top of his head. He put on his dark blue hat and started towards the door. 'See you later, Maggie!'

'See you later, love,' shouted Maggie from the other room. 'I'll try and get us all back before midnight.'

Snap Potts headed off to work, whistling a tune, the same tune that he always whistled.

Henry was itching to get going. 'I'm so excited, Loppy, not long now and we'll be on our way to the contest! I think it's gonna be even better than last year, Loppy, don't you?'

'Yeah, I suppose,' said Penelope.

Henry continued. 'Mind you, I wanted that boy from the Patellas to win. What was his name now?'

'Clifton,' said Penelope.

'Yes, Clifton, that was it,' said Henry, 'Clifton Smith, but bloomin' crappy Crail went and won it though, didn't he? I still don't know how he managed to come first in the physicals. All of the others seemed to be much stronger than him. Anyway, who do you think is gonna win it this year then, Loppy?'

'Oh, I don't know, Henry. Won't there be some of the same people who competed last year?' said Penelope. 'Aren't they allowed to do it again?'

'They're only allowed to compete twice, Loppy, everyone knows that. So Clifton Smith will be able to do it again if he's got the points, of course, but the other four will all be newcomers to it,' said Henry.

'Well I'll have to say that Clifton will win it then, won't I, Henry?' said Penelope. 'Because I don't know who any of the others are, do I?'

'Oh yeah,' said Henry glumly. 'I suppose you don't, do you?'

'Anyway, he did have a lot of support last year didn't he?' said Penelope. 'Not many people seemed altogether happy when they announced Cornelius Crail as the winner; not the most popular of choices I must say.'

'Especially not from around here anyway,' said Henry. 'He was always bragging about one day winning the contest and being up there in Central Head, and now he's sitting alongside the great Sananab. Sometimes life just isn't fair, Loppy.'

'Er, doesn't that sound a little bit familiar, Henry?' said Penelope spotting the sudden irony. 'I think we both know someone who is always saying that one day they are going to win the contest, and that one day they will be working in Central Head. Somebody who happens to be sitting not very far from here right now.'

'Who, me?' said Henry.

'Yes, you!' said Penelope.

The similarities had suddenly dawned on Henry, even though he felt pained to admit it.

'Oh yeah, well ok, I suppose you're right. But I still don't think he deserves it anyway,' he said.

'You'll win it one day, Henry, I'm certain of it,' said Penelope comfortingly. 'Anyway, let's hope for some good luck. Today is when they announce the successful trialists, isn't it?'

'Yes, after the contest,' said Henry. 'I'm very confident though, Loppy, I think I'll be ok.'

Penelope looked disappointed. 'What about me then?' she said. 'There's never been a girl who has won the contest before, has there? What chance have I got? I'd hate to have to stay here for the rest of my life. How boring would that be? I mean, I love Mother and Father very much, but there's no life for me around here. I need something to do.'

Henry realised that he'd been a little selfish with his last remark. He knew that he and Penelope felt exactly the same about the Luglands and there were certainly other places that they both wanted to see. Things that they both needed to do. They were best friends and always had been. They both wanted the same thing, and things were always much more achievable when they did them together.

'But there have been plenty of girls who have entered the trials, Loppy. There seem to be more and more each year, in fact, it's more popular now than it's ever been. I'm sure you'll get in to the trials. In fact, I'm sure we will both get into the trials, together,' he said.

'Oh, I do hope so, Henry, I really do,' she said.

'Yes, we'll be ok, Loppy. We've always stuck together, haven't we?' said Henry.

'Yes, we need to look out for each other. Like Father says, stick together,' said Penelope.

Maggie came back in from the kitchen, fully dressed and ready to go. She was carrying two huge bags under each arm. Inside were enough sandwiches and snacks to feed an entire army.

'Right then, all done, a bit of a rush though. I reckon this should be enough to get us to Central Head. I'm sure there'll be a few pies when we get there, if we run out. That's if the tight buggers don't scrimp on the spread again this year,' she said.

'Now come along you two, we best be off. And I think you're right, Henry, perhaps I slightly underestimated the amount of time we had. My body clock is all over the place at the moment. We were supposed to meet Winnie ten minutes ago, she'll be wondering where we are. You know how she frets and all.'

Henry was up and at the door before she had even finished her sentence. He didn't need a second invitation. 'Today is the first day of the rest of our lives, Loppy!' he said excitedly. 'Let us march towards our future!'

'Er, right, ok, Henry, if you like,' said Penelope, slightly uncomfortable with her friend's new found profundity.

Maggie looked puzzlingly at her daughter, who shrugged her shoulders in return. She shook her head and said, 'Ok, whatever, right come on or we're gonna miss the boat!'

The three of them left the house and hurried off down the road. Henry was running on ahead, the other two trying their best to keep up.

Winnie Drum was waiting at the end of the road, along with her nephew Ronnie and some of his friends. It was his band. They were playing a song whilst Winnie was dancing around them like a giddy little girl. She twirled around and around as if she didn't have a care in the world, then she fell over.

'Oh no, I think Winnie is drunk again Henry. Look she's fallen over,' said Penelope, as they neared the others. 'And look at the time, it's only ten past eight.'

'Is this it?' said Maggie helping her friend to her feet. 'I thought we were all going together, what's happened to the others?'

'They've all gone on ahead,' said Ronnie without missing a beat. 'You are cutting it a bit fine, Mrs Potts. It's just gone ten past, and the boat will be leaving any minute.'

'We would've been fine if these two hadn't eaten all the bloomin' grub,' said Maggie, pointing at the two culprits. 'Right come on then, we'll be ok if we hurry. Come on everyone, we'll be buggered if we miss this!'

They started to run. As fast as their legs could carry them, they made their way down towards the harbour. Maggie, already slowed down by the sheer weight of food she was carrying, was trying to help Winnie who was slowed down by the sheer weight of booze that she had. The children were ok but Maggie and Winnie, wheezing and breathless, were struggling to keep up.

'Come on, it's just about to leave!' shouted Henry desperately.

'Alright, keep your hair on,' said Maggie, just as she and her friend reached the harbour. The boat was ready and waiting for them.

'See, I told you we'd be ok, didn't I?' said Maggie. 'No sweat!'

Lugland Harbour was not the busiest in The Will but it was quite beautiful, nonetheless. It was situated at the bottom of the Eustachian Hills and the river flowed out into the Auricular Valley.

Most min tended not to travel very far, on account of most of them living and working in the same place, but some min did travel for work, for leisure, and for other activities.

The easiest way to get around The Will was to walk, and it was also free which is why it was the most popular form of transport. If anybody needed to go that little bit further though, the best way to do that was to go by boat. The only major route out of the Luglands was indeed the harbour and travelling by boat was also a very pleasurable way to get around.

The boats travelled through the blood system. The blood system was a very simple one, as long as you remembered which way you were going. There were two ways you could go. The veins took you towards the centre of The Will, The Heartlands, and the arteries took you away. Another way to tell was the colour of the rivers. The veins were a deep dark red colour, yet the arteries were a bright shiny red. So depending on the colour of the river you were in, you had a pretty good idea of which way you were going. All of the ships, boats and ferries were coloured the same way.

There were millions of veins and arteries inside The Will, but not all of them were wide enough or strong enough to carry a boat. Still there were thousands of ships and boats travelling up and down The Will at any one time. It was an extremely important part of the day-to-day running of things. Some boats carried people and some carried cargo, and they ranged in size from the smallest cutters to the largest liners.

The blood network was controlled by Central Head and the timing of such a complicated network was crucial. A boat being only seconds too early or a minute too late could be disastrous. It could cause chaos to the network.

'Mother?' said Penelope cautiously.

'Yes, dear?' replied Maggie.

'Why is this boat empty and that one over there is full of people?' said Penelope.

Maggie looked around. There did seem to be an awful lot of people over the other side of the river she thought, and not very many on the side which they were stood.

'Well they're probably going the other way, aren't they?' she said. 'Mind you, I don't know why anyone wouldn't be going towards Central Head, on today of all days, do you?'

'No, Mother. Which is why I asked,' said Penelope rather worriedly.

'Are you sure we're on the right side of the river, Mrs Potts?' said Henry.

'Of course, we're on the right side of the river, Henry. Don't you think I know my way around the veins? I've been using these boats since I was a...' she stopped in mid-sentence. The doubt suddenly jumped up and down on her brain like a trampoline. She walked over to the boat. 'Excuse me, love?'

The Harbour Master was standing at the side of the boat in his immaculate uniform and shiny peaked cap. 'Yes, madam, how can I be of service to you today?'

'Where does this boat go to?' said Maggie, now getting nervous.

'This is the 8.15 express to Heartlands East, Madam. We'll be leaving any second now, so best hurry and get aboard if you don't want to miss it?' said the Harbour Master.

'You mean it's not going to Central Head?' said Maggie.

'Central Head?' said the Harbour Master. 'Why no, Madam, this is a Vein-line vessel, this side of the river is Heart bound. If you're going to Central Head, then you want an outbound ticket. You'll need to take the Artery ferry, Madam,' he turned and pointed across the river. 'It's that one over there.'

They all looked across at the other side of the river, where the ferry was packed with min. They heard it start up its engine and watched as it gently began to pull away from the harbour.

'You'll have to hurry though, Madam, it's just about to leave,' said the Harbour Master again.

'Is there another one after that one, Sir?' said Henry.

'Oh yes, son, of course there is. There'll be another one leaving at...' he looked down at his watch, '...6.15 this evening.'

'Oh Will's bloody teeth!' shouted Maggie. 'Come on, we've got to get on that boat or else!'

They ran along the dockside to the huge set of steps which lead up to the bridge. Maggie was running like she was thirty years younger, out-sprinting all of them. The bridge today seemed like the longest bridge they had ever seen, even though it was the same size as it had always been. They eventually reached the other side, a few sandwiches lighter as the odd one or two had fallen out of the bag in the hurry. The ferry was now about two feet away from the quayside.

'Right jump!' said Maggie.

'Jump?' said Penelope. 'What do you mean jump? I can't jump that!'

'If you don't jump then I'll bloody-well throw you overboard, now jump! And that goes for the lot of you!' said Maggie, again.

'Oh please don't let me die!' shouted Ronnie Drum as he prepared himself. 'And please don't let me break my drum!'

Billy the trumpet player shouted, 'It's a big B flat, lads!'

'Ooh, this is exciting, isn't it?' said Winnie.

'Now!' shouted Maggie, again.

They all took a run towards the edge of the quayside. If they would have had any time to think about what they were about to do, then they would have definitely stayed where they were. This was insane. But the adrenaline of the run, coupled with the threat of Maggie Potts throwing them into the river if they didn't do as she said, made them jump. They all did as they were told. It was a leap of faith.

Henry closed his eyes and hoped for the best. Penelope wanted to cry but then thought better of it. The clanging of musical instruments, followed by the thud of thick cut sandwiches and bottles of beer, could be heard as they each came down and landed in a heap on the ship's deck.

'Now then, who's for a sandwich?' said Maggie as she sat upright. She was as calm as you like.

Nobody else said a word, although the sound of a cork being pulled from a bottle, followed by a glugging noise meant that Winnie was ok. The rest of the min on the boat just stared in disbelief.

Chapter Seven

Almost the entire Lugland population was on the ferry. The contest was the biggest day out any of them ever had, and it was the highlight of their year. It was the one day of the year that they didn't have to go to work, apart from the skeleton crew which would take turns each year. Snap Potts was of course always on the skeleton crew.

Another Earside worker who was always on the skeleton crew was Ollie Gimble, but today he was absent and he wasn't very happy about it.

'This is not good, Stony, Mr Grip won't be pleased. I mean I've never been off work when I'm not supposed to. It's not right,' he said to Stony as they walked.

'Oh stop your whining, Ollie,' said Stony Pickles. 'Anyway, old Georgie boy won't be doing many more days work around here for a while now, will he? Haven't you heard? He's gone, done a runner, been exiled or something like that. Been a naughty boy, hasn't he Curley?'

'Yeah, Stony, gone forever and good riddance I say, about bloody time,' said Raymond Curley.

'Now come on you two, I won't have a bad word said about Mr Grip like that. He was always good to me he was, always gave me jobs to do. He's a good min, Mr Grip is, whatever they say he's done then, then, then they're telling lies they are, telling lies,' said the gentle giant.

'Oh stop bloomin' going on about it will you? Doing my head in now you are, Ollie,' said Stony. 'Anyway, where's that place you said, Curley? Round here somewhere, it's got to be hasn't it?'

'Yeah, just on up ahead I think. It's a bit dark down here, it's a long time since I've been and I can't really see properly,' said Curley.

'Where's that light, Ollie? Get that lantern lit so we can see what we're doing, will you?' said Stony.

'I don't know what you're bringing me down here for anyway,' said Ollie. 'Why have I got to come?'

'Because, Ollie, you're bloody-well big and hard, aren't you?' said Stony. 'And it's right dangerous down here. A few nasty types lurking around these parts, isn't there? And we need you to, well, look after us if there's any trouble, like.'

'Oh, right,' said Ollie. 'Where are we anyway?'

'We're down in the East aren't we? This is Oesophagus country, this is. Lots of unsavoury types down here though, got to have your wits about you down here, you have. It's always bloomin' dark down here too, even in the middle of the day. That's why it's so dangerous.

They say that even Leopold Schmidt and his min won't come anywhere near here. The Oesophagus people sort of get left alone to look after themselves,' said Curley.

Stony held up the now illuminated lantern. 'That's better. We can see where we are now. We can see what's around us....' He cut short his sentence immediately.

Holding up the lantern had revealed that circling the three Luglanders were about a dozen or so of the unsavoury types Curley had previously mentioned, and each one of them had a knife pointing to the throats of the three min.

Stony gulped with fear. 'Are these friends of yours, Curley?' he said.

One of the min leaned closer to Curley's face with his knife and gestured to him that he could easily slit his throat with one flick.

'Who are you? And what the hell are you doing in my territory?' he said.

Curley could barely speak with fear. 'Er..., we're, er..., looking for Mr Yanich, Sir, and I was told I could, er..., find him around here?'

'Who told you that?' asked the min.

'Er, Scooper told me, Sir. Scooper Barnes from up near the canal. He says to say that he sent us, Sir,' said Curley.

'Scooper sent you here? Unarmed? You must be mad. Give me one good reason why we shouldn't kill you all now?' said the min. He seemed to be the leader of the unsavoury types.

Curley was petrified with fear and said the first thing that came into his head. 'Because we've got something, Sir, something of value for Mr Yanich to see.'

Stony gave him a kick. He wanted to keep the diary a secret, until he had to hand it over to someone who could read it to him, of course. He certainly didn't want to let a dozen knife wielding bandits in on it.

'Ah, you do, do you?' said the bandit. 'And what is this object of value, I ask you?'

Stony perked up some courage, a lot of courage considering the situation they were in.

'We won't show it to anyone but Mr Yanich,' he said thinking on his feet. 'Now please take us to him, he is expecting us.'

'Oh he is, is he?' said the bandit. 'Well we'd better not keep him waiting then, had we?' He gestured to the other bandits. 'Take them to him and we'll see what he has to say about this. If they are lying, we'll kill them.'

They walked under escort for a little while until they reached a small house. Outside there were two more bandits standing guard at the entrance. It was a quaint little house, not one that you would expect an evil bandit to live in. From the outside it looked like a typical country cottage. The garden was well kept and there was a little window box filled with flowers. There was a post-box at the end of the lawn with the word 'Yanich' neatly written on it and a small winding path which lead to the door.

'Tell Mr Yanich that he has visitors,' said the bandit to the guards at the door. 'They say he's expecting them.'

The guard nodded. He turned around, knocked on the door and went inside.

After a few minutes he came back out followed by a small min with long grey hair, tied back in a pony tail. He was very well dressed and impeccably turned out, not a hair out of place.

He wore a brilliant white shirt, the creases down the arms were perfectly symmetrical and the first couple of inches of sleeve were rolled up to reveal his wrists. On top of this he wore a black sleeveless waistcoat with white pinstripes running down it from top to bottom. On it were three black buttons, all neatly fastened. A small red handkerchief could be seen poking out of the small left side pocket. He wore black trousers and black boots. He walked to the end of the path where the others were standing.

'Lance tells me that you've brought some visitors to see me, Mr Quick, and that I should be expecting them. However, I can assure you that I am not expecting anyone today, let alone these three strangers,' said Mr Yanich.

'I knew it!' said Mr Quick. 'Right lads, let's do them in!'

'Wait, wait, wait!' said Curley desperately. 'We have something we need you to look at, Mr Yanich, it's a book. A book with loads of things in it. Could be dead important this could, dead important!'

Mr Yanich held out his hand. 'Leave them be for a moment, Mr Quick. A book you say, of importance? I'm intrigued, where is this book?'

'It's here, Sir,' said Stony, as he pulled the huge diary from under his tunic.

Mr Yanich stared at the book for a moment, his eyes lit up with excitement. He could tell straight away that this was no ordinary book.

'You speak the truth, Sir. This is indeed a book of importance. A book like this could only have come from one place. This book is from Central Head, am I right?'

'Er, yeah, that's right,' said Stony.

Mr Yanich turned and started to walk back into his house. 'Bring it inside gentlemen. Come we have a lot to discuss, this is a rare find. Lance, show the min to my study and make some tea would you? We might be here for some time.'

Stony, Ollie and Curley followed him down the winding path to his door, and started to make their way inside.

'Fat lot of good you were and all, Ollie. I thought you were supposed to protect us?' said Stony.

'I'm not stupid, Stony, that min had a knife he did,' said Ollie.

Stony pulled a face at Mr Quick as he went past, much to Mr Quick's annoyance. Lance went inside also, shutting the door behind him and leaving one remaining guard outside.

Outside of the cottage Mr Quick turned to his gang. 'So our friend thinks he's got one up on me does he? He will find out, however, that Zachary Quick has a long memory. A very long memory indeed. He'll keep, for now. Our paths will cross again, I'm certain of that. Sharpen your blades, min; I've a feeling that we might be needing them soon.'

He and his min headed off into the darkness.

Inside, the house had much the same appearance as the outside. It was more of a country cottage than a house and, indeed, it seemed a lot bigger on the inside than it did on the outside. Everything was pristine and there was not a speck of dust on anything. This was the home of somebody who was obsessive about cleanliness. There were dozens of books on the shelves around the room. This was the home of an educated min.

'Please, gentlemin, have a seat,' said Mr Yanich.

Stony, Ollie and Curley sat down where they were told.

'Thank you, Mr Yanich,' said Ollie, ever the polite child.

'Now, let me see this book of yours,' said Mr Yanich, as he sat down.

Stony handed it over to him and then sat back down in his seat.

'So tell me, boys, why have you brought this to me?' said Mr Yanich.

'Well we wanted you to read it for us like, Sir. So as to sort of tell us what it says like, Sir. On account of us not being very well educated in that sort of thing, Sir,' said Stony.

'But you come here at great risk, do you not?' replied Mr Yanich. 'Don't you know how dangerous it is around here? You could be killed. Either you are very foolish or very brave. You may have a plan to try to trick me, which one is it I ask myself? Foolish or brave?'

He looked at the three blank faces sitting opposite him. 'Perhaps it is the former,' he added confidently.

'Yeah, it'll be one of them formers, Sir, I reckon, yeah,' said Curley. He obviously didn't have a clue what he'd just said.

'So who sent you here?' said Mr Yanich.

'Er Scooper, Sir. Scooper Barnes from up near the canal. He sent us, Sir. He said you would help us, Sir,' said Curley.

'Scooper Barnes? But he's from the Luglands, is he not? You mean to say you've come all the way from the Luglands?' said Mr Yanich.

'Yes, Sir,' said Stony

'You were not followed, were you? None of the Zamindar's min saw you come here, did they? Mind you, if you were followed they wouldn't get past Mr Quick, anyway,' said Mr Yanich.

'No, Sir, we weren't followed. We came on foot, Sir, so we could make sure of it,' said Curley.

'On foot? From the Luglands? You must have been walking all night to get to here, that is quite a journey,' said Mr Yanich.

'Yes, Sir. We have been walking all night, and all day, and all bloomin' night again, because someone get us lost, didn't they?' said Ollie, looking accusingly at Raymond Curley. 'And I ain't had any grub for hours, I'm bloomin' starving!'

Raymond Curley looked away in embarrassment, 'Sorry.'

Mr Yanich shouted to the guard who was still in the other room. 'Lance, could you bring some food for our guests please? Along with the tea, thank you.'

Ollie was overjoyed at the thought of finally getting some food, an instant smile appearing on his huge face. 'Thanks, Mr Yanich, Sir!'

'Scooper Barnes, you say? Ah, we were good friends once. We were in prison together, you know. Shared a cell we did. We looked after each other back then. Got me through it he did. How is he these days, still demanding money with menaces?'

'Yes, Sir,' said Curley.

'Ah, good,' said Mr Yanich.

Ollie looked puzzled. 'Hang on a minute, isn't he that fella who...'

'Ahem!' Stony interrupted him by clearing his throat very loudly. 'Er, so the book, Mr Yanich, what is it then?'

Ollie was put out by his friend's interruption, but his head was quickly turned by the food which had just been brought in by the guard. He started to tuck in.

Mr Yanich read out the title of the book from the front cover. 'Montague Schmidt's Journal. Vol IX.' He then opened the book and started to flick through the pages.

'So it's a diary, and not just anyone's diary either. This is the diary of Montague Schmidt, son of Leopold Schmidt. The most devious and corrupt min I've ever had the misfortune to meet. Feared and hated throughout The Will, and the person responsible for my ten year incarceration in the hell that they call prison. Do you see these scars?'

He rolled back his sleeves to reveal the most brutal and vicious scarring on his forearms and wrists. 'Chained and beaten every day of my life for ten years, stripped of my dignity and left to rot by this min. Leopold Schmidt, he is worse than any criminal alive today. I despise that min. The mere mention of his name fills me with anger.'

Stony and Curley listened with great interest, only to be interrupted by the sounds of Ollie Gimble munching away on his grub and slurping his tea. They each gave him a despairing look.

Mr Yanich continued to flick through the diary. 'So tell me, exactly how did you come across this diary. Did you steal it? And more importantly do they know it's missing?'

'Well, there's a bit of a funny story about that like,' said Stony. 'You know the other day when we all had to go up to you know where? When what's his name messed the alarms up or sommat?

Well anyway, I was just sitting there minding my own business, like, as you do, and the next thing I know, the bloody great thing came down and smacked me on the head. Could've been the end of me that, you know? I mean the size of the bloomin' thing! I said to Curley didn't I Curley? I'm going to have to have a few weeks off work with my head now like. You'd think they'd have some sort of health and safety in place up there, wouldn't you?'

'But do they know it's missing?' said Mr Yanich.

'Er, I reckon so, like. I mean there was a lot of commotion at the time wasn't there, Curley? People running about all over the place,' said Stony.

'Ah, so they are looking for it? Good, very good. That means that there is something of value in here. Something that Mr Leopold Schmidt doesn't want us to see.'

Mr Yanich continued to turn page after page. His eyes were glistening with every ounce of new information gathered. 'This is good, boys, very good indeed. You have done well by bringing this to me; you chose the right min.'

'So what are we going to do with it, Sir? Can we sell it and split the profits?' said Stony.

'Ha, ha, sell it?' said Mr Yanich. 'Sell it? Sell it to whom, and for what price? Are you mad? Don't you realise what this is? This could be worth more than all of the money in The Will. There may be information in here that could change things forever. As long as I have this book then I have something that they don't have, and that, my friend, is priceless.'

'Er, you, Sir?' said Stony.

'I'm sorry?' said Mr Yanich.

'Well you said that as long as *you* had it, Sir. Well it's not exactly yours is it, Sir? It's ours,' said Stony.

Mr Yanich paused for a moment. 'But you're forgetting something, young min. You brought this to me, did you not?'

'Yes, Sir, but only so you could read it to us like, not for keeps, Sir. We want it back,' said Stony.

The tension in the room was starting to mount. Stony and Curley were beginning to feel uncomfortable.

'You are very brave to make demands in my house, young min, very brave indeed. You must know that you are not in any position to bargain? The odds are stacked heavily in my favour,' said Mr Yanich.

'Well we just want our book back, Mister, that's all. Just want it back, like,' said Stony Pickles.

'Now, now. Let's not get upset about this now, shall we? We're all on the same side after all,' said Mr Yanich, trying to calm the situation. 'Now, I believe that it's probably going to take me a few days to read through all of this material and really work out what we're going to do with it all. We're all friends here, aren't we?'

The three friends didn't really have much choice but to say yes.

'Yeah, I guess so,' said Stony reluctantly.

'Good, good,' replied Mr Yanich. 'Now, here's what I want you to do. I want you to go back to the Luglands for a couple of days, and leave this book with me. In return, I will give you some things of value which you can trade or sell if that's what you want to do. I'll send for you again when I know more about the diary. In the meantime, I will put the feelers out around the place. Send a few of my min up north; see if there's anything happening out there. How does that sound?'

'Well I'm not really sure...' said Stony. He looked up to see that two guards had suddenly appeared from nowhere with two rather large looking spears; rather large and threatening looking spears. 'Er, yes, Mr Yanich, I think that sounds like a good plan to me. Just what I was going to say, actually,' he added.

'Good,' said Mr Yanich. 'Lance, give them something to take with them.'

The guard nodded.

'Er, excuse me, Sir?' said Ollie, blissfully unaware of the rising tension.

'Yes, what is it?' replied Mr Yanich.

'Can I take some of that nice grub with me, Sir? It's a long way back and we're bound to get hungry on the way,' said Ollie.

'Of course, it would be my pleasure to provide for you on your arduous journey,' said Mr Yanich. He gestured towards his guards again. 'Lance.'

The guard nodded once more and proceeded to present a gleeful Ollie Gimble with a bag of food.

As the min left the room, Mr Yanich sat reading the diary. Every page gave him something more, something that he could use against Central Head, and more importantly something that he could use against Leopold Schmidt. He thought to himself, if they're looking for it, then there must be something that they don't want us to see. Something important. Something really, really important. But what was it? It must be in here somewhere, somewhere in the pages of this diary. He would just have to find out what it was.

Ollie, Stony and Curley were stood outside in the forest.

'Jeez, I'm glad to get out of there. Aren't you Curley?' said Stony.

'Not half,' said Curley. 'I thought something was going to go off in there.'

'Yeah,' said Stony. 'The only thing going off was his bloomin' chops though, weren't they?' He was pointing at Ollie. 'Never stopped eating!'

'Well I was hungry, wasn't I?' said Ollie. 'Hadn't had any grub since yesterday? And my mamma always says I'm a growing lad and that I should always have plenty to eat. It's not good for a lad like me to go without.'

'A growing lad?' said Curley. 'Blimey, how big are you gonna grow?'

'Oh well, at least we're out of there now, anyway. But did you see his face when he was reading that diary? I think he's right, boys, there's definitely something important in that book, and something they don't want us to see. I knew it the minute I saw it, I knew it was important,' said Stony.

'Yeah, I think you're right,' said Curley. 'But we haven't got it anymore, have we? He's got it now. '

'I know, Curley. But we left on decent enough terms, so I think we may be able to get it back from him, and if he don't give us it back, then we'll bloomin' well steal it from him won't we?' replied Stony.

'Too bloomin' right we will!' said Curley.

Stony looked around at the dark and very unfriendly surroundings of the Oesophagus Forest. It suddenly occurred to him that they were not out of the woods yet. In fact, they were still stuck slap bang right in the middle of them.

'But at the moment that's the least of our worries,' he said to the others. 'We've still got to get out of here with a pocket full of swag, while there's that nutcase Quick lurking about.'

'Oh yeah, I forgot about him,' said Curley.

'Yeah, I don't reckon he's forgotten about us though, do you? And he's not the friendliest of folks now, is he? Right, come on, let's get out of here before he comes back,' said Stony.

The three min ran off into the darkness.

Chapter Eight

Leopold Schmidt was in his office. He was sorting out the ever-increasing pile of jobs he had to do ahead of the contest. He was extremely annoyed about having to go to the prison, and at this moment in time was extremely annoyed at Cornelius Crail. It seemed that he was the one who had told Sananab about the unrest thus making up the Master's mind that a trip to the prison was needed. And that was just it, the unrest? There wasn't any unrest of real significance to speak of. Just the usual nonsense of prisoners trying to escape and that was always dealt with by administering a vicious beating, which always did the trick. So what was the big issue this time?

This was the busiest time of the year for his office and this inconvenience could cause all sorts of problems for him. And to make matters worse, the guards had still not managed to find his son's diary either and that was another headache which he could do without right now. All in all, Leopold Schmidt was not in the best of moods today. He was sitting at his desk signing the last few trial papers when there was a barely audible knock at the door. The sound of the feeble hand on the other side was familiar to him; it could only be Cornelius Crail.

'Enter, boy,' he said. Cornelius came in and shut the door behind him. He was very apprehensive about the meeting as he knew the Zamindar would not be happy with him and Leopold Schmidt was somebody who you did not want to get on the wrong side of.

'Good morning, Sir. You sent for me?' said the boy.

'Yes, sit down,' said Leopold, without looking up from his papers.

'Is there anything in particular I can help you with, Sir?' said Cornelius.

'Yes, there is, Cornelius,' said Leopold angrily. 'There is something that you can help me with. Just the small matter of the contest to manage today, that's all!' He took the paper he had just signed, moved it across the table and slammed it down on to another pile, still without looking up from his desk.

'Oh very good, Sir, and how can be of service to you? To work alongside a min as great as yourself is a huge honour, Mr Schmidt, Sir. I am learning from you every day,' said the boy. Crawling was his speciality.

'What are you after, Crail?' said Leopold, finishing his last signature and finally looking up at the boy.

'After, Sir? Why I'm not after anything, Sir. I'm not entirely sure what you mean.' Cornelius put on his pre-rehearsed innocent look. 'I am here just to serve you and the Master, Sir. That is all. And to serve The Will of course, Sir,' he said.

Leopold Schmidt had been around the block a few times, and he wasn't about to fall for the boot licking which was taking place. He knew the boy was up to something.

'And this mention of the so called unrest at the prison?' said the Zamindar.

Cornelius knew this question would come, and was well prepared for it. 'Well I felt it only my duty to point it out, Sir. The Master must be informed of everything that goes on inside The Will and indeed it seemed he was unaware of the situation. Therefore, my divulgence on this matter was clearly needed, and perfectly justified. But if I spoke out of turn, Sir, then I apologise profusely. It was never my intention to put you at any inconvenience, Mr Schmidt, Sir,' he said, backing into a corner.

'Well you have put me at an inconvenience, Cornelius. There's no doubt about that now, is there? Having to go to the blasted prison at this time is a disruption I can well do without,' said Leopold. He was gathering all of the signed papers together and tying them together in a bundle.

'I am deeply sorry, Sir. If there's any way I can help you out, then I'll be only too willing,' said the boy.

'Well you can help me by being at my side today, Cornelius,' said Leopold. 'There's so much to do for the contest. As my Thought Apprentice, I need you to do everything I ask of you today. It is so important because I have to leave tonight, therefore I can't afford for anything to go wrong. The contest requires a lot of organising. There are the contestants, and the judging, and the trials; not to mention the thousands of people that will be there. Today is the busiest day of the calendar.'

'As you wish, Sir, but it is all arranged,' said Cornelius. 'I spoke to Mr Pothackery yesterday, I'm going to take on most of the business today and then I shall move on to the trials tomorrow.'

He knew that Leopold didn't know anything about this, and he was slightly worried about how he would react to it.

'You're going to do what?' said Leopold. This was obviously news to him.

'Look after the trials, Sir,' said Cornelius. 'Sananab's orders, Sir. Mr Pothackery is to assist me this year, he has been briefed of his revised duties and it's all been taken care of.'

Leopold was surprised to say the least. He had to check that he wasn't hearing things. 'You're going to be looking after the trials? You, Cornelius?'

'Yes, Sir. I'll be in complete control, the Master himself appointed me yesterday,' said the boy. He showed a piece of paper to the Zamindar confirming the fact.

Leopold read through the official document carefully, muttering aloud some of the major points as he read.

'I immediately appoint the Thought Apprentice for Central Head, Mr Cornelius Crail as the official Overseer of the contest trials, Will year '34. Etcetera, etcetera, all previous edicts shall be withdrawn and replaced by law 9623.6 of the Will,' he said, somewhat perplexed.

'And what has he asked you to do for the contest?' he added, as he handed the boy back the document.

'Oh, just to assist you and Mr Pothackery, Sir. I only want to help you in any way I can,' said Cornelius. He had to think very carefully about what he was going to say next, as it could cause a stir. After a brief pause, he dared to go on.

'However, I've already taken on some key duties which will be solely my responsibility, of course. And I must have things done the way I ask,' said the boy.

'Key duties? And what are these duties?' said a bewildered Leopold Schmidt.

Cornelius showed him another piece of paper on which all of his duties were clearly laid out; including a lot of the things which Leopold would normally take care of himself. He had obviously been relieved of them, as of today.

'The Master has signed it, Sir. It's his orders, see,' said the boy, as he pointed out Sananab's signature on the document. He knew that Leopold couldn't do anything about it. He'd got one up on him and was very pleased about this fact. But this was Leopold Schmidt he was dealing with, and even though Cornelius's devious, power crazed mind had somehow managed to get one over on him, his cowardly, spineless body was still very much afraid of him.

Leopold read through the second document carefully and then handed the boy back his paper. He closed his desk drawer and got up from his chair. Leopold Schmidt didn't hold his reputation for nothing; he was certainly a tyrant and definitely not a min to be messed with. But he was also an extremely intelligent min and this was something which struck him as odd. Why had Cornelius suddenly been given extra responsibility? And why was he not consulted about it? What was the Master doing here? And more importantly why was he doing it? There was obviously a reason behind this, a reason that he was not privy too. He decided to ignore those questions for now, he would return to the issue later. Now was not the time, the contest was only hours away.

He walked around to the other side of the desk where Cornelius was still sitting in his chair. 'Well it seems that you have been promoted, Cornelius. Well done, my boy, well done indeed,' he said, patting the boy on his shoulder.

'This calls for a celebration but it must wait until after the contest, I'm afraid. There will be plenty of time for your exaltation then, I'm sure,' he added.

This was not the response Cornelius was expecting. He was expecting one of pure anger or at least extreme dissatisfaction and it put him off guard a little. 'Er, thank you, Sir. Yes, thank you indeed,' he said rather unconvinced.

'Now come, Cornelius, we've a lot to do,' said Leopold. 'We must get to Thalamus immediately, Mr Pothackery and his team will be already there waiting for us. Come along, come along, boy, we must make haste.'

Leopold shot out of the door like a rocket on its way to the moon. Cornelius hurriedly followed him, still confused about the mood of the Zamindar. He'd started off angry enough, he thought, but then his emotions changed, firstly to surprise, and then to a confused fervour. He was somewhat thrown by this, but he quickly cast it aside. There were more important things on his mind. He had a job to do, and his orders had come from the highest place. Higher even than Leopold Schmidt. He would do what was asked of him and he would make sure that he did it well; alongside his own devious plan of course. Today was the first day of the plot, the first day that he could do what he was born to do. Every min would know who Cornelius Crail was, he thought. One day he would be as powerful as Sananab himself. Today was the start of his journey towards that design, and he would enjoy every single crooked minute of it.

Tuesday 30th October, 9:30 a.m. Limbic Mountains, Central Head.

The Central Limbic Mountain Province, a bit of a mouthful for most min and generally shortened by everyone to just the Limbics, was the only mountainous region of Central Head. It was regarded as one of the very few so-called holiday destinations because it was one of the most beautiful and picturesque places in the entire Will. It was also one of the areas which Leopold Schmidt looked after as head of the Security Council and he considered it to be his domain; taxing travellers accordingly.

A holiday, however, was something most min never really took to; they didn't see the point. The majority of the working min just stayed at home because it was less hassle, and there was always plenty of food too which was another good reason not to leave. Min tended to get very anxious if they didn't know exactly when or where their next meal was coming from.

Some of the more adventurous types would endeavour to 'Go Abroad' whenever they could, however, but they always tended to bore most people to tears with their stories once they returned. Having to work with someone on their first day back after a holiday would often be a very dull day indeed. Some would even bring in pictures to show everyone; like they thought anybody would be interested in that? Nothing cleared a staff canteen quicker than the sight of someone getting their holiday snaps out.

Mount Thalamus was the epicentre of The Limbics and the mountain on which the contest took place every year. It was also the place where the main camp for the trials was located, Hippocampus, and a place Cornelius knew very well, having spent all of his time there during last year's trials. The mountains were covered with snow all year round and at their peaks, they could be quite hazardous and tricky to negotiate, which is why the physicals were always set there. It would take a lot of nerve, strength and skill for a contestant to come first in the physicals. These were the most difficult tests of all, and the tests which would often separate the min from the boys and the womin from the girls. All the more reason then, that more than a few people were fairly surprised at last year's winner.

Mount Thalamus towered above the magnificent bay area below. The focal point of which was the resplendent golden bridge stretching far across the blood red river which flowed through it. The huge spandrel walls which built up from the gigantic rocks at the banks formed at the centre to create the striking, capacious double archway in-between.

The faint remainder of a distant twilight was being slowly replaced by the incoming brightness of the morning. The boats in their hundreds were cruising in and out of the bay, the river split with colour. From the commanding Heart-bound vessels sailing along the dark red venous river on the one side, having dropped off their passengers and heading back for more, to the bright, glistening shiny red river boats of the Arteries bringing in thousands more min every minute. The bay was packed with eager travellers, each and every one of them brimming with excitement for this year's contest.

On the Head-bound side of the river were the houses of the rich. Central Head had its fair share of wealth, and anybody who had enough money to live in and around Mount Thalamus Bay had an awful lot of wealth indeed.

It was also where the centre of the Security Council was and a highly taxable area to boot. There tended to be only two types of min who lived there; Security Council personnel or tax dodgers. Except tax dodging was not a very advisable thing to do for a min, lest you wanted to spend a few years in the Stomachic Sea or you had permission of course. The only person who could give you permission was the head of the Security Council; none other than Mr Leopold Schmidt himself. Therefore, the rich people who lived in Mount Thalamus Bay were the very elite few who were allowed to. Either way they were controlled by the Zamindar, whether they liked it or not, and he had his reasons for this. The rich Bay Area residents watched from their privileged positions in their privileged homes by the sea.

To the Heart-bound side of river, lay the enormous banks of grass where the thousands of ordinary min would gather to watch every year. These would be the min who mostly worked outside of Central Head, although not exclusively. Depending on how early the people arrived, would determine the quality of the view they would have, as there were no benches, grandstands, or indeed seating of any kind provided for them.

The min tended to get up extremely early on contest day, as the last thing anybody wanted was to be stuck at the back of the crowd with a lousy view. Nor did anybody want to get right down to the front either. The reason for this was simple. If there was any particular moment of excitement during the contest, the people at the back of the crowd would generally push forward to get a better look. Once this happened, the people in the middle of the crowd would have no choice but to follow, and the people at the front of the crowd would have no choice but to end up head first in the river. So there was always an awkward stand off as to who would go down to the front, and who would hang back for the middle spots. Normally the excited youngsters who didn't know any better would end up at the front; they would learn from their mistake and change their approach the following year.

Across the river, at the foot of the mountain was the Amygdala Arena. This was where it all happened; this was where the action was. The contestants and their families were the only non-members of Central Head who were allowed in except for the few privileged min who helped to run the contest.

At the heart of the arena was the grandiose Cerebellum Dome with the distinctive Temporal Tower adjacent to it. This was where the important people viewed the contest and this was where the dignitaries sat. On contest day, this would consist primarily of the five judges, Mr Pothackery and his staff, although they were often busy down below with the contestants, Leopold Schmidt and the winner of the previous year's contest, by coincidence this year it happened to be Cornelius Crail. There were always a few seats put aside for guests, usually taken up by previous winners who worked in Central Head or anyone deemed influential enough to be there. But the most important seat on the balcony was for the most important one of all, the one who everyone feared, the mighty Sananab.

Leopold and Cornelius arrived at the Cerebellum Dome where the viewing gallery windows had already been retracted in preparation for the big day. Mr Pothackery and his team where busy adorning the area with the last few finishing touches to decorations and hanging the banners for the contest.

'Good morning, Mr Schmidt. Good morning, Mr Crail,' said Mr Pothackery.

'Ah, good morning, Charles,' said Leopold.

'Good morning, Mr Pothackery,' echoed Cornelius.

'How are things shaping up then, Charles?' said Leopold, 'We will be ready to start on time, I trust?'

'Yes, Leopold, everything is in order. We are running exactly to time,' said Mr Pothackery. 'To the second, Sir.'

'Good, good.' Leopold looked out at the assembling crowd below, 'I see the rabble have already started to congregate?'

Mr Pothackery was a forthright and honest min. Having worked in Central Head for many years running the trials, he had made friends with many of the contest winners and saw the trials as a way of making someone into a better person, through hard work and with honour and dignity.

He was an extremely popular figure amongst past winners and was a firm believer that once a friendship had been established he would remain a friend for life, no matter what. He loved his job very much and did everything he could to make the trials a happy place to be, even for those trialists who would sadly not make the grade.

He was wise, he watched and listened, and he had seen a lot of folk come and go over the years. He, like most in the camp, was still not sure how Cornelius Crail managed to come through on top last year, nevertheless, any winner of the contest deserved his respect and that is what he gave him.

The use of the word 'rabble' from Leopold Schmidt was slightly uncomfortable to him, knowing that most of his own friends and family would undoubtedly be in amongst it, but he rose above the Zamindar's jibe.

'Er, yes, Sir. They've been here for hours most of them, Sir. We've had boats arriving all morning,' he said.

'Perhaps they thought to abandon their usual tardiness for an occasion such as this but you can bet your life they will be back to their customary standards of chronometry when it comes to turning up for work again tomorrow,' said Leopold. 'And to think that they actually get a full day's allowance for today. The Master must be mad to continue to endorse this. If I had my way I'd charge them all an entry fee.'

There was a sudden silence. Nobody ever heard anyone say a bad word about Sananab in public, even if it was Leopold Schmidt.

Cornelius Crail piped up. 'Er, if the Master has endorsed it, Sir, then it can only be in the best interest of The Will itself, could it not?'

'Indeed, all things are for the good of The Will, my Zamindar, otherwise I would not allow it, Cornelius is right and we will all do well to remember this,' said Sananab. He had appeared behind the min from out of nowhere.

Everyone spun around in amazement. How did he do that they all thought to themselves? Where did he come from, and how long had he been standing there?

None more so, than Leopold Schmidt. 'Ah, Your Eminence. I did not hear you come in,' he said gingerly.

'Obviously not, Leopold,' said Sananab taking his seat at the centre of the gallery. He waited for a moment before continuing to speak. 'Mad you say? Mad indeed. Madness can behold such a beautiful and strange innocence, yet it can also be considered an expensive liability. Maybe I am mad to allow such insolence and from such a senior figure? A trusted senior figure, and in front of the min too?'

'Ah, please accept my apology, Your Eminence. I clearly spoke out of turn. It must be the pressure I'm under at this busy time. It won't happen again,' said Leopold.

'I trust it will not, my Zamindar. I trust it will not,' said Sananab. Everyone else in the room stood in silent fear. He turned to the Thought Apprentice. 'Now, Cornelius, I hope everything is in place for you. After all, it is your first day in charge of the contest and such an important day in the career of my young Thought Apprentice. Have you have informed Mr Schmidt and Mr Pothackery of your new role?'

'Yes, Sir. I did exactly as you told me, Sir,' said Cornelius Crail.

'Ah good,' said Sananab, he once again turned to Leopold Schmidt, and continued. 'And I have given Cornelius a few extra things to take care of this year, Leopold. You work so incredibly hard as my Zamindar and I thought I would help you to lessen your load somewhat. The pressure you speak of is undoubtedly taking its toll. I trust that you find this to your satisfaction?'

Leopold was still trying to work out where the Master had emerged from, yet he was extremely relieved, as he seemed to have escaped any recoil from him after his outburst. 'Yes, Sir. I do, thank you. Although it did come as a bit of a surprise to me, Your Eminence. If you would have consulted me on this matter, I might have been able to offer some support to you, been of some help perhaps?' he said.

'It is you that I am helping, Leopold,' said Sananab. 'By taking away some of your strain. And it is time our young Thought Apprentice, here, earned his title. After all, you selected the boy yourself. 'One day I will need a successor,' you said. 'One day I will have to hand over my baton,' you said'. And this is the boy who will succeed you, Leopold. This is the boy who you have chosen, picked by your own hand, my friend.'

There was an indescribable silence which filled the air. Nobody would dare say anything. The only sound which could be heard was the general rumble coming from the crowd below who were all eager for the contest to start, and by this time were starting to get a little impatient.

'But that day will come many years from now, my Zamindar. Many, many years from now,' said Sananab.

'Indeed, Sir,' said Leopold. He didn't really know what else he could say, and it was not often that he was stuck for a response.

Leopold Schmidt *did* handpick Cornelius as his successor; this much was true. He possessed all of the qualities needed to succeed, but only because his own son would not be up to the task. He always hoped that one day Monty would follow him but he also knew that, sadly, this day would never come.

'But today is a day for celebration, Leopold. The day in which we will find another who is worthy to take their place alongside us. Someone who will achieve distinction as a deserving winner of the greatest of all contests, as our young Thought Apprentice himself has done so very well,'

Sananab turned to the boy, 'Now, Cornelius, I believe it is time to begin. At your command, my Thought Apprentice.'

'Yes, Master, I believe it is,' said Cornelius. 'Mr Pothackery, are we ready?'

'Yes, Mr Crail. We are ready and waiting for when you give the order, Sir,' said Mr Pothackery.

Being called 'Sir' by Mr Pothackery was an instant shot of power to Cornelius Crail, and giving an order to Leopold Schmidt was something he had dreamed of for a very long time. Power, authority, influence, prestige, domination, supremacy, yes this what he was born to do. His eyes glistened with pleasure; an evil grin appeared on his face,

'Zamindar, start the proceedings!' he barked.

Leopold was livid. He was boiling up inside but what could he do at this stage? The answer was, of course, nothing. He nodded to Mr Pothackery to get his min ready then stood up and walked to address the crowd. Mr Pothackery pointed to his min to begin the fanfare. Everyone on the balcony stood as the trumpeters played, when they had finished Leopold shouted to the crowd,

'All shall stand before His Eminence!'

The thousands of gathering min below stood in silence to hear Sananab speak.

'I stand before you, all good min of The Will, on this very special day. Today we will find a winner; someone who is worthy to stand alongside me. Someone who is worthy to serve you and most importantly of all, someone who is worthy to serve The Will,' said the Master. He managed a brief glance across to Cornelius Crail, who smiled back at him in his own contemptuous manner. Sananab held out both of his hands over the vast crowd below, as if they were tiny puppets controlled by his skeletal fingers, 'Nos Numquam Immutare Voluntaten!'

The thousands of anxious min in the bay beneath repeated the motto with military accuracy. 'Nos Numquam Immutare Voluntaten!'

Sananab repeated the motto. 'Nos Numquam Immutare Voluntaten!'

The crowd duly repeated on cue. 'Nos Numquam Immutare Voluntaten!'

For a third time Sananab called out the unwritten law of The Will. 'Nos Numquam Immutare Voluntaten!'

Once more the thousands of expectant min below obeyed their Master. 'Nos Numquam Immutare Voluntaten!'

'Let the contest begin!' roared Sananab.

The congregation cheered with excitement as the mighty Sananab announced that the proceedings were underway. The noise was deafening. The band of Central Head started to play the Contest March as the five contestants each walked out onto the arena to take their place. The flags of each of their respected areas flying high with pride, their families sitting proudly watching their children take centre stage.

This was the day that could make them or break them. It could change their lives forever. Nobody ever remembered the contestants who failed but everyone remembers the ones who won.

Each contestant was cheered by the thousands of min rooting for them. Everyone had their favourites, for this was a day where sitting on the fence was unheard of. Some were even chanting for their favoured athlete with pre-rehearsed mantras and songs carefully adapted to suit the names of their choice.

The rules of the contest meant that any athlete could compete for a maximum of two years and if he or she didn't win at the second attempt, then that was that. It was incredibly rare for someone to win the first time around, however, so most of the past winners did indeed achieve their goal at the second attempt.

This year, four of the contestants were competing for the first time and one of them was returning from the previous year. His name was Clifton Smith. He was a large boy, very well built and quite mature for his age. He came from the Patellas and had worked alongside his father as a Jointsman. Like many min hailing from that part of The Will, he needed to be strong. The joints in the Patellas were a very important part of the general workings of The Will. They were always on the go and they never really stopped from morning until night. They were enormous joints to handle; supporting the weight of the entire upper divisions of The Will and it took hundreds of exceptionally strong min to operate them. The complexity of the joints operations in the Patellas was mind-boggling and it took a min with the same amount of mind-boggling strength to even attempt to work inside them.

He was determined to win this time around and so were his supporters. He couldn't believe that he came second in the physicals last year. Especially as the winner turned out to be Cornelius Crail but then again nobody else could really believe it either.

The other four contestants were debutantes, each believing that this year would be their turn to shine. The exuberance of youth was very much on their side.

Cornelius Crail stepped up to the edge of the balcony to speak. 'Ladies and gentlemin, it gives me great pleasure to introduce to you this year's contestants!' he said.

The crowd once again cheered.

Cornelius continued to speak. 'Your first contestant, and returning from last year, who gave a good account of himself but was beaten by the better min, from The Patellas is Clifton Smith.'

Clifton gave the Thought Apprentice an angry glance, but properly took his place in the arena to the joy of his adoring fans who cheered him like he was already the champion.

Meanwhile, one of Clifton Smith's adoring fans was not cheering him into the arena, far from it. In fact, right at this moment he wasn't very happy at all, it was Henry Grip. The boat from the Luglands was just docking into the bay and to Henry Grip it seemed like the end of the world was happening right now. 'Oh, I knew it, we're late! Look, Mrs Potts, it's already started!' he moaned.

'Well it's not my fault that we got the slowest bloomin' boat in the world, now is it?' said Maggie.

'We're never going to get a good spot now, are we? There's thousands here already, we'll be lucky if we see anything at all now,' moaned Henry again.

'Well there's no use moaning and staying on the bloody boat is there? Come on, let's see if we can find a way in,' said Maggie.

All of the Lugland folk jumped off the boat as fast as they could and started making their way towards the arena. The seemingly impenetrably thick wall of bodies spread out in front of them. They tried to push their way in without success.

'Here, what's your bloomin' game?' said one of the min standing at the back.

'You'll stand in line like the rest of us,' said another, 'We've been here all morning, I'll have you know!'

'You're not bloody-well pushing me out of the way!' said another angry member of the crowd as she pointed an accusing finger at the party.

'Every bloomin' year you always get someone trying it on,' said the first min again. 'Well you're not getting past me, I say, not this time.'

'It's no use, Mother,' said Penelope. 'We'll never get through, there's too many of them.'

Henry put his head in his hands. He had been looking forward to this day for a whole year and all he could see was the back of somebody's head. It was a disaster. For a brief moment he wanted to cry, albeit a very brief moment, as suddenly things took an unexpected turn for the better. There was a strange noise, followed by what sounded like a few very displeased voices.

'Oh my word, what's that?' said one.

'Ugh, that is disgusting,' said another. 'I think I'm going to be sick!'

Henry looked up to see everyone in the vicinity of them holding their noses to avoid a very unpleasant smell. The crowd parted in two, creating a large crack down the centre. In the middle of this newly parted stretch was a rather embarrassed Winnie Drum.

'Oh excuse me,' she said. 'Better out than in, eh?'

Not being slow to seize upon an opportunity, Maggie grabbed Henry and Penelope by the hands and dragged them into the crowd. 'Quick everyone,' she said. 'They don't normally last that long. It'll be gone in a minute, better get in while we can!'

Winnie and Ronnie Drum followed closely by his band, with Maggie, Henry and Penelope already ahead of them, quickly made their way into the area vacated by masses. Each of them trying not to breathe in as they settled on a spot halfway through the pack.

'Ah, you see, I told you, Henry, there's more than a few tricks to getting to the front of a crowd,' said Maggie with a wink. 'Just listen to your old Auntie Maggie.'

'You mean you actually planned that?' said Penelope, daring to open her nostrils once again. 'Mother, that is disgusting! I can't believe you did that.'

'Well, no, we never actually planned it exactly like that, but your old

90

mother would've got us in somehow. Anyway, you can't look a gift horse in the mouth, can you? Even if it is a drunken one with no teeth,' said Maggie. 'Besides, we're here now, aren't we? Winnie, I think that calls for a drop of ale, don't you?'

'Oohh I reckon so, Maggie. I reckon so chuck!' said a happy Winnie Drum. They each opened up a bottle of something and took a huge swig. 'Any pork pies going?'

'Loppy, look, there's crappy Crail on the balcony,' said Henry, happy now that he could see. He was pointing up at the Cerebellum Dome. 'I wonder why he's leading the contestants out. It's normally Leopold Schmidt what does it.'

Penelope looked up to find Cornelius Crail continuing to read out the roll call.

'Your second contestant, his first time in the contest, from the Clavicle City is Maximillian Silverdale!'

Each of the contestants were cheered on by the huge crowd, and adored by their individual supporters, as they entered the arena.

'From the Nation of Arms, Florence Seybold,' continued Cornelius, pausing for each batch of cheers. 'From the Knuckle Valley, Marshall Stanley.'

'Come on Marshall, come on Marshall, come on Marshall!' came the chant from a large group of supporters who were standing right next to Penelope, she was almost deafened by them.

'Oh look there's a girl competing this year, Henry, and you said that a girl would never win,' she said. 'Well I hope she wins it, I really hope she does. Come on Florence, come on Florence!' she shouted.

Maggie and Henry both looked at each other, they were dumbstruck, never thinking that Penelope would ever show this much emotion, the occasion was quite clearly getting to her.

'And your final contestant from the Liver Counties is George Tobias,' said Cornelius, as the last contestant took his place on the podium.

'George Tobias, I've heard he's quite fancied to win it this year, Loppy. I think Clifton Smith will beat him though. He'll have too much for him in the physicals, I reckon,' said Henry.

'What is the first test, Henry?' said Penelope.

'There are two physicals first, Loppy; both endurance tests. First the run and then the swim,' said Henry eagerly.

Penelope thought about the word endurance. 'That doesn't sound like much fun at all,' she said.

'On my whistle,' shouted Cornelius from the balcony, 'the first physical will begin!' He held up the whistle to his mouth, the contestants waiting anxiously on their marks, the crowd hoping that their chosen competitor would make a good start.

'Three, two, one, and....' Cornelius blew his whistle.

Chapter Nine

The crowd burst into rapturous cheer as each contestant leapt off their podium and started to run. The first test was a physical and one of the toughest to get first up, it was the endurance run. Every hopeful would have to negotiate their way around a set trail and return to the arena, the first back would be the winner; very simple. The only problem was that the route which had been set for them involved climbing the very dangerous, and sometimes treacherous, Hypothalamus Mountain.

Hypothalamus was the slightly smaller of the two Thalamus Mountains but with its razor sharp ridges and potentially deadly slippery glaciers, it wasn't for the faint hearted. It would generally take at least a couple of hours to complete. In fact, nobody in the history of the contest had ever done it in less than two. Some contestants, especially debutantes, never made it back in any fit state to carry on. Mount Hypothalamus had broken many a min before.

The spectators settled themselves down for the wait and started to open their sandwiches. Some, like Ronnie Drum and his band, started to sing a few songs to pass the time, and everyone around them would join in.

Some min would even take bets on who would win, although it was strictly illegal and if Leopold Schmidt's min were to catch them they'd throw them in jail. To the bookmakers however, that risk was always one which was worth taking. Bookmakers never seemed to be short of a bob or two, there was perhaps a good reason for that.

The contest was a day of celebration and everyone was enjoying themselves immensely. One boy, a small but seemingly well fed boy, with red rounded glasses perched in the middle of a rather red rounded face, was sat in a small corner of the bay, away from most of the spectators but not so far away as he couldn't see. He was writing down everything that he saw in a huge book.

The six tests which the contestants had to take were divided up into categories. Five of the tests were fixed, three of them were physicals and the other two were psychological. The sixth test could be either physical or psychological and the nature of this test was decided by a committee. A committee which consisted of Sananab, Leopold Schmidt and the previous year's returning contest winner. If there was an outright winner based on the results of the first five tests, there would be no need to take the sixth challenge. But if there was a five way split, which there sometimes was, then the sixth challenge would become the all-important deciding tiebreaker test.

After a couple of hours of eating, drinking , illegal gambling and generally enjoying a day off work, the crowd suddenly started to stir as the people in front rose to their feet. The noise gradually rising as the first glimpse of a returning contestant appeared in the distance. The roar of his supporters becoming ever greater as they all realised who he was.

The first to make it back to the Amygdala Arena was Clifton Smith. He jogged back to his place, with his arms held aloft, the sign of a winner. He stood on the podium and punched the air with delight as his supporters chanted out his name. 'Clifton, Clifton, Clifton, Clifton!'

From the Cerebellum Dome's balcony above, Cornelius Crail announced his arrival. 'Ladies and gentlemin, the winner of the first test and in record time of one hour and fifty seven minutes is Clifton Smith!'

This brought a rapturous roar from the banks of grass as the spectators realised that they had actually been there to witness a world record. The previous record had stood for twenty years.

'A world record, Loppy, and under two hours, I can't believe it!' said Henry.

Clifton Smith was quickly followed by George Tobias, who was only a few minutes behind him. Ordinarily a time of two hours would have been more than enough to win the first physical, but this time he had been devastatingly pipped to the post. The loyal supporters from his birthplace of the Liver Counties cheering him on as he took his place back on the podium.

The Liver Counties were a very proud nation; they'd had many a previous contest winner and it was the dream of every boy and girl who grew up there to one day represent their people in Central Head. His aides were patting him on the back and congratulating him on his wonderful achievement, but he was obviously disappointed not to finish in first place. He nodded to his camp as they towelled him dry; this was an obvious setback to the boy who had come to win.

After about twenty minutes or so, the next contestant returned from the first physical. It was Marshall Stanley, who was immediately followed by Maximillian Silverdale. The two of them almost identical with their finishing times, only seconds between them.

Then there was another wait, quite a long wait, especially for the supporters of Florence Seybold. They were getting more than a little anxious as to why she hadn't returned. Another half an hour went by and she still hadn't come back. It was now an hour since the first contestant had returned and everyone was getting worried, even on the Cerebellum balcony.

'Mr Crail, Sir, it's been three hours now, I think we should go and look for her, she could be injured,' said Mr Pothackery.

'If she can't manage the physicals then she shouldn't be here, Sir,' said Cornelius Crail heartlessly.

'But, Sir?' said Mr Pothackery.

'You can leave her there to rot as far as I'm concerned. She's obviously too weak to compete,' said Cornelius.

Sananab was considered by most to be a ruthless leader, but even a ruthless leader knew that if he didn't have the people on his side, then his leadership would be worthless.

'Perhaps an accident has occurred. This could be a serious matter. We should send someone.' he interrupted. 'We don't want to be seen as uncaring now do we, Cornelius Crail?'

'Very well, Sir. If you think it best?' said Cornelius.

'Right you are, Sir,' said Mr Pothackery.

'Er, Charles?' said Leopold Schmidt.

'Yes, Mr Schmidt, Sir?' said Mr Pothackery.

'I'll, er, come with you. I know these mountains like the back of my hand, and my min too, we can take a face each,' said Leopold.

'Ok, Leopold, that will certainly help us,' said Mr Pothackery.

'Very good, my Zamindar,' said Sananab. 'We will look after everything else from here. Cornelius is doing a wonderful job so far, don't you think?'

'Sir,' said Leopold Schmidt who was becoming increasingly uncomfortable around Sananab and Cornelius of late, and saw this as an opportunity to get away from them both for the time being and perhaps gather his thoughts elsewhere.

He and his min, along with Mr Pothackery and the rest of the contest organisers, made their way down to the arena where the family of Florence Seybold were starting to panic. Their little girl was lost in the treacherous mountain which loomed menacingly above them.

'Don't worry, Mrs Seybold,' said Mr Pothackery. 'We have min who know every inch of these mountains; we'll have her back here in no time.'

No sooner than Mr Pothackery had finished speaking, their anguish turned to relief as the diminutive figure of their daughter moved into view.

'No need, Sir, she's here!' said Mrs Seybold, with joy.

'Oh that is a relief,' said Mr Pothackery. 'Quick let us help her to the tents.'

Florence Seybold hobbled back to the arena. She was covered in cuts, bruises and scratches, and was quite clearly exhausted.

Mr Pothackery and his min took Florence Seybold off to the medic's tent, accompanied by her family. 'Come on now, Florence, my girl, we'll get you sorted out,' said Mr Pothackery.

'Thanks, Mr Pothackery,' said Florence. 'I'll be alright. I just lost my step and fell down a rock. Couldn't get back up for ages; think I've hurt my ankle. I can still carry on though, can't I sir?'

'Well I don't think you're in any fit state to go swimming in the river now, do you?' said Mr Pothackery.

'But, Sir, I've got to, Sir!' said Florence.

'I'm afraid it's not possible, Florence. I mean you would never get through it. Your leg clearly needs attending to, it must be bandaged up immediately,' said Mr Pothackery.

'But I can still do the mental, Sir, can't I? That's my strongest test, that's what I'm good at,' said Florence Seybold.

'Well I suppose that's up to your mother now, Florence,' said Mr Pothackery. 'But there's no way that I can stop you, I'm afraid it's not my decision.'

'That blasted mountain, she's lucky to be alive! No, I'm afraid my daughter is too precious to me to lose her to this damn contest. No I'm taking you home, Floppy, back where you belong, with Mummy and Daddy,' said Mrs Seybold.

Florence was crestfallen. 'But, Mummy, I've trained all year for this. It's what we've always talked about; it's what I've always wanted. Just to compete with the others is a dream come true for me. I can't stop it now, I've come so far.'

'But darling, you could have been killed up there. It's too dangerous, it should be stopped all this nonsense if you ask me, once and for all,' said her mother.

Mr Pothackery, who had seen Florence train every day for the past year, knew how much she wanted to compete and he knew how much it meant to her to be the only female competitor. She wanted to be involved so much, to try and stand up for the rest of the womin who had gone before her. Even if she didn't win, just to be in the final five was a great achievement in itself and it would set a precedent for future generations.

He offered a solution. 'Well, there is a way she could still compete, Mrs Seybold. If she were to miss out the remaining physicals, then she could still attempt the remaining mental tests. There is no rule against that, after all she already has one physical test under her belt, and even though she didn't come back first, she could still win the two mentals. Providing all of the other contestants are in agreement, of course?'

He looked across at the rest of the group for confirmation. Every one of the other contestants was in complete agreement. They were rivals, of course, but they had all come through the trials together and every one of them knew how much it meant to Florence to compete.

Mrs Seybold looked down at her daughter. How could she deny her now?

'Don't think she'd ever really forgive me if I said no, do you?' she said to nobody in particular. 'But no more physicals for you, lady. I think we've seen just about enough of those for one day.'

'Very well, Mrs Seybold, I shall inform Mr Crail,' said Mr Pothackery, he turned to one of his min. 'Er, can you please tell Mr Crail that Florence will be taking no further part in the physicals today, but will still be exercising her right to enter in the psychological tests? Thank you.'

The messenger nodded and made his way back up to the Cerebellum Dome balcony.

Cornelius Crail announced the news. 'Ladies and gentlemin, it seems that the first test has taken its toll on one of our contestants, Ms Seybold has obviously not got what it takes to win this contest and hasn't the strength or indeed it seems the courage to continue with the physicals. I doubt Central Head will be any worse off having seen the first of this year's losers.'

This announcement was met with abject dislike, especially from the thousands who had travelled from The Nation of Arms to support their sister. A chorus of boos immediately began to ring out towards the balcony and a few were shaking their fists angrily in the air. The judges and dignitaries in the dome looked extremely uncomfortable in their seats as a few missiles were thrown towards the balcony, even the mighty Sananab looked a little uneasy.

Down in the arena, Leopold Schmidt and Mr Pothackery were both surprised at Cornelius's choice of words. The former looking more concerned at the unhappy gathering of spectators milling around him.

Sananab looked angrily towards Cornelius, but quickly got up from his seat and addressed the crowd. 'Ladies and Gentlemin, we will now have the next test, the endurance swim.'

The boos from the crowd suddenly turned to cheers as the next eagerly anticipated test was about to begin. A slightly embarrassed, but even more cowardly Cornelius prepared to start the countdown again.

'On my whistle, the second physical will begin. Three, two, one...' He blew his whistle and the remaining four contestants leapt from their podiums and made their way down to the water's edge, each one diving into the deep red river to begin the arduous swim.

Each contestant had to swim five times around the bay and the first to return was the winner. The blood red river was dense and thick, and around the rocky areas near the bridge it was filled with deep clots which were extremely difficult to get through. This was a tough test at the best of times but considering each competitor had only just completed the mountain run, this was going to be all the more difficult. The waves at this time of day were also at their highest and it took a min with immense upper body strength to swim through them.

The first contestant back was George Tobias, much to the delight of his followers. They cheered as the sodden figure climbed out of the river and clawed his way up the slippery bank. He wearily made his way back to the arena and collapsed in a heap against the podium. He could barely raise his arm above his head with sheer exhaustion but he managed a small fist of victory as he acknowledged his adoring public.

'Ladies and gentlemin, the winner of the endurance swim is George Tobias!' announced Cornelius Crail from the balcony as the crowds were still cheering.

Second to return was Clifton Smith, and it was soon becoming clear to everyone that these two boys could barely be separated. They were far and away miles above the other contestants when it came to their physical strength. In third place came Maximillian Silverdale and last to finish the endurance swim was Marshall Stanley. Each contestant being cheered on by their partisan supporters.

'So that's one each for the big two in the physicals, Loppy' said Henry. 'There's not much separating those two, is there?'

'No, Henry, there isn't,' replied Penelope. 'They weren't exactly the most interesting of challenges though, were they Henry? They're all brute force and ignorance, if you ask me.'

'Ignorance?' said Henry Grip, he wanted to ignore his friends comment but somehow couldn't allow himself to.

Back on the balcony, Cornelius Crail was about to announce the start of the third test; the mental arithmetic test. The contests were now coming round thick and fast and there was little or no time for any respite in-between rounds.

'Ladies and gentlemin, we now have our third test and the first psychological test. Written on this scroll is a problem, a mathematical problem, the first contestant to give me the answer is the winner.'

He pointed up at the giant scroll which was rolled up and attached to the side of the enormous temporal tower.

'Are you ready?' he said to the masses below. A huge roar came back from the crowd as he gave the order for the scroll to be released.

One of Mr Pothackery's min pulled on the giant golden cord and the enormous scroll rolled open, unfurling itself down the side of the magnificent tower. It unravelled at lightning speed as it revealed the gigantic numbers and symbols of the biggest mathematical equation that anyone had ever seen. Each of the five contestants stared at it with deep concentration as they tried to work out what it all meant.

Clifton Smith and George Tobias both turned to look at each other as they shook their heads in defeat. There was no way that they were ever going to work out what this meant. Even if it meant staying there until next year's contest, they still wouldn't have a clue. They both stepped down from their podiums and stood at the side with the rest of the spectators inside the arena.

Marshall Stanley was the next to drop out. Deciding that this test wasn't for him, he reluctantly climbed down from his podium to join the other two boys, leaving only Florence Seybold and Maximillian Silverdale as the last two remaining participants in the test. This, however, was their speciality test; this was what they were good at. They both knew that they wouldn't be able to compete with some of the others when it came to the physicals but they also knew that the others wouldn't be able to beat them in the psychological tests either.

Each of them was stood on their podium frantically working out the sum in their heads. Their eyes visibly moving up and down and side to side as each line of the problem was figured out. Under her breath Florence

Seybold was sounding out numbers to herself, which could be heard by the people nearby in the arena including Maximillian. He looked across at her peevishly as he was clearly distracted by her muttering yet she carried on regardless.

'The square root of the quadratic, divided by the sum of the adjacent side, multiplied by the six plus the forty-seven, gives us the one, nine, five which means that the overall size of x plus the triangle, divided by the other side, multiplied by the square root of one, two, three....' she suddenly stopped mumbling and shouted aloud. 'I've got it! The answer is seven-hundred and sixty-four squared!'

There was a sudden silence as everyone waited to see if she was correct. Maximillian Silverdale was furious. He was angry at having allowed himself to be put off by his biggest rival.

On the balcony, Cornelius Crail spoke once more. 'We have an answer from The Nation of Arms. If this is the correct answer, Ms Seybold will be the winner. If it is incorrect, however, Master Silverdale shall be the winner. Can we please reveal the answer?'

The two contestants waited with baited breath.

Placed directly in front of the scroll which contained the question was another gigantic scroll which contained the all important answer. The same contest worker, who had earlier revealed the gigantic equation, once again stepped up to take hold of the rope. He pulled the massive blue cord to unfurl the other scroll. The enormous numbers were written on it for all to see, seven-hundred and sixty four-squared.

'We have a winner. Ms Seybold is correct,' said Cornelius Crail from the balcony.

Florence Seybold raised her fists in the air with joy as her loyal supporters cheered and applauded her magnificent victory. Henry and Penelope were applauding like crazy, especially Penelope who had been rooting for her all along.

'I knew she could do it, Henry, I knew she could,' she said.

'Yes, well done to her, Loppy. Well done indeed!' said Henry.

'Let the next test begin!' said Cornelius Crail, the pace between rounds was now so quick that the participants could hardly think.

'The fourth test is another mental examination and one which each of our contestants must be well prepared for,' he continued. 'Each player must ask one other player a question. If they answer correctly then they stay in the test. If should they answer incorrectly, then I'm afraid they must bow out. This is a test in which strategy will play a major part.'

Henry turned to Penelope. 'What he means Loppy is that...'

'I think I've worked that one out for myself, Henry. It's simple they just ask their biggest rival the most difficult question and if they get it wrong then they're out. However that would only work if they got the question wrong. If they were to get it right then it could seriously backfire, therefore I think I would perhaps take a different approach. It makes perfect sense to me,' said Penelope.

Henry looked confused, but didn't dare to argue. Penelope wasn't stupid so there must have been some sort of logic to it he thought.

The five contestants handed their questions to Mr Pothackery, each of which had been previously written down on the contest cards. He picked up the megaphone and addressed the crowd.

'Ladies and gentlemin, I will pick a card at random and ask each contestant their questions accordingly. I will continue to ask the questions until such a time as we have an eventual winner. These questions can be on any subject and to any recipient of the particular individual's choosing. The first question is from Florence Seybold to Clifton Smith.'

There was an expectant silence as the thousands waited to hear what the first riddle was.

'The question is: What five letter word becomes shorter when you add two letters to it?' said Mr Pothackery.

'That's simple,' said Penelope to Henry. 'The word is short, and the letters are 'e' and 'r'.'

Clifton Smith answered immediately. 'That is a trick question, there is no possible answer, how can you make a word shorter by adding letters to it? Why it can't be done.'

He looked around to his supporters with a more than confident look on his face.

'I'm afraid that is incorrect, Mr Smith,' said Mr Pothackery. 'The answer to the question is the word 'short'. By adding the letters 'e' and 'r' to the word 'short', you get the word 'shorter'.

The crowd gasped and applauded as some of them now realised what the question had meant but most of them just applauded because everyone else around them was doing so. The vast majority of them they didn't have a clue about this sort of thing but didn't want to appear dumb. There were people shouting, 'Ha, I knew it all along,' and, 'Jeez, is he bloody stupid or what?' Even thought they didn't have the foggiest idea of what was going on. The people from the Nation of Arms applauded Florence Seybold with extra vigour as she had managed to knock out one of her main rivals already. The strategy which Cornelius Crail had mentioned was certainly coming into play from the start. Now she just needed to get her question right.

Mr Pothackery continued. 'The next question is from Clifton Smith to Maximillian Silverdale. The question is: If a speeding Heart-bound boat was to crash somewhere along the border of The Patellas and the Thighlands, where would you bury the survivors?'

'Oh please, that's so easy,' said Penelope. 'Only a fool would get that question wrong.'

'Yeah, even I know that one, Loppy,' said Henry.

Maximillian Silverdale smiled the huge smile of a boy who knew exactly what the answer was and wanted his questioner to know it. 'The answer is that you do not bury survivors. And in any case, it wouldn't be a Heart-bound boat there anyway, it would be a Vein-Line vessel, and Head-bound as it would be on the wrong side of the river.'

'Correct!' shouted Mr Pothackery through his megaphone. The citizens of the Clavicle City were ecstatic in their celebrations as their boy took one step closer to winning this test.

Clifton Smith was deeply disappointed especially as Maximillian Silverdale had also made him out to look a little stupid too, but his main rival was George Tobias and he would have to hope that his question was a tough one.

Mr Pothackery continued. 'The next question is from Marshall Stanley to George Tobias. The question is: Mr and Mrs Stanley have seven children, half of them are boys, how is this possible?'

There were people in the crowd at this point who were counting their fingers on each hand. Some were even counting their friends' fingers too as if it would help to find the answer. Some had taken their shoes off in utter confusion and couldn't remember which foot was which.

George Tobias looked utterly perplexed. 'Er, is it because one of them is a girl?' he said, somewhat bewildered.

'Oh this is easy, Henry,' said Penelope. 'They're all boys, aren't they? They must be. That is the only possible explanation.'

'I'm afraid that is incorrect, Mr Tobias. The correct answer is that half of them are boys and so are the other half. They are all of them indeed boys,' said Mr Pothackery.

George Tobias cursed as he realised his mistake. 'Ah, that's a bloomin' trick question, innit!?' he said angrily. That could have clinched it for him but now he would have to hope for a tie in order to take the contest to the sixth challenge. But he did still have his own question up his sleeve.

'Bad luck, George,' said Mr Pothackery, trying to play down tension.

'Yeah, ok, Sir, whatever,' said George Tobias, still angry with himself. Clifton Smith was suddenly a happier min; the huge smile on his face was confirmation of this.

'The next question is from Maximillian Silverdale to Marshall Stanley,' said Mr Pothackery, once again through his megaphone. 'The question is: If nine Clavicle workers meet each other for work one morning, and each shakes hands only once with each other, how many handshakes will there have been in total?'

Predictably the people in the crowd started to shake hands with each other but most of them couldn't count up to nine anyway so it was purely a waste of time. They were enjoying themselves immensely, nonetheless.

Penelope whispered into Henry's ear. 'Thirty-six,' she said.

Marshall Stanley eventually answered the question. 'Er, I think the answer is forty -three, Sir,' he managed.

'I'm afraid the answer to the question is thirty-six times, Marshall,' said Mr Pothackery.

'See I told you, Henry, thirty-six,' said Penelope. 'I don't really like those endurance tests very much but these ones are great fun!'

Henry had only got one of the answers correct so far and half of the crowd had got that one right, including Winnie Drum and that was saying something. He was being completely outshone by his friend and he knew it.

'The next question is from George Tobias to Florence Seybold. The question is: Name one eight letter word which has 'kst' in the middle, in the beginning and the end,' said Mr Pothackery.

Florence Seybold looked puzzled. 'Er, can you repeat the question please, Sir?'

'Of course, Florence,' said Mr Pothackery. 'Name one eight letter word which has 'kst' in the middle, in the beginning, and the end.'

'If she gets this one right then she'll be tied with Whatshisname wont she, Henry?' said Penelope.

'Yes, Loppy. It would have to go to another question, I think?' said Henry. 'I don't know who would ask it though, do you know the answer?'

'No, this is a hard one this, Henry,' said Penelope.

Florence Seybold was completely flummoxed, she didn't have a clue. 'I'm sorry, Mr Pothackery,' she said. 'I'm afraid I don't know the answer.' Her adoring crowd sighed with disappointment, including Penelope Potts.

'The eight letter word is 'inkstand', 'in' is at the beginning, 'kst' is in the middle, and 'and' is at the end,' said Mr Pothackery.

George Tobias had a smug smile on his face. He'd obviously got that question from somebody else; there was no way that he could have thought up a question like that. And what was more, everybody else knew it. Florence gave him a discerning look.

All of this meant that there was an outright winner for this test. Cornelius Crail, from the balcony once again, addressed the thousands of people below. 'Ladies and gentlemin, we have a winner. Having got one question correct without any challenge from the other contestants, the winner is Maximillian Silverdale!'

There was a huge cheer from the people of the Clavicle City, they had a winner, and more importantly now had a chance of their min going through to Central Head.

Chapter Ten

A few hours had passed since the start of the contest and for many of the spectators the time had simply flown by. Four of the fixed challenges had already taken place, which meant that there was only one remaining.

'Ladies and gentlemin, we will now have our final fixed challenge!' roared Cornelius Crail from his lofty position on the balcony. 'Contestants, you will take your places for the bulldog run!'

The crowd gave out an enormous cheer as the fifth test was announced. This was an extremely tough physical challenge but one which was always enjoyed by all. It was the test in which tactics played a major part in winning or losing, one where the minds of the contestants were tested also. Not by mental examinations like in the mathematics equation or the riddles test but by choosing which person they would side with. In the bulldog run, previous contestants had been known to go all out to win at any cost but the wilier of competitors had also been known to go all out to stop somebody else from winning; and that was where the skill lied. What was needed to succeed in the bulldog run was the combination of both the psychological and the physical tests together and to treat them as one. To use the strengths of your competitors against the weaknesses of your rivals; it was tit for tat, cat and mouse, and more often than not, the mice were never seen again.

'Oh, I remember this one, Henry. This is where they have to stop one another from getting across to the other side, isn't it?' said Penelope. 'This could get quite nasty if last year was anything to go by. Folks ganging up on each other out there as I recall and some of the people in the crowd don't look too friendly either.'

Henry looked around at the mob surrounding them. 'No they don't look too friendly to me neither, Loppy,' he said.

Some of the chants in the crowd had started up as the heavily biased supporters started to once again rally for their heroes. Some of them even had money riding on the outcome of this test, as this was the one on which most of the illegal betting took place. There was much more to have a flutter on than just the winners and losers in this round. Among the most popular of these bets was the one where the punters would bet on which contestant was going to get knocked out first. Knocked out, meant being physically knocked out cold, as opposed to meaning being eliminated from the contest.

Mr Pothackery was standing at the bulldog run finish line where he picked up his megaphone once again to speak to the crowd. 'Ladies and gentlemin, a recap of the rules for the fifth and final fixed test are as follows. Each contestant will try as they may to get from the two tall trees at the water's edge to a straight line anywhere between here and the start of the concourse, without going to ground. They must get past the other remaining contestants whose job it is to stop them in any way they see fit. Should one of our contestants succeed in getting through, they will be awarded the winners medal. If more than one contestant gets through, then the honours shall be shared. However, if nobody gets past the bulldog or goes to ground in their attempt, then this test will not be counted in the final scores.'

There was a murmuring throughout the crowd as they all realised that the stakes were very high for their athletes at this crucial stage.

Mr Pothackery continued. 'May I remind you that Ms Seybold cannot take part in this test due to her injury, so the chances of someone getting through could be a little higher than normal? May I also remind you that three of our contestants in this test already have one completed test victory to their name, and only need one more positive result to go their way for them to be crowned as this year's champion? If Mr Stanley were to achieve victory in this test however, then that would give us a five way split and should that eventuality unfold, then we would need the all important sixth tiebreaker test.'

There was another enormous cheer from the thousands of eager spectators as the smell of victory became ever closer. Yet the possibility of going into an agonising tiebreaker was something that none of them wanted, especially the contestants. All except for Marshall Stanley, of course, as this was now his last chance to win.

Mr Pothackery's trusty megaphone was held aloft once again. 'The first runner is Clifton Smith competing against the bulldog of Maximillian Silverdale, Marshall Stanley and George Tobias.'

There was another roar as the contestants too their places. The bulldog formed in a 'V' formation with George Tobias at the head, flanked by the two smaller boys. Clifton Smith started to run. He headed straight for his main rival, George Tobias, thinking that if he were to get past him then the other two would be child's play; they were physically no match for him and they knew it. George Tobias stood firm at the centre of the track as Clifton Smith headed straight for him. There was an almighty crack followed by the sound of silence as the unstoppable force collided with the immovable object. The two boys staggered around in a daze for a few seconds before they both hit the floor with an almighty thud. Nobody in the vicinity could stop themselves from making a kind of wincing facial expression followed by a prolonged painful hissing sound, as they sucked in a gasp of fresh air through their teeth. This seemed to say to anybody observing that added together these two actions both made up the well known phrase, 'I bet that bloody hurt!'

'Aren't they supposed to, like, dodge round each other or something,

Henry? I mean it doesn't take much tactical awareness to run straight into a bloomin' brick wall, does it?' said Penelope.

'Yeah, I thought he'd have a lot more about him than that, Loppy,' said Henry disappointed, 'I mean that's it now isn't it, he can't win unless it goes to a tie? I can't believe it, I really can't.'

'Oh look, they're back on their feet, Henry. They're walking a bit like Winnie Drum when she's had a few too many. I wonder if they are going to carry on?' said Penelope.

Mr Pothackery was thinking exactly the same thing; he walked over to greet the two boys.

'Are you two alright?' he said. 'I mean you must have both taken an awful bump to the head there. Are you ok to carry on? You're up next George, it's your run?'

'Yes fine, yes, I am, Sir. Fine, yes I am,' said George Tobias. He was quite clearly not fine, not fine at all.

'Very well then, I suppose you'll have to go through with it now anyway,' said Mr Pothackery rather reluctantly. He once again raised his megaphone. 'Ladies and gentlemin, the next runner will be George Tobias and the next bulldog will be Clifton Smith! If he can walk that far that is,' he added under his breath. 'Along with Maximillian Silverdale and Marshall Stanley.'

The crowd cheered as the contestants took their places. This time the bulldog was made up of more of a two-pronged attack rather than three, with Clifton Smith barely able to stand up and wandering aimlessly in the middle of the track.

'On my whistle,' said Mr Pothackery. 'Three, two, one, and....'

He blew his whistle. George Tobias started to run towards the others but his run soon turned into more of a walk, and then to a gentle stroll. He reached the stationary figure of Marshall Stanley who gently held out his arm in front of him. Without any force or effort, George Tobias walked straight into it and proceeded to fall flat on his back. Marshall Stanley held up his hands in a slightly apologetic manner, but the bulldog had won through again, although a Chihuahua would have probably had the same effect on poor old George who could visibly see stars circling around his own head. The bookmakers at this point were cursing their luck as the odds on George Tobias falling first were very high indeed.

'Two down and two to go,' said Mr Pothackery. 'The next runner is Maximillian Silverdale, against the bulldog of Clifton Smith, George Tobias and Marshall Stanley. Perhaps it is just one against one who can tell anymore, I don't know..? Anyway on my whistle, three, two, one, and...'

Maximillian took off like a rocket towards the other side of the track, standing in his way was a solitary Marshall Stanley, who knew that the other two were neither use nor ornament to him right now, and he would have to do this on his own. Maximillian was past him before he could see him and in a last gasp attempt to bring him down he threw himself into a magnificent full length dive to his left. His fingertips somehow managed to wrap themselves around the trailing shoelaces of Maximillian and he just about had enough grip to hold on and pull his competitor down as he ran. Maximillian Silverdale with his arms outstretched in front of him fell inches short of the finish line as he slid along the grass. He had been an arm's length away from winning the contest outright, he was distraught. Marshall Stanley sportingly went over to the dejected figure and held out his hand to help the boy up; they walked back to the start line to rapturous applause.

'Ladies and gentlemin!' said Mr Pothackery. 'Our fourth and final bulldog! Running will be Marshall Stanley, and the bulldog will be, will be...' he looked around to see Clifton Smith and George Tobias sitting on the floor with their heads in their hands, they were clearly not going to play any further part in this test. 'Well, the bulldog will just be Maximillian Silverdale, I suppose?'

This was certainly a first for the cheering crowd, a bulldog run with only two remaining contestants. 'I've never even heard of this before, Loppy,' said Henry. 'A bulldog one on one, who would have thought it possible?'

'But it all seems a bit barbaric, Henry. No place in Central Head is worth all of this surely? It's all supposed to be a contest, a game. It's more like a bloomin' battleground than a contest. I just hope someone wins it now so it doesn't have to go to another one, I hate seeing people get hurt,' replied Penelope.

'But it's what the trials will prepare us for, Loppy, when we both get chosen,' said Henry rather brashly. 'It's what the contest is all about, the challenge, the honour, the battle, the winning!'

'I just don't like to see people get hurt, Henry. I don't think it's right, that's all,' said Penelope.

Henry and Penelope were suddenly interrupted by the megaphone of Mr Pothackery. 'Ladies and gentlemin, on my whistle, three, two, one, and....'

The two boys stood still, each waiting for the other to make the first move. After a few seconds, Marshall Stanley started to walk slowly towards his rival who stood firm and unmoved. Marshall Stanley then started to quicken up, moving first to the left and then to the right. Each move was counteracted by the agile Maximillian Silverdale. The runner immediately gathered his pace sprinting wildly off to the far left of the concourse before suddenly stopping in his tracks and adroitly switching his balance and heading off in the other direction. Maximillian Silverdale was up to his task, however, and each twist and turn of direction was cancelled out by the ever-alert opponent from the Clavicle City. Marshall Stanley decided that perhaps a change of approach was needed. He stopped in the centre of the track, turned a hundred and eighty degrees and started to walk back to the starting line. Maximillian Silverdale, along with everybody else in the arena, and the surrounding areas were puzzled. He turned to face his opponent again and started to run. As fast as he could possibly manage, he ran straight towards the bulldog.

'What's he doing, Loppy?' said Henry. 'He's not going to do the same as Clifton Smith, is he? He'll knock himself out like the other two did.'

Marshall Stanley who was gathering pace ran straight at Maximillian and by this stage in the proceedings he was becoming more than a little uncomfortable. Just as the two boys were about to collide, Marshall Stanley threw his arms towards the ground, and like an enormous spring he somersaulted himself high over the head of his opponent, coiling his body together as he rolled five times through the air with such grace and landed perfectly on his feet no more than six inches away from the finish line. He turned around to face his stunned opponent once more, gave him a wink with his left eye, turned back around and stepped calmly over the line. The crowd erupted.

Cornelius Crail who had been quiet for some time while this lengthy test had been taking place, once again addressed the now ecstatic crowd from the balcony. 'Ladies and gentlemin, we have another winner! The only person to complete the bulldog run without a challenge is therefore winner of our fifth and final fixed test! Marshall Stanley!'

The boy from the Knuckle Valley went back to his podium and took the applause like a true champion. His friends and family were congratulating him on his wonderful achievement and also wondering where the bloody hell he learned gymnastics from.

'What happens now then, Henry? It's honours even,' said Penelope.

'I'm not really sure, Loppy. It's a tiebreaker I think, dunno, I've never seen a tiebreaker before,' replied Henry.

The first five tests each had a different winner which meant that now there would have to be a sixth and all important tiebreaker test. Mr Pothackery and Leopold Schmidt hurriedly made their way back up the Cerebellum Dome where Cornelius Crail was with Sananab and the rest of the judges. They would have to decide on the manner of the sixth test. Whether it would be physical or psychological would depend on the committee's decision. The discussion had already begun with Cornelius Crail making his position known early on.

'The endurance run is definitely the best choice for the sixth. Whoever comes through it will be a deserving champion, as I was last year,' he said.

'That's absurd,' said Leopold Schmidt. 'There's not enough time to complete another run, it will take too long.'

'I'm afraid I do agree with Leopold, Sir,' said Mr Pothackery. 'Surely a shorter test would be more suitable for us at this time? The people will want to get back to their homes; some of these folks have got a lot of travelling to do, some of the boats have already started to leave.'

'Nonsense! They will go when the contest is over. The decision is not theirs to make, it is ours,' said Cornelius.

'I think a mental test would be the best option. It will take no time at all,' said Leopold Schmidt.

'There is also the matter of the injured contestants too, Sir. If we have another physical then three out of the five would simply not be able to compete,' said Mr Pothackery.

The judges all nodded in agreement.

'But a mental test would play into the hands of the other two, would it not?' said Cornelius Crail. 'It would surely be to their advantage?'

'With all due respect, Sir, I don't think any of today's contestants would gain any advantage no matter what we did next. They are all quite clearly shattered, and the end cannot come too soon for them, I fear. This year, I think we may have asked too much of them,' said Mr Pothackery.

Sananab joined in the debate. 'We are looking for somebody with both physical and mental strength, are we not? And the contestant who wins the final challenge should have an abundance of both. I do not wish to have somebody who is weak, who cannot fight, nor somebody who cannot find the mental strength required to overcome their pain. Cornelius is right; a physical test should be the final challenge. However, the Zamindar is also correct, the run will take too long, therefore the final test will be the endurance swim. I have made my decision and that is final. Cornelius, inform the people of this,' he said.

'Yes, Sir, right away, Sir,' said Cornelius. He walked out on to the balcony to announce the decision. 'Ladies and gentlemin, the sixth and final tiebreaker test will be a repeat of the endurance swim.'

The announcement was met with mixed response. Some of the crowd were overjoyed at another physical, but most of them were not. Especially the people from the Nation of Arms as this meant that Florence Seybold could now not win the contest. Leopold Schmidt and Charles Pothackery were both none too pleased about it either.

'Can the remaining contestants take their places on their podiums?' said Cornelius again. 'On my whistle the test will begin, three, two, one, and....'

Once again the four remaining contestants leapt from their podiums and headed down to the river. George Tobias dived into the water but could barely keep himself afloat. Seeing that he was struggling, Clifton Smith who had still not entered the water held out his hand and pulled his rival out of the river. Another few minutes and the boy could have drowned. The contest was over for both boys, the injuries sustained in the bulldog run were too much for them to carry on and they both walked back to the arena arm in arm as friends. Maximillian Silverdale and Marshall Stanley were the only two remaining contestants physically able to start the test, although they were both completely exhausted and not in the best shape to swim. They both jumped in and started the arduous task. After one lap of the course, Maximillian could compete no more: He climbed out onto the bank where he was helped up by some of Mr Pothackery's min. His contest was also over.

Marshall Stanley was the only one left in the race now. Even though he was unaware of Maximillian's exit, he finished the last lap of the swim and reached the finish line. He was completely exhausted.

'Ladies and gentlemin, the winner of the contest is Marshall Stanley!' announced Cornelius Crail.

The victorious Marshall Stanley made his way back to the podium; he was the champion. The people from the Knuckle Valley were going bananas, cheering home their beloved son. His arms were held aloft, he had done at against all odds, his first time in the contest and he was the champion. He was led up the steps to the Cerebellum Dome where he was greeted by the official judges. The band was playing a victorious salute to the boy who had won.

He began his victory speech. 'Ladies and gentlemin, first of all I want to thank my family and friends for all of the wonderful support that they have given me throughout the trials, and I want to thank Mr Pothackery for all of his help during the last year. I want to thank you all for the wonderful support that we have all had today, but most of all I want to thank Clifton, George, Maximillian and Florence for making it such a wonderful day. I know we will all stay friends for a long time to come, thank you all!'

There was an almighty roar from the crowd as they cheered on the great speech Marshall had made.

He continued his speech. 'And now the moment all of you hopeful trialists have been waiting for. As is tradition on this day, the contest winner always reads out the names of the one hundred min who have made the trials. Starting from tomorrow, the people on this list will spend the next year as trialists. The names are as follows.'

Maggie Potts knelt down to speak to Henry and Penelope. 'Now you listen here to me, you two. If your names get read out in the next few minutes, it will be the greatest day of your lives. If they don't though, there's no shame in it you hear? If they don't, then you're still the best two little people in my life, you got that? No matter what happens, you've both got nothing but goodness to give to this world and ain't nobody gonna take that away from you. And if one of you is to get picked and the other one doesn't, then that's just how it is and there ain't no use complaining, ok?'

'Yes, Mother,' said Penelope.

'Yes, Mrs Potts,' said Henry.

'Right, come on then. We'll stand together as a family.' Maggie stood up and put her arms around each of the children. The three of them stood together and listened as the names were read out.

'The first three names on the list are three of my fellow contestants who qualify as debutantes for the trials again next year. They are of course, Florence Seybold, George Tobias and Maximillian Silverdale,' said Marshall Stanley, he paused for their applause. 'And in no particular order the rest of the names are Monty Schmidt...'

'Hey, there's that name again, Monty Schmidt. It must be the same boy mustn't it, Loppy?' said Henry.

'Yes, I suppose it must be,' said Penelope.

'Sshh you two, we need to listen out for ours,' said Maggie.

Marshall continued. 'Samuel Appleby, Audrey Atkins, Robinson Sneed, Angus Murphy, Henry Grip...'

'Yes, Loppy, I've done it, ha, ha! I can't believe it! I've actually been picked!' said Henry. He was jumping up and down with excitement.

'Well done, Henry, love! Well done! Here, Winnie, our Henry has been picked!' said Maggie.

'Yes, well done, Henry. I knew you would get picked, well done, I know you'll make a great trialist,' said Penelope.

Maggie could sense that although her daughter was pleased for Henry, her name had still not been read out and she knew how much she wanted this. She squeezed her daughter to her just that little bit tighter, gave her a kiss on the cheek and then gave her a little wink.

Marshall Stanley continued with his list of names. As each name was read out Penelope got a little more anxious when her own name was not included.

'Owen Smallhaven, Danny Cow, Diggy Johnston, Henry Gold, Tom Sticks, Penelope Potts...'

'Yerse!!!' Maggie Potts screamed at the top of her voice, she was jumping up and down on the spot and doing a sort of dance by kicking up her knees as high as they could go. 'Yes, yes, yes, yes, yes, Penelope, love! You've done it, love! You've done it; you've only gone and done it! Woo hoo!'

'Well done, Loppy, I knew we could both do it! I knew we could!' said Henry.

Penelope was almost speechless. 'I'm just so relieved, Henry. It's amazing and we can go together like we said, me and you like always!'

Marshall Stanley finished reading out the last name on the list and then held up his fist in victory once again as he left the Cerebellum Dome to enormous cheer.

Sananab stood up to address the crowd for the final time. 'Ladies and gentlemin, we have found a winner. A boy who will wear the uniform of Central Head and who will honour and serve The Will from this moment on. The contest is over, Nos Numquam Immutare Voluntaten!'

The crowd for the last time responded in unison with the motto of Central Head. 'Nos Numquam Immutare Voluntaten!'

The band played on as this exciting contest had come to an end. The thousands of spectators started to make their way back towards the waiting boats.

'Winnie, love, open another bottle. We're having a party!' said Maggie.

'I'll drink to that, Maggie Potts. I'll certainly drink to that!' said Winnie Drum.

Chapter Eleven

It was the most beautiful sunny autumn morning. Today somehow even the dark gloominess of the Luglands seemed like the brightest place in the entire Will. Especially to Henry Grip because today was different to any other day in his life, today he was going to the trials. The day he had waited his whole life for had arrived.

He had been awake for hours. In fact, Penelope wasn't sure if he had actually gone to bed. It was very late when they eventually arrived home from the contest and by the time they had dropped Winnie and Ronnie Drum off at the canal, it was well after midnight. She'd had only a couple of hours sleep herself and, deep down, was almost as excited as Henry was but she didn't want to show it.

Henry was dancing around the room and singing to himself. 'We're going to the trials, we're going to the trials, ee aye adio, we're going to the trials. We're going to the trials, we're going to the trials, ee aye adio, we're going to the trials.'

'Good morning, Henry. Did you sleep well?' said Penelope.

'Hey, Loppy,' replied her friend. 'No not really, I was too excited about today, I can't believe it, we are actually going to the trials, we are actually going to be there today! We're going to the trials, we're going to the trials, ee aye adio, we're going to the trials.'

'Where did you learn that song from, Henry, I've never heard you sing that before?' said Penelope.

'I heard someone singing it in the crowd yesterday, Loppy. Some of the supporters where chanting it and it just stuck in my head. It's good, isn't it?' said Henry, before continuing with his song. 'We're going to the trials, we're going to the trials, ee aye adio, we're going to the trials.'

'Not really,' said Penelope. 'I think it's starting to give me a headache.'

'Headache?' said Maggie, as she walked in from the other room. 'Oh Will's teeth, have I got a bloody headache? I think I've got more than one in fact. Oohh, how many headaches can you have at once?'

She was rubbing the side of her head with her hands and groaning all the time she was doing it.

'One, Mother, as you've only got one head,' said Penelope. She knew her mother had got something which she called a hangover and she only got one of those when she had been drinking with Winnie Drum.

'Oh, well I think I've got someone else's then and all, love. Ooh Will's

110

teeth, it's like someone's inside my head trying to punish me and it's bloomin' well working and all,' she said, feeling sorry for herself.

'Someone inside your head, Mrs Potts? That would be weird. Who would ever think that they could have people inside their head?' said Henry puzzled before going back to his singing. 'We're going to the trials, we're going to the trials, ee aye adio, we're....'

'Alright, Henry, love, quieten it down for your old Auntie Maggie, eh? I'm feeling a bit delicate this morning, aren't I?' said Maggie. She too was starting to get a bit annoyed with the song.

'Shouldn't have had all those bottles of grog then should you, Mother,' said Penelope. 'You and Winnie Drum had loads.'

'Well, we were celebrating, weren't we?' said her mother. 'It's not every day that your one and only daughter gets to go to the trials, is it? And my surrogate son here, of course. It was a special day, wasn't it? Had to have a few drops of the old Drum brew, didn't we? Anyway speaking of which, have you both packed? It must be getting on a bit. What time is the boat coming for you?'

'I think we've got about half an hour, Mrs Potts. They're sending one especially for us, can you believe it? They're actually sending a special boat just for us two. Me and Loppy!' said Henry. 'But we don't want to be late, like we were yesterday, do we?' he added.

'No, love, you don't,' said Maggie, remembering the boy's sulking from twenty-four hours earlier, and she didn't fancy a second helping of it today. 'Ok, give us a minute to get dressed and I'll walk down with yez to see you off. Have you seen your father this morning yet, Penelope, love?'

'No, he was on earlies, Mother. He left a note though. He says to pop into work on the way down to see him before we get on the boat,' said Penelope.

'Righty ho.' Maggie went into the other room to get dressed.

Penelope turned to Henry. 'Well this is it then, Henry. Off to the big city for a whole year, and I never thought this day would ever come.' She looked around her home for the last time before she would have to leave it behind.

'I never thought I would ever hear myself saying this, but I'm going to miss it you know, Henry? I really will miss it. I've got great memories of this place, this room. Really fond memories of it. It's been my home for ever and now I'm going to leave it. I'm really nervous now, Henry, are you?'

'We'll be fine, Loppy, me and you against the world, eh? And Central Head is only a day's sail away from here if we ever want to come back for any reason. It's not as if we're going to the Stomachic Sea or the Patellas, or even down to the Foothills or anywhere as far as that now? It's what we've always wanted, Loppy, to get away from here and to see the rest of the world! It's what we've always dreamed of,' said Henry. He wasn't nervous at all, he just wanted to get going, he couldn't wait for the trials to start.

'Yeah, I suppose you're right, Henry. We'll be ok, won't we? We'll look after each other, won't we?' said Penelope.

'Always do, Loppy. Always do,' said Henry.

'Right come on then, you two. If we've got to pop into see your father, we best get a move on,' said Maggie, as she appeared from the other room. She still had her nightgown and slippers on but with a coat over the top to try and hide the fact.

'Mother, you're not even dressed properly,' said Penelope embarrassed.

'Oh it'll do, Penelope, love. Anyway, who's gonna notice? Besides I'm going straight back to bed when I get in, with my head I can tell you. Have you got everything now?' replied Maggie.

'Yes, I think so, Mother. I've checked about ten times already,' said Penelope, trying not to look at her mother's appalling dress up.

'What about you, Henry, love?' said Maggie.

'Yes, Mrs Potts. I've definitely got everything, I've double checked everything again this morning after I packed it all last night,' said Henry.

'Right, Ok then. Come on, let's get a move on then,' said Maggie as she ushered the children out of the door.

They walked down the hill towards Luglands Harbour. Situated a few yards from the end of the road was the entrance to the Earside Left Working Department of The Will. This was where half of the entire Lugland population worked, the other half of course worked over the other side. Snap Potts was in charge of the Left Ear Department, and for once he wasn't being as strict as he usually was towards his workers. In fact he was being quite lenient today, some might say that he was even in a good mood and that was extremely rare, because today he was expecting two rather special visitors.

Maggie, Penelope and Henry went inside. They were greeted by the sight of the entire Earside Left workforce standing as one and applauding the two trialists. There was a huge banner on the wall which read 'Congratulations to Henry and Penelope on your acceptance to the trials, good luck from everyone from the Left Ear Dept!' Somebody had even tried to draw little pictures of the Limbic Mountains on it to try and include some geography in the work, although they just looked like some funny little triangles. Everyone was clapping and cheering like crazy. Two of their own had made it into the trials, and they were all celebrating this wonderful achievement.

Snap came over to greet them. 'Hello, Penelope, love. Hello, Henry, son. We all just wanted to wish you luck in the trials. Make us all proud, eh?'

'I don't know what to say, Father,' said Penelope. She had a tear in her eye and was trying her best to hide it.

'Just do your best, love. That's all you can do. You too, Henry, son. Do your best, and make your dad proud, eh?' said Snap.

Henry too was slightly overcome by emotion but fifteen year old boys were not supposed to show their feelings so he too was trying his best to hide it. 'I will, Sir. Thank you, Mr Potts.'

Snap gave them both a big hug and then reluctantly steered them back towards his wife. 'Right go on then, off you go, before you miss the boat.'

Deep down he didn't want them to go and they both knew it but he was also a father. As his friend George Grip had once said to him, 'How could any father ever stand in the way of his daughter's dreams?' He turned around to face his still cheering workforce.

'Right, you lot, back to bloody work, that's enough skiving for one day! And you there, Johnny, where's your bloody hat? You're supposed to be wearing a safety hat! This is the third time this week I've had to warn you!'

Maggie and the children walked off down the lane towards the harbour where the boat, which had been specially sent from Central Head, was waiting for them. The Harbour Master was standing ready to greet the two of them. Everybody in the Luglands knew about their two trialists and they were all very proud that they had two representatives from their home town.

'Good morning, Miss Potts. Good morning, Master Grip,' he said as he bowed his cap.

'Good morning, Sir!' said Henry and Penelope in unison.

'Your vessel awaits you. Please may I take your bags and load then on to the ship for you?' said the Harbour Master.

'Thank you, Sir,' said Penelope as she and Henry handed him their cases.

'Look, love,' said Maggie. 'There's a few people come down to see you off.'

Henry and Penelope looked over to see a small crowd of people had indeed gathered at the side of the river. They were waving and clapping just like the Earside workers had done earlier. The two felt slightly uncomfortable at their new-found celebrity status.

'How does everybody know, Mrs Potts?' said Henry. 'I mean we only found out ourselves last night.'

'I dunno. Somebody must've told 'em, I suppose?' said Maggie innocently. 'Anyway, they're all proud of you, aren't they? Everyone is proud of you, none so more than me.'

She knelt down to give the children a hug, she was crying. Her baby was about to finally fly the nest and no matter how much she had prepared herself for this moment, it was still heartbreaking to let her go.

'Now you listen here, you two. You'll be the best two kids that those buggers up there have ever seen, I'm certain of that. And I want you to know that there are a lot of people around here that love you very much. And no matter what happens, no matter how it all turns out, you'll always belong to the Luglands and you'll always belong to me. I want you to remember something; probably the most important thing that you will ever learn is to never forget where you are from and never be ashamed of your roots. This town is what made you both, and you'll do well to remember that whenever times get hard. This place will always be your home.'

'We won't let you down, Mrs Potts, and we'll try our best,' said Henry.

'Yes, Mother. We'll make sure we look after each other like Father said,' said Penelope.

'Right, come here give your old mum a big kiss,' said Maggie as she squeezed the two children into her face. 'Well you better get on the boat before it goes without you then, eh?'

Henry and Penelope climbed aboard the magnificent Central Head-bound vessel as it started up its engines and got ready to leave. Maggie stood with the crowd of people who had come to see them off. She was crying floods of tears as she waved her daughter and surrogate son off on their new adventure. Henry and Penelope waved back as the boat hauled up its gangway, closed up the gate and sailed off along the river toward the sunlit horizon.

'There's no turning back now, Loppy,' said Henry as he looked towards his friend.

'No, Henry,' said Penelope as she wiped away a tear from her eye, 'no turning back now.'

Wednesday 31st October, 7:40 a.m. Trials Office, Central Head.

The first day of the trials was always an immensely busy one for Mr Pothackery and his colleagues, and today would be no different even though Cornelius Crail was going to be in overall charge of proceedings this time around.

It was early, very early and considering all of the hard work that had gone into the organisation and running of the contest only twenty-four hours previously, it seemed like there had barely been an hour in-between the end of one engaging night and the onset of another industrious morning. Time seemed to be in a hurry to get somewhere else all of a sudden and Mr Pothackery was doing his best to try and keep up with it.

He was on his way to Mount Thalamus Bay to greet the trialists as they came in off the boats. This was customary on the first morning of the new trial season. But before he could meet with tradition, however, he had to go to Central Headquarters to pick up some official papers first. He preferred this time of the day as there were not that many people around. The Will's busy period didn't really kick in for another hour or so and this was the best time of the morning to get anything done.

Having collected the necessary documents, along with a few of his own bits and bobs, he closed his brief case popped a sweet into his mouth and started to make his way back to The Limbics. On his way out, he happened to walk past the office of Leopold Schmidt and noticed that the door was open. This was very unusual as the offices around here were always kept locked, especially along this particular corridor of the Neocortex. Even if there was a meeting taking place inside, the doors were kept firmly shut to avoid any stray ears from picking up something that they should not be privy too.

He heard various noises coming from inside, ranging from what sounded like the opening and closing of drawers to the repeated opening and slamming shut of cupboard doors. He could also hear the sound of a voice coming from inside, a voice which did not sound particularly happy with the world. Mr Pothackery curiously popped his head around the door to see what was going on. It was Leopold Schmidt and he was obviously looking for something but seemed to be having a bit of trouble finding it.

'Leopold, is that you?' said Mr Pothackery.

Leopold was startled by the voice. He spun around on the spot and looked straight at Mr Pothackery.

'Will's teeth, Charles?' he said.

Mr Pothackery was a little startled himself. 'Yes, Sir. Er, are you alright, Leopold? I thought you had gone to the prison,' he managed.

'Oh the prison? Yes I am going this morning. Just getting a few things sorted out before I leave,' said Leopold.

'I thought you were travelling last night, Leopold, on the last boat?' said Mr Pothackery.

'Yes, I was supposed to be going last night, Charles, but by the time the contest finished, what with the extra test and everything then it was too late. The boats were packed. So I thought it better to go first thing this morning instead,' said Leopold, as he turned back to his searching.

'Ah ok,' said Mr Pothackery. 'Would you like to accompany me to the bay on your way Leopold? It's such a lovely morning outside.'

'Er, no thank you, Charles. I will go straight from here, I think, but thanks all the same,' said Leopold, he was still obviously looking for something.

'Have you lost something, Leopold?' said Mr Pothackery.

'Ah yes, well you could say that, Charles. Yes, you could say that,' said Leopold Schmidt, still frantically searching.

'What is it, Leopold? I could help you look if you want. I can spare a few minutes before I have to go,' said Mr Pothackery.

'Ah, it's no use,' said Leopold as he gave up his search and sat down at his desk. 'I've looked everywhere; it's nowhere to be seen.'

'Oh,' said Mr Pothackery. 'I'm sure if we both looked then we might stand a better chance, Sir. Two heads and all that, eh? That's if I knew what I was looking for mind.'

'Ah, I suppose you had better know. Its Monty's diary, isn't it Charles,' said Leopold. 'You know he keeps a running journal of everything he ever does, sees or hears? Writes everything down in his books? Well he's gone and lost one, hasn't he? Heaven knows how he's managed to do so, mind you. I mean the size of the blasted things alone. How anyone could ever miss a book of that size is beyond me but we've looked everywhere and we can't find it.'

'I'm sure it will turn up somewhere, Leopold, these things often do,' said Mr Pothackery.

'Yes, but that's just it, Charles. Where *will* it turn up? And in *whose* hands will it *end* up? That is what I'm worried about,' said Leopold.

'Well I'm sure it will be fine, Leopold. There can't be anything interesting in there, surely? It's only a boy's diary. I mean I often see him sitting down quietly and just writing down the day to day running of things, no harm in that. There are hundreds of people here that do the same thing every day, filling out ledgers and transcripts. It's just the same boring old mundane tasks which we all have to do to ensure The Will runs smoothly. There are no secrets here after all,' said Mr Pothackery.

'If it was only the mundane ledgers and transcripts that was in it, then I wouldn't be worrying, Charles. It is everything else that he writes down that I'm concerned about,' said Leopold.

'I don't quite follow, Sir. What else is in it?' said Mr Pothackery.

'Well the truth is, Charles, is that I don't actually know what is in it. It could be anything. I just know that there could be things in there that other folk are not meant to see. Things which could be of a more delicate nature, shall we say?' said Leopold.

Mr Pothackery, intrigued by what Leopold had said, decided to sit down to give this conversation a bit more attention. 'Sir?'

'Well he writes *everything* down, doesn't he? Absolutely everything that the boy sees. Only last month I was having a meeting with Cornelius about a few important matters, confidential matters, extremely confidential matters I might add. The meeting lasted quite a while, Charles, a couple of hours at least. It was only when we had finished up and Cornelius had gone that I noticed Monty. He was sitting behind that bench over there filling in his diary. I took the book from him to see what he'd been doing only to find that he had written it all down, word for word. Everything that I had said and everything that Cornelius had said, in its entirety.

Of course I pulled the pages out. I couldn't risk anybody reading what was in there. I mean if that sort of information got into the wrong hands then we could have a war on our hands, an uprising, who knows what else? But that was only a few pages, Charles. These diaries date back for years, he's been filling them in as long as he could read and write,' said Leopold.

'Ah, I see your point, Leopold. This is a delicate matter, an unfortunate situation indeed,' said Mr Pothackery.

'I've tried to stop him doing it, Charles, I really have. But when I do he doesn't speak to me, he just ignores me. It's the only thing that makes him happy. He doesn't really say much to anyone at all so the only time I know that he's truly happy is when he's writing. He's all I've got, Charles. He's the one thing left that's good about my life,' said Leopold sincerely.

'Now come, Leopold, don't be too hard on yourself. You have a very difficult job to do, everyone knows that. I'm sure nobody thinks badly of you,' said Mr Pothackery.

'Ah, Charles, you are a good friend, and you always see the good in people, no matter what. But even I know most of the people hate me in this world, and it's ok, you don't have to make excuses, I know how it is. I've made enemies over the years, Charles, many bitter enemies,' said Leopold.

'But it is a job of such importance that you have to fulfil, Leopold,' said Mr Pothackery. 'You are bound to have ruffled a few feathers along the way. It's par for the course. I'm sure nobody really means what they say about you.'

'Dear Charles, no matter what I do, you are always there for me, as a friend. I will always appreciate your kindness. But I chose my path, I knew which way it would lead and I walked down it a long time ago. I have done things which cannot be undone and I must accept that I shall always be hated in this world. It doesn't affect me so much anymore,' said Leopold.

'Well, you are not hated by me, Sir,' said Mr Pothackery comfortingly. 'Once a friend always a friend, that's what I always say. We had some good times during the trials, Leopold, tough times and competitive times, but good times, nonetheless. I shall always have fond memories of our year together and I shall always try to stand by you if I can.'

'Thank you, Charles, thank you indeed,' said Leopold. 'There is one thing you can do for me, however, something that would mean a great deal to me?'

'Yes, Leopold, what is it?' said Mr Pothackery.

'Keep an eye on Monty for me,' said Leopold Schmidt. 'I am not really sure how he will fair during the trials. He's not generally very good at mixing with other folks of his age; in fact he's not really good at mixing with anyone at all, no matter what age they are. I fear that he might be a target for some of the others because of who his father is. Perhaps they may try to take out their hatred for me on young Monty. He is my only son, Charles, my flesh and blood. One day I had rather hoped that he could take over from me and have an important position here but I don't think that will ever happen somehow. The trials are the last chance I have to make something of him. I don't expect him to win the contest, of course, but I am hoping that maybe this can bring him out of his shell a little.

Ordinarily I would be there to check on him myself, but as you know I shall be away for at least a month with this wretched prison business. You are the only person in this world who I trust, Charles, and after everything that I have put you through over the years, I wouldn't blame you if you turned your back on me like so many others have done.'

'Of course I will keep an eye on him, Leopold,' said Mr Pothackery. 'He is a good boy; he's got the build his father had during his trials and he certainly came through it alright. Don't worry Sir, he'll be ok.' Mr Pothackery got up from his seat. 'I'm afraid I am going to have to get going now, Leopold, I have to meet the trialists as they get off the boats, they will be coming in any minute.'

'Ok, Charles, I am going to have to leave any second anyway,' said Leopold. 'Oh, and there is just one other thing I would like you to do for me Charles?'

'Yes, Sir?' said Mr Pothackery.

'Keep an eye on the contemptible Cornelius Crail,' said Leopold.

Suddenly the loving and caring voice of a father had turned back into the ruthless speech of the Zamindar.

'I don't know what he is up to but he is certainly up to something. My having to go to the prison, just as you are demoted from Trial Overseer, and his promotion to the role, does that not strike you as odd? Yes, very odd, very odd indeed. There is definitely something going on here, Charles, and what's more, I know that the Master is in on it too. And if the Master is in on it, then it must be important. I don't know what it is yet but you can be damn sure I am going to find out. I am much too long in the tooth to have the wool pulled over my eyes, Charles, and I sense something in the air, something which I haven't sensed for a long time. They want me out of the picture for some reason but I can have eyes and ears wherever I need them. There won't be much that evades me this time. You mark my words.'

Mr Pothackery was a little shocked at the sudden attitude change in Leopold. Seeing how a min could change as quickly as that was the reason why a lot of people did, in fact, have a deep hatred for him, and was also the reason most of the population were terrified of their Zamindar.

He decided to try to avoid the question as best he could. 'Well I'll certainly do my best, Sir. But I really must be getting along now or I fear that I may be late. Have a safe journey, Sir. I'll see you in a month or so.'

Mr Pothackery ran out of the door as fast as he could without looking back, he disappeared around the corner and out of sight. Leopold Schmidt grabbed his things, slammed his office door shut and quickly marched away in the opposite direction.

Chapter Twelve

Raymond Curley was on his way to find his irreverent sidekicks, Stony Pickles and Ollie Gimble. He was in a hurry, he'd had a visitor. The three young min had been waiting for word to come from their new found comrade of sorts, Mr Yanich, and it had been more than twenty-four hours since they had left Monty Schmidt's diary in his possession. He had told them he would need a couple of days to read through it but they had already decided that the time was up and they wanted to know just what this book was all about.

Raymond was running as fast as he could manage, while at the same time trying to look vaguely inconspicuous. He wasn't doing a particularly good job of either. He reached their usual point of rendezvous, the clearing at the foot of the Eustachian Hills, where the other two were conspicuously waiting for him.

Stony Pickles, not bothering with the pleasantries of a greeting, got straight to the point. 'So what did he say then?' he barked rather impatiently.

'Who?' replied Curley, catching his breath and turning around to see if he had been followed.

'Scooper, of course,' said Stony. 'You said that you had a visit off Scooper Barnes, that's why we're here, innit?'

'Yeah, he knocked round this morning, like, first thing. I'd only just got up, hadn't even had my breakfast,' said Curley, his breathing becoming a little more regular. He sat down on the wet grass.

'That was quick, Curley,' said Ollie.

'And?' said Stony getting even more impatient. 'What's the score like, what did he say?'

'Well he reckoned that Johnny Forks from down near the forest, had told Eddie Forks, their kid, like, to tell his Mrs, to tell her mate Reenie, to tell her fella Billy Jones, to tell his mate Potty Stevens, to tell Gordon Le Blue, you know Gordon Le Blue from the valley, the one with all the funny pictures? Anyway to tell Gordon Le Blue, to tell Natty Pikes, to tell Ernie Bottles, to tell Scooper to tell me like,' said Curley.

There was a moment of silence as the other two tried to understand what he had just said.

'Tell you what?' said Stony Pickles, utterly confused.

Ollie Gimble was even more bewildered, he was still trying to get from Eddie Forks to his Mrs.

'Well, he didn't say too much, on the count of him not really knowing anything, like,' said Curley.

'He, what?' said Stony, now completely perplexed.

'But he did say that Mr Yanich wants us to go to his place again, he reckons he's got some news about the book. He said he couldn't tell him what it was coz he was only the messenger, like, but we're to go to his straight away he said and he'll tell us when we get there,' continued Curley.

'Ooh, I knew it, Ollie, I told you so, didn't I, son? That's got important bloody stuff in it that book has. I knew it the minute it whacked me on the head!' said an excited Stony Pickles, his eyes lighting up with mischief.

'Yeah, Stony, you did, didn't you?' said Ollie.

'I wonder what it is, boys. It could be anything couldn't it? It could even tell us where the keys are kept to the vault that has all the money in Central Head!' said Stony gleefully.

'Yeah, imagine all that money, Stony,' said Ollie Gimble. 'I could give some to my mamma and we could always have loads of grub to eat whenever we wanted to!' He was licking his lips and had a look of unadulterated longing on his face.

'Do you ever think about anything other than stuffing your bloomin' chops, Ollie?' said Stony.

'It's got to be worth something that book hasn't it, Stony, no matter what Yanich says. There must be some money to be made out of this, like?' said Raymond Curley, quickly changing the subject.

'Yeah I reckon so, Curley, and I reckon he might be just trying to keep all the dosh for himself too' said Stony Pickles.

'But Mr Yanich seemed like such a nice min to me. He was very kind to us! I don't reckon he'd cheat us, Stony,' said Ollie Gimble, still trying to work out whether the last comment about him stuffing his chops was a compliment or an insult.

'Cheat us?' replied Stony. 'I reckon he'd cheat his own bloomin' mother him, and what's more I reckon he's already planning to do us out of what's rightfully mine, er what's rightfully ours.' Stony Pickles paused for a second before continuing. 'The best thing we can do is to get there as quick as we can, boys, coz I don't trust that fella one bit. What d'you reckon?'

'Yeah come on, Stony. Let's go and see him and if he doesn't give us the book back, we'll bloody-well take it won't we?' said Curley.

'Yeah, too right, Curley!' said Stony Pickles.

'Yeah!' said Curley.

'Yeah!' said Stony again.

'Yeah!' said Ollie Gimble enthusiastically. He was trying to fit in with the others even though he didn't particularly know what he was agreeing with.

'Mind you, we'll have to wait until he tells us what it is first like, on account of none of us having a bloomin' clue how to figure out what's in it,' said Stony.

'Yeah, you have got a point there, Stony,' said Raymond Curley.

'Tell you what though, boys, I am not looking forward to meeting that fella Quick again. He's a right bloomin' nutcase that one, I tell you! I reckon he's got it in for me and all,' said Stony.

'Yeah I didn't like the look of him either, Stony,' said Ollie. 'That min had a knife pointing at me, I don't like it when people are pointing knives at me Stony, it's not very nice you know?'

'Well he's not very nice, is he Ollie?' said Curley. 'Must've been dropped on his head or sommat him, like, mixed all his brains up.'

'Well the one thing that we have on our side, lads, is that Mr Yanich seems to be his mate, like, so as long as he's his mate, while he's still our mate, then I reckon we'll be ok,' said Stony Pickles.

'I've got nice mates, I have Stony!' said Ollie Gimble, suddenly quite contented with the world.

Stony and Curley looked at each other confused.

'What d'you mean Ollie?' said Curley. 'We're your only mates, me and Stony aren't we? And ain't nobody ever called us nice before?'

'Yeah Curley's right, Ollie,' said Stony. 'We're not nice, we're mean and nasty and ruthful and ain't nobody gonna mess with us if they know what's good for them, innit?'

'Less, I think isn't it, Stony?' said Curley.

'Eh? Less what?' said Stony, not appreciating the interruption whilst he was mid-flow.

'Less, not full I mean,' said Curley.

'What are you going on about now, Curley?' said Stony.

'Less I think, isn't it? Ruthless not ruthful. You said ruthful and I don't think I've ever heard of that, like, I've heard of ruthless though. I think it means that you're dead hard and stuff, like?' replied Curley.

'Yeah, ok, whatever, well we're dead hard and mean and ruthless then, aren't we boys?' said Stony again, particularly emphasising the syllable 'less.'

'Er, Stony?' said Ollie.

'Yeah, what is it now, Ollie?' replied Stony Pickles.

'I know someone called Ruth,' said Ollie. 'She works with me sometimes in Earside Right. She's ever so nice, Stony. Mind you I don't know what her second name is, like. I don't think it's less though, or even full come to think of it?' the look of permanent confusion quickly returning to his face.

'Oh I think I know her too, Ollie, is she a big girl? From over near our way, walks with a limp, talks with lisp?' said Curley.

'Yeah that's her, Curley, she's ever so nice. I sometimes sit with her when we have our butties at dinner time, like,' said Ollie, brightening up again.

'Oh yeah, nice,' replied Curley.

Stony Pickles interrupted the seemingly private conversation. 'I can't believe you two sometimes. What the bloody hell has Ruth whatever her name is got to do with anything? Jeez, I thought we we're going on about getting the book back in case you never noticed, not your bloomin' dinner time again, Ollie! No matter what the subject is, it always gets around to your bloomin' belly!'

'Well...,' Ollie was about to respond to his friends accusation, before he was instantly cut short by Stony. 'And don't tell me, you're a growing lad, aren't you?'

Curley had a huge grin on his face, the same grin that he always wore when it was somebody else being made fun of instead of him. This didn't happen very often.

'Now I don't think it's right you making fun of me all the time, Stony, on account of me being a growing lad and all, it's not my fault is it? I just get hungry sometimes that's all, and when a min gets hungry then a min's got to eat, hasn't he? Besides, I've got more room to fill than you two haven't I? So I need more grub to fill it, stands to reason, doesn't it?' said Ollie Gimble.

'Ollie, you're not gonna grow anymore, mate. That's just something what your mamma tells you when you're hungry. Blimey, you're as big as a tree now, you can't get any bigger than that!' said Stony. He was however a little worried what Ollie's response would be. He could be very sensitive about his mamma and everyone knew it. Stony backed away a little just in case his giant friend took offence to what he had said and smacked him round the head.

'No, you're wrong, Stony! My mamma wouldn't say anything if it weren't true. I'm a growing lad, and I'm gonna grow up to be big and strong just like she says I am. And you, or Curley, or nobody else can say otherwise, got it?' said a more aggressive Ollie Gimble. He pointed towards the other two boys; his finger was big enough to cover them both.

'No problem with me, Ollie, just like you say!' replied a suddenly frightened Stony Pickles.

'Tree? You'll be like a bloomin' forest once you get going, Ollie, plenty more growing left in you I reckon! What, there'll be leaves and branches everywhere before too long!' added Raymond Curley, he also knew when to agree with the big min.

Stony Pickles decided that this would be a good time to change the subject. 'Er, right then, boys, er, I reckon we should be making tracks then, eh? Got a long way to walk before we get to the forest again, haven't we?'

'Yeah, Stony, I reckon that's a good plan like, what d'you reckon Ollie?' said Curley trying to get on the good side of his friend.

'Er? Yeah, that's what I reckon will be a good plan too, Curley, yeah. Let's make, er, some tracks then,' replied Ollie, in a confused voice.

'Right then, let's get on it. This way innit, Curley, if I remember right?' said Stony Pickles, pointing towards the thick trees at other side of the clearing.

'Er, hang on a minute. Yeah definitely this way Stony, that's the way we went last time,' said Curley.

'Right,' said Stony.

The three min started to walk. They headed vaguely towards the edge of the grass.

'Stony?' said Ollie Gimble.

'Yeah, Ollie, what is it?' replied Stony.

'Er, how do I make tracks like?' said Ollie.

Stony Pickles looked across at Curley. For one brief moment he thought that it would be really clever to poke fun at their hefty friend and his latest remark, and then he immediately thought better of it. 'Er, it's ok Ollie, we'll show you on the way, like, won't we Curley?'

'Er, yeah, Ollie, we'll show you on the way,' said Curley.

Wednesday 31st October, 2:30 p.m. Mount Thalamus Bay, Central Head.

Mr Pothackery arrived at Mount Thalamus Bay where the magnificent boats of Central Head were busy dropping off all of the trialists. The early afternoon sunshine showing off the magnificent golden bridge in all its glory as the ships and boats sailed gracefully beneath its arches. The nervous faces of a hundred teenagers were reflected in the waters of the blood red river as they timorously peered out over the side.

The first morning of the next year of their lives had started early for most of them, including Henry and Penelope. Some of the trialists had even travelled through the night, having had to come from places a lot further away than the Luglands. This year's elite had come from far and wide, from every corner of The Will, and many of them would not even arrive until much later as their journeys would take several days, even weeks.

Some of the one hundred were already there of course. They were the three returning trialists who had competed in the contest. For Maximillian Silverdale, Florence Seybold and George Tobias, it was hardly worth travelling home as there would not be enough time for them to return for the start of the trials. Each of them having said their farewells to their families after the contest had decided to stay at Hippocampus.

One more trialist who was already there was the one boy who had only to step out of his nice and pleasant, rich and luxurious home to arrive at the bay in plenty of time, Monty Schmidt. He stood there awkwardly alone, too afraid to talk to anyone else and too frightened to run away, clutching his diary to his chest as if it was the most precious thing in the world to him.

'Welcome, welcome, welcome everybody!' said Mr Pothackery as he helped some of the teenagers from the boat. 'Come along now everyone, this way, that's it join the others over there, and we'll be leaving any minute now. Hello young min very pleased to meet you too, very good yes. Such a lovely day today, don't you think? Right, how many have we got here now, one, two, three, four, five, six, seven? Ah, are you two for the trials, too, young lady?'

'Er, yes, Sir, I'm Penelope Potts and this is Henry Grip,' replied Penelope.

'Ah, Penelope and Henry, let me see now,' he looked down at his clipboard, ran his finger down the list of names until he came to theirs and promptly put a tick next to them. 'Ah from the Luglands I see? Such a lovely part of The Will. Very pleased to meet you. My name is Charles Pothackery and I will be looking after you today. Can you please make your way over to the others there? Thank you.'

Henry and Penelope walked over to where the rest of the trialists were standing.

Mr Pothackery continued speaking to nobody in particular. 'Right, I do believe that could possibly be everyone,' he looked up from his clipboard to address the waiting group. 'Well, we're expecting just over half of our party today and the rest will be following on, so I think that is everyone accounted for. Right, so on we go!

If you would all like to follow me. It's only a short walk to Hippocampus from here. Just across the other side of the bay and it's right there at the foot of the mountain.'

Mr Pothackery started to walk and gestured to the children to follow him. Everyone obliged except for Monty Schmidt; he stood still as if he was stuck to the floor.

Henry and Penelope instantly recognised him as they walked past the lonely figure. They had heard his name being called out at the contest on the previous evening and had therefore deduced that perhaps it was probably going to be the boy with the curious book that they had stumbled upon at the hearing a few days earlier. However, as soon as they saw him again with the enormous diary clutched firmly to his chest, they knew that this couldn't possibly be anybody else.

'Hey, Loppy, it *is* that boy Monty Schmidt. Look, he's got his big book with him again,' said Henry.

'Yes, Henry, I thought as much. There can't be too many boys with that name I suppose, it had to be him really,' said Penelope. 'He seems frightened of something though, doesn't he? Look, he's frozen to the spot.'

'Yes, Loppy,' said Henry. 'He looks bloomin' terrified if you ask me!'

Mr Pothackery turned around and also noticed that the boy hadn't moved; he walked back towards him. 'Come along, Monty, there's a good chap, eh. It won't be long before we get there, and then you can get settled in to your new room and meet all of the others.'

Monty just stared at the min without speaking; he was clearly afraid.

'Try and join in, eh, Monty,' said Mr Pothackery. 'It'll be good for you to mix with the others, make some new friends. I guarantee that you'll be having fun in no time.'

Monty stood, staring down at the floor, motionless.

'I did promise your father that I'd look out for you, Monty. Perhaps you could just give it a try, eh?' said Mr Pothackery. Monty looked up at the min and then started to walk. The mere mention of his father seemed to coax him into action.

'That's the spirit, young Monty. Why don't you walk with Henry and Penelope, here, while I go on up ahead? I'm sure they wouldn't mind the company and it won't be long before we get there now, eh,' said Mr Pothackery. He quickly ran back to the front of the group, leaving Monty in the company of the two friends from the Luglands.

The three trialists continued to walk on for a few minutes in a rather awkward silence. Henry and Penelope were somewhat intrigued by Monty Schmidt but they were even more intrigued by his diary. They wanted to ask him all sorts of questions like, 'Why was he spying on them last week at the trial?' and, 'Why did he run away from them when they confronted him?' and, 'Why in Will's name did he carry that big bloomin' book around with him all of the time?' Somehow, though, it didn't seem the time to ask, considering that right now Monty Schmidt looked like a frightened little boy trying his best not to be noticed in the middle of a crowd.

'Are you ok?' offered Penelope. 'Er, Monty isn't it?'

Monty looked up at Penelope and nodded meekly in response. His round red face was the same colour as the river which flowed behind him.

'This is my friend Henry,' added Penelope.

Henry smiled at the boy.

'Hello,' managed Monty. He barely looked up from the ground, still tightly clutching on to his diary.

'Me and Loppy are from the Luglands. We've travelled all morning to get here, it's been quite a journey hasn't it, Loppy?' said Henry.

'Yes, quite,' said Penelope as she nodded towards the boy.

'Where have you travelled from?' inquired Henry.

'I live here in the bay, with my father,' replied Monty.

'Oh, so you've not travelled very far at all then?' added Henry as they walked. He was becoming slightly bored with this small talk and was eager to get to the camp.

'Are you sure you are ok, Monty?' said Penelope. 'It's just that you seem a little, well, nervous?'

'Do I?' said Monty nervously.

'Well, yes, a bit,' said Penelope. 'But if it's all the same, then I am a little bit nervous too. This is the first time I have ever been away from home and Henry too. Isn't it Henry?'

'Yes, Loppy, but I'm not nervous,' said Henry quite dismissively. 'I'm just looking forward to getting stuck into the trials. I want to get out there on to the mountain and start training for the physicals, work up a sweat, and show Mr Pothackery that I've got what it takes! No I'm not nervous, Loppy, I'm just really excited! Aren't you?'

Penelope was half expecting a response of similar nature from her friend, she knew him all too well. 'Well all I am saying, Henry, is that it's ok to be nervous, isn't it? No shame in it, that's all.'

'Anyway we're almost there, look. I think I can see Hippocampus from here!' said Henry excitedly.

'Yes it does look rather daunting, doesn't it?' said Penelope 'And to think that we are going to be here for a whole year, that seems like forever.'

'Yes it does,' said Monty. 'I wish I could go back home.'

Just as Penelope had managed to get Monty to say slightly more than two words to them, Henry stepped in with a predictable response.

'Daunting?' he said. 'What do you mean daunting? It's going to be the best year of our lives, Loppy. I don't know what you're worried about. It's going to be fantastic!'

Mr Pothackery interrupted the trio as he suddenly shouted from the front of the group. 'Right, here we are then everyone. Welcome to you new home for the next year. This is where you are all going to be staying from now on, the famous Hippocampus of the Central Head Trials!

Now I would like you all to make your way over to the accommodation areas where you will be shown to your individual commorancies. The girl's rooms are over towards the top of the grounds there and boy's rooms are down here on the right hand side. Once you have settled yourselves in, we will all meet up again at the Central Fornix Hall, situated just over there between the edge of the camp and the start of the mountain pass.

Now I know this all seems a bit strange to you right now, but I promise you that you will know your way around the camp like the back of your hand before long. If you have any questions, or if you are unsure about anything, please don't be afraid to ask one of the trial stewards who will be only too willing help you in any way they can. Now we will be dining at around five o' clock so you haven't got long to get yourselves unpacked before we sit down to eat. So off you go then, and as quick as you can before somebody else hogs all the lovely food!'

The mere mention of food was enough to kick start the young hopefuls into action; the love of all things culinary is an ingrained feature of any min's internal make-up. Henry, Penelope and Monty started to make their way towards the accommodation blocks where all of the other trialists were already vigorously battling with each other to try to bag the best rooms. The individual cabins were filling up very quickly.

'Well I guess I'll see you in a little while then, Henry,' said Penelope, 'I think I've got to go over there to the girl's area. We've got to meet at Central Fornix Hall, Mr Pothackery said. It must be that building over there, I suppose?' she pointed to a large building in the distance.

'Yes I think so, Loppy,' said Henry. 'The boy's rooms are here anyway.'

'Ok then, cheerio. Cheerio, Monty, and good luck,' said Penelope.

'Yes, cheerio,' replied Monty.

'Good luck, Loppy,' said Henry. 'See you at five o' clock.'

Penelope wandered off to the other side of the camp, leaving the two boys alone.

One of the trial stewards was busy helping the last few boys into the remaining rooms. 'That's it now, boys, as quick as you can. You'll soon be settled in, there you go,' he looked up and seemed surprised to see Henry and Monty still standing outside. 'Have you two boys not found a room yet?' he said.

'Er, no, not yet, Sir. We were just saying goodbye to our friend,' said Henry.

'Well you haven't got time for that now, you need to find a room, quickly. Come on now, chop chop,' said the steward. 'Hang on a minute you must be the last two lads without accommodation. All of the other chaps are already unpacking. Oh well, you will have to take that room at the end there now. The one next to the flagpole, do you see it? It's the only room left on this block now, I'm afraid.'

'Ok, thank you Sir,' said Henry.

Henry and Monty started make their way towards the flagpole the steward had pointed to.

'Well it looks like we are sharing a room then, Monty,' said Henry.

'Er, yes I suppose it does,' replied Monty.

Hippocampus was now buzzing with activity. As the two boys walked, they peered inside the dozens of open doorways. They could see the other trialists eagerly unpacking all of their things and settling in to their new homes. Henry was brimming with enthusiasm and his excitement was increasing more and more as they went past each open door.

When Henry and Monty reached their allocated room, they could immediately see why it was the last one. It was much smaller than all of the other rooms, and the reason why all of the other boys had been scrambling to find their rooms first was now becoming all too clear. It wasn't anywhere near as impressive as Henry imagined it would be.

There were two small beds inside, one either end of the room and next to each bed was a small cupboard. On top of each cupboard was the standard Central Head stationery pack which was issued to every fledgling trialist. This consisted of writing paper, an ink pad and a pen, all with the motto 'Nos Numquam Immutare Voluntaten' emblazoned upon every piece in bold letters for all to see.

There was a rather old and somewhat rickety looking table in the middle of the room and two even older looking wooden chairs beside it. The table was a sort of half diamond shape, and it had the look of something which at one time was two different things but had now been cobbled together to form one. One of the chairs looked like it had been fashioned for a giant, and the other one for a small child. On top of the table, there was a lantern and next to it was a large open book.

On the opposite wall to the door was an arch-shaped window with its shutters fully open to let the afternoon sunlight stream in to the room from the outside. On the back of the entrance door there were two hooks to hang a hat or coat and written underneath these were the words 'Broom Cupboard'.

'Oh no!' said Henry looking around. 'This must be the worst room in the camp. Look at it, Monty, it's tiny! I can't believe it. I think my room back at home is bigger than this! No wonder everyone was running around trying to get the other rooms, they've beaten us to all the best ones. This is the pits!'

Monty scurried over to the bed in the corner and laid his diary upon it. He opened it up and frantically started to write.

'I guess I'll take this bed then,' said Henry sarcastically, as he placed his belongings on top of the remaining bunk. He started to unpack his things from his bag and put them in the small cupboard next to the bed.

Monty looked up from his book. 'Would you like to take this bed, Henry? We can swap if you like, I don't mind,' he said.

'No it's fine, this'll do,' mumbled Henry. He was clearly unimpressed by his new lodgings.

'Well if you're sure?' said Monty, as he quickly returned to his writing.

'Maybe they're just putting us here temporarily until a better room is fixed or something? Yeah, it must be that. We'll probably get moved to somewhere better then, yeah, that'll be it I reckon,' said Henry mumbling to himself.

The only sound coming from Monty's bunk was the frantic sound of scribbling.

'Aren't you going to unpack, Monty?' said Henry glumly.

'No, I'm not bothering,' replied Monty without looking up. 'I need to update my diary. I haven't got the best of memory, you see, so I need to fill in what's happened so far today before I forget it.'

'Do you write everything down, Monty?' said Henry, 'I mean absolutely everything that you see or hear?'

'Yes of course, Henry, don't you?' replied Monty.

'No I don't, Monty,' said Henry. 'But if I did, I'd be writing down how crummy this bloomin' room is I can tell you that for nothing.' He carried on filling his cupboard with his few remaining belongings.

Monty looked up at Henry as if to acknowledge his remark and then immediately disregarded it as unimportant. He went back to his scribbling.

'I can sense that I'm not going to be getting much conversation out of you for a while, Monty,' said Henry sulking, 'I wonder if Loppy has found a roommate yet.'

Penelope Potts had found her way over to the girl's accommodation block. The area itself was much smaller than the boy's area and the main reason for this was that there never seemed to be as many female trial applicants as there were male, so there was never as much demand for rooms. This was something that Mr Pothackery had done his best to try to change, however, and over the last ten years or so he had made great strides forward in this regard. Nowadays, there were generally a lot more girls applying than there used to be before which was a great testament to Mr Pothackery and his efforts. But despite the positive upturn in figures, the numbers were still a little male heavy.

Penelope walked up to the block of cabins and noticed straight away that from the outside the female rooms seemed to be a bit nicer than the ones the boys were staying in. The individual cabins tended to be a little more spaced out than in the boy's area and things didn't seem as cramped. In addition to this there wasn't the added inconvenience of dozens of testosterone-filled teenage boys tripping over each other, whilst running around and battling for the best rooms either. This side of the camp was much more welcoming.

She noticed that there was a girl standing outside one of the cabins. Penelope instantly recognised her as Florence Seybold, the sole female representative from the contest and also the person who Penelope had been unashamedly rooting for throughout the day. Standing before her was someone she admired immensely for showing her that an ordinary girl like her could, in fact, compete in the traditionally male dominated contest and have a chance of winning. She was a role model for any girl who wanted to enter the trials, and she was standing right in front of her.

'Hello there. My name is Florence, what's yours?' said Florence Seybold as she held out her hand for Penelope to shake.

Penelope reciprocated the gesture. 'Hello Florence. My name is Penelope Potts. I'm very pleased to meet you,' she said nervously.

'And I'm very pleased to meet you too, Penelope Potts,' said Florence. 'I think that you are the first of the new girls to turn up today, I believe that the others are following on, so Mr Pothackery tells me anyway. I know there is someone coming from the Thighlands and another from the Mental Region. I think there is someone from Shin City due to arrive too, and there is even a girl coming from The Foothills, you know? Gosh, that is exciting isn't it? All the way from The Foothills? I've never met anyone from as far away as the Foothills before, have you?'

'Er, no. Can't say I have,' replied Penelope.

'There are going to be quite a few of us this year, by all accounts. Jolly good, hey?' said Florence.

'Er, yes, jolly good,' replied Penelope.

'And where are you from, Penelope Potts? If you don't mind me asking,' said Florence Seybold.

'Er, no. I'm from the Luglands, do you know it?' replied Penelope.

'Ah, yes, The Luglands I do know it. Yes there was a boy from the Luglands who won the contest last year. Do you know him?' said Florence.

'Well, yes, I know who he is. Cornelius Crail is his name, but I don't really know him if that's what you mean. My friend Henry knew him though,' said Penelope.

'Oh well we can't know everyone, I suppose. Big Will and all that, hey?' said Florence. 'Well seeing as the others won't be getting here for a few days or more, would you like to share my cabin Penelope? I can help you settle in. I know where everything is you see, as I was here last year.'

Penelope was amazed at how friendly the girl was because back home in the Luglands she only had one friend and that was Henry. And to meet someone new who would go from heroine to roommate in less than twenty-four hours was something which didn't happen very often to a girl like Penelope. 'Yes, thank you very much, Florence. That would be very nice of you.'

'The pleasure is all mine, Penelope, this way. Mine is the one in the middle, it's not much to look at, I know, but one does what one can,' said Florence.

The two girls walked over to the cabin which was situated in the centre of a row of five. Florence opened the door and went inside; she was quickly followed by Penelope.

'Home sweet home!' said Florence as she stepped through the door.

'Wow!' said Penelope.

The room seemed as if it were ten times bigger on the inside, than it could have possibly been from the outside. It was fantastic. It was something Penelope Potts couldn't have even dreamed of, it was like a different world. She could never have imagined that she would be able to live in a place as amazing as this.

In the centre of the floor of the huge cabin was the most magnificent square shaped carpet which covered almost the entire stone floor beneath it. It was deep blue in colour, with tinges of yellow and white throughout. Around each edge of the rug was the motto of Central Head 'Nos Numquam Immutare Voluntaten' written in bold black letters, and beautifully embroidered in the centre was the gigantic symbol of the crossed keys in silver and black.

The deep stone walls rose up from the ground and towered over her head until they reached the impressive high ceiling above which boasted an opulent chandelier hanging way down below. There were hanging lanterns fixed around every wall and beneath each one was a picture or portrait of an important figure of Central Head.

The focal point of the room was the great fireplace on the central wall with the large portrait of Sananab himself hanging above it and looking down at everything in the room. Next to this, on either side were two striking bookcases filled from top to bottom with more books than Penelope had ever seen in her life.

There was a large wooden bench against one of the walls with the initials of Central Head embossed on the back rest. Penelope shuffled over to it and sat down. Her jaw had dropped and her mouth was wide was open; she was speechless.

Florence walked over and sat down on the huge wooden chair which was next to the bench. 'Do you like it, Penelope?' she said.

Penelope looked at her new friend; she wanted to reply but couldn't quite manage it.

Florence smiled at her and chuckled to herself. 'It's not bad, is it? Actually I think this is the best room in the camp. Most of the rooms over this side are like this and they're a lot better than the ones over there, I'll tell you. We girls get looked after quite well here, on account of there not being that many of us you see. Life does have its little perks sometimes.'

'Florence, this is incredible. I mean it's just magnificent. It is everything I could've ever wished for and more. It's unbelievable, thank you ever so much,' said Penelope.

'Don't thank me, Penelope, thank Mr Pothackery. He is the one who makes all of this possible; he is the one who we all need to thank. Not forgetting the good people of Central Head who chose us all in the first place of course,' said Florence. 'Anyway, when you've been up on that mountain for six hours and your body is aching like it's never ached before then you won't be thanking me then, believe me. What you will be longing for then is that bed over there.'

Florence pointed over to the far wall where there were two luxurious looking beds. Next to each bed was a small cupboard and on top of each cupboard was a jug of water and a cup. Dividing up the sleeping area was a large round table in the centre and on top of which were the two obligatory Central Head stationery kits, one for each trialist.

Florence continued. 'I'll take the bed on the left again, if it is ok with you Penelope? I had the same bed last year you see so we might as well do the same again to make things easier, so yours will be the one on the right, there in the corner if that suits you?'

Penelope was still awestruck by the whole experience. She would have slept on the floor if she had to and it would still have been like a palace to her. 'Er, yes, Florence, yes that's perfectly fine, thank you.'

'That's great then, Penelope. And it will also make sure that I don't get mixed up when returning from the, er..., during the night,' said Florence. 'Oh talking of which, the, er, lavatory is just through that door there. One good thing is that we don't have to share like the boys do, we get one to ourselves.'

'Oh great,' said Penelope. She had never heard of the, er, lavatory before, as Florence had called it but she was an intelligent girl and guessed that she probably meant the lavvy.

Florence stood up and walked over to the fireplace. 'Whatever you need, Penelope, you just give me a shout and I'll help you if I can. We're all friends here, you know. Competitive, yes, but friends all the same. Mr Pothackery drums it into us you know. 'A friend is for life, not just for Christmas' he says, I'm not sure I know exactly what he means by that but I can understand the sentiment alright. You need friends in this Will, Penelope, and Mr

Pothackery is certainly a good friend to us all. And now we are going to be roomies, you and I, so we are now officially friends too!'

There were two small shots of what looked like liquor on top of the fireplace. Florence picked up both of them and brought them back over to the bench where Penelope was sitting. 'And here is your welcome drink from Central Head, Penelope, a toast to our new friendship. To Florence Seybold and Penelope Potts, roomies extraordinaire! Jolly hockey sticks, hey!' She gave one of the tiny cups to Penelope and raised the other one up in the air.

'Jolly hockey sticks, is that what this is then, Florence?' said Penelope somewhat confused, as she took the shot from her new friend. She had never heard of anything like this before.

'No, not jolly hockey sticks, ha, ha! No that's just a saying, Penelope. 'Jolly hockey sticks' is a saying from back home. I like to keep up the old traditions, you know how it is. Now we must drink a toast to us!' replied Florence.

Penelope stood up from the bench and the two girls touched their tiny cups together.

'Is it liquor then, Florence?' said Penelope.

'No, of course not,' replied Florence. 'It's bambury juice. It's good for you; they make it here in the mountains, you know? Anyway, bottoms up, hey!'

'Oh, ok, here goes then. Bottoms up!' said Penelope. She didn't really know what she was doing but, nevertheless, it seemed like a lot of fun.

The two girls drank a toast to their new found friendship. Penelope Potts stood for a moment and thought about where she was and what she was doing. This was a dream come true for her and she had only been at the trials for half an hour.

Two weeks earlier she wasn't even remotely interested in being a trialist; two weeks ago she was preparing herself for a future of working with her father at Earside Left. Two weeks ago the highlight of her week would have been looking forward to going to the bingo with her mother and Winnie Drum. Two weeks ago she was bored silly. Now everything was different. Everything had suddenly changed. It was magical; it was beyond her wildest dreams.

She had already met new friends and new adventures would surely come. And what was more, she was with her best friend too. She closed her eyes and thought of her mother and father and how they had worked so hard to bring her up as an honest girl. She thought about how her mother had said that there was adventure in her, and that she would always want to go and explore, and she also thought about how her father had not wanted to let her go anywhere near Central Head. She was very happy at this moment in time, however, that her father had never got his wish. She would make him proud though, she thought. She would make them proud. She would make them both the proudest parents in the entire Will. She would not let them down.

Chapter Thirteen

Sananab got up from his chair and walked towards the thick, heavy door of his office. He scrunched up the piece of parchment he had in his hand and threw it on to the floor behind him. As he got to the door, he hesitated for a moment as his hand turned the brass doorknob. He seemed to think of something; he looked puzzled in some way. After a few seconds he opened the door and left his office.

He strode down the well-lit corridor of the Neocortex, and made his way around the corner where he came upon another door. It was similar to the one that barred the way to his own office, yet if anything it seemed more important. A door that had history deep within its heart. This could indeed be considered more important than his own, even if he was the most important person in The Will. This was not the door to just any old room; this was the door to the most important room of all, the nerve centre of the Neocortex. This was the Lobe Room. This was the room in which all of the millions of messages sent to the brain every single minute of every day were processed.

Sananab opened the door and went inside. As he entered, he was greeted by the sight of hundreds of min going about their daily routine, processing and configuring all of the millions of messages which were being sent there every minute. Each one was dressed immaculately in the prestigious black and red uniform of Central Head. The Lobe Room was vast. It was the biggest room in the whole of Neocortex: In fact, the Lobe Room was so big that it was even bigger than some actual towns or cities situated in certain parts of The Will. It was divided up into different areas, each one responsible for a different part or function of The Will. It was an information highway, a sheer continent of thought. The min who worked in the Lobe Room were handpicked by Sananab himself; only the trusted were allowed to be this close the thoughts of The Will itself.

Sananab made his way straight to the area of the Lobe Room that was of particular interest to him, the Frontal Area. He sat down in the throne-like seat in the centre of the Frontal Lobe Area and he watched. He didn't say anything to anybody, he just sat and watched. He watched as the thousands of messages travelled through the nerves before his very eyes and were processed and moved on to other parts of The Will. He watched with great interest, very great interest indeed. He was looking for something.

At the heart of Hippocampus was the impressive Central Fornix Hall. It was one of the oldest buildings in the camp and the rest of Hippocampus had been built up around it. Over the years accommodation blocks, sports fields and running tracks were added as the popularity of the contest had grown. This gave the architecture a somewhat mixed-up feel, yet the blend of old and new was something which for many visitors gave the camp its unusual charm.

Along the two sides of the hall there were a series of huge arch-shaped windows and each one had the symbol of the crossed keys colourfully etched in stained glass. The vast high ceiling was painted in white and gold and towered above the area below.

At one end of the hall were three large statues looking out over the entire room. The statue furthest to the right was a life sized sculpture of Sananab, current ruler of Central Head, and the other two looming figures were sculptures of its previous two rulers, Geffron Scolt and Triston Clearwater Snr respectively.

The floor was a beautiful polished wood and the history of The Will could somehow be felt within the thousands of scratches, indents and subtle idiosyncrasies of the thirty-four years of wear and tear it had been made to endure.

Inside the hall was a long table which had been set for dinner. The elegant tablecloth which sat upon it, like many other items at the camp, was adorned with the motto of Central Head. There were several candles placed along the centre, in-between which the plates and cutlery had been meticulously laid out for the guests. It was large enough to seat more than the one hundred trialists quite easily and would still have room besides. There were still a large amount of people yet to turn up and even with all of the trial stewards it was nowhere near to its capacity.

Penelope and Florence were already seated, along with most of the other trialists, when Henry and Monty appeared at the door. They were late. The two boys scurried into the hall and quickly sat down in the seats which Penelope had saved for them.

'Where have you been? Everyone's been waiting for you?' said Penelope.

'Well I was ready ages ago, Loppy, but we had to wait for someone to fill his bloomin' diary in, didn't we?' said Henry, looking accusingly at Monty Schmidt.

Monty didn't say anything, he just clutched on to his diary as he sat down.

Mr Pothackery began to speak. 'Ah, Henry, Monty, you're here. Better late than never, eh? Ha, ha, jolly good. Now then here we all are, welcome to Central Fornix Hall everyone. This is the place where we hold our group meetings every day so you will all become familiar with it very soon. It's also the place where we eat together too so you will all be spending a lot of time in here. We trialists do like our food you'll all be glad to know. Ha, ha!

Now we like to be as informal as we can here, guys, we all sit at the same tables. There's no separation of teachers and trialists or anything like that and we're all friends here so we all muck in together so to speak. The stewards, teachers and I are always here for you should you need us, anytime day or night. You just come and knock at the door and we shall help you in any way that we can. Can I also introduce you to a new member of the team this year? To my left here is Mr Cornelius Crail, who will be...'

Cornelius Crail interrupted Mr Pothackery before he had a chance to finish his sentence. 'I will be in charge, total charge. I shall be in complete control of everything that happens on this camp. Complete control, do you hear? And if anybody should need anything from me, I expect you to make an appointment. Knocking at my door in the middle of the night is not acceptable is that clear? My time is precious to me and I don't expect to be awoken at any hour by some weak, homesick child who misses their mother.'

Everyone in the hall was shocked to say the least; nobody was expecting an outburst of such rhetoric. The look of sheer confusion was sitting uncomfortably on everyone's face. Mr Pothackery was especially surprised but he was more embarrassed than anything else. Unfortunately he was not in charge of the trials anymore and Cornelius Crail was making it quite clear that he most definitely was. He couldn't do anything about it other than to sit there and listen like everybody else and try to do the best that he could for the trialists.

Cornelius continued with his speech. 'I can assure you of this, the next year of your life is going to be extremely tough and hard and nobody should be expecting an easy ride from me. I triumphed as the deserving winner of the contest because I was mentally prepared. I showed no weakness, and I proved to be the best; head and shoulders above anybody else. Unlike the rest of the pathetic finalists I was strong and mentally tough. Things are going to change this year and you all had better get used to it. Things are going to get done my way, and by my rules. Anybody who shows any sign of weakness will be punished and left to rue their mistakes. There is no place in Central Head for the weak; we have no time for losers. Have you all got that?'

Some of the trialists nodded in reply, too scared to say anything.

'Now I have important business to attend to with Sananab; the greatest mind that The Will has ever known. I shall return tomorrow and I shall be watching everyone very carefully. If you don't think that you've got what it takes to be a true champion like me, then you're not worthy of a place at this table. Think on it.'

Cornelius stood up and walked off towards the door. On his way past the table he kicked the chair that Henry was sitting in, causing him to get squashed between the chair and the table. Cornelius stopped and gave him an evil stare. He said nothing and left.

Mr Pothackery was speechless. The atmosphere was suddenly very bad. He looked around at the frightened faces of the trialists sitting at the table. He had to do something to change the mood, but didn't know quite what to do. 'Er, I think that perhaps we should bring out the food now. Yes, can we have the food now, please?' he said.

The stewards did as Mr Pothackery had suggested and started to bring out the food.

'Er, once you have finished your meals, you may return to your cabins. The rest of the evening is yours to do as you wish, er, feel free to mingle,' said Mr Pothackery quite glumly. Cornelius Crail had certainly made an impression on his first day in charge, nobody could deny that.

'And you are all to meet back here at 9:00 a.m. in the morning for your first seminar, I will see you all then,' continued Mr Pothackery. He then got up and left the hall, shaking his head. He had the look of somebody who had suddenly lost their appetite.

'What a ghastly little min,' said Florence. 'Are you alright?'

'Er, yes I'm ok,' replied Henry, rubbing his chest.

'Henry, that was awful. He did that deliberately, I swear it,' said Penelope to her friend.

'Yes, I think he did,' said Henry. 'It wouldn't be the first time though, would it? He's always had it in for me that Crail has. Of all the people who could be in charge, why does it have to be him? Not bloomin' fair, Loppy.'

'I'm sorry, you actually know each other?' said Florence, quite confused at the situation.

Penelope thought that this would be a good time for introductions. 'Oh of course, you haven't met yet have you? Florence, this is my friend Henry Grip, he is the one I was telling you about. We're both from the Luglands, you see, we've travelled here together, and Henry, this is my new roommate, Florence Seybold.'

'How do you do? Pleased to meet you, Florence,' said Henry as he offered his handshake.

'Very pleased to meet you too, Henry,' said Florence as she shook his hand.

'Florence was in the contest, Henry, remember? She won one of the psychological tests,' said Penelope. 'The one with the numbers?'

'Oh yeah, of course,' said Henry, suddenly a bit more excited. 'I can't believe I'm actually sitting next to someone who has competed in the contest! What was it like? You have to tell us all about it?'

'Jolly hard I can tell you that!' said Florence. 'But you'll soon get to know all about that first hand, I'm sure.'

'And this is Monty,' added Penelope. 'We've only just met today, haven't we, Monty?'

'Hmm,' said Monty. He was suddenly a lot more interested in the food that had just reached them rather than the pleasantries of the conversation.

Henry too had noticed this. 'Monty is my new roommate but he doesn't exactly say much at all, do you, Monty?' he added as Monty started to tuck in to his grub.

'Well it's jolly nice to make friends with you all. I just know that we'll have a jolly spiffing time together. Hey!' added Florence.

'Yes we will,' said Penelope. 'Jolly hockey sticks too!' she added, trying desperately to fit in with her new friend.

'Ah, that's the spirit, Penelope. Yes, jolly hockey sticks. What!' said Florence.

Henry looked utterly confused, 'Er, yeah ok.' he said.

By this time they had all been brought food and were eagerly tucking in.

'So tell me, Henry,' said Florence, 'this min Crail, you say that you know each other, from the Luglands? He doesn't seem the type of chap that you and Penelope would want to get yourselves mixed up with. Forgive me for being quite forward here but I've only just met you two, and you seem jolly nice people to me, yet that min seems such an odious little fellow; not very nice at all.'

'No, he isn't very nice at all, Florence, you've got that right,' replied Henry. 'I only know him because he grew up in the same place as me, Earside Right. He is a couple of years older than me and he always used to make fun of me. He picked on me quite a bit when we were younger. I was the only boy from the Luglands who grew up without a mother, you see, so there was only ever me and my father. Cornelius used to call me names and stuff. He never liked me from the beginning. Father used to tell me to just ignore him and he would eventually go away but he never did; he was always there picking away at me.'

'Henry, that is dreadful. How awful it must have been for you,' said Florence. 'What an absolute rotter that min is.'

'I grew up without a mother too,' said Monty Schmidt, hardly looking up from his plate.

'Did you, Monty?' said Penelope. 'What happened?'

'I don't know. Father wouldn't tell me so I never knew,' said Monty.

'I didn't know that, Monty,' said Henry. 'I'm sorry to hear that.'

'Well you just sort of get used to it, don't you? I expect you must know all about that,' said Monty. He went back to his plate.

'Yeah, I do,' replied Henry.

'And do you know what happened to your mother, Henry?' said Florence.

'No, not really, Florence,' said Henry. 'In fact nobody really knows. It's a bit of a mystery apparently. One minute she was there and the next minute she was gone. She just wasn't there anymore. Some people say that something must have happened to her, I mean min don't just disappear, do they? But I'm not sure myself. It was just after I was born so I didn't really know anything else but Father reckons she is out there somewhere. He says that one day she will come back.'

'I know she will come back one day, Henry, I'm certain of it,' said Penelope reassuringly.

Henry just smiled. Thinking about his mother made him a little upset so he tried not to do it very often, Penelope knew this too but whenever they met new people, which wasn't very often, the subject did often tend to come up.

'Even if she did come back now, who would she come back to?' he said. 'I mean, after last week, Father has gone too hasn't he? That stupid hearing and the sentence, and that horrible Zamindar and...'

It had suddenly dawned on Henry that the reason why his father had gone away was due to the actions of the patriarch of someone who was sitting not a million miles away from him; he looked across his roommate who was also beginning to put two and two together.

'Oh, so it was your father that was sentenced last week was it, Henry?' said Monty, as he looked up from his food.

'Yes, it bloomin' well was, Monty!' exclaimed Henry. Penelope and Florence were feeling very uncomfortable at this point but not as uncomfortable as Monty Schmidt.

'I'm sorry, Henry, I really am. My father is not the most popular of min, and I know that all too well. In fact, I don't think I have ever met anyone who actually has a nice word to say about him. I know that people despise him, and I can see why. If it's any consolation, Henry, then he has never really been much of a father to me.'

Monty paused for a second before continuing. 'If I were not related to him then I probably would hate him just as much as everybody else does. As it is, we don't really speak anyway. I suppose the only true friends I have are my diaries and he tries to take them away from me too. He punishes me with them you see, takes them off me when I don't speak to him because he knows that it will hurt me. I'm only here because Father made me come. I'm an embarrassment to him and his pride. He thinks this place will toughen me up. I'm sorry about your father, Henry, but please don't think any worse of me for who I am; I wish I could've been somebody else but I can't.'

Henry listened to Monty quite carefully and reluctantly conceded that the two boys were very similar in many ways. Henry wasn't a vindictive person, and no matter how tough it was for him, he couldn't blame Monty for his father's actions; it just wasn't right. 'Ah, it's ok, Monty. I don't blame you; it's not your fault, is it?'

'Thanks, Henry,' said Monty. He was starting to feel that for the first time in his life, he could possibly be making friends with someone other than a book.

Penelope was beginning to see that there was something about Monty Schmidt. He was kind and gentle, and somebody not unlike herself. The curious boy, whom they had stumbled upon from a few days ago, was beginning to appear different. He was becoming interesting all of a sudden.

She smiled at Monty, and for the first time he seemed like a friend. He smiled back a friendly smile.

'Well I, for one, am jolly pleased that I have met a wonderful bunch of chaps such as you! What a jolly nice time it's been meeting you all, and I know that we are all going to be such good friends this year. A toast to the four of us, raise your glasses!' said Florence.

The four friends raised their glasses for the toast. 'Hurrah!' said Florence.

'Hurrah!' said the other three.

Some of the trial stewards appeared and began to clear away the plates and cutlery that were left on the table. Most of the trialists had finished their meals and were starting to head back to their cabins. Henry, Monty, Penelope and Florence got up from the table and made their way towards the door.

'Right then, I suppose we'll see you all in the morning at nine then?' said Henry.

'Yes, Henry, I'm actually really looking forward to it now,' said Penelope.

'See, Loppy, I told you it was going to be great, didn't I?' replied Henry.

'Does anybody know what we are going to be doing then?' said Monty.

'Yes, I do chaps,' said Florence. 'First up for you guys tomorrow morning is the history of The Will. It's designed to get your minds ticking over for the mental tests you see. It's actually a jolly good lesson, if you ask me. I always enjoyed the history seminars I did; you'd be surprised what you actually know, as opposed to what you don't know. You can gain a lot of knowledge from the history seminars and Mr Pothackery leads them too so it's all jolly good fun to boot!'

'Wow! That sounds amazing. I can't wait!' said Penelope. Knowledge was something she craved.

'It's physical training for us three though, the three returning from the contest I mean. That's if I can manage it. My ankle still a bit sore you see.' Florence pointed to the strapping which was still on her injured ankle.

'Perhaps I might just sit the day out tomorrow, see how I am in the morning,' she added.

'See you at nine then, Henry, Monty,' said Penelope.

'Yes, cheerio,' said Monty.

'Ta, ta for now!' said Florence.

'Bye, Loppy. Bye, Florence,' said Henry.

The two girls walked off towards their cabins, with the two boys heading off in the opposite direction.

Chapter Fourteen

Thursday 1st November, 6:58 a.m. The Oesophagus Forest.

The Oesophagus Forest was dark, it was always dark. Even though it was early in the morning and the rest of The Will was waking up to a world which was bathed in bright sunshine, everything here was different. Nobody really knew why it was always dark, some say that it had something to do with the fact that everybody who lived here had a particularly dark outlook on life and that their dark thoughts had turned the skyline black. Others thought it was because of the dark deeds which had been cruelly done by the evil min from days gone by to anyone who had dared to cross them. Most folk, however, just thought it was dark because it was downright scary. Not many people went in to the Oesophagus Forest unless they really had to and, more importantly, not many people ever came out of there unless they were allowed to.

The three wanna-be villains from the Luglands, Stony Pickles, Ollie Gimble and Raymond Curley, were stumbling around in the gloom trying to find their way to Mr Yanich's cottage. But with their combined sense of direction not exactly leaping directly from the pages of the latest Boy Scout manual, they were not having a particularly easy time of finding it.

'Ouch! Was that you again, Ollie? I'll bloody swing for you in a minute, I will,' said Stony Pickles.

'Well it's not my fault is it? I can't see where I'm bloomin' well going, can I?' replied Ollie Gimble.

'If you step on my toes again, Ollie, there'll be nothing left of 'em! That must be about the hundredth time in the last hour, jeez!' said Stony Pickles.

'Ah come on, Stony,' said Ollie. 'It's not that many times is it? Nowhere near a hundred, more like about five or something I reckon, if that, like.'

'Well it bloomin' well feels like a hundred, doesn't it?' said Stony jumping up and down on one leg and holding his other leg in his hands.

The sound of a snigger came from a few yards ahead of the two min. It was Raymond Curley, he had wandered a few paces further on whilst the commotion ensued.

'And what are you laughing at, Curley?' said Stony. 'It's you that's gone and got us lost again anyway, innit? Fat lot of good you turned out to be.'

'We're not lost I've told you. It's around here somewhere, any minute now we'll be there, you'll see,' said Raymond Curley.

'See? I can't see anything, can I?' said Ollie. 'Bloomin' pitch black, innit? Why can't we light the lantern, Stony?'

'Yeah he's right you know, Stony,' said Curley. 'Just light it and we can see where we're going then. Be there in no time then, wont we?'

'I've told you two, we are not lighting that lantern, right?' snapped Stony. 'You know what happened last time, don't you? As soon as we lit the match then that bloomin' psychopath Quick turned up, didn't he? He must have seen the light you see, alerted him to our presence, like. So we need to keep a low profile, don't we? Try and stay under the radar... Aaaghh!'

The very brief period of time that elapsed between the end of the word 'radar', and the beginning of the word 'Aaaghh' contained the sound of a very loud thud and, if anybody could've actually seen it, the actions of a min walking straight into a tree. Stony Pickles was lying in a heap on the ground, completely dazed.

'Are you alright, Stony?' said Curley into the darkness.

'Oohh, no, I'm not alright, Curley. Oh my poor head, I think I can see stars,' said Stony.

'You've got bloody better eyesight than me then,' said Curley under his breath. 'Why, what've you done?' he then added a bit louder, trying to be a little more sympathetic towards his injured friend.

'Dunno, reckon I must've walked into a tree or something, mustn't I?' said the wounded min. He was still lying on the floor and rubbing his head.

Ollie Gimble was finding this all completely hilarious. 'Ha, ha, what a dummy. Ha, ha, Curley, fancy walking into a tree. Ha, ha, what a big dummy!' He was stumbling around laughing at his friend's misfortune. There was then another brief sound which filled the air but this time it was more like the sound of a giant figure kicking a min squarely in the head whilst lying powerless on the ground.

'Aaaghh, what the hell was that?' said Stony Pickles from his lowly position as Ollie Gimble's foot collided with his skull. 'Oohh wait a minute, I think I know what it was. Oh, Will help me.'

The realisation of what had just happened quickly dawned upon him. No more than a mere millisecond before he finished his sentence, the giant frame of his lofty friend came crashing down on top of his helpless body.

Thump.

'Aaaghh!'

'Sorry, Stony, I think I must have tripped over something,' said Ollie.

'Yeah, you did, my bloody head!' said a muffled voice from underneath the enormous whale-like body of Ollie Gimble. 'Curley, will you get this big idiot off me?'

Curley wandered over to the spot where he thought that the sound had vaguely come from, he was still sniggering. 'Don't know how I'm gonna pull him off you, Stony, he's heavy you know. Anyway I can't see a bloomin' thing in this place. Look, why don't you just let me light the lantern?'

'No, don't light the lantern. We'll get caught by the other fella if you do,' said Stony, still muffled due to the fact that there was a twenty five stone min lying on top of him.

Ollie was trying to get up, but wasn't having much luck. 'I think my arm is stuck, Stony, there's a hole or something here and it's stuck down it. I can't pull it out,' he said.

'Well just give it a try, will you? I'm nearly suffocating down here,' said Stony.

'I am, Stony, I'm trying,' said Ollie whilst struggling to free his arm from the hole. 'Ah, there you go, its free now.'

With this he yanked his arm out of the hole with great force, whereupon it collided with an unsuspecting Raymond Curley who instantly dropped his lantern and doubled over in pain.

'Oohh!' he cried out in agony.

'What's up, Curley?' said Stony.

'Oohh! Something's just whacked me right in the goolies!' said Curley, through his pain.

'Ha, ha, serves you right for laughing at me, doesn't it,' said Stony as he struggled to his feet. 'Oohh, he's took one right in the nuts, Ollie, ha, ha. It's got to hurt that, son, hasn't it, eh? It's got to hurt that, ha, ha.'

'Ha, ha, yeah, Stony. Right in the goolies, ha, ha, ha!' said Ollie Gimble, blissfully unaware that it was he who had struck the heavy blow.

'Ah, it's no use. I think you're right, you know, we're gonna have to light the lantern. Can't see a bloomin' thing at all now,' conceded Stony. 'Ollie, pass me that lantern before someone goes and falls over again.'

'There you go, Stony,' said Ollie. He reached down to the ground, picked up what he thought was the lantern, and handed it to his friend.

'Ollie, that's not the lantern, it's a ruddy great piece of tree! It's probably got a bit of my head stuck in it. And its, urgh... it's got all stuff all over it, yuck,' said Stony. He dropped the branch on the ground, and started to wipe his hands on his tunic. 'It's over there somewhere, Ollie, I heard it drop.'

Ollie fumbled around on the ground until he found the lantern, 'There you go, Stony.'

Stony Pickles took the lantern from his friend and proceeded to light it. 'There you go, that's better, lads. At least we can see what we're all... aahh...'

His sentence was suddenly cut short. Now that the three min could finally see, they instantly wished that they were still in the dark. They were greeted by the sight of Zachary Quick and a dozen of his cut-throat gang members. Each one was wielding a sharp knife and was it pointing ominously towards their throats.

Raymond Curley was still doubled up with pain but as he began to straighten up the realisation of what was happening, coupled with the threat of a viciously sharp blade held inches away from his face, was enough to make him quickly forget about his injury.

'I knew it, I bloomin' well knew it. I told you, didn't I?' said Stony.

When the opportunity of saying 'I told you so' comes along, it is very rarely passed up. And the satisfaction gained from saying 'I told you so' is considerably more rewarding to most people than being afraid of a dozen knife-wielding bandits. Stony Pickles was no different. As soon as he had inflated his own ego by proving to his friends he had been correct with his prediction, he quickly realised the severity of the situation they were in and went back to being scared. He gulped with fear as Mr Quick leaned closer.

'Oh, how I am going to enjoy watching you die,' said Mr Quick.

'Er, now let's not get too hasty here, Mr Quick. We're all friends here, aren't we?' said Stony.

Mr Quick pressed his knife closer into the neck of Stony Pickles, until it just pierced the skin. 'No, we are not all friends here, Lugland boy, we are most definitely not.'

Raymond Curley intervened. 'Er, we've been sent for haven't we, Quick, by Mr Yanich. He wants to see us, doesn't he? Sent a messenger, said we had to come and see him, like. Urgent, like.'

Mr Quick relaxed his grip on Stony and stood back. 'I don't know what Mr Yanich has in store for you three but he obviously thinks that it's important, otherwise you would have been disposed of long ago. Very well, take them to Yanich's cottage, min, let him have his wish. Only once he has finished with them, then we shall *finish* with them.' With this, he made a gesture of cutting Stony Pickles' throat with his knife and then pushed him forward forcing him to walk. They all walked along the short path until they reached Mr Yanich's cottage where the two guards were once again standing outside his door.

'These idiots are apparently expected,' said Mr Quick to the guards. He then gave Stony Pickles a shove towards the cottage.

The three Lugland min walked down the winding path to the door, one of the guards opened it and they went inside. The well-lit interior of the cottage was as immaculate as it was before. There wasn't a thing out of place, not a speck of dust anywhere.

Mr Yanich was sitting down on a large chair in his study. He had the open diary on his lap and was reading it intensely. He looked up to find that his visitors had arrived.

'Ah, you've made it, I see,' he said. 'Do come in and sit down. Make yourselves comfortable, gentlemin. Lance, er, some tea for our friends please.' He gestured towards one of the guards who had also come in from outside with the hapless trio. He could see from out of the corner of his eye that Ollie Gimble was staring at him open mouthed in expectancy for something. 'Oh and perhaps something to eat for our large friend here too, I think.'

A beaming smile instantly appeared on Ollie Gimble's face.

'It's comforting to know that the welcoming committee from outside haven't lost any of their delightful charm then, Mr Yanich?' said Raymond

Curley sarcastically. 'That Quick fella had a knife in Stony's neck, it looks like he's drew blood there, you know.'

Stony Pickles quickly examined his neck wound with his finger. He noticed that there was indeed a bit of blood, although it was barely a scratch. 'Yeah, he has and all you know, Curley, look.' He showed his friend the faint drop of blood on his finger. 'I might have to have a week off work with that, I reckon. Could even be a fortnight with an injury like that, you know!'

'Ah yes, Mr Quick can be a little... overzealous shall we say. But he is loyal, nonetheless, and he does keep the forest clear of any unwanted guests, which is our primary concern after all. And I have seen him do a lot worse than that with a knife, my friend. You can count yourself lucky that he stopped there,' said Mr Yanich, quite unsympathetically.

'So you, er, sent for us then, Mr Yanich? We came as soon as we heard, like,' said Stony, quickly changing the subject. 'What's it, er, all about then? The book, like.'

'Yes, my friend, I did send for you, and you've arrived a bit sooner that I had envisaged too, I might add. This certainly does make fascinating reading,' said Mr Yanich as he turned the pages of the big book.

Stony Pickles looked across at his two friends. 'See I told you didn't I, boys? I knew there was something in this; I could feel it in my water.'

'But we drank the last of the water last night, didn't we, Stony?' said Ollie Gimble. 'I didn't think we had any more.'

'No I didn't mean the water that we had; I meant that I could... Ah forget it, Ollie, it doesn't matter anyway,' said Stony. He was getting tired of having to explain almost every phrase or saying to his less than intelligent companion.

'So what is it then, Mr Yanich? What's in it, like?' said Raymond Curley, getting back to the subject.

Mr Yanich leaned forward. 'Contained within the pages of this book here, gentlemin, is information, a great deal of information. Written down in this diary are some of the most closely guarded secrets of The Will. Central Head will have you believe many things, my friends, many things which they say that they have no control over; this however is a lie. Recorded here are the transcripts of meetings which have taken place, meetings between some of the most trusted senior figures from Central Head. Some of these are meaningless to us, I'll grant you, merely mundane procedural matters but others are pure gold.

'One of them, in particular, has turned out to be rather interesting. In fact, it has turned out to be very interesting indeed. Our friend here, the young Mr Schmidt, has provided us with a very detailed account of a significant encounter between the Zamindar and the most powerful min of all, the Ruler himself.'

'What? You mean pointy head?' said Stony.

144

'I mean Sananab, my Lugland friend, the one who cannot be touched,' said Mr Yanich.

'Jeez, what did he say then Mr Yanich, in this meeting like?' said Curley.

The guard, who had been entrusted with bringing the tea suddenly appeared from the other room. He laid out the tea things on the table and handed a huge plate of sandwiches straight into the grateful arms of Ollie Gimble.

'Ah thank you, Lance, you're very kind,' said Mr Yanich.

'Thanks, Mr Yanich, Sir!' said Ollie Gimble as he began to shovel the sandwiches directly into his face.

'Never stops bloomin' eating this fella, Curley,' said Stony Pickles in disgust.

Raymond Curley just shook his head in response.

'Perhaps gentlemin, it would be easier if I were to read it out for you so that you can take it all in?' said Mr Yanich.

'Yeah, that sounds like a plan, Mr Yanich,' said Curley.

'Yeah, I'm up for that as well, like,' said Stony, in agreement with his friend.

'Very well then, sit back and listen carefully, my friends, for this is certainly a tale worth hearing.' Mr Yanich began to read...

'Diary entry for Friday 26th October, time is 11.47 a.m. Father was sitting at his desk in his office and he was filling out some forms. I was hiding in my usual speck, behind the big chair in the corner, and I was reading my book. He didn't know that I was there.

The door of the office opened suddenly and Sananab came rushing in. He was not his usual calm self, he seemed excited about something. Father looked up from his paperwork. 'Good morning, Sir, are you alright? You startled me a little; I didn't think we were supposed to meet until later on.'

'Yes, Leopold, I am fine. In fact, I am more than fine. I am happy, very happy, I am very happy indeed,' said Sananab.

'Well that is good, Sir, is it not?' said Father, a little unsurely.

'Sananab sat down on the chair on the opposite side of the desk to Father. 'Yes, my Zamindar, it is very good, very good indeed,' he said.

Father still looked a little confused. 'Sir?' he said.

Sananab cupped his hands together and leaned a little bit closer to my father. 'Leopold, I have done it. At last, I have finally done it, the breakthrough I have been waiting for, all these years and now I have succeeded,' he said.

'Succeeded in doing what, Sir?' asked Father.

'You may ask my friend, yes you may ask. I have succeeded in doing something that we have always wanted, Leopold, always dreamed of. I have changed The Will,' said Sananab.

For a moment time seemed to stand still, there was an eerie silence which filled the room.

Father was completely shocked; he sat back in his chair. 'You have done what?' he said.

'This morning,' said Sananab. 'I did it. I have managed to change The Will. I made it do something that was not its will but mine. I controlled its thoughts, and I controlled its actions. I made sure that it did not hear the alarm this morning. It was me who made that happen, Leopold. It was me who did it.'

'But how, Sir? I mean that's impossible,' said Father. He was absolutely astonished at what he was hearing.

'Nerves, Leopold, it's the nerves. You have to be able to control the nerves. It's so simple when you think about it, yes so simple. I don't know why it has taken me so long to understand it. But now I have,' said Sananab.

Father was still shocked; he didn't really know what to say. 'But I still don't understand, Sir,' he said.

'You have to be able to manipulate the thought process, Leopold, control the nerves. If you can control the nerves, you can control the min and if you control the min, then you can control The Will itself.

'Take this morning, for instance. The alarm was sounded but The Will never heard it, at least that is what everyone thinks. The truth is that The Will did hear the sound; it's just that it was not detected here in Central Head. While the message was on its way to its usual destination, it was intercepted. I intercepted it and sent it off somewhere else. It was sent to another part of The Will, to a place where the min didn't know what to do with it so it just got lost.

'That is why Central Head never got the message and that is why The Will never actually heard the alarm. Simple minology. But minology which had been manipulated and controlled by me, it was easy. '

Father got up from his chair and began to pace around the room. 'Master, this is a very serious matter indeed, I mean this is huge, colossal, this could change everything,' he said.

'Yes, Leopold, it has changed everything,' said Sananab. 'Don't you see what this means? It means we can carry on the work we initiated all those years ago, you and me. We can finish what we started. This is the breakthrough that we've been waiting for; the catalyst for our success!'

Father looked a little uneasy; he had deep concern in his voice. 'Wait a minute you don't mean...? Surely you don't think we can go through all of that again? Not with you and me and...? It was so dangerous, Sir, I mean you know how it turned out before. It was so terrible for everyone, especially poor old...' He looked down at the floor and held his hand to his forehead.

'But it is different now, isn't it my friend? Now that we can control The Will, we can make it do anything, whatever we want it to. We never had this before, did we? And that is why, well, that is why the events of all those years ago happened as they did. It will work this time, my Zamindar, this time we will succeed. This time we have the power to achieve anything,' said Sananab.

'I'm not sure, Sir, I'm really not sure,' said Father, 'I mean changing The Will, what if someone else had seen you do it? This could cause mayhem throughout the entire body. Perhaps we should inform the people that it was all a misunderstanding, play it down.'

Sananab carefully got up from the chair that he was sitting in and walked around to the other side of the desk where Father's chair was. He very slowly and calmly sat down in it. His voice changed from one of previous excitement into one of cold calculated thought. 'As you are so keen on informing the people, my Zamindar, perhaps we should also inform the people of the role you played in those unfortunate events of fifteen years ago? Perhaps we should inform the people of the active part you took in the entire episode? Perhaps we should inform them of the particular lengths that you went to, in order to set up that dreadful deed?'

Father walked over to the other chair and sat down. 'Very well, I shall do whatever you ask of me, Sir,' he said.

'Good, Leopold, that is very good. Now that's more like it, isn't it? Your initial reluctance disappointed me so. I do like things a lot better when we are friends, don't you?' said Sananab.

'Yes, Sir,' said Father. 'What do you want me to do?'

'I have seen something, Leopold, something deep within the nerves. I have foreseen something that will have a devastating effect on the entire Will. In three years' time, every single one of us is going to be damaged by this, and that is why we need to carry on with what we started all those years ago. This is big, Leopold, it is the biggest thing that we will ever have to deal with in our lives, and it can't be stopped. We cannot tell anyone about this or we will have an uprising on our hands. We are not prepared for such an eventuality now, and we never have been. If we do not find a solution to this then I cannot see a future for the min beyond it,' said Sananab.

Father looked worried. He looked more concerned than I have ever seen him in my whole life.

'Sir, what is this you speak of? This is catastrophic news,' he said.

'I still don't fully understand it myself, Leopold, and I need to do some further investigation. I must gain the knowledge, have togetherness with the nerves, live and breathe them. Become as one with The Will itself, until I can see exactly what this is,' replied Sananab.

'Sir, this sounds like something that will take more than your good self to work out,' said Father. 'Can I not assist you with this?'

'Possibly, my Zamindar, yes very possibly. We shall see in due course but first of all I need you to do something for me,' said Sananab.

'Yes, Sir, anything,' said Father.

'We need someone to take the fall for this morning's little indiscretion, Leopold. Nobody must know that we have changed The Will. Nobody must ever find out that it was us, do you hear? Therefore somebody else needs to take the blame, and quickly. Somebody needs to be seen by everyone else in the entire Will that it was them who caused the alarm not to be heard. Somebody here has disgraced the sacred motto of The Will and broken the unwritten law. 'Nos Numquam Immutare Voluntaten', Leopold, the most powerful rule of all! We need a very public scapegoat, my Zamindar. We need an unsuspecting victim, a min to take the rap,' said Sananab.

'Ah, I see Sir. Yes, a public scapegoat. That is a good idea. Perhaps a trial of some sort? Yes you leave it to me, Sir, I will create something public. I will make sure everyone sees it and I will make everybody knows who is guilty alright. Ha, ha, yes, Sir, you leave it to me, I think I know just the min,' said Father.

'Very good, my Zamindar, I knew I could rely on you. We must act swiftly on this, it is time to set the wheels in motion,' said Sananab.

The two min got up from the table and headed towards the door. 'Right, now where has Cornelius got to? I'll be needing him to help me with this one,' said Father as the two min left the office and shut the door behind them...

Mr Yanich closed the diary and addressed his three guests. 'Well then, my three Lugland warriors, what do you make of that?' he said.

The three min sat open mouthed. They were shocked at the revelations of the diary. Even Ollie Gimble was shocked; and given that there were still a few uneaten sandwiches left on the table, this was a good indication of just how shocked he was.

'Woah, so it was him who messed up the alarm the other day, Pointy Head? Jeez, and all the trouble what that caused as well,' said Stony.

'That's not fair, Mr Yanich,' said Ollie. 'Coz Mr Grip, he got the blame for that thing with the alarm, didn't he? And all along it wasn't him, that's not bloomin' fair. He's a nice min, Mr Grip is. He was always nice to me and he shouldn't have had to go away!'

'Yeah, so old Georgie boy took the fall for something he didn't do, eh? That certainly is a turn up for the books. Juicy bit of gossip you've got there, Mr Yanich, so who else knows about it, like?' said Curley.

'I don't believe that you truly understand what you have just heard, my friends, and it is more that a juicy bit of gossip, Mr Curley. A hell of a lot more than that believe me,' said Mr Yanich. 'I do believe that we have stumbled across something here which could affect our lives forever. To change The Will is one thing, something which is unthinkable; the mere mention of it would get you a one way ticket to the Stomachic Sea, without question. It is a crime so epic that nobody would ever even begin to conceive of it. But the thing that is even more remarkable in all of this, my friends, is the question which you seem to have initially overlooked. Let me read it to you again.'

He reopened the book at the page where he had been previously reading from, and carefully ran his finger down the page until he found the appropriate paragraph. 'In three years' time, every single one of us is going to be damaged by this and that is why we need to carry on with what we started all those years ago. This is big, it is the biggest thing that we will ever have to deal with in our lives and it can't be stopped. If we do not find a solution to this then I cannot see a future for the min beyond it.'

Mr Yanich closed the book again and looked at the others. 'What is going to happen in three years time? What is it that can't be stopped? If this is indeed as catastrophic as the loathsome leader predicts, then this could be then end for all of us. This is something a lot bigger than changing The Will, my friends, as ludicrous as that may sound.'

'So what does it all mean then, Mr Yanich?' said Stony. 'What's going to happen, like?'

'I must have read this diary a hundred times since you brought it to me, gentlemin, and this is the only mention of it. Apart from the passage I have just read to you, at no other place within the pages of this book does it contain any reference to any information concerning the next three years. So the simple answer is that I don't really know what it means yet. But we need to find out exactly what is going to happen in three years' time, my friends, that much is certain,' said Mr Yanich.

'So what are you going to do then, Mr Yanich?' said Ollie Gimble.

'Yeah, what *are* you going to do then?' said Raymond Curley.

'Yeah and, er, more importantly, where exactly do we fit into all of this, like?' added Stony Pickles.

'Ah, ever the concerned citizen, Mr Pickles, your mother must be so proud,' said Mr Yanich.

'What the hell has she got to do with it? Stupid old bag,' replied Stony. Ollie Gimble gave him stern look. He hated anybody disrespecting their mother.

'Quite,' said Mr Yanich. 'What I am proposing to do gentlemin is to find out just what the hell is going on. They speak of avoiding an uprising; well once we have finished with them they won't know what has hit them. We have the power of knowledge, my friends, one word from us to the right sort of people and there will be an uprising before they can blink. Yes, I'll wager that once Mr Leopold Schmidt and company find out just what we know, they will be powerless to resist us. We will gather a posse together and march to Central Head and confront the enemy head on. We will force them to tell us what is unfolding there and we won't stop until they tell us exactly what is going to happen in three years' time. We have the threat of insurrection on our side, gentlemin, we hold all the cards. We will fight them if necessary; with all of the force that we can muster. Once and for all, Mr Leopold Schmidt will get what has been coming to him for many a long year. We will not stop until he is kneeling before us and begging for mercy. He has many enemies in this Will, my friends, and there is a long queue of min who would not hesitate to strike him down. We will leave immediately.'

As soon as Raymond Curley and Stony Pickles heard the word 'fight', the cowardice from within came rushing to the surface.

'F, f, f, fight, what you mean us? You mean you want us to go up there and, er, like have a proper fight, like? With all that lot?' said Stony Pickles.

'Yeah, I mean there are a lot of soldiers in the Security Council, aren't there? And they've got, like, spears and things, haven't they? I don't know whether we're really cut out for this fighting lark you know, Mr Yanich, maybe we should just, er, sit this one out like, you know?' said Raymond Curley, cementing his cowardly ways.

'Well my mamma says that fighting is wrong, Mr Yanich, and that only bullies fight but I don't reckon its right what happened to Mr Grip, and I reckon that Mr Schmidt, well he sounds like a bully to me right enough, so if it's all the same with you, Mr Yanich, Sir, then you can count me in!' said Ollie Gimble.

Mr Yanich smiled at the three min. 'Ah it seems that Mr Gimble, here, has more courage in his rather large little finger than the both of you two put together, young sirs. I think you should take heed from your friend, for he speaks wisely.'

Stony and Curley both looked at each other. Neither of them knew how they were going to get out of this one but they were still going to give it a try.

'Well I still think it might be a bit...' said Stony, before he was immediately interrupted by Mr Yanich.

'Boys, boys, boys. Fear not, my young Lugland comrades, fear not. For you might yet be spared the inconvenience of the dreadful combat you so desperately wish to avoid. I do believe there is a way you can assist me without donning your battledress.'

'What's he on about, Curley?' said Stony confused as he turned to his friend.

'Er, I think he means there's a way that we mightn't have to fight, Stony,' replied Curley.

'Oh good,' said Stony under his breath. 'Coz I thought he was gonna make us wear a dress for a minute then, like.' He immediately turned back to Mr Yanich. 'Yeah, that sounds like a good scheme that, Mr Yanich, I reckon we should, er, have a listen to this new idea, like.'

Mr Yanich continued. 'What I need from you three is a way in. I am well known to Leopold Schmidt, as are most of my min. We simply would never get past the Security Council without being recognised. They would raise the alarm straight away and the whole operation would be compromised. You three, however, are unknown to them or at least I think you are. Therefore, you must create a diversion to attract the attention of the Security Council whilst my min and I gain entry to the compound and confront the Zamindar.'

Stony Pickles was trying to visualise this in his mind. 'So let me get this straight,' he said. 'You want us three to distract the guards from the *outside*, while you lot then go *inside* to fight Leopold Schmidt and his min there while we are all still on the *outside* where there's *no* fighting going on? Me and Ollie and Curley?'

'That is exactly what I want you to do, Mr Pickles,' said Mr Yanich.

'Well I reckon that's definitely a pretty good scheme that, Mr Yanich, Sir. What d'you reckon, Curley?' said Stony, nodding his head vigorously.

'Yeah, that's sounds like a proper good plan to me, that one, like. How about you, Ollie?' added Curley, also in agreement with his cowardly friend.

Ollie Gimble looked puzzled but his confusion was suddenly diverted by Stony Pickles who pointed to the tray on the table and said, 'There's some sarnies left there you know, Ollie?'

Ollie Gimble dutifully picked up the tray and began to eat.

'Well then my friends, that's settled then,' said Mr Yanich. 'We leave today. We travel to the Limbics. First we go on foot, then by boat. I do believe that the Central Head Trials have already started for this year and the Overseer of the trials is none other than our detestable Zamindar, Mr Leopold Schmidt himself, and that my friends, is where we shall find him.

Lance, will you make the necessary preparations for our journey please? We have no time to lose.'

'Hang on a minute,' said Stony. 'You know what you said you and your min? Well the name of one of those min doesn't happen to be Mr Quick, does it? He's not coming with us, is he? He's off his bloody head him, you know?'

'Of course he is travelling with us, Mr Pickles, why wouldn't he be? After all, he is my number one fellow. You don't have a problem with that, I hope?' said Mr Yanich.

'No, it's not me that's got the problem though, is it?' said Stony. 'It's him that's got a problem with me!'

Chapter Fifteen

The official trialists of Central Head had already spent their first night in the bright new surroundings of Hippocampus. The initial formalities of the previous day had now been completed and the fresh roots of new friendships had already started to grow. It was a new and exciting world for most of them and even though many were still settling in to their new cabins, today was the first day of official training so there were still a few nervous teenagers around the camp.

One of the trialists suffering the effects of first day nerves was Monty Schmidt. He was still in his room, sitting up on the end of his bed with his legs crossed, reading his diary. He was less than impressed with the occasion. On the opposite side of the room was somebody who was most definitely not suffering from first day nerves, in fact quite the opposite, it was Henry Grip. All night he had been dreaming of trying on the new uniform which had been laid out for him. He had now been standing in it for almost an hour. It was the proudest moment in his life.

'Come along, Monty,' said Henry. 'Aren't you excited for the first proper days training? I know I am. I can't wait to get stuck in to the trials! Mind you, 'The History of The Will' isn't really my ideal way of starting off. I'd much rather be climbing up into the mountains and taking on all of the physical training drills straight away but I guess you have to start somewhere I suppose.'

He caught a glimpse of himself in the mirror and started to practice shadow boxing with himself.

'Mmm,' replied Monty Schmidt. He never looked up from his diary.

'Come on, Monty, we've got to get over to Fornix Hall by nine. It's nearly five-to, and you haven't even got your uniform on yet,' said Henry, carefully wiping a speck of dust from the left shoulder of his brand new trialist jacket, whilst standing proudly in front of the mirror.

'Er, I'm not really feeling very well, Henry,' said Monty. 'Why don't you go on without me? I'll just stay here.'

'What? Stay here? What's the matter with you, Monty? You can't miss your first day, what will Mr Pothackery think?' said Henry, turning around.

'I'm just not feeling up to it, Henry,' said Monty.

'What do you mean you don't feel up to it? Are you ill?' said Henry, as he walked over to Monty's bed.

'Yes, Henry, I'm ill,' said Monty, rather unconvincingly.

'You don't look very ill, Monty, apart from maybe your face looks a bit red but then it always looks a bit red, doesn't it?' said Henry. Being tactful wasn't his strongest point.

'Does it Henry? Does it really? I've never noticed,' said Monty, awkwardly examining his own face.

'Well, only a bit red,' replied Henry sheepishly, realising that he had slightly embarrassed the boy. 'I imagine most folk don't even really notice it actually,' he added, trying to make his new friend feel a bit better about himself.

'It's probably just a bit of tummy ache, Henry. I expect I'll be ok after a bit of rest. Perhaps you could tell Mr Pothackery for me, that I won't be able to make the first seminar today? Tell him I'll make up for it tomorrow, Henry,' replied Monty.

'Well if you're sure, Monty?' said Henry.

'Yes, I'm sure, and thank you, Henry,' replied Monty. 'I do hope you enjoy your first day.'

'Right, ok then, Monty. Well cheerio then and, er, get some rest then I suppose, eh?' said Henry.

Monty went back to reading his diary whilst Henry darted out of the door and headed towards Fornix Hall.

Henry couldn't quite work out whether Monty's sudden illness was genuine or not but got the impression that he was somehow faking it. His brain wouldn't allow him to understand why somebody would not be chomping at the bit to get started with the trials and would rather stay in that crummy little room all day instead. Some people were strange, he thought.

The walk from the boys' cabins to Fornix Hall was a relatively short one and the journey would only take a few minutes. Henry was walking with a purpose, he had spring in his step and he couldn't wait to get there. He reached the end of the commorancies block and made the sharp right turn towards the hall. As soon as he turned around the corner, he tripped over the outstretched leg of Cornelius Crail and fell flat on his face on the ground. He looked up to see the wiry little min staring down at him from above.

'Oh dear me, look what I've done. I really mustn't leave my foot in places like that now, should I Henry? How silly of me, people might trip over it when they're not looking. Tut, tut, tut. And look, you have gone and made all of your new clothes dirty too. What will Mr Pothackery say?' said Cornelius. He walked off with an evil grin on his face but not before kicking a patch of dirt into the face of Henry while he was still on the ground.

Henry sat up. He looked down at his now dirty uniform. He began to dust himself off and slowly got to his feet. He sighed a huge sigh. It was moments like this that he wished he had known his mother for he was sure that she would have known just what to say, and it was moments like this that he wished he could talk to his father as he was certain that he would have known what to say.

He looked up at the sky. He suddenly remembered the words that his father had said to him before he left. 'You only have to close your eyes to see'. Henry closed his eyes tight shut and immediately pictured an image of his father, smiling at him in his new trialist uniform. His father winked at him and said the words, 'You can do it.'

Henry opened his eyes and saw the back of Cornelius Crail as he was walking into the building of Central Fornix Hall just across the way. 'You are not going to spoil this for me Cornelius Crail, no matter how hard you try. I will try harder. I will do my family proud,' he said.

Henry marched over to the hall and went inside. He wasn't the last to enter as there were still a few stragglers making their way in alongside him. The hall was huge but the trialists who were already there had congregated in a small section down in the front left corner. He made his way down to the front where the others were.

The area had been set out like a classroom of sorts, only there were no chairs or tables laid out as a conventional classroom would have had. Here everybody was sitting cross legged on the floor, including the staff and stewards, although they were slightly higher up on a long raised step. He could see Penelope already there waiting for him and he went over to her and sat down.

'Are you on your own, Henry? Where's Monty?' said Penelope.

'He's, er, he said he's not feeling very well, Loppy, so he's not coming,' replied Henry.

'What's the matter with him?' said Penelope. She was genuinely concerned for their new friend.

Henry was still slightly confused as to why Monty hadn't made it. 'To be honest with you, Loppy, I don't think there's anything wrong with him. I just don't think he likes it here. Mind you, you should see the state of our crummy little cabin, I think it's a bloomin' broom cupboard!' he said.

'Oh well I do hope he's ok, Henry. I mean he shouldn't really be missing the first day, should he?' said Penelope. As she was talking she looked down at Henry's uniform and noticed that it was dirty. 'What's happened to your uniform, Henry, it's all dirty. Are you alright?'

'Yeah I'm ok, Loppy, I'll tell you later,' replied Henry as he continued to dust off his jacket. He looked up to find that Cornelius Crail was now sitting down next to Mr Pothackery. He was grinning at him.

Mr Pothackery addressed the group. 'Now I think that we are all present and correct, aren't we trialists?' He looked around and noticed that Monty Schmidt was not there. 'Er, Henry. Is Monty not with you?'

'Er, no Sir,' said Henry. 'He's, er, not feeling very well, Mr Pothackery. He says to tell you that he hopes he will be better tomorrow, Sir, and that he will make up the time then.'

'Oh that is a concern,' said Mr Pothackery. 'Perhaps we should send someone to check up on him, see if he needs any help?' He then noticed

Henry's uniform. 'Are you ok, Henry?' he added, pointing at his dirty clothes.

Henry looked down at his jacket. 'What? Oh, yes Sir, it's nothing,' he said, wiping a bit of dirt from it with his hand. He looked up to see that Cornelius was still wearing his smarmy grin.

Mr Pothackery waved over to one of the trial stewards who was standing at the side of the hall. 'Er, Mr Adamson, could you go and check on Monty and see if he's alright, please? Thank you so much.'

The steward went off to check on the boy.

Mr Pothackery continued talking. 'Right then, trialists, welcome to your first day of learning. I trust you have all settled in well and all had a good night's sleep. Your first seminar of the year is one of the most important ones of all in my book, 'The scientific history of The Will'.

Now then, every morning this week we will cover a wide range of topics, including how we came to be here, how the min exist as we know them today and how The Will itself came into being. All of these are very exciting topics and are essential knowledge when it comes to the all important psychological tests you will have to face during the contest, should you make it that far of course.

Now this will be a very informal learning group, as are all of my seminars. It will be catered to your own requirements, after all this year belongs to you trialists. We may all speak at different times during the next few hours and therefore you need to pay attention in case you miss anything. That is very important.

Now a lot of this could indeed come from the floor, so should you wish to make a contribution to the group then feel free to just go ahead and shout out whenever you feel the need. Class participation is encouraged and indeed necessary, that is how we learn after all...'

He could feel Cornelius Crail's gaze burning into the side of his head and decided to change tack somewhat.

'Ah, and as you can see trialists, Mr Crail will be very kindly observing with us today. Should you would wish to speak to him personally, in light of last night's comments, perhaps you could, er, make an appointment?' Mr Pothackery's voice trailed off at the end of the sentence, where it became more of a question directed towards Cornelius Crail.

The Thought Apprentice responded accordingly. 'Yes, as I said yesterday, you will make an appointment to speak to me, and it had better be important otherwise you will be wasting my precious time.'

Cornelius Crail was not the most gifted of public speakers, and he rather let his mouth run away with itself before his brain ever had the chance to catch up. He was suddenly faced with a room full of expectant students and he didn't have the faintest idea of what he was going to say next. The silence made him uncomfortable. He decided that he should perhaps let someone else take over, somebody who was good at this sort of thing after all. He thought about what Mr Pothackery had just said. 'And, er, today I will be just, er, observing. Yes, just observing. Well, carry on then, Pothackery,' he added.

'Yes, well. Very well then,' said Mr Pothackery rather uncomfortably. 'I suppose this would be a good time to, er, begin.'

Mr Pothackery stood up and walked over to a huge scroll positioned on an enormous wooden stand behind him. He pulled the cord at the side of the scroll and it unravelled itself revealing a giant map of The Will.

'Now then trialists, here we have a map of The Will. Now this map contains every place in the entire Will as we know it today. Magnificent, isn't it? Yes, I'm sure you will agree. But it hasn't always been like this, has it?' He looked around at the blank faces in front of him. 'Who can tell me why?' he said.

There was no response from anyone.

'Ok, let me rephrase that. Who can tell me when The Will was formed?' he said. The room was still filled with silence. 'Oh come on trialists, somebody must know, its basic minology this stuff. Is there anyone who can tell me when The Will came into being?'

Penelope Potts raised her hand.

'Yes, Penelope?' said Mr Pothackery enthusiastically, as he pointed across the room to her.

'Well, The Will was formed on the first day, January the first in the year zero-to-one, sir. Everyone knows that,' she said.

'Yes, of course it was Penelope, well done. That's the spirit. Now to everybody else here, I want you to all get involved in this, like Penelope. Don't be shy there trialists,' said Mr Pothackery. 'Right now, so we've established when The Will came into being, now can anybody tell me when The Will was actually formed?'

There were blank expressions upon the faces of everyone in front of him.

'No? Right ok, let me give you an example, er...' Mr Pothackery looked around frantically for something to help him. He spotted a leaf on the floor which had just blown in from outside. 'Ah.' He rushed over and picked up the leaf from the ground.

'Now this leaf here which I hold in my hand was, only five minutes ago, on that tree there outside. And now it is in my hand. Now if we were to go back even further, say twelve months ago, this leaf didn't exist at all, yet five minutes ago it was on that tree. So there was a period of time between the non-existence of this leaf and the existence of this leaf now, and that period is called its growth period, its life cycle. You all understand that things must grow, they can't just exist out of nothing, right?'

The trialists all nodded and murmured in universal acknowledgement, even though some of them still looked slightly confused.

'Right, good, ok,' said Mr Pothackery. 'So, therefore it was exactly the same with The Will. There was a period of time when The Will, like this leaf, didn't exist. And there was also a period of time that The Will, like this leaf, had to grow. When its life actually began. Unfortunately, the life of this leaf is now over because it is no longer attached to that tree over there but the life of The Will, is very much ongoing. Is everybody following me so far?'

The general murmuring from the group had now turned into more of an overall 'Yes, Sir,' with additional nodding becoming more and more noticeable.

'Right, good, yes, very good. So as Penelope has already brilliantly pointed out, the first day of The Will as we know it today, began on the first day of January in the year zero-to-one. But as we have also just established, there must have been a period of time before that day, otherwise how could The Will have got here? So can anybody tell me how long that period of time was? Can anybody hazard a guess?' He was looking around at the trialists, hoping that somebody would give him an answer. 'A day, a week, a month, a year? Anyone?'

Penelope thought about this. She had always been able to remember a lot of stuff, and even though she didn't know if she was entirely right with this one, somehow a number just popped into her head. She held up a hand slightly hesitantly. 'Er, forty weeks?' she said.

'Well done, Penelope!' said Mr Pothackery. 'Yes forty weeks exactly. Well done indeed. I see the Lugland education system is still going strong these days, ha, ha!'

Henry turned to Penelope. 'How did you know that, Loppy?' he said with a certain amount of envy.

'I don't really know, Henry. It just sort of popped into my head,' said Penelope. The only Lugland education system she knew was listening to her mother and father arguing whilst trying to read a book.

Henry was a little unimpressed at being outdone by his friend so early on.

'And does anybody know what we call this period, what it is more commonly known as?' said Mr Pothackery.

One of the other boys, who was sitting not too far away from Henry and Penelope, decided to join in the class. His name was Samson Pocket.

'Sir, it is known as the Gestational Age, Sir,' he said rather proudly.

'Well done, Samson. Yes, well done indeed!' said Mr Pothackery. 'We do have a bright bunch of trialists this year, don't we?'

Samson Pocket seemed rather pleased with himself, as another general murmur went around the room. Everybody was now beginning to feel a bit more involved in the class, all except for Henry Grip. His competitive instinct was taking a bit of a beating seeing as he didn't know any of the answers so far.

Mr Pothackery unravelled another scroll next to the giant map. It was another map of The Will, quite similar to the first one but this one had been split into three different coloured sections.

'Right, so we have established that exactly forty weeks before the first day of the year, zero-to-one, The Will had already started to grow. This was also quite rightly identified by Samson, here, as the Gestational Age. It was in this age period that everything else started to grow with it. The trees, the rivers, the mountains and the seas, everything that we see today had its origins in this forty week cycle. Is everyone still following me?'

The universal nodding continued amidst the general mutterings of, 'Ok, that makes sense,' and, 'Yeah I'm with you, Sir.'

A girl from the front of the group raised her hand.

'Yes, Constance?' said Mr Pothackery as he noticed her.

'Sir, why is the second map split into three parts? With different colours,' she asked.

'Ah yes, good question, Constance, good question indeed. The second map is split into three different parts, as you say, because the Gestational Age was itself split into three smaller periods. They were called the trimesters and the three trimesters represent the three different periods of growth.

For example, in the first trimester The Will was a very primitive place indeed, this was a time before even some parts of Central Head existed. And through the weeks and months that followed, the rest of The Will was built up around it. When we eventually got to the third trimester, at the end of the forty weeks, then The Will was fully formed,' said Mr Pothackery.

Constance Futtock was a very inquisitive girl. She was born and raised in Regio-Mentalis, situated at the southernmost tip of Central Head. Technically it was still classed as belonging to Central Head, even though it was hundreds of miles away from The Limbics but the people who lived there would never admit it. They were a proud nation and liked to be kept away from the bureaucracy of Central Head. Some would say they were all anti-establishment. It was an area of The Will sometimes cruelly described by many as the 'Mental Region'. This was because most of the min that came from there tended to be quite impatient with each other and were never easily satisfied. Nobody ever argued with anybody from the Mental Region if they could help it.

She once again raised her hand. 'So who formed it then, Sir? I mean the trees and rivers and things can grow on their own yes, but what about the towns and cities and buildings and everything else? Someone must have made them, Sir? Otherwise, how would they have got there?'

Mr Pothackery was now beginning to get really excited, even though he had talked about these subjects hundreds of times before; he never got tired of teaching and learning. His face was lit up with enthusiasm.

'Constance Futtock, you are asking all of the right questions today, my girl. Oh how I love this fascinating subject. Right, so now this is to everyone. Constance has just posed a wonderful question to us, who was responsible for all of the things that she has just said? Responsible for the building that we are now in now for example, or the great Cerebellum Dome magnificently looking down on us from out there through that window? Who made all of these great things? It couldn't have been us now could it? None of us were here until the first day, were we?'

A boy near the front of the group raised his hand.

'Yes, Angus?' said Mr Pothackery, bouncing with energy.

'Can I go to the toilet please, Sir?' replied the boy.

Everybody instantly roared with laughter. That is everybody except poor old Angus and Mr Pothackery.

'Yes, Angus, run along,' said Mr Pothackery. 'There's always one, isn't there? I don't know, perhaps it's the mountain air what does it, affects the nerves or something. Now back to the subject at hand. Come on settle down now. Right, does anybody know the answer to Constance's question? Who made all of this possible?'

Henry was racking his brain trying to find any shred of information he could, in order to get involved with the class, unfortunately he could not. He turned to Penelope to ask if she knew the answer but he could see her hand already on its way up. He rolled his eyes. 'Tut, might have known,' he said under his breath.

'Ah, Penelope?' said Mr Pothackery as he spotted her raised hand.

'Er, I think it was the Tri-min, Sir?' she said. 'They were the things which pre-existed the min, Sir. Up until day one.'

Mr Pothackery cupped his hands together with delight. 'Penelope Potts, you are a credit to the good people of the Luglands, well done indeed! Yes, that is exactly the answer I was looking for, in fact I couldn't have put it better myself!' he said.

Penelope was blushing, next to the extremely jealous Henry Grip.

'How is it you know all of this stuff, Loppy? You've never bloomin' talked about any of this before,' said Henry.

'I don't know, Henry,' replied Penelope. 'It's just there, I suppose, at the back of my head. I don't know where I learned it, I just did. Maybe it was from one of your contest books, Henry. After all, I've gone through the questions enough times with you, haven't I?'

'Yeah, I suppose so,' Henry managed in reply.

Mr Pothackery excitedly continued with his lesson. 'The Tri-min are the only reason why we are here today, ladies and gentlemin. It was the Tri-min who were responsible for all of this. Everything that we have today, everything which exists in the entire Will is because of the efforts of these wonderful creatures, all those years ago.

The continents and oceans, land and cities, rivers and towns were all thought up and designed by the Tri-min. The language we speak, the air we breathe, the food we eat, the water we drink is all down to them. They taught us how to live, how to exist, and more importantly, how to serve The Will. Even the name given to our world was at the hands of the Tri-min. I bet that most of you don't know this but before the time that it became known as The Will, our world was previously known as something else. It was called The

Womb. And it was only some time after the first day of the year zero to one, that it was decided that it should be re named as The Will by the first official min of Central Head.'

Cornelius Crail was paying careful attention to the group. Sananab had told him to look out for someone, with a thirst for knowledge as he had put it. Today's lesson had certainly flagged up a couple of potential candidates. So far it had been an interesting morning. He was making notes, taking down the names of certain people. Perhaps there was someone who might be just what the Master was looking for.

'The Tri-min, Sir, yes, my father told me about them, Sir,' said Samson Pocket. 'He said that because The Will was created on the first day, then the Tri-min all died, Sir. Is that true?'

Mr Pothackery responded to the boy. 'Yes, Samson. Well your father is quite right in many respects and I suppose that you could say that the Tri-min all died for us. Yes, that's true, but I like to think of it as them coming to the end of their cycle, so we as min could begin ours.

After all, we needed to be able to operate from day one, did we not? Otherwise The Will couldn't have functioned. We have to serve The Will, it is our duty. There was a sort of changeover, if you like, just like in a shift changeover at work. You are all very familiar with those, I trust? The Tri-min finished their shift, and then the ordinary min took over from there. Simple minology really when you think about it. That is why some of the older min, like myself, cannot remember our early childhood because we didn't have one you see. We were already children when The Will came into being.

Your father himself, Samson, must have been born a child, and yours, Penelope, and yours, Constance, and your mother, George, and yours too, Danny. It is a fascinating world in which we live, trialists, and it's fascinating that we can be allowed understand it.'

Penelope raised her hand again. 'Sir?'

'Yes, Penelope?' said Mr Pothackery.

'This is certainly fascinating, I agree, and very enjoyable to listen to, but can I ask how we come to know all of this information about the Tri-min etc? I mean yes some of it has been passed down, and some things we can remember but who says that it's all true? I mean, how do we know what we are told hasn't been made up, and it is indeed the truth?' said Penelope.

Everybody in the room was more than surprised at the question, nobody ever questioned Central Head. There was a brief silence that only lasted for a few seconds, but to Penelope it seemed like hours. Cornelius Crail suddenly became a lot more interested in Penelope Potts.

Mr Pothackery looked slightly puzzled, as Penelope's question was one he was not expecting. 'That is an interesting theory, Penelope. To question minology itself is indeed an odd thing to do, especially at such a young age. Better not let anyone in Central Head hear you ask questions like that now hey? Ha, ha! But there is a simple explanation that will satisfy your curiosity and I can indeed show you the answer right now.'

He walked over to the end of the hall where the three statues were standing proudly and looking over the room. He stood next to the first statue and patted it on the back.

'This min here is responsible for all of the knowledge we have about the Tri-min and the early days of The Will. My friends let me introduce you to the great Geffron Scolt, the first ruler of Central Head. This min and his colleagues made sure that every single piece of information regarding the beginnings of The Will, and afterwards of course, was written down and kept logged in the chronicles of Central Head.

Every single piece of information regarding the formation of The Will, the Gestation Age, the Tri-min, and everything else from the very first day onwards, can be found in those books.'

Everybody in the room gasped, they were thoroughly impressed.

'Wow, Sir, and where are these books kept? Have you seen them yourself?' said Penelope.

'Why, they are kept in Central Head, of course. In the Neocortex, where all of the important stuff happens. And yes, I have been fortunate enough to have had the privilege of seeing the chronicles first hand, Penelope, and I can assure you what I have told you here today is very much the truth, exactly how it is written.'

'Do you think any of us might be able to see them someday, Sir?' said Penelope. She was showing her excitement at the discovery of these books.

'Perhaps, Penelope, who knows?' said Mr Pothackery. 'If you happen to be the winner of the contest then I'm certain of it.'

He looked around at the rest of the group. 'Perhaps that could be an incentive for you, trialists, to work hard and succeed. Now I do believe that we have reached the end of this morning's lesson. I'm sure you will agree that it has been an enlightening one for us all. We shall gather here again at the same time tomorrow morning to further our studies.

Now this afternoon, I do believe the more sporting types amongst you will be happy to know that we shall be heading up into the mountains for some endurance training. So Mr Johnston will meet you all outside the hall at two o' clock sharp and don't be late.'

This news was greeted with a communal cheer. The loudest voice of them all belonging to Henry Grip.

'Now go on, off you go, trialists, and thank you for an excellent morning's work,' said Mr Pothackery.

Henry was overjoyed at the thought of going into the mountains. He'd had enough of history for one day. 'Top of the class on your first day hey, Loppy? Bloomin' show off!' he said sarcastically.

'What do you mean, Henry?' replied Penelope, 'I was only answering questions, wasn't I? That's why we are all *here*, Henry!'

'Yeah, right,' said Henry dismissively. 'Anyway, I can't wait to get up in those mountains, Loppy. Better than boring old history any day!' He seemed to brighten up mid sentence with the thought of physical training.

'Well, I thought it was a fascinating lesson, Henry, very useful indeed. Mr Pothackery was very nice. And I, for one, am not looking forward to going up there in a hurry. That's for sure,' said Penelope as she pointed towards Mount Thalamus.

Cornelius Crail quickly scurried off out of the hall. He looked like he was headed somewhere important. On his way out he walked past Henry and Penelope, where he gave them a curious look. 'Nice uniform, Grip, ha, ha!' he said sarcastically.

Penelope suddenly realised what must have happened.

'Did he do that to you, Henry? Cornelius Crail,' she said.

'Yeah, he bloomin' tripped me over, didn't he?' said Henry.

'Henry, we've got to tell Mr Pothackery, it's just not fair. I mean we just can't let him get away with that,' said Penelope.

'No, Loppy, that will only make things worse I reckon. Just leave it, eh?' said Henry.

'Well I don't like it, Henry, I don't like it one little bit,' replied Penelope.

'Yeah neither do I, Loppy, but I just don't want to let him get to me. I've waited too long for this and I'm not going to let him spoil it,' said Henry. 'Anyway, forget about that now. Come and have some lunch, eh? I'm bloomin' starving.'

Henry and Penelope walked out of the hall together.

Chapter Sixteen

Cornelius Crail was running as fast as he could in order to get to his pre-arranged meeting with Sananab. He had made his way over from Hippocampus and was now heading for the restricted zone of the Neocortex. He was under orders to keep the Master informed of proceedings on a daily basis, and this was to be the first of his progress reports.

'Good afternoon, Mr Crail,' said a Head-worker as he went past.

'How are you this afternoon, Mr Crail?' said another.

Cornelius ignored the pleasantries from the hardworking min of Central Head and continued to walk. He reached the beginning of the corridor which led to the Neocortex, typed in his pass-code on the wall-mounted keypad and went through the gate. It was dark here for some reason, which wasn't normal. Usually it was a very bright area but today the light had seemed to have gone elsewhere. He couldn't quite see where he was going for a moment and he was trying to feel his way to Sananab's office from memory, his arms stretched out in front of him so as not to bump into anything. He knew this place like the back of his hand but he only knew the back of his hand when he could see it, in the dark it could have been anybody's hand.

He had got halfway down the corridor, or at least he thought he'd got that far. 'What the hell's going on with the light here today?' he said to himself. 'Can't see a damn thing.'

He thought that he may have gone too far along the corridor so he decided to go back to where he had started from and try again. He turned around and walked straight into the tall, commanding figure of Sananab who was standing right behind him in the middle of the corridor.

'Aaaghh!' said Cornelius as he fell flat on his back on the ground. 'Master, you scared me!' he said. His heart was beating like crazy.

'Perhaps you ought to train your eyes to see in the dark, Cornelius, it is a trait which has served me well in the past,' said Sananab.

He reached out and opened the door to his office; they had been standing directly outside of it all along. Cornelius picked himself up off the floor and they both went in.

It was lighter inside the office and Cornelius could at least now see what he was doing. He sat down at the desk.

'So, Cornelius, what have you got to tell me? I want news of our young hopefuls. Have you found me someone?' said Sananab, as he followed the boy into the office and sat down opposite him.

athetic fool that he was. However, the love he showed her was not reciprocated I'm afraid and she had married another min without his knowledge. Leopold was furious with her and when he found this out, he turned his back on her.

So it was down to me to complete the task which I did successfully, Cornelius. I transferred her. She has gone forever. Leopold still harbours pathetic tears of regret for her even now. I don't know why, she chose someone else instead of him but he still says he loved her, whatever that means. He hasn't got the backbone for the task, Cornelius, he never has and he never will, unlike you, my young Thought Apprentice.'

'Ah I see, Sir. So it is possible and very much achievable as you have already proved? So we should go now, transfer as soon as we can! Why must we wait, Sir?' said Cornelius.

'We must wait, Cornelius, until we have successfully transferred another min, one more time,' said Sananab. 'You see, fifteen years ago I didn't know where our friend was going to be transferred *to* exactly; I just knew that I could do it, and I succeeded of course. But when you and I are to be transferred, Cornelius, we need to know where we are going to go. In fact, we will choose our destination and choose it wisely for we cannot just end up anywhere, the risks are far too great.

Therefore what I need, Cornelius, is *somebody else* to transfer. To see if I can choose the destination this time, to see if it will work. If it goes wrong then so be it, we will have lost another min, they are worthless to me anyway and we can just try again with another, and another, and another. We have plenty of time to perfect it, three years in fact. But if it is a success, then we can choose to transfer whenever we want to Cornelius, you and I.'

The devious mind of Cornelius Crail was beginning to work overtime. 'Ah, and the person you wish to transfer is the person I must choose from the trials, Master? That is why you have chosen me for this task, that is why I am the Overseer,' he said. 'An ingenious plan, Sir, if I may say so.'

'Indeed, my young Thought Apprentice, we are on the same path now I see, thinking the same things at last,' said Sananab. 'But this person must be bright and clever, and they must be as intelligent as they come, but still have the thirst for even more knowledge. That is imperative, otherwise it won't work, Cornelius. The person who transfers must have deep intelligent thought, be perceptive and wise, otherwise they cannot manipulate the nerves enough to transfer.

But we must not let them know our devious plans for them, or everything will be ruined. We must make them somehow believe that they are helping The Will, fulfilling their duty to the min. Perhaps we could go so far as to have them 'saving the world', it has such a nice ring to it, don't you think?'

'Ha, ha, ha! Master, this is an excellent plan, I only wish I could have thought up something like this myself!' said Cornelius.

'Have you seen enough of the trialists already to choose somebody who

'What, already, Sir? I mean I've barely started. It is still only the first day after all,' replied Cornelius.

'Perhaps we need to act sooner than we first thought, Cornelius, get things moving along,' said Sananab.

'Er, yes, Master, as you wish. Has something happened then, Sir?' said Cornelius.

'Cornelius, when I asked you if you were loyal to me, you responded in the way I had hoped, and I thank you for your loyalty, Cornelius. It means a great deal to me,' said Sananab.

'Of course, Sir, it is an honour. As I have already said, I live to serve you,' said the crawling Thought Apprentice.

'Indeed. And in return for your loyalty, Cornelius, I am going to reward you. I am going to reward you in a way that you cannot possibly imagine. I am going to give you the gift of life!' said Sananab.

'Sir, I don't follow?' said Cornelius cautiously. He thought that life was something that he already owned and would rather have liked to hold on to it as long he could.

'Cornelius, last time we spoke I told you that something had happened, something that will have a great significance to The Will, something bigger than anything we have ever encountered before. Yet I did not divulge the details of this occurrence,' said Sananab. 'My friend, I am now going to tell you something which will surprise you, possibly shock you somewhat.'

Cornelius's eyes narrowed, as he prepared himself for something bad.

'In less than three years time, Cornelius, The Will is going to die. I have seen it in the nerves. There is nothing we can do about it, it cannot be changed. Three years from now The Will is going to perish and every single min in the entire Will is going to die with it,' said Sananab.

Cornelius was flabbergasted. He sat back in his chair. He was open mouthed, he was speechless.

'Yes, indeed, my Thought Apprentice. It is a lot to take in. I myself was shocked when I first learned of this tragedy, however I have now come to terms with it, so to speak,' said Sananab, without any emotion.

'Sir, are you sure? Can this not be a mistake?' said Cornelius hopefully.

'I'm afraid there is no mistake, Cornelius. I have seen it in the nerves, with my own eyes. We are all going to die,' said Sananab. He didn't seem concerned in any way. He spoke as if he was merely saying good morning to somebody.

Cornelius was on the opposite side of emotion, he was panicking and shaking at the news that he had just heard. 'Will's teeth, I can't believe it, Sir. What are we going to do? Master, this is... it is... I mean this is..., oh no! Who else knows about this? Does Mr Schmidt know? Have you told him?' he said.

'Er, not exactly,' said Sananab, with slightly more feeling. 'He knows that there will be a significant event in three years time, yes, but he does not know what it is, and we need to keep it that way, Cornelius. He must not know the truth. The Zamindar is old and faded and of no use to me anymore. He has out-served his purpose, Cornelius. You are the one who is loyal to me now, remember?' He leaned closer to the boy, staring directly into his eyes.

'Yes, Sir, forever,' said Cornelius nervously.

'And you will be rewarded for it, Cornelius, as I have promised you,' said Sananab. He got up from his chair and began to circle the room. 'Have you ever heard of something called transference, Cornelius?'

Cornelius was suddenly intrigued. 'Er, yes, Sir, I have heard of it, yes. Some people talked about it when I was a child, Sir, but it doesn't exist, does it? It is just a myth surely? It is an old wives tale, a story made up to frighten the children into doing as they were told. Nobody ever believed it was real.... Sir....' he said.

'On the contrary, my young Thought Apprentice, the ability to transfer a min from this Will to another is most definitely not a myth. It is not an old wives tale, and it is not a feeble story, my friend, it is very much possible,' said Sananab.

Cornelius was now very interested in what his Master was saying. 'Sir, this is something that I never believed could happen, this is mind blowing, this is astonishing...' He stopped mid sentence as it suddenly dawned on him what the Master was actually alluding to. 'Ah, Sir, forgive me if I'm wrong here but I think I know what you may be getting at. You say that The Will is going to die, and there is nothing that any of us can do about it, and then you tell me that transference is possible. Master, are you saying that we should all transfer? To another Will, Sir?'

'No, Cornelius Crail, I am not saying that we should all transfer. I am saying that *we* should transfer, not everyone else, just you and I. This will be your gift of life!' said Sananab.

The evil and devious mind of Cornelius Crail immediately came rushing to the surface, and what was more, the mighty Sananab himself wanted to include *him* in his plans.

'Yes, Sir, this is indeed a great idea. We could leave all of these pathetic little cretins behind, yes be rid of them forever. You and me, Sir. I would love to see their faces when they are about to meet their maker, when they are all about to die!' said Cornelius. 'But where would we transfer to, Sir? I've heard of there being another world outside of The Will but nobody has ever seen it, have they? Do you know if one exists?'

Sananab returned to his chair at the desk; he was now a little more excited. 'Cornelius, I have another surprise for you, my young Thought Apprentice. Something else that will make your head spin, but something that I can teach you. Something that you never thought was possible in your wildest dreams. I have the ability, Cornelius Crail, to change The Will. I can do it, whenever I choose to. In fact, I have already done it. Last week, the missed alarm and the hearing at Central Head, that was me. I did it. I changed The Will.'

Cornelius was shocked at this latest revelation, but immediately wan know more. 'You did, Sir? You ch... ch... changed The Will, b... b... how?' he said.

'The details of how, Cornelius, do not matter at this time. The fact matter remains that I *can* do it, and I can teach *you* how to do it too there are definitely other worlds out there. That is for certain, my fri have seen them, through the nerves. As I have seen many great through the power of the nerves.

Do you see what this means? You and I will have the ability to tr and when we do, Cornelius, we will also have the ability to control t Will. Take over it, rule it as we wish. We can do whatever we cho nobody can stop us!'

'Yes, we can rule over everyone, we can make them do whate want. We can do whatever we choose and nobody can stop us Cornelius excitedly. He had to repeat the words so that he could truly them. He could now picture himself as the leader. He would finally everything he had hoped for, all powerful.

'But when would we go, Sir. I mean three years is a long time should we not just go now? Leave these fools and everything else beh

'Ah, your thirst for power is refreshing, my friend, but I fea patience is called for here. There are things that we must do, certai must be put into place before we can leave The Will. After all I need you how to manipulate the nerves, how to change The Will,' said Sar

'Ah, yes, Sir. Forgive my impatience. I am just excited for what t will bring us. What is it that you need me to do, Master? I will do that is required,' said Cornelius.

Sananab again got up from his chair and started to circle the began to speak. 'Fifteen years ago, Cornelius, the Zamindar and little... experiment. A successful experiment, I might add. It s purpose at the time; it was something we needed to do.

There was a womin, a womin that Leopold knew, somebody tha for the task at hand. She was a willing participant in our experime least at the beginning she was anyway. She had a thirst for k Cornelius, something that not many people had at that time. She know everything, all that the wonders of knowledge could bring.

The idea was to transfer her to another Will. She was excited first womin to have ever been transferred, and we too were excite the first to try it. Everything was going according to plan encountered a slight problem. We discovered that if we transferre could be a remote possibility that perhaps we would not be able t back.

Once she discovered this, of course she didn't want to go b and I were too far down the line to stop there, we had to carry work. But Leopold had a thing for her, you see. He had fallen

possesses these qualities? Your friend from the Luglands, perhaps? The one who you asked me to put through, the Grip boy?' said Sananab.

'Er, Henry Grip, Sir? No I don't think that he is the type of person that you are looking for. I can think of a different plan for him, something much more satisfying. Perhaps we should go for somebody else. Yes, if you want somebody who has intelligence but still has this thirst that you speak of, Sir, I think I know just the person you're looking for,' said Cornelius.

'Then bring them to me, Cornelius,' said Sananab, as he smashed his hand down on to the desk. 'Tomorrow, we shall get started straight away. We have no time to lose.'

'Yes, Sir, of course. I shall take her from Pothackery's seminar first thing, Sir. Pathetic excuse for a lesson that is, always babbling on about history. She seems to know more about it than he does anyway,' said Cornelius.

'Ah, so it is a girl that you speak of Cornelius, another girl? Interesting Cornelius, that is very interesting. Pray tell, who is this girl?' said Sananab.

'Er, the Potts girl, Sir, Penelope Potts, from the Luglands. She seems very bright, more so than any of the others, Sir,' replied Cornelius.

'Ah yes, the girl with the yellow hair, the one who the Zamindar was so keen for us not to put through. I sensed something about this girl, Cornelius, at the hearing. Perhaps I should see this knowledge first hand? Yes that is what I will do. I shall make an appearance in this seminar tomorrow, watch proceedings for myself, and see if this girl has indeed got what it takes,' said Sananab.

'As you wish, Master,' said Cornelius.

'Now run along, Cornelius, I have things to prepare,' said Sananab.

Cornelius bowed to his Master, got up from his chair and walked towards the door. After struggling to open it, he managed to sneak through the gap and headed off into the darkness.

Sananab sat back in his chair. He was rolling the spherical ornament, which had been sat on top of his desk, round and around through his fingers. 'What a pathetic excuse for a min you really are, Cornelius Crail. And you think I am going to take you with me? You think that I would actually share The Will with you? No, my young Thought Apprentice, if you believe that then you are even more of a fool than I thought you were.'

Thursday 1st November, 11:09 p.m. Oesophagus Forest.

The newly formed posse made up from a mixture of cut-throats and cowards was on its way to Central Head. They'd had to move on foot for the first part of their journey, as that was the only way to get through the Oesophagus Forest, there were no transport links of any kind in or out of bandit country. They had reached the end of the thick, dark trees and the trio from the Luglands could now finally see where they were going, just as nightfall came.

'Typical innit, Curley? Can't see a bloody thing all day long in there, and as soon as we get out its gone flaming dark again!' said Stony Pickles.

'I'm just happy to get out of there, Stony, can't see them bloomin' knives that they've got in there, can you?' replied Raymond Curley. 'Mind you, can't really see them too well here neither,' he added, looking around for the glint of a blade.

'What time d'you reckon it is now, anyway?' said Stony. 'We must have been walking all day again by the looks of it.'

'Yeah I reckon we have, Stony,' said Curley. 'Getting a bit sick of it now, like, my legs are killing me.'

'Yeah me too, Curley,' agreed Stony.

'How do you think I feel?' said Ollie Gimble. 'I haven't eaten anything for hours, I'm bloomin' starving, I am!'

'Oh shurrup, Ollie,' said the other two min in unison.

Ollie Gimble was very put out by his friends' command but he did as he was told.

Mr Yanich and the rest of the posse had stopped up ahead, where the trio caught them up.

'Well gentlemin, the first part of our journey is complete. Now we must look to find a boat,' said Mr Yanich.

'That will be nice, Mr Yanich. I ain't never been on a boat before! Going to Central Head on a boat, that will be lovely! I wish my mamma could come with us too, coz she ain't never been on a boat neither, and she said she always wanted to ride in one like,' said Ollie.

'I'm afraid this is not a holiday excursion, Mr Gimble. Unless your mother can throw a spear directly at the heart of enemy from a hundred feet, then I suggest she stays at home,' said Mr Yanich.

'Ollie's mamma could throw a spear from a lot further away than a hundred feet, Mr Yanich,' said Stony. 'Come to think of it, she could probably batter you to death with the other end of it from that far an' all.'

'Yeah, spot on that, Stony,' said Curley.

Ollie Gimble nodded his head and smiled. He stood immensely proud, as everything that Stony had said about his mother was very true.

'Ah quite,' said Mr Yanich. 'But I'm afraid you'll have to wait a few days for your seafaring arrival at Thalamus Bay, Mr Gimble, because we have to make a slight detour first.'

'But I thought we were going straight to Central Head, Mr Yanich, to the trials?' said Curley.

'Do you think we could take on the might of the Security Council by ourselves, Mr Curley?' said Mr Yanich. 'There are not even twenty of us here, and I'm afraid we are going to need a lot more than that. No, we must get some reinforcements first, my friend, build up an army.'

'An army?' said Stony Pickles. 'Ooh I don't like the sound of that, boys, sounds like someone might get hurt.' His true cowardice was showing through.

'Ha! Somebody *will* get hurt Mr Pickles, that's the whole point. Many people will get hurt and many people will die! They will meet a horrible and sticky end, and that is why we are going there, this is a war!' said Mr Yanich.

The three friends from the Luglands looked at each other with concern. They certainly hadn't signed up for any war, not one that they knew about anyway.

'Now, I have arranged to meet a few friends of mine up ahead. They have already put the word about that we are looking for a few more to join our little crusade, and the word back is that the numbers are very promising. At the moment, there are a couple of hundred more recruits waiting for us in the city of Regio-Mentalis. We must pick up my friend Mr White, who is waiting for us up ahead at the Cut Throat Valley and from there we must take a boat to Regio-Mentalis. This will take a couple of days, my friends, but when our army is complete, we can take on the might of Leopold Schmidt and his Security Council. In fact once our army is complete we can take on anyone!' continued Mr Yanich.

The rest of the posse all cheered with delight and punched their fists up in the air as Mr Yanich finished his sentence, everyone except for the Lugland trio. Although, Ollie was trying to join in belatedly, not because of the sentiment that it represented but because everybody else was doing it.

'The Mental Region? Bloody hell everyone is off their bleeding heads in the Mental Region. They're all nutcases, worse than Mr Qu...' Stony stopped mid sentence when he realised what he was about to say. 'But yeah, reinforcements, Mr Yanich, yeah that's...er... yeah, a good plan I reckon, that one.'

He looked around to see if Mr Quick had picked up on his near mistake, but the bandit hadn't noticed anything. He seemed to be occupied by staring longingly at his knife, so a relieved Stony Pickles thought that he must have got away with it for now.

'But, er, that's, er, quite a way from here though, Mr Yanich, and, er, forgive me if I'm being stupid here like, but where are we gonna get a boat from?'

'You are quite right Mr Pickles, and you are stupid, but I forgive you,' said Mr Yanich quietly. 'In answer to your question, that's easy, we are going to steal a boat, and you my friend are going to help us steal it.'

'Steal a boat! How in Will's name are we gonna steal a boat?' said Curley. 'They're about a bloomin' hundred feet long with Central Head-workers running up and down them all day long, aren't they? You can't just slip one under your tunic when no one's looking, like, can you?'

Mr Yanich calmly responded to Raymond Curley's question. 'My friends, you don't seem to realise that things are now going to get very serious for you, very serious indeed. From this point on, your involvement in all of this is not up for discussion. You are very much part of this posse, and very much a part of our army. We will steal a boat, Mr Curley, by slitting the throat of anybody who tries to stop us from stealing that boat. Yet, if they co-operate then we shall be merciful and let them live. And if anybody else wants to get in our way then we shall slit their throats too. It's quite simple. It's kill or be killed. We must find out what is going to happen to The Will, and nothing shall stand in our way. Do I make myself clear?'

The bandits all raised their knives up in the air as one. The three Luglanders nodded in reply, too afraid to do anything else.

'Good, that's very good, gentlemin,' said Mr Yanich. 'Now, we must make our way to the Cut Throat Valley, where we are expected. Come along, comrades, we must make haste. Mr Quick, I suggest you stay at the back of our little group, just in case any of our three Lugland guests decide that they should want to, er, wander off at any point.'

'Oh it will be my pleasure, Sir,' said Mr Quick. He walked over to the trio. 'Please let them run my friend, please let them run so that me and you can have a good day,' he said to his knife.

The posse continued to walk on towards the Cut Throat Valley. Stony, Ollie and Curley were sticking together like glue, with the daunting figure of Zachary Quick looming closely behind them.

'I tell you what, boys,' whispered Stony to the other two. 'I'm beginning to wonder whether that flaming book is worth all of this, like. I'm starting to have second thoughts about it now.'

'Yeah me too, Stony,' said Curley.

'And me,' said Ollie. 'I don't like it, Stony, I don't like it one bit. I didn't even want to come in the first place.'

'But we can't do anything now can we, Stony?' said Curley. 'Got us by the balls now, haven't they?'

'Yeah you're not wrong there, Curley,' said Stony. 'And that Yanich fella is starting to turn a little nasty, isn't he? I, for one, am starting to think that we might be better trying to get the hell out of it as soon as we can. Far away from any bleeding nutcase who carries a knife! What about you two?'

'Yeah, I would like to go back home now, Stony. I don't like this anymore, all this talk about killing folk and stuff. That's not right that, Stony,' said Ollie.

'Yeah too bloody right, Ollie,' said Curley. 'They're all bleeding mental.'

'You think these are mental, just wait till we get to the Mental Region, I've heard that they're worse! They hate anyone from Central Head, there you know. Off their heads the lot of them,' said Stony.

'So what are we gonna do, Stony?' said Ollie. 'Have you got a plan, like? Coz I reckon now would be a good time for a plan, Stony.'

'Yeah, Ollie, you're not wrong there. Now would be a bloody great time for a plan, like. In fact, now would be the best bloody time in the world for a great big stonking, clever and brilliant plan. Only trouble is, I haven't got one, have I?' said Stony.

'Oh,' said Ollie, glumly.

'But it doesn't mean that we can't think of one, does it?' said Stony.

'Let's just do a runner now, Stony. They'll never catch us, come on I reckon we can make it!' said Curley.

'You're joking aren't you, Curley? There's nothing that bleeding Nutty Nigel behind us there would like more than to come chasing after us in the dark with a bloody knife, and it would be a bloody knife and all d'you get what I'm saying?' said Stony. 'No boys, we need to just keep our heads down for the time being until we come up with a way of getting the hell out of here. Let's just keep quiet for now until we work out what we're gonna do, ok?'

'Yeah ok, Stony,' said Ollie.

'Ok, sound,' said Curley. 'But we'll have to come up with something soon, or we're gonna end up on a boat with hundreds of bleeding nutters!'

'Yeah I know, Curley, but let's not just think about that for now, eh?' said Stony.

'Oh, and I wanted to go on the boat, and all!' said Ollie disappointingly.

'Where the hell did you get him from, Stony? He lives in a different bloomin' world to everyone else,' said Curley, shaking his head.

'Oh I dunno, Curley, but I wish I could bloomin' take him back there sometimes,' said Stony.

'Well I ain't never been on a boat, have I? I was looking forward to that,' said Ollie.

'Oh shurrup, Ollie!' said the two min together.

The three min continued to walk together under escort, desperately trying to figure out what to do.

The posse reached the end of the track where they could see the waves of the blood red river shimmering gently in the moonlight. Waiting for them at the jetty was a boat which had been tied up to the shore. At first there didn't seem to be anyone on it, and it was only when they got closer that they could see the terrified figure of the ship's Captain kneeling down on the deck with another min standing behind him holding a knife to his throat.

The other min was quite similar to Mr Yanich in many ways. He too was impeccably dressed in a smart shirt and waistcoat. He seemed a bit younger than Mr Yanich though, and his hair was much shorter.

'Ah, Mr Yanich,' he said from the boat as he saw them approaching. He waved to the group with his other hand.

'Ah, Mr White, so good to see you, it's been a long time! And I see you have saved us the trouble of stealing a vessel, for you have already done it yourself. How very kind of you, Sir,' said Mr Yanich as he boarded the boat.

'Ah don't mention it, my good man, it was no trouble,' said Mr White. 'The other fellow that was here seems to have run away.'

One of the bandits leaped on board and immediately took over from Mr White. He led the Captain inside to the control room and readied him for the off.

'How are you, my friend?' said Mr Yanich with his arms outstretched.

172

Mr White walked over to Mr Yanich and gave him a huge hug. 'I am well, my friend, very well indeed. I am looking forward to getting into a bit of action again though, it's been a while. Where is this diary you speak of? I am very much looking forward to seeing it.'

'It's here, my good friend,' said Mr Yanich as he pulled the huge diary from his bag.

'Well now, this is some find, Sir. A rare treat indeed!' said Mr White as he gazed at the book.

'Yes, my friend, it certainly is that. But enough for now, I can show it to you on the way. We will have plenty of time to talk on our journey.' Mr Yanich turned around to the posse. 'Right, everyone on board please, we sail straight away. Regio-Mentalis is more than two days sail from here; we must not waste any time.'

Everybody else climbed aboard the boat, including the Luglanders, closely followed by Mr Quick.

Mr Yanich spoke once more as he gestured to the control room. 'Captain, if you would be so kind as to set a course for the Regio-Mentalis that would be splendid. Thank you, my good man!'

The Captain, with a knife held to his neck set the controls and they were off.

Chapter Seventeen

The official trialists of The Will year '34/'35 had once again gathered at Central Fornix Hall and were congregated down in the front left hand section ready for their second seminar with Mr Pothackery. The previous day's session had proved extremely interesting for most of them. Learning about the history and formation of The Will was something that many of them had enjoyed. However, not all of them were as easily impressed.

Henry Grip was sitting next to his friend Penelope Potts and he was not looking forward to another uninspiring history lesson.

'I can't believe we've got to sit through another boring old science and history of the bloomin' boring old Will again, Loppy. As if yesterday wasn't bad enough, it's so bloomin' boring!' he said.

Penelope, who had enjoyed the previous day's seminar immensely, responded in her own unique fashion. 'You just didn't like it, Henry, because you never got any questions right and everybody else did!'

Henry's competitive side came charging to the surface. 'Well who wants to know about all of that boring stuff anyway? And nobody else got any of the questions right, Loppy, it was only you! Will only knows how though, bloomin' teacher's pet already,' he said, with more than a tinge of jealousy.

'I want to learn about it, Henry, because I happen to find it all very interesting,' said Penelope. 'Just because you find it boring, doesn't mean that everybody else does. And it was you that wanted to come here in the first place anyway, that's the only reason why I am here after all. If it wasn't for you, then I wouldn't even be here!'

'Yeah well just remember that, Loppy,' said Henry.

Penelope looked angrily at him. 'And just what is that supposed to mean, Henry?' she said.

Henry was searching his head for a response. 'Yeah, whatever,' he managed.

'I just don't get you sometimes, Henry,' said Penelope. Then she suddenly realised that Henry had come to the hall unaccompanied again today. 'Anyway what's happened to Monty, is he ill again?' she added.

'Well, yeah he says he is, but I don't reckon there's anything wrong with him. Maybe he's just trying to get out of this boring old lesson. I wish I'd said that I was ill too now,' said Henry.

'I do hope he's ok, Henry. I mean he looks so scared all of the time. He must really hate it here, the poor little thing,' said Penelope.

174

'Why do you care anyway?' said Henry in an overly uncaring fashion, which didn't really befit him.

'I care, Henry, because he is our friend. Just like I would care about you if it was the other way round! And you should care too, he is your roommate, you know?' said Penelope.

'Well there's nothing wrong with him, is there? He's just putting it on,' said Henry.

The argument was rather conveniently interrupted.

'Right then, trialists, good morning once again, and how are we all today?' said a voice from the front of the hall. It was Mr Pothackery. He had just come in from outside and had taken his place on the step at the front of the group, where a couple of trial stewards accompanied him. He seemed a lot more relaxed than he did on the previous day, probably because Cornelius Crail was not in attendance this morning.

The children responded with their communal mutterings.

'Ah, jolly good,' said Mr Pothackery. 'And how was the endurance training yesterday? Did you all have a good time up in the mountains?'

'Yes, Sir, it was great. Are we going up there again this afternoon?' said Henry eagerly.

'Yes indeed you are, Mr Grip,' said Mr Pothackery. 'The mountain air is so good for the soul, don't you think?'

'Yes, Sir, I can't wait to go again,' said Henry happily.

Mr Pothackery too noticed that Henry wasn't accompanied by his roommate. 'Er, still no Monty today, Henry?' he said.

'No, Sir, he's still not well, Sir,' replied Henry.

'Oh dear, Mr Adamson, would you be so kind?' Mr Pothackery gestured to one of the stewards, who promptly left to attend to the apparently sick boy.

'Ok then, trialists, now let us continue where we left off from yesterday's seminar,' said Mr Pothackery to the congregation as a whole.

Henry tutted to himself, and put his head in his hands, 'Oh no.'

Mr Pothackery walked over to the maps of The Will, which were still on the stand from the previous day. 'So can anybody tell me where we got to yesterday?'

Angus Murphy put up an eager arm.

'Yes, Angus?' said Mr Pothackery.

'Sir, can I go to the toilet please?' said Angus.

Mr Pothackery rolled his eyes. 'Yes, Angus, off you go,' he said, to the obvious amusement of the rest of the group.

Constance Futtock then raised her hand. She was sitting a little closer to Penelope today. The Lugland girl's contribution to yesterday's lesson had made an impression on her.

'Yes, Constance?' said Mr Pothackery.

'Sir, we got up to understanding about the Tri-min and how they formed

The Will, Sir, and about how we were born and how our parents were born, Sir,' said Constance.

'Yes jolly good, Constance,' said Mr Pothackery. 'And anything else?'

'Yes, Sir,' said Penelope. 'You told us about the first ruler of Central Head, Geffron Scolt and about how he wrote everything down in the chronicles, Sir, in the Neocortex.'

'Yes, very good, Penelope, indeed I did,' said Mr Pothackery. 'And I do believe that is about where we got to, is it not?'

'Yes I think so, Sir,' said Penelope.

'Right, ok then,' said Mr Pothackery. 'So the wonderful Mr Geffron Scolt, as Penelope has pointed out, was indeed the first ruler of Central Head and he ruled for the first five glorious years of the life of The Will. It is down to him that we have so much freedom and choice in this world, for he was a great min, a brilliant min, full of vision and hope.

And it was also the idea of Geffron Scolt to hold the annual contest, which you all obviously will be hoping to enter into next year. Without him, none of us would be sitting here today.'

All of a sudden, Henry became a little more interested. Penelope looked at him with a typical frown.

'It was his idea that we should choose a worthy apprentice, to nurture and train in the ways of The Will, and that we should do this each year so as to make The Will a better place for all to live and work in. It was such an honourable gesture on his part, don't you think, trialists?' said Mr Pothackery.

Everybody agreed. After all, that was why they were there.

'Yes, it was in those first five years that we learned how to use everything that had been given to us by The Will. How to build up our own lives, and give ourselves some comfort and luxury, at the same time as fulfilling our duty to The Will.

Yes, Geffron Scolt taught us that we should enjoy our work as much as we can, and that we should try to make our lives better. We learned how to build from materials such as wood and stone, how to forge steel for ships and boats, and how to use the rivers for transport and for travel. Luxury trades such as carpentry and blacksmithing were created, to aid the growth of the min.

We learned how to use the food and water, which is given to us every day by The Will, to take it and store it, and transform it into the luxury items that we have today. Where do you think your favourite sandwiches came from, trialists? Before Geffron Scolt, we didn't even have sandwiches. They hadn't been thought of by then!' said Mr Pothackery.

After mentioning sandwiches, he had everybody's undivided attention. The min were always quite partial to a sandwich.

A large boy from the back of the group raised his hand. His name was Danny Cow.

'Yes, Danny?' said Mr Pothackery.

'Sir, how come Mr Scolt isn't ruler anymore?' said Danny Cow.

'Well after five years, Danny, he decided that he should step down and let somebody else take over. He thought that once the Will was moving forward in the right direction, he should pass it on to somebody else and let them bring in their new ideas, keep a fresh approach to things. And that person was this fellow.'

Mr Pothackery walked over to the central statue of the three, and put his hand around its shoulder. 'Triston Clearwater Snr.'

'So how come that he isn't ruler anymore then, Sir?' said Constance Futtock.

'Well, Mr Clearwater Snr ruled for ten years Constance and he ruled very well, just as his predecessor had done, but like Mr Scolt before him, he decided that he should pass on the baton to somebody else. It was thought he would hand it over to his son, Triston Clearwater Jnr, but they say that he somehow decided to rule himself out of the running at the last minute, nobody really knows why, everybody thought that he was rather nailed on for the job,' said Mr Pothackery, he looked slightly puzzled.

'So what happened then, Mr Pothackery?' said Penelope.

'Well, Penelope, that was in the year '15 and it was then that our current leader Sananab, very kindly accepted the chance to take up the mantle. He has been ruler ever since, for nineteen years now,' said Mr Pothackery, pointing at the third statue.

'Yeah and I bet that's when the Zamindar came into power too,' said Danny Cow, 'and started to bully everyone into doing what he wanted them to, taking all their taxes off them, and throwing them in jail. That's what my dad says anyway.'

A few of the trialists seemed to agree with Danny Cow's interpretation of events, the rest of the group gasped in surprise at the boy's outburst.

'Now, now Danny Cow, we'll have none of that sort of talk in here, we must not disrespect our Zamindar, it is not becoming for an official trialist of Central Head to speak in such a way, no matter what your father says,' said Mr Pothackery.

'Yes but its true though, Sir, isn't it?' said the boy.

Everybody eagerly stared at Mr Pothackery for his response.

'Well if you mean that the Zamindar and the Master both came into power almost at the same time, then yes it is true, Danny. But that is merely a coincidence. Mr Schmidt did become Zamindar during the same year that Sananab became leader but that was just the way things turned out. Mr Schmidt is a good min. He is just under a lot of pressure that is all. I do agree that perhaps his tactics can be sometimes, a little, how shall we say, heavy handed, but he is a good min underneath I can assure you. It is the pressures of the job, which can sometimes take their toll on a min,' said Mr Pothackery.

'Well if it's the pressures of the job what does it, Sir, how come Mr Scolt was so great? He must have had the same pressures and I bet he wouldn't have sent poor old Henry's dad into exile would he?' said Danny Cow.

Henry looked up at the boy, and even though they had only briefly met the day before on the mountain, he didn't realise that he had already made another friend.

'Now that was an individual case, Danny, and we should not really comment on it, should we? Even though, I do have to agree with you there, it is a rather desperate punishment, which poor old Mr Grip has had to endure, a very unfortunate set of events all round I fear.' Mr Pothackery briefly glanced over at Henry, and sighed with regret before continuing. 'But I can assure you all that Mr Schmidt is a good min deep down. He was once a trialist himself you know, and a previous contest winner to boot! He and I were trialists together, we were roommates in fact, and he holds all of the honour and virtues that you yourselves hold as trialists today, even if they are a little hard to find at times.

Once he became our Zamindar, well, Central Head rather took over his life. Became a burden somewhat, rather changed him, I fear, but he is still a previous contest winner and as Zamindar of The Will, he deserves your respect.

Now enough talk of that, let us get back to the subject in hand. Let us get back to talking about the growth of the min,' said Mr Pothackery.

At the back of the hall, completely unnoticed by anybody else, two figures had suddenly entered the fray and were watching proceedings from afar, with a great deal of interest. They were Sananab and Cornelius Crail. They stood still and said nothing.

Penelope raised her hand once more.

'Ah yes, Penelope, not another question about the Zamindar I hope?' said Mr Pothackery.

'Er, no Sir, but it is sort of related to what happened with the alarm last week,' said Penelope. 'I wanted to ask you about what happens when the min don't do as they are supposed to, Sir?'

'I'm sorry, Penelope, I don't quite follow you?' said Mr Pothackery.

'I would have thought that was obvious, the Zamindar bloomin' well throws them in jail,' said Danny Cow sarcastically.

The rest of the group murmured in general agreement.

'No, Sir what I mean is, well if for instance someone deliberately didn't do their job, Sir. If they deliberately didn't do as they were supposed to, then what would happen to The Will, Sir?' said Penelope.

'Are you talking about something specific here, Penelope?' said Mr Pothackery.

'Well I've heard about something, and I'm not sure if it's true or not, Sir, but it's something called...,' she paused for a second before saying the next word, 'instinct, Sir. Do you know what that is?'

Everybody in the room turned to look at Penelope, as they waited with baited breath for Mr Pothackery's response, including a fairly confused Henry Grip, and two very interested onlookers from the back of the hall.

'This certainly is quite advanced thinking, Penelope, something that many second years, even past trialists don't fully understand, but I can see that you certainly have a thirst for knowledge, young lady,' said Mr Pothackery. 'And yes, in answer to your question, there is such a thing as 'instinct' as you quite rightly say.

Geffron Scolt wrote about it in the very first chronicle in fact. It was passed down from the last of the Tri-min to us that 'instinct' is something believed to have the power to *take over*. It has the capacity to take over The Will when there is a threat to its being, or to its function. If it were in danger of any kind, and the min were somehow absent from duty, not at their post so to speak, then 'instinct' would strive to take over The Will, let it run itself. But only for a split second is it thought instinct could work, any longer than a few seconds and it couldn't cope. That's why it relies on the min to survive. That is why we are here after all. Simple minology you see, Penelope.'

'But if that is the case, Sir, why did it not take over last week when the alarm didn't go off?' said Penelope.

'To tell you the truth, I don't exactly know, Penelope. Perhaps it wasn't deemed as a great enough threat, who knows? All I know, is that it was a very rare thing indeed that happened last week, wasn't it? We as min are always at hand to fulfil our duty to The Will, and that is why we have lived for thirty-four years without incident. That is why it is such a wonderful place for us all. Nos Numquam Immutare Voluntaten, eh?' said Mr Pothackery.

'Nos Numquam Immutare Voluntaten,' said everyone in reply.

'Nos Numquam Immutare Voluntaten is indeed a motto which you will all do well to remember, young trialists,' said Sananab as he emerged from the shadows.

Everybody immediately turned around to see where the voice had come from, and they gasped in awe as they realised who it was.

'Oh, Loppy, look who it is!' whispered Henry excitedly.

Sananab walked to the front of the hall, closely followed by Cornelius Crail, who glowered at Henry and Penelope as he passed them.

'Your Eminence, it is certainly a great honour for you to come and visit us today. The trialists are very privileged,' said Mr Pothackery.

'Yes, Mr Pothackery, I thought I would come along and see for myself how they are settling in,' said Sananab. 'Cornelius tells me there are one or two students who are already showing some promise.' He looked directly at Penelope. He could see into her mind. At the same time, she could feel him inside her head, working his way through her thoughts.

'Ah yes, Sir, we do have a wonderful group of trialists this year, and I know they will all do well,' said Mr Pothackery proudly.

'Yes, but perhaps one or two of them will do rather better than some of the others, Charles, in particular a young lady who seems to be asking all the right questions,' said Sananab. He started to walk towards Henry and Penelope.

'I have been listening to your seminar this morning Charles and I am impressed by what I have been hearing.' He stopped directly in front of Penelope. 'Miss Potts, how are you today?'

To say that Penelope was a little scared was an understatement, for anyone to be this close to Sananab was terrifying.

'Er... I am fine, Sir,' she said.

'Now, my dear girl, please relax, and do not be alarmed by my presence. I am merely taking an interest in the trials this year, a more direct interest than I might have done in the past. The winner of the contest will be working alongside me in Central Head after all, and I only want to make sure that we find the right person for the job. There will be a rather special position created for this year's winner, one with a bit more of a, shall we say, an overall importance,' said Sananab.

'Ok, Sir,' managed Penelope, she couldn't think of anything else to say.

Henry was sitting next to her. He was shaking at the thought of being this close to Sananab, he couldn't believe his eyes.

'The things you speak of, Miss Potts, the questions you ask, they interest me. You have intelligence, a curiosity. Perhaps you could come to my office to talk some more? I would like that.' Sananab turned to the front of the hall where Mr Pothackery was standing. 'Mr Pothackery?'

'Er, yes, Sir?' said Mr Pothackery.

'Would you mind if Miss Potts here was to come to the Neocortex with me to talk some more?' said Sananab.

'Er, no, Sir, whatever you wish, Sir,' said Mr Pothackery.

'Good, that's settled then.' Sananab turned back to Penelope. 'My dear, would you be so kind as to accompany Mr Crail back to my office when it is convenient for you to do so? Your training must come first of course.'

Penelope was speechless. She just sat there in shock.

'Fine, after today's lesson would be convenient for me too. Thank you so much,' said Sananab. He spun around on the spot and strode off towards the doors at the end of the hall, on his way out he shouted to the Thought Apprentice. 'Cornelius, could you please escort Miss Potts to my office when today's lesson is over? Thank you.'

Sananab left the hall. Everybody inside was in complete shock.

Mr Pothackery turned to the group and said, 'Er, well, trialists, I rather think that may be enough for today. Yes, I think now would perhaps be a good time to, er, break for lunch.'

He, like everybody else, was shocked at the appearance of Sananab in his classroom, in all of the years that he had been overseeing the trials he had perhaps seen the Master once or twice at most.

'So we'll meet here again tomorrow trialists? In the meantime, you are to meet outside here again at two o' clock for the endurance training.' He walked off with the other trial stewards towards the doors.

'Woah, what was all that about, Loppy?' said Henry.

'I don't know, Henry, but I'm scared,' replied Penelope.

Cornelius Crail made his way over to the pair. 'Come on then, *Miss Potts*, you have an appointment to keep and we mustn't keep the Master waiting now, must we?' he said.

'But do I *have* to go?' said the frightened girl.

'Of course you *have* to go,' snapped Cornelius. 'You can't disobey the Master, now come on we haven't got all day!'

Penelope reluctantly followed the boy out of the hall.

Henry stood and watched her go. For a split second, he was confused. He didn't know whether to feel concerned for her as his best friend or to be jealous of her. Deep down he would have loved to have had a one-to-one with the mighty Sananab but he didn't get the opportunity, did he? That particular privilege had gone to the teacher's pet. And to make things worse, she was with that horrible bully Cornelius Crail too.

'Oh well, go and have your little talk with him and crappy Crail then. See if I care, I've got training to do!' he said.

Henry turned around and saw the rest of the group making their way out of the hall. 'Hey, Danny, hang on a minute, I'll come with you!' he shouted.

Friday 2nd November, 3:09 p.m. Neocortex, Central Head.

Cornelius Crail and Penelope Potts had made their way over from Hippocampus to the offices of Central Head, and they were now in the restricted section of the Neocortex. Penelope was scared. In fact she was terrified, yet she couldn't help feeling slightly curious at the same time. Only this morning she was sitting in Mr Pothackery's seminar, enjoying herself immensely and learning all about the wonderful things that The Will had to offer. Now she was standing outside of Sananab's office with the despicable Cornelius Crail at her side. Things here moved very quickly. This place was different to anywhere she had ever been before; there was something strange about it. She could feel the sheer weight of knowledge, circling above their heads and whizzing through the air. It was invisible to the naked eye and she couldn't touch it with her hands, but she could feel it inside her head.

Cornelius feebly knocked on the door.

'Come in, Miss Potts,' said a voice from inside.

They opened the door and went in. Penelope gazed around the room in amazement. There were hundreds of books filling the shelves from floor to ceiling. Every inch of the circular room was filled with something, whether it was a book or a chart or an object of importance. This room held millions of pieces of information in one form or another. She felt that it somehow had a history to it.

Sitting behind the beautiful and ornate wooden, circular desk was Sananab. 'Ah, Miss Potts, welcome to Central Headquarters. Please do have a seat,' he said.

Penelope sat down on the chair on the opposite side of the desk from Sananab. Cornelius Crail stood at the side of the room next to the giant shelves, which dwarfed him in size.

'Miss Potts you are a very acute young lady,' said Sananab. 'Cornelius informed me yesterday that you had a certain amount of curiosity in you, yet your knowledge about The Will was second to none. Naturally I had to see for myself so I decided to come to the seminar this morning to observe, and let me tell you that I was not disappointed.'

Cornelius grinned with derision from the side of the room.

'Er, thank you, Sir,' replied Penelope nervously.

'Penelope, oh, may I call you Penelope?' said Sananab.

'If you like, Sir,' said Penelope.

'Thank you. Now that we are friends Penelope, I think that I can describe to you, how you feel sometimes, how your mind works and how you think about certain things,' said Sananab.

Penelope twitched nervously in her chair. 'Sir?'

'Penelope, I know that you can hear things and feels things that not many other ordinary people can feel,' said Sananab. 'You are special, Penelope, you have a gift. You can *listen!*'

Penelope leaned back in the chair, quite uncomfortably.

'You can listen to the nerves. Even outside of this room, just a second ago, you were listening to the nerves. You could feel the flow of information that runs through these walls, and you could feel it flowing through you. Am I right, Penelope?' said Sananab.

Penelope had never met anybody else in her life before who knew that she could do this, apart from her mother and the only reason that her mother knew was because Penelope had told her about it. She was intrigued to know how Sananab knew this, but more than that she was extremely excited about the fact that he did.

'But how do you know?' she asked curiously.

'Because I can feel them too, Penelope. I can listen in just as you can. You and I are the same. We both have the gift,' said Sananab excitedly.

'But nobody else has ever been able to do it, Sir, not like me. I have never met anybody who thinks like me. And whenever I have tried to tell anybody about it, Sir, then they just laugh. They think that it's... well, funny,' said Penelope.

'That is because they are ignorant to your gift, Penelope, not everybody is blessed with the talent that comes with listening to the nerves, not everyone has got what it takes. But you have my dear. You have the ability to make a difference, you have the ability to change the world!' said Sananab.

Penelope started to laugh nervously. 'What change the world? Ha, as if,' she said.

Sananab leaned closer to her. 'I do not think you fully understand why you are here, do you, Penelope? When I say that you can change the world, I mean it!'

'But I don't understand, Sir. How could I ever do anything like that? I'm just a girl? And I'm not sure if I would ever want to change the world anyway,' said Penelope, somewhat apprehensively.

Sananab got up from his chair and walked over to one of the bookshelves at the side of the desk, he began to run his fingers along the spines of all of the books packed into the shelf.

'Do you see these books, Penelope, and these charts, and these maps, and all of this information which is gathered here on these shelves? Well, it took a wealth of intelligence firstly to collect it, and secondly to write it all down for us to see and preserve it; many min with the gift of knowledge that we both have. Many people before us have devoted their lives to ensure that we have enough philosophy to survive and to serve The Will. They gave us a chance in this life to make The Will a better place for our families and friends! And you sit there and mock them?'

Penelope suddenly became a little more scared than she already was.

'Er, no, Sir, I'm not mocking anyone. It's just all a bit of a shock, that's all. I'm just a bit nervous,' she said.

'If I were to say to you the phrase Nos Numquam Immutare Voluntaten, would you understand what it meant, Penelope?' said Sananab.

'Yes, of course I would,' said Penelope. 'It is the law, the written law and the unwritten law. It means we can never change The Will. Everyone knows that.'

'But what if I were to say to you, that for one time, and for an extremely important reason, that we must ignore our famous motto,' said Sananab.

'But you can't, nobody can change The Will. It's not allowed or even possible, is it?' said Penelope.

'Oh it is possible, my dear, very much so in fact. Penelope, I am saying to you that we *must* change The Will,' said Sananab.

Penelope was extremely surprised by what she had heard, but she was also very clever and she thought that perhaps this might be some kind of test. 'Is this a trick, Sir?' she said. 'Coz if it is then I'm not falling for it.'

'I'm afraid it is not a trick, Penelope, it is the truth. Let me assure you that it is indeed possible to change The Will, and it is also imperative that we do so. And what's more, Penelope Potts, I want you to help me do it,' said Sananab.

'Sir, if it's all the same to you I think I would like to go back to the camp now, Sir. I'm not sure that I like the way that this conversation has turned out,' said Penelope desperately, as she started to get up from her chair.

Cornelius walked over to the chair from the side of the room. 'You will go back to the camp when the Master says you can, ok?' he said, pushing her firmly back in her seat.

Penelope didn't reply. She was now very, very frightened indeed. All that she could think of was her mother and father, and the thought of being back home in the boring old Luglands seemed like the best thing in the world to her right now.

'Cornelius, my dear boy, please relax. Penelope is our guest, after all, and we don't want to make her feel uncomfortable now do we? What would her parents think?' said Sananab.

Cornelius went back to leaning on his perch at the side of the room.

'Now, Penelope, I need you to help me change The Will because it will die if we don't,' said Sananab. There was not an ounce of emotion in his voice.

Penelope looked at him in horror, she didn't say a word.

'You are the one person that I have met Penelope who has the gift. You can see into the nerves, just as I can, and I have seen it in the nerves, The Will is going to die. I will show you Penelope, you will be able to see it as I have, nobody else will be able to see, other than you,' said Sananab. 'But if we work together, you and I, then we can prevent it from happening. You and I can change The Will.'

'Sir this is… this is… I... I... I... I don't' kn...kn...kn...kn... know what to... I don't know… Sir, this is not happening. Sir,… this is horrible…' said Penelope. She was scared and she was shaking. She was beginning to cry.

Sananab interrupted her, and he began to get louder. 'This morning Penelope, you talked about instinct and what it can do. Well, very soon, Penelope, instinct is going to make a decision for The Will and that decision will spark off a chain of events that will result in the death of The Will. I don't need to tell you, Penelope, that if this is allowed to happen we will all die with it. Your mother and father, your friend Henry, all of the people that you hold dear back at home, they will all die! Unless you agree to help me, Penelope.'

Throughout this speech Penelope was squirming in her chair; her whole body was in pain, every word from his lips made her feel like she was about to explode. It seemed like he was mentally torturing her in some way. It was making her dizzy, she couldn't focus on anything in the room, her eyes were rolling round and round trying not to hurt.

The tirade continued.

'The future of the entire Will is in your hands, Penelope. What do you want to do? Ask yourself that question. Do you run back to the trials and pretend that this isn't happening? Do you go back there, knowing that each and every one of your friends will die because of your actions? Do you sit there like a coward and ignore your fate, and the fate of everybody else? Or do you help me save your family and friends, and everyone else who deserves the right to live in this world, to honour and serve The Will? Do you take the easy option and hide from the truth, or do you stay with me and do what is right?'

'Ok, ok, ok, I'll do it, I'll do it!' shouted Penelope from the chair.

Sananab's words had penetrated her brain. She could feel the pain of the sharp edges from the words as they swirled around her very soul. She just wanted the pain to stop. She would say anything just so the pain would stop. She paused for a moment and waited for her heart to stop racing.

'What do I have to do?' she said.

Sananab went and sat back down in his chair; he had got his min.

Cornelius grinned at him from the side of the room. Sananab acknowledged the Thought Apprentice's gesture with a smile of his own. He then looked at Penelope who was still terrified in her chair.

'The first thing you must do, Penelope, is not to breathe a word of this to anyone, do you understand? If this were to get out then it could ruin everything, and we wouldn't have the chance to act in time save The Will.

Then you must return here every day after your training. Cornelius will escort you, for as long as it takes. Penelope, we must listen to the nerves together, try to find a way in which we can stop this event from taking place, by thought manipulation, we must conquer this; the future depends on it. And every day, Penelope, we will learn together and I will try to show you how to change The Will!'

'But how do you know that it will work, Sir. How do you know that we can change The Will? I mean it's never been done before, has it? What if we don't succeed? What then?' said Penelope.

'We will succeed, Penelope,' said Sananab, 'I am certain of it, in fact, because I know that it has been done before. I have seen it with my own eyes!'

'What, it has? But when?' said Penelope, she was completely astonished at these revelations.

'Oh, come, come, Penelope, you are a very intelligent girl. Surely you do not need me to tell you that? With the knowledge that you possess, I think that you already have a pretty good idea as to when it happened,' said Sananab.

'Oh no!'

It suddenly dawned on Penelope that the missed alarm last week was no coincidence. Everything that had happened to Mr Grip, and to Henry and to her mother and father, and everyone else from the Luglands was down to this. She started to cry.

'But, Sir, please no! I don't think I can go through with it. Look what damage it has already caused, to my friends and family. This is horrible!'

'If you don't go through with it, Penelope, you will have no friends and family left. They will all die, as will you and I. How do you think your family would feel if they knew that you were the only person in The Will who could save them, but that you turned your back on them?'

'But, Sir, there must be somebody else who can do it? There are thousands of other people in The Will, why does it have to be me?' she said, still crying.

'No, Penelope! You said it yourself, you are the only one with the gift, it must be you,' said Sananab.

'Ok, Sir, I will do what I have to do,' said Penelope reluctantly.

'Now not a word of this to anyone, Penelope, remember? The future depends on it. I shall see you back here after the trials tomorrow afternoon,' said Sananab. 'Cornelius, would you escort Miss Potts back to Hippocampus please? Thank you.'

The two Luglanders left Sananab's office, leaving the Master sitting there alone at his desk. He sat back in his chair and put his arms behind his head.

'One by one the pieces fall neatly into place, very soon this artful jigsaw will be complete,' he said to himself.

He picked up the ornament that was sitting on the top of his desk and he rolled it around in his fingers a couple of times. After a few seconds, he hurled it at the wall as hard as he could. It smashed against the wall and fell into a thousand pieces on the floor.

Chapter Eighteen

Sunday 4th November, 8:20 a.m. Regio-Mentalis.

The hijacked boat containing the belligerent posse from the Oesophagus Forest pulled into the picturesque quayside of Regio-Mentalis. Standing by the water's edge was a band of almost two hundred merciless, ruthless and homicidal savages, waiting for its arrival.

Stony Pickles, Ollie Gimble and Raymond Curley were sitting at the back of the boat, under the watchful eye of Zachary Quick and his trusty knife, and from this situation they were not about to attempt an escape at anytime soon.

One of the bandits tied a rope to the jetty as the boat slowed to a halt. Mr Yanich and Mr White came out from one of the inside cabins to greet the awaiting reception.

There was a large figure standing at the front of the group, and he seemed to be the one in command. He was a well-built figure, with huge arms full of thick bulging muscles and covered with tattoos. His skin was dark and he had a peaked cap covering his bald head. The rest of the army were all dressed similarly, although not identically, in clothes which looked worn and dirty, and everybody there looked as though they had seen many a battle in their time.

'Are you Yanich?' said the leader.

Mr Yanich stepped forward. 'Yes, I'm Mr Yanich, and you are?'

'Chinner,' said the min, as he held a clenched fist up to his own chin.

'Ah, Mr Chinner, we meet at last,' said Mr Yanich. 'I've heard a lot about you over the years, your reputation precedes you, Sir. You are famous amongst our kind, some would say legendary.'

'No mister, just Chinner,' said Chinner.

'Ah yes, of course, how silly of me,' said Mr Yanich. 'And I do believe you have already met Mr White?'

Chinner held out his huge hand for Mr White to shake, he then made a fist and they both tensed the muscles in their hands and punched fists together.

'How are you, Whitey? It's been a long time.' said Chinner.

'Yes, indeed it has, my good man, and yes, I am well, Sir, very well,' said Mr White.

'So what's the plan then?' said Chinner. 'I was told we were gonna go and kick some arse up in Central Head, is that right?'

'I do believe that is the general gist of the idea yes, Mr Chinner, are your troops ready to fight?' said Mr Yanich.

'Ready and able Yanich, and there's no mister, just Chinner. Where d'you want us then?' said Chinner.

'Well on the boat would be a good start,' said Mr Yanich, he looked around at the size of the boat. 'It will be a bit of a squeeze I'm afraid, but you'd better get everyone aboard as soon as you can and we can get going straight away. It is almost a week's sail to The Limbics from here so we've no time to lose. Perhaps we can chat about the killing on the way?'

Chinner waved to his waiting army. 'Come on, lads, everyone on the boat, and bring your weapons. There's gonna be some blood spilled by the time we've had our say!' he shouted.

There was an almighty roar from the army as they started to climb aboard the vessel.

Stony Pickles whispered to his two friends as he watched the army board the boat. 'I'll tell you what, boys, this lot look even more mental than I thought. Look at that fella at the front, he's got arms as big as you, Ollie. And look at that fella there, and those two behind him, I think they've only got about three eyes and four arms between them. Jeez, they've been in some battles this lot, I tell you.'

Zachary Quick heard Stony Pickles whispering and he immediately hauled him up off his feet and dragged him along the deck to the Captain's cabin. He pushed his face so hard into the glass that it almost cracked, and squeezed the back of his neck until he nearly choked. He scraped his knife along the top of Stony's head, drawing blood as he went.

'You listen to me, Lugland boy! When we get to The Limbics I am going to skin you alive and throw you into the river. I don't care what Yanich has in store for you. I am going to take pleasure in watching you die, do you hear me?' he said menacingly.

'Don't think that you are going to come back from this trip alive, you filthy little creature, or any of your idiot friends neither. I promise you that your days are numbered, boy, so make sure you spend the last of your time wisely, because in a few days' time you are a dead min!'

With this, he cut off a huge chunk of Stony's hair and threw him to the deck where Ollie and Curley were sitting. He then threw the clump of hair after him as he fell.

Ollie tried to stand up to retaliate but as he did, two dozen knives immediately appeared directly in front of his face. He sat back down on the deck.

Mr Yanich walked past the dejected figure of Stony Pickles on his way to the inside cabin, accompanied by Mr White and Chinner.

'What on earth are you doing down there, Mr Pickles? And you seem to have lost a lock of your hair. Mr Quick, you really should look after our guests a bit more. Ha, ha, come along gentlemin, we have things to discuss,' he said as he opened the cabin door. 'Tell me, Mr Chinner, I've always wanted to know, how did you escape from prison?'

188

'There's no mister, just Chinner,' said Chinner.

Mr Yanich gave the order to the Captain to set sail. The boat started its engines, and headed off up the river on its route towards The Limbics.

'Are you alright, Stony?' said Curley. 'Here, let me help you up, mate. Ollie, give us a hand will you?'

The two min helped their friend up from the floor.

Zachary Quick stood back with the rest of his team of bandits. They watched and laughed as the three friends moved to a quiet corner of the boat, slightly further away from them.

'Look what he's done to you, Stony, he's cut your bloomin' hair off! And your head, it's all cut, like,' said Curley.

'Yeah, Stony, are you ok? I don't like that fella, Stony, he's gonna get me really angry one of these days,' said Ollie.

Stony Pickles was terrified, he was shaking like a leaf. He had never experienced anything like this before in his life and he wasn't enjoying it at all. 'I can't believe him. What have I ever done to him, like?' he said.

'Well, we'll do a runner when we get there, Stony. Away from all these bloody nutcases, just wait till we get there and we'll be away,' said Curley.

'Yeah, just leave me alone for a while, boys, eh? Just leave me alone for a while,' said Stony.

He huddled himself into a corner next to a coiled rope and a few shipping crates and closed his eyes. There were a few drops of blood seeping out from under his hood.

Raymond Curley looked up at the band of cut-throats that were taunting and laughing at them. He knew they were powerless to stop them. Things had definitely taken a real turn for the worse that was for sure. Somehow finding out what was in the diary meant nothing anymore. He knew that they just had to sit and wait for their chance to run, to get away from these maniacs for good. But the chance would come, that he was certain of. He just wished that it would bloody-well hurry up and get there, that was all.

Saturday 10th November, 5:38 p.m. Hippocampus, Central Head.

Cornelius Crail was escorting Penelope Potts from the Neocortex back to Hippocampus as instructed, much to her obvious displeasure. She hated the fact that she was so close to his loathsome, contemptuous, little face, and she wasn't afraid to let him know it too.

'Why do you insist on taking me back to the camp, Cornelius? I know my way around, you know? You don't have to follow me like a bloomin' shadow!' said Penelope.

'Because it is the Master's orders, that is why. I am to escort you to and from the camp every day, you heard him yourself. And if the Master wishes it, then I am to do it,' replied Cornelius.

'Yes, but it's been over a week now, Cornelius, and I think you can safely say that I'm not going to run off anywhere, am I? Can't you just walk on ahead or something? You're really starting to creep me out,' said Penelope.

Cornelius was clearly put out by the creepy comment. Nevertheless, he continued to walk alongside her.

'No I cannot, *Miss* Potts!' he said. 'And anyway, everyone can see that we are friends now, can't they? So we must walk together as friends do. We can hold hands if you like?'

Penelope gave him a look, and if looks could kill he would have already been dead by now.

'And we must keep up the show, mustn't we? Especially for little old Henry. Yes, everyone knows who your friends are now. They can all see that you have definitely gone up in the world, Penelope. Everybody can now see where your loyalties lie!'

Penelope stopped dead in her tracks. 'Let's just get one thing straight, Cornelius, once and for all. I am *not* your friend, nor will I ever be. So you had better get used to it. I am only doing this because I have to. If there was any other way then I wouldn't be within a million miles of you, got it?'

They continued to walk on.

'But that's not what everyone else thinks is it, Penelope?' said Cornelius. 'Especially Henry Grip. Ha, ha! Little old Henry has made new friends now though, hasn't he? He's left you behind. I don't know why you ever bothered with him anyway. He's weak and stupid, and he hasn't got what it takes, you're better off without him.'

Penelope stopped again. 'Henry Grip is ten times the person you will ever be, Cornelius Crail, so you just leave him alone, and leave me alone while you're at it!'

'Well maybe I should tell the Master what you think, Penelope. I'm sure he would be interested to know how you feel about all of this. Perhaps I should tell him that you're having second thoughts? Tell him that you just want to be left alone?' said Cornelius threateningly.

'No, perhaps not Cornelius,' said Penelope. 'I just want this all to be over with that's all, so everything can go back to normal.'

'There will be no getting back to normal though, will there?' said Cornelius. 'Especially when we've transferred from this dump,' he added under his breath.

Penelope wasn't exactly sure if she had heard him correctly. 'What did you say, Cornelius?' she said.

'Eh, What?' said Cornelius, realising that he had said something that he shouldn't have.

'What did you say, just then?' said Penelope.

'Er, I said there will be no getting back to normal,' he said nervously, hoping that she hadn't heard the second part.

'No, I mean after that, you said something else after that,' said Penelope.

'Er, well I think you know your way back from here anyway, don't you?'

said Cornelius. 'Er, I've got some important business to attend to so I must be off.' With this, he scurried off in another direction, trying to get away from Penelope as fast as he could.

Penelope continued back towards Hippocampus alone. She knew that Cornelius Crail was a devious little so and so, and she knew that he had probably said something important; otherwise he wouldn't have run away like that.

'Hmm, transferred?' she said to herself. 'I wonder what he meant by that?'

She got back to Hippocampus where all of the trialists were out in the arena practicing their athletics training on the playing field. It was a beautiful day, and everybody was hard at work in the afternoon sunshine.

Henry was with Danny Cow. They were throwing a ball to each other from one side of the field to the other. When they saw Penelope approaching they came together in the centre of the field.

'Oh here she is, Danny,' said Henry. 'Been to another one of her private sessions again, I bet.'

'Yeah I reckon, Henry. She hasn't got her friend with her today though, has she?' said Danny Cow.

'Yeah, they've probably had a lover's tiff!' said Henry.

The two boys laughed.

'Hello, Henry, hello, Danny,' said Penelope, pretending she hadn't heard their jibes. 'How's the training going today, are you having fun?'

'Well we were, until you showed up,' said Henry.

'Oh come on, Henry, don't be like that. I've told you it doesn't suit you,' said Penelope.

'Oh doesn't it now?' said Henry. 'Well maybe you should go and tell that to crappy Crail instead, he's your new friend now isn't he? You spend enough time with him these days.'

'No, Henry, he is not. You're my best friend, and you always have been, remember?' said Penelope.

'Yeah, well you could've fooled me! Nobody ever sees you round here. Every day you go swanning off with him to Will knows where. You never do any lessons anymore. Special treatment all the time for you now, *Penelope*!' said Henry.

'Yeah, what is it that you do all day long anyway? What's so important?' said Danny.

'Nothing, it's just, well something that I am helping him out with, that's all,' said Penelope.

'Well if it's nothing important, why can't you tell us what it is then?' said Henry.

'I've already told you, Henry, I can't. They made me say so, otherwise....' said Penelope before she was interrupted by Henry.

'Ah, forget it anyway, Penelope. We've got better things to do, haven't we Danny?' he said.

'Yeah, come on, Henry, let's get back to training,' said Danny.

'No wait, there is something that I need to tell you Henry. Something that I've only just heard, right now coming back from...' said Penelope.

'Ah, save it for lover boy,' interrupted Henry. 'I'm sure he can't wait to hear all about it. Come on Danny, I'll race you to the end of the track.'

The two boys raced off towards the arena, leaving Penelope stood alone in the centre of the playing field.

She had been friends with Henry all of her life, and they had never fallen out before. Yes they'd had the odd disagreement over the years; which two friends hadn't? But this was different, it was as if he never wanted to be friends with her ever again, and it hurt. She wanted to tell him what she was doing but she knew that they wouldn't let her. She had never felt more alone than she did right now. She needed someone to talk to. She couldn't go to Florence because she was up in the mountains with the other second years and even if she could, Florence had also taken a bit of a dim view of her recent activities and they hadn't exactly spoken much over the last week as a result of it. She had always wanted a friend like Florence, and now that she had got one, it looked like she was probably going to lose her too.

She turned around and started to walk back to her cabin, when she saw Monty walking towards the boys' commorancies. He wasn't dressed in his training uniform, so she guessed he had probably told them that he was sick again and therefore had been excused from the lesson. Perhaps Monty would listen to her? Yes, there was something about Monty that appealed to her; even though everybody else thought that he was a little odd, she quite liked that about him. She liked the fact that he was a bit different.

She followed him back towards his room, and as she turned the corner she saw Monty go inside.

'Hi, Monty,' she said as she got to the door. It was still open.

Monty was sitting at the table, he was writing in his diary. He looked up as he heard Penelope's voice.

'Oh hi, Penelope, come in,' he said. 'I'm afraid Henry isn't here though, I think he is out training with the others.'

'Yes, I know, I've just seen him. Actually it wasn't Henry I came to see, it was you, Monty,' said Penelope as she walked towards the table.

Monty looked worried. 'Me, Penelope?' he said.

'Well, I just need a friend to talk to Monty, because it seems that everybody else has turned their back on me. You are the only person that is still speaking to me,' said Penelope as she sat down.

She then quickly realised that she hadn't put that quite as intended. 'Er, not that I wouldn't have came to you anyway, Monty, even if they were still talking to me. I mean, oh I didn't mean, oh, I don't know what I mean anymore, it's just all so horrible,' she added.

'It's ok, Penelope, you can talk to me anytime you like, I don't mind. In fact, nobody really talks to me either most of the time, so I guess we're both in the same boat. Why is Henry not talking to you anyway? You two are best friends normally. What's happened, have you fallen out?' said Monty.

'Oh, it's all gone wrong, Monty. Henry is not speaking to me because I was asked to, well, help out with something by Sananab and Cornelius Crail. I mean I never wanted to be chosen or anything, honest I didn't, but how can you say no to Sananab? Last week after the second history seminar it was. They urged me to help them with some, er, research and they made me swear not to tell anyone what it was all about, and so I didn't, and so now nobody will speak to me anymore because of it. But it's really important, Monty, what I'm helping them with. I mean, it's really, really important, otherwise I wouldn't be doing it, I just wouldn't.'

'Oh, I see,' said Monty. 'Well if those two have asked you then I suppose it must be important, and yes I don't suppose they would take too kindly to being refused. Can you not just explain to Henry about it, and tell him what they said?'

'Oh I've tried, Monty, but I can't get more than three words in before he just stops me in my tracks. And then he goes and runs off playing bulldog with Tom Sticks or Danny Cow or one of that lot. He doesn't want to listen to me; he's already made his mind up about it,' said Penelope glumly.

'Ah, that is a problem, Penelope, and Cornelius is such a brute to Henry all the time too. I've seen it myself. I suppose that doesn't help matters either,' said Monty.

'No, it doesn't. Oh what a mess, Monty, what a bloomin' mess!' said Penelope. She was almost in tears.

Monty Schmidt didn't have many friends. In fact two weeks ago, he didn't have any so he wasn't quite sure how to comfort one, especially a friend of the opposite sex who he happened to be quite fond of. This was a situation that was completely alien to him as he had never come across one before in his entire life. He nervously looked down at his book.

'What am I going to do, Monty?' added Penelope.

'Well I believe you, Penelope, and you can always talk to me about it if you want?' said Monty, comfortingly.

'Thanks, Monty. It means a great deal to have somebody to talk to. You have a good way of listening to people, not many boys have that I must say,' said Penelope. 'Anyway you must have been around Sananab and Cornelius and, er, your father too so you must have a good idea of what they can be like. More than most I'd bet.'

Monty looked up from his book. 'I don't like him, Penelope, Cornelius I mean. He's not very nice to anyone at all. And I don't really like Sananab either, he makes fun of Father a lot of the time, and I know he doesn't like it much but he just ignores it and carries on doing what he is told to. Yes it's true that Father and I don't really see eye to eye, but at the same time I don't really like seeing anybody made fun of; it's just not right. To be perfectly honest, any combination of the three of them can mean trouble for somebody that's for sure.'

'Well it's a combination of two that are making trouble for me at the moment, Monty,' said Penelope. She looked down at the table and stared at it for a minute when she suddenly had a thought. 'Monty?'

'Yes?'

'You must have been in your father's study at times when there have been conversations going on between Sananab and your father, or Cornelius and your father, or whoever else and your father, right?'

'Er, yes, Penelope, lots of times. I hide behind the table in the corner of the room and listen in sometimes,' said Monty.

'So you must have heard what they were saying at these meetings then, Monty?' said Penelope.

'Oh yes, sure, Penelope.'

'And were these meetings generally ones of importance, Monty?' asked Penelope.

'Er, yes I suppose so, Penelope,' said Monty. 'But Father and Sananab have been in office for years, ever since I can remember. There have been a lot of meetings, and a lot of conversations. Some more important than others, I guess. Why?'

'And can you remember any of these meetings directly, Monty? Or anything specifically mentioned during the conversations?' said Penelope getting a little excited.

'Well I haven't got the best of memories you see, Penelope, so I'm afraid I don't really remember much at all afterwards,' said Monty.

Penelope sighed. She was hoping that Monty could've given her some information about what Cornelius had said. She looked back at the table. Her disappointment didn't last long however and her hopes were suddenly raised again as Monty spoke once more.

'Which is why I write everything down you see, before I forget it,' he said pointing to his diary.

Penelope raised her head once more. She was suddenly fascinated as to what could be written inside the pages of this book.

'Do you mean to say that in that diary you have the transcripts of meetings and conversations between Sananab and your father and Cornelius, and Will knows who else?' she said.

'Yes,' said Monty. 'But probably not in this one, because I only started it last week, but certainly in my other diaries, yes, the ones which are now all completed. Well all except the previous one, I lost it you see before I had the chance to fill it in properly, they normally last me for a whole year.' He was overjoyed that somebody was actually showing interest in his diaries.

'Monty, have you ever heard of something called transference? I mean have you ever heard of somebody being transferred?' said Penelope hopefully.

'Transference, Penelope?' replied Monty. 'Isn't that just an old wives tale?'

'Well that's what I thought, Monty, but it was something that Cornelius said earlier you see, he said something like, 'It won't matter when we've all been transferred.' Now if it was anybody else saying it then I wouldn't even bat an eyelid but this is Cornelius Crail we are talking about, and I don't trust him one little bit, do you?'

'Well you've got a point there, Penelope, but I don't think it is possible surely? It's just a made up story, isn't it? A bit like the bogey man,' said Monty.

'Well maybe it is and maybe it isn't, Monty, but I for one want to find out. Can you have a look back through your diary to see if there is anything in there about transference?' said Penelope, eagerly.

'Well yes, Penelope, of course, but like I say I only started this one last week so there won't be anything in this one, because I have been here, haven't I? It would be in one of the others, if at all,' said Monty.

'Well where are the others kept, Monty? Do you have them here?'

'No I'm afraid not, Penelope, I can only just about carry one at a time as they're so big. The last one unfortunately got lost somewhere and I don't have a clue where that one is, and the others are all kept locked in Father's study, and only he has the key. He takes them away from me you see, and locks them away so I can't get to them again. The best bet would have been my last one, but like I say it got lost,' replied Monty.

Penelope remembered what had happened at the hearing. They'd actually had the diary in their hands. Henry had said that they should keep it, but she had disagreed with him and tossed it away. If only she would have listened to Henry. 'Aaaghh, Henry!' she said out loud.

Monty looked around to see if Henry had come in but there was nobody there. He was momentarily confused.

'So that's it then,' said Penelope. 'We'll never know unless we ask one of those two and I'm certainly not going to do that, am I?' She was sitting with her head in her hands, and her two elbows perched on the table.

'Well we may not have my diaries anymore, Penelope, but there may be another book which has that kind of information in it,' said Monty.

Penelope peeled her face out from underneath her hands. 'Yes?'

'The chronicles of Geffron Scolt. They might have it in, Penelope. If it were written anywhere it would be in those I bet.' Monty had a cheeky smile on his face.

'What, you know where the chronicles are, Monty?' said Penelope.

'Yes!' said Monty. He was now beaming. 'And I can take us there too.'

'Monty, are you saying that you know how to get to the chronicles of Geffron Scolt?'

'Yes, of course,' replied Monty.

'Well what are we waiting for? Let's go! I mean, where are they? I mean, if we can get there of course, I mean, oh my! Sorry I'm so excited,' said Penelope.

'They are in the Neocortex, deep in Central Head. But that is where Sananab and Cornelius will be so we can't go now otherwise we will be seen. We must go at night. We can go tonight if you like, Penelope?' said Monty.

'Yes definitely, tonight! Oh I'm so excited! I'm going to see these wonderful books, Monty. I'll meet you on the corner as soon as it gets dark, but not a word to Henry, ok?' said Penelope.

'Right, Penelope, not a word. I'll see you there. It shouldn't be too long before dark,' said Monty.

Penelope left the boys' cabins with a spring in her step, she decided to rush back to her room to get ready and wait. As she turned the corner of the accommodation blocks, she almost ran into Mr Pothackery who was coming the other way.

'Penelope, where are you going in such a rush? You almost knocked me over, my girl, and it's almost time to eat. Ah, perhaps there lies the answer to my question, I should've known,' he said.

'Er, sorry Mr Pothackery, got to rush!' she said as she continued past him.

Mr Pothackery waved to her as she went.

'Er, jolly good, enjoy your food, Penelope,' he said shaking his head. As he turned back he was greeted by the sight of the onrushing figure of Mr Adamson who was hurtling towards him with a piece of paper in his hand, he was waving it the air. 'Why is everyone in such a rush to eat tonight? It's not soup again, I hope,' he said.

'Mr Pothackery, Sir, Mr Pothackery, you've got to see this!' shouted Mr Adamson as he got nearer to him.

'Er, yes, what is it Mr Adamson? Not this evening's menu, I hope?'

'No, Sir, it's from Mr Schmidt, Sir. You must read it, Sir, look!' said Mr Adamson, as he handed him the piece of paper.

Mr Pothackery looked concerned as he started to read.

'It's from Mr Schmidt, Sir,' said Mr Adamson again. 'He says he's had word that there is an army, Sir, on its way here to Thalamus. He said they're going to attack us, Sir. There is a posse of bandits and they are on their way here to attack *us*, Sir. They think that Mr Schmidt is hiding here so they are going to try and get in, Sir. What are we going to do?'

'Oh my word, Jon, this is dreadful,' said Mr Pothackery as he continued to read aloud. 'This is a message from Leopold Augustus Schmidt to Charles William Pothackery. This is a code red seven message. I have received word that an army of bandits is to attack the province of Thalamus Bay. This attack will take place at night and the bandits will be arriving by boat. The precise time and which night is unknown to me, as yet, but it will be soon. You must alert the Security Council immediately and put them on full alert. I have word that they will not only attack the Security Council building, but they will also target the trials as well. You must gather any stewards who are able to carry a shield and hold a spear, and prepare them for an attack.

All trialists must be kept safely locked up inside their cabins, and any activities must be stopped immediately. This is a very serious threat and must not be taken lightly. I am currently on my way back to Thalamus as I write, but I am still a few days' sail away from you. I have sent the fastest messenger in The Will to bring you this letter. The last part of the journey is quicker on foot so I hope he will get there in time. I trust I will only be a few hours behind him at the most. Do all you can to defend Hippocampus, Charles. The future of the children is in your hands. These bandits are some of the worst criminals The Will has ever seen. Good luck, Charles, Leopold Schmidt.'

'Sir, what are we to do?' said Mr Adamson.

Mr Pothackery looked at the letter again. 'This is dated six days ago, Jon. They could arrive at any minute. Oh Will's teeth! Right, take this over to the Security Council building and show it to the General immediately. Ask him to send any spare soldiers they have over here, once they have secured their building. In the meantime, I shall go and round up all of the stewards and get the trialists locked in their cabins straight away. Or perhaps they should all be inside the hall? Yes, that's what we'll do. We'll lock them all in the hall together in one safe place. Oh Jon, this is dreadful. We must defend this camp with everything we've got, come on!'

The two min ran off towards the hall, as fast as they could manage.

Chapter Nineteen

The dim light of the early evening was casually making its way into Thalamus Bay, where dozens of scattered lanterns were starting to burn into the dusk. Two thirds of the blistering sun had already disappeared over the horizon, and the rest of it was following rapidly. The blood red river was shimmering gently underneath the magnificent golden bridge, and the sound of the waves could be heard rolling up against its banks.

About half a mile down river from the bay, was a boat. It was the same boat that had been hijacked only a week earlier at the Cut Throat Valley, but had since detoured via the Regio-Mentalis. It was now carrying some of the most vicious mercenaries The Will had ever seen, and hidden amongst them were three not-so-vicious, but very unwilling scallywags from the Luglands.

Mr Yanich came out of the indoor cabin and walked out onto the deck. He was accompanied by Chinner and Mr White. They filed up to the bow of the boat and looked out towards the bay area, which lay further upstream.

'By the looks of it, gentlemin, our beloved Security Council might have got word of our arrival. Look there,' he said pointing out towards the hill.

There was a line of armed soldiers all around the perimeter of the building and its grounds. Hundreds of min were standing guard.

'But how the hell did they get word, Yanich? Who could've known?' said Mr White.

'I don't know, Mr White, but somehow they have; that much seems all too clear. And that certainly puts plans to our element of surprise, doesn't it? Our cunning subterfuge may have to be rethought.'

'How do you mean, Yanich?' said Chinner.

'Well, Mr Chinner, we were going to use our three friends over there as a way in. Come up with a clever ruse of some kind to get us through the gates and inside the camp, but I'm afraid that may not be an option anymore,' said Mr Yanich.

'No mister, just Chinner,' said Chinner.

'Well there is always the old fashioned approach, Mr Yanich,' said Mr White helpfully.

'What's that, then?' said Chinner. 'Run up to 'em and smash 'em over the head with a spear?'

'Precisely, Mr Chinner,' said Mr White. 'It has never let me down yet.'

Mr Chinner had a smile on his face. 'No mister, just Chinner!' he said through a bloodthirsty grin.

'Well there's no other way for it. We shall wait here until the sun has completely set, gentlemin. Then, once we are ready, we shall sail up to the bay, jump out of the boat and charge them at full speed. Mr Chinner, you keep half of your min back as a secondary line of attack. Once me and my soldiers make the charge, you maintain a spear attack from the rear. Can your min throw that far?' said Mr Yanich.

'Oh yeah, don't you worry about that, Yanich, they can throw alright!' said Chinner.

'Good,' said Mr Yanich. He turned to his friend. 'Mr White, you take the rest of the army and head for Hippocampus. Take Mr Quick and his gang with you; they'll make light work of anything that stands in your way. Oh and, er, if our three friends from the Luglands happen to accidentally fall on a spear and drown in the river, then I wouldn't be too worried. It seems that they might have outlasted their purpose now anyway. It is a bit of a shame, however, as I was becoming rather fond of the tall chap, but I suppose there's no room for sentiment here.'

'I think I would have to fight Mr Quick for the privilege first,' said Mr White.

'Very well, let him have his day, but be sure that it doesn't get in the way of our main objective,' continued Mr Yanich. 'In the meantime, I am going to confront Mr Leopold Schmidt. But alas, however much pleasure we get from slaughtering the Security Council tonight, it still doesn't tell us the one thing which we came here to find out does it? Just what is going to happen to The Will in three years' time? We must find that out, Mr White, or our battle will be pointless. That knowledge is power my friend, and could well be used to our advantage later on. Under no circumstances must the Zamindar be killed, he must be kept alive so we can torture him until he tells us what we want to know. Is that clear?'

'As you wish, Mr Yanich, he will be spared,' said Mr White, 'but only him.'

'Yeah!' said Chinner, as he held his fist up to his chin.

'Prepare for battle, gentlemin, the night is closing in,' said Mr Yanich.

Sitting at the back of the boat, in amongst the ship's remaining cargo were Stony Pickles, Ollie Gimble and Raymond Curley. Stony was still very scared after what had happened to him at the hands of Zachary Quick. He was sitting with his hood up. The bleeding from his head wound seemed to be getting worse and there was blood on his hands where he had been trying to stem the flow from under his hood. Ollie and Curly were sitting opposite him.

'What do you think they're saying, Stony?' said Curley.

'I dunno, Curley, but I don't reckon it's about collecting flowers, do you? They keep looking over so they must be talking about us,' replied Stony.

'My mamma collects flowers, Stony,' said Ollie. 'She sometimes puts them in a book.'

'What? Flowers in a book?' said Curley, suddenly baffled by Ollie Gimble's latest revelation.

'Yeah, in a book. What's wrong with that?' said Ollie.

'Well nothing but they'll just get all squashed, won't they?' said Curley.

'Well I don't know, do I?' said Ollie. 'All I know is that she puts them in a book.'

'The world's gone mad,' said Curley shaking his head. 'What next? People will be putting stamps in a book or coins even?'

'Sorry to spoil the party but I think we've heard enough about books for a bloomin' lifetime, don't you, boys?' said Stony.

'Yeah, you're not wrong there, Stony,' conceded Curley.

'S'pose, Stony,' said Ollie.

Raymond Curley noticed the blood slowly trickling down the side of Stony's face. 'Are you alright, Stony? I reckon that bleeding is getting worse, you know?' he said with concern.

'Yeah, I'll be fine,' said Stony, trying to wipe the blood from his cheek. 'Now listen here, you two, I reckon the best thing that we can do now is the minute we get of this bloody boat, we all do a runner right?'

'Sounds good to me, Stony,' said Ollie.

'Yeah and me, like. These fellas look like they'd stick you on a butty for breakfast,' said Curley.

'What?' said Stony. 'A bloomin' butty, what are you on about, Curley?'

'Well I just meant that...'

'Oh never mind that now, we haven't got time,' interrupted Stony. 'Anyway, now I'm no expert in battle, right, although I reckon I could hold my own if it came down to it, like, but if you look up there on the top of that hill you can see at least a hundred soldiers with spears. You see 'em?'

The two min looked up at the hill.

'Now if there is a hundred soldiers standing on a hill with spears, that tells me that they are expecting something; and if they are expecting something then there's no way of surprising them, is there? And if there's no way of surprising them like Yanich wanted *us* to do, then there's not much bloody use for us in his little plan anymore, is there? So what do you reckon they'll have in store for us instead?'

'Er, I dunno,' said Curley worriedly.

'Well neither do I, Curley, but I don't particularly wanna stick around to find out, do you?' said Stony.

'Er, no, not really,' said Curley.

'No, not me neither, Stony. I wanna go home,' said Ollie.

'Yeah, I'll second that, Ollie,' said Curley. 'Probably should've stayed there in the first place.'

'Right, well I might have a bit of a plan there. Have you seen what's inside these bags here, boys?' said Stony, pointing to a stack of cargo he had been leaning against at the back of the boat. He slowly peeled back the top of one of the hessian sacks to reveal its contents. 'Sand, innit? And you know what sand does when it gets in your eyes?'

'You can't see anything when you've got sand in your eyes, Stony,' said Ollie. 'It makes you fall over.'

'Exactly, Ollie,' said Stony, pointing at his friend.

'Ah, I think I'm with you now, Stony,' said Curley. 'We throw some sand in their eyes and then we bleeding do one!'

'You're not a soft as you look you are you, Curley?' said Stony. 'That's exactly what were gonna do, and it might just give us enough time to make a run for it. Now it's getting darker by the minute, isn't it, so once were away from them they'll never find us, will they?'

'Yeah that's a good plan, Stony, I like that plan,' said Ollie.

'Right, then fill up your pockets with as much of this sand as you can boys but don't let them see you, for Will's sake. If Quick finds out were up to something he'll have our goolies dangling from them trees!' said Stony Pickles.

Raymond Curley and Ollie Gimble both winced in pain.

'Let's make sure we're ready, boys. I can't see them waiting much longer, it's nearly dark now.' With this, Stony Pickles emptied a handful of sand into his pocket. It wasn't as fine as it was when it came out of the bag, as it was getting clogged up with the blood from his hands.

Saturday 10th November, 11:23 p.m. Hippocampus, Central Head.

It was now pitch black at Hippocampus, and it was so dark that Penelope could hardly see further than end of her own nose. She managed to reach the corner of the boys' commorancies block where she had previously arranged to meet Monty.

She thought she would have had to secretly sneak past everyone through the camp so as not to be seen, but for some reason there was hardly anybody around at all. They all must have been tucked up in their beds, she thought.

Monty suddenly appeared from out of the darkness. 'Hello Penelope, are you ok?' he said.

'Ooh, Monty, you scared the hell out of me!' said Penelope, as she nearly jumped out of her skin.

'Sorry, Penelope, I didn't mean to, it's just so dark. Are you ready to go then?' said her friend.

'It's ok, Monty. Yes, of course I am. I can't wait to see the chronicles! How long will it take us to get there?'

'Oh not that long, I know a few short cuts. I've been finding my way around the corridors of the Neocortex ever since I can remember,' said Monty. 'It's not that far. Mind you, finding our way out of the camp in the dark won't be easy.'

'This is so exciting, Monty, we're actually going to see the chronicles of

201

Geffron Scolt. All of the information contained within those pages, all of that knowledge, it's going to be wonderful,' said Penelope enthusiastically. She looked around in the gloom and was still surprised by the lack of people, even at this time of night. 'I did think that there would have been a few more folk out and about tonight though, didn't you? It seems very quiet,' she added.

'Yes, it is quiet, Penelope. I haven't seen Henry since he went up to training, he must be with Danny Cow again, he seems to spend a lot of time with him,' said Monty.

'Yes, well, they're a perfect match, aren't they? Anyway, I don't suppose we've got time to stand around here all night talking, have we, Monty?' said Penelope. 'Come on let's get going before somebody sees us.'

'Yeah I suppose you're right. Come on then, this way,' said Monty as he started to walk. He was suddenly stopped in his tracks when Penelope pulled him back towards the wall.

'Quick, Monty, someone's coming,' she said.

A trial steward came running out of the darkness at full speed. He sped past them and headed towards Fornix Hall.

'Who was that?' said Monty, after he had gone.

'I don't know, it must have been a steward I suppose,' replied Penelope.

'Jeez, he nearly knocked me over,' said Monty.

'Yeah, but I don't think he saw us, that's the main thing,' said Penelope. 'Come on! Let's get going before he comes back.'

The two friends ran off towards Central Head.

The steward made his way into Fornix Hall where a few members of the Security Council were standing guard at the entrance. All of the trialists had been told to make their way there immediately by Mr Pothackery and his staff, and everyone had obeyed. Everyone except for Monty and Penelope, although amongst the initial excitement and general confusion, their absence had not been noticed.

The children were getting restless. Some of them were excited and some of them were scared; but they were all together and in one place which meant that Mr Pothackery could protect them.

Henry Grip stood up from the centre of the group.

'Sir, just what the hell is going on? One minute we're out on the mountain training, and the next minute we're all dragged in here. What's happening?' he said.

'Yeah, if something is up, Sir, then we've got a right to know,' said Danny Cow.

'Ok, ok, calm down, trialists, and I will let you know what is happening,' said Mr Pothackery calmly. 'Now I need you all to be strong and courageous tonight, my friends, for I have something rather concerning to tell you.'

The trialists looked at each other, worried.

'I'm afraid that we have received some terrible news, trialists, and I don't really know how to put this in any other way but to come right out and say it. We are about to come under attack. Right now, there is an army of bandits who are about to try to invade the camp. We believe that the attack will take place this very evening, and we must do everything we can to defend ourselves,' continued Mr Pothackery.

The children gasped in horror at the news.

'Yes, this is very grave news indeed, trialists, which is why I have gathered you all here. You must all stay here inside the hall, for it is the safest place on the camp for now. You will be guarded by Security Council personnel who will be posted around the perimeter of the hall and there is no way that any bandit will get even close to here. You will be completely safe here, trialists, I will make sure of that.

These bandits threaten the very core of what we believe in; everything that is good and honourable about the trials and we must not let them succeed in damaging anything inside this camp. This is our home, and we will defend it with everything that we have got.'

Henry stood up again.

'Sir, if the camp is under threat then I want to help defend it. I want to fight,' he said.

'Yeah, so do I,' said Danny Cow.

'Yeah, and me,' said Angus Murphy.

A chorus of approval rushed around the young group of trialists even though most of them were surprised that Angus did not just want to go to the toilet again.

'As much as your enthusiasm for the fight is very much appreciated, trialists, I'm afraid it is out of the question. It is far too dangerous. It is my duty to keep you all safe, and that is exactly what I shall do. You are to stay inside this hall and you are not to go anywhere unless I specifically tell you to, is that clear?'

'But, Sir, we all want to...,' said Henry.

'No buts, Henry, you will do as I say,' said Mr Pothackery.

'Yes, Sir,' said Henry reluctantly.

The rest of the children started to talk amongst themselves. They were frightened and scared. None of them had ever been in a situation like this before.

'Now we must be strong, trialists. Stay with your friends and keep each other safe. For now, we must wait,' said Mr Pothackery. There was a feeling of deep concern etched on his face.

Saturday 10th November, 11:41 p.m. Carotid Artery River.

The hijacked boat containing the bandits was already heading upstream towards Thalamus Bay. Mr Yanich and his band of cutthroats were poised for an attack.

Chapter Twenty

Monty and Penelope had entered the offices of Central Head, and were heading towards the restricted section of the Neocortex. Nobody was allowed in there except for Sananab and the few Head-workers that he kept close. Usually Leopold Schmidt would have been constantly at his side, but as the Zamindar was occupied elsewhere, the Master's personal guards were the next best thing. Two of them were standing at the entrance to the restricted corridor.

'How are we going to get past those guards, Monty?' whispered Penelope.

She and Monty were peering out from behind a concealed corner of the adjacent corridor.

'To tell you the truth, I'm not really sure, Penelope.'

'Well we'll have to think of something, Monty, otherwise we'll never get through. Where are the chronicles kept anyway? Are they somewhere down that corridor? I know that's where Sananab's office is and Mr Schmidt's too, but I've never been further than the Lobe Room. Even though I've never been allowed inside it,' said Penelope.

'Yes, it's past the Lobe Room, Penelope. Right down towards the end of the corridor. There is a bridge we have to go across, and then there is an enormous room on the other side called the Corpus Callosum. That's where all the important stuff is usually kept, and that is where the chronicles are,' said Monty.

'Well how are we going to get in there without those two seeing us?' said Penelope.

'We could try a diversion of some kind? I don't know, maybe throw something to make a noise so they go and investigate?' said Monty.

'Do you really think that they would fall for that old chestnut, Monty?' said Penelope. 'Are they really that dumb? They would've had to have come from the 'I'm so stupid that I'd fall the bloomin' obvious' school of guarding to swallow that one.'

'Well it's worth a try, I suppose. Can't do any harm, can it?' said Monty.

'It could do plenty of harm, Monty. Especially if they catch us doing it, then there would be a distinct possibility that they could do plenty of harm to us!' replied Penelope, somewhat sarcastically.

'Well I don't know what else to suggest, Penelope,' said Monty.

'Well neither do I, so I suppose we'll have to try it,' conceded Penelope. 'What can we throw then?'

'Er, I've got some sweets,' said Monty, helpfully.

'Sweets! We're not bloomin' Hansel and Gretel, Monty. Haven't you got anything else?' said Penelope.

'Hansel and who?'

'Oh never mind,' said Penelope. 'I suppose they'll have to do. Here, hand them over.'

Penelope held out her hand as Monty gave her the bag of sweets. She emptied half of them out of the bag and threw them down the corridor.

The two guards immediately heard the noise of the sweets skittling across the polished floor. One of them gestured to the other to go and investigate, and he duly obeyed.

Monty and Penelope stayed hidden from view.

The investigative guard picked up one of the sweets and immediately realised what it was. Any type of food to most min was something which could not be passed up; no matter what the situation. Sweets were also seen as a bit of a luxury item, as they were something other than the staple diet of sandwiches.

'Hey, these are sweets, Bobby! Kola cubes, if I'm not mistaken,' said the guard.

His friend immediately left his post and ran towards the scattered confectionary.

'Kola cubes, Yerse! That'll do me Eddie!' he said as he frantically tried to gather up anything that the other guard had missed.

Monty and Penelope scurried out from their hiding place and ran along the corridor while the guards were busy picking the sweets up from the floor. Monty keyed in the security code on the keypad mounted on the wall, and they made their way through the now open doorway into the forbidden corridor of the Neocortex. When they were out of earshot they stopped outside the Lobe Room.

'I can't believe they fell for that, Monty. Are they stupid or what?' said Penelope.

'You did save some though, didn't you Penelope? I mean you didn't throw them all away, did you?' said Monty. 'I am very fond of a kola cube.'

Penelope opened her hand to reveal the few sticky sweets that were left. 'Of course I didn't, Monty, what do you take me for?' she said.

'Oh good,' said Monty with a smile. He took a sweet from Penelope's hand and popped it into his mouth.

Penelope looked up to see the Lobe Room in front of her. 'This is the Lobe Room isn't it, Monty? This is where it all happens; this is where all the decisions are made. I wonder what is going on inside there right now?' she said curiously.

Just as Penelope had finished speaking, the huge door knob of the Lobe Room door began to turn, and a tall thin slither of light appeared as the door started to open from the other side.

'Quick, Loppy, we have to go! Somebody's coming!' said Monty. He grabbed Penelope by her skirt and they ran off towards the bridge at the end of the corridor. They managed to get on it without being seen.

As they were halfway across, Penelope stopped and turned to Monty. 'Did you just call me Loppy, Monty?'

'Er, I'm not really sure, did I?' said Monty. 'I didn't mean to offend you or anything, I mean I know Henry calls you that and I didn't want to seem too familiar or anything...'

'It's ok, Monty, I like it,' interrupted Penelope. 'But don't overdo it.' She was smiling.

Monty smiled back at her. There was a sparkle in his eyes that had never been there before. He was happy. 'Ok, Loppy,' he said.

They continued along the bridge until they reached the other side and there it was waiting for them, the door to the Corpus Callosum.

'This is it, Penelope, this is where the chronicles are kept. This is the Corpus Callosum,' said Monty. 'Come on let's get inside before those guards come back!'

They opened the huge door and went inside.

This place was different, somehow unequalled. It was as if this room had been conceived in an altogether separate age. Penelope had never come across a place like this anywhere before. It seemed old, even older than The Will itself, if that were at all possible. It was as if the walls themselves had memories. It was as if they had once lived.

She expected there to be books, hundreds of books, thousands even, but in truth there were not that many. There were some, yes, but not anywhere near as many as there were back in her cabin at Hippocampus. She was somewhat disappointed by this, but at the same time excited about actually being there.

'I never expected it to be like this, Monty. Somehow I thought it would be, well, different,' said Penelope as she gazed around the room.

'What did you expect, Penelope?'

'Er, I don't know, Monty. I'm not really sure, just different I suppose, less empty. I thought there would have been more books here for a start,' she replied.

'Yes, I did think that too when I first came in here, years ago. There used to be more, but Father said that Sananab had them moved to his own office. That is why most of the shelves are empty,' said Monty. 'In fact, he also took some of the furniture from here too; his desk and his chair came from in here. He even took the door and had it swapped for a different one, nobody knows why. Some say he took all of the feelings out of place. I'm not really sure what they mean by that but it does seem rather empty now, doesn't it?'

'Yes, it does. But why do you think he did that? Why didn't he just use this room as his office?' said Penelope.

'I don't really know, Penelope. Perhaps he didn't like the room but still wanted all of the contents for himself?'

'Yeah, perhaps he just wanted all of that knowledge for himself too, Monty?' said Penelope. 'To use it against people, to manipulate folk.'

'Maybe, but he didn't take the chronicles though, Penelope, they are still here.' Monty walked over to a large cupboard standing alone against the wall, looming high above his head. He opened the two doors towards himself and there on the shelves inside were the twelve volumes of the chronicles of Geffron Scolt, filed in consecutive order. 'Here they are, all twelve of them.'

Penelope walked over to the cupboard and ran her hand along the edge of the books. They too were old, the bindings were worn and aged, and there were markings and symbols on the spines that she couldn't make out. But they were magnificent all the same. She felt privileged just to be able to touch them.

'Wow, this is incredible, Monty, but twelve of them? I didn't know there would be so many, where do we start?' she said.

'I don't know. At the beginning, I suppose?' offered Monty.

'We'll never get through all of that information, Monty. It'll take us weeks to read even half of them.'

'Well we've got to start somewhere, I guess, Penelope,' replied the boy.

Penelope agreed. 'Ok, we'll have to do our best in the time we've got. You take the first half and I'll take the second. Here, help me get them to that table over there. We are just going to have to scan through them as best we can. Look for anything that talks about instinct, or transference, or anything like that. Any mention of either of those words should tell us something about what Sananab and Cornelius are trying to do. It's got to be in here somewhere, Monty; it's just got to be.'

'Ok, Penelope, but we'll have to be quick. It won't be long until those guards get through my kola cubes!' said Monty.

Penelope laughed. She now felt completely comfortable with Monty, even though there was the distinct possibility that they could be caught at any minute. They took the chronicles from the cupboard and placed them on the table. They both began to read.

Penelope flicked through the first book. 'It looks like these are all about the Tri-min, Monty. Everything that Mr Pothackery said is true, it's all in here. Everything from the formation of The Will to the trimesters, everything is here just like he said.'

'Yeah, and this one too, Penelope. Wow, it really is interesting stuff, isn't it?' said Monty.

'Is there anything about transference in yours, Monty?' said Penelope.

'No, not yet.'

'No, me neither,' said Penelope, as she put down the first volume and picked up the next.

Monty did the same with his. He picked up another from the bottom of the pile and started to flick through it.

'Wait a minute, Penelope, I think I've found something here, look,' he said pointing to a page.

Penelope dropped her book and leaned closer to Monty.

'Oh yeah, Monty, I think this could be it,' she began to read aloud from the book. 'When the work of the Tri-min is complete, the end of the third trimester must facilitate the transference of time. The world which is to be known as 'The Will' shall come into being on the first day of the first month of the first year and the world of the Tri-min shall cease to be.

To sustain the creation of the new world, the Tri-min must first aid the creation of a paradox, which shall forever be known as 'instinct'. This is the window which will allow the transference to take place. The window can only remain open for one thousandth of a second after an instinct occurs then it will shut forever. Instinct is irreversible and can never be undone. The Tri-min shall make way for the birth of The Min; who shall exist to serve The Will.'

Penelope turned to Monty. 'That's what they must be trying to do Monty, they're trying to transfer. Don't you see? It says here that there is a window, of a thousandth of a second after an instinct takes place, which will allow transference to happen. That's what they're looking for, that window of opportunity.'

'But why, Penelope, why would they want to transfer?' said Monty.

'Well, because Sananab told me that something bad is going to happen, in three years time. He said that The Will is going to die.'

'What?' said Monty. He was flabbergasted.

'Oh yeah, sorry, you didn't know, did you? Because I never told you, did I? Sorry, yeah, The Will is going to die, with everyone in it,' said Penelope, quite matter-of-factly.

'No, you didn't, Penelope! What do you mean The Will is going to die?' There was more than a hint of panic in his voice.

'Well, that's why I'm helping them you see; to try and change The Will,' said Penelope.

This was even more of a revelation to Monty. 'What? Change The Will. W... w... w... what are you talking about, Penelope, that's just not possible?'

'Well it is possible because Sananab told me he's already done it, but anyway, Monty, I don't believe them for one minute. You see Cornelius mentioned something about transference to me on the way back today which got me thinking. And now that I've read this about instinct in the chronicles, then I think I know what they're really up to. I'm convinced that instead of me helping them to change The Will like they say I am, they actually want to transfer out of The Will. And if it really is going to die in three years time, like they say it is, then I reckon that's what they want. They want out! Just like it says here, and it looks like they're going to leave us all behind to face the music.'

'And The Will does play a wonderful tune, Penelope, don't you think?' said Sananab as he slammed the door shut.

Monty and Penelope turned round to see Sananab, Cornelius Crail, and the two guards standing next to the door. They both gasped in horror.

'Guards, seize them!' cried Sananab.

The two guards ran over to the teenagers and grabbed them by their arms.

'Cornelius, put her in that chair,' said Sananab, 'and make sure she doesn't move. In fact, tie her down. We might be here for some time.'

'Certainly, Sir, but what about him?' said Cornelius pointing to Monty.

'Let him go, Cornelius, he is of no use to us,' said Sananab.

'But, Sir, what if he speaks to someone?'

'Nobody will believe the ramblings of a pathetic bookworm who hardly says a word to anyone, Cornelius, let him go,' replied his Master.

'As you wish, Sir.' Cornelius grabbed hold of Monty by his collar and threw him out of the room. Monty sped off along the corridor and out of sight.

'Monty, you've got to get help, find Henry and Mr Pothackery!' shouted Penelope from the chair.

'Help, ha, ha! I'm afraid there's not going to be anyone helping you now, Miss Potts. Besides, Mr Pothackery and your little friend might be a little preoccupied with other things at the moment. I've arranged for a little visit to take place at Hippocampus tonight; they're going to need all the help they can get for themselves,' said Sananab.

Cornelius looked immediately confused. 'What visit is this, Sir?' he said.

'Oh I put into place a certain chain of events a little while ago which will culminate in a few hundred bloodthirsty villains trying to take over the camp tonight. But don't you worry, by the time they've finished killing each other we shall be long gone, Cornelius. Far away from this world.'

'Ah, I see, Sir, so we go tonight, that is excellent news! It's about time we left this crummy place behind. But I would have loved to have been there to see Henry Grip bite the dust,' said Cornelius.

'You leave Henry alone, you little worm!' shouted Penelope in his ear.

Cornelius tugged harder on one of the ropes binding Penelope's arms to the chair. Penelope winced with pain as they started to press into her skin.

'Guards, wait outside and do not let anybody into this room, do you hear me?' said Sananab.

'Yes, Sir,' said the first guard. They both walked out of the room and shut the door behind them.

'Now, Miss Potts, you are indeed a very intelligent young lady,' said Sananab. 'I never doubted for one second that you were unerringly astute, but to work out everything about our impending transference merely from reading the chronicles is indeed inspiring. Even if it seems you had a bit of help from Cornelius' unfortunate slip of the tongue.'

Cornelius cowered behind the chair.

'But no matter, what's done is done, and we cannot change things now can we?' Sananab continued. 'But what you haven't quite realised yet, Miss Potts, is that Cornelius and I are not the only ones who will be privileged enough to attain transference from The Will this very night. Oh no, the first to achieve that particular honour will be a certain pretty little girl from The Luglands.'

Penelope started to scream as she realised what was happening. 'No, no! You can't, no you can't do it!'

'Oh but we can, Penelope Potts, and we will,' said Sananab. He walked over to the side of the room and ran his fingers along one of the empty shelves. 'This room was once filled with memories, more complex than we ever could have imagined. Thoughts so intricate that no ordinary min could ever have come up with, not in their wildest dreams. This is where all of the wisdom was stored, the knowledge which the Tri-min so dutifully handed down to us. The information contained within these memories seeped out from the books and manuscripts in which they were stored, and made its way out into the very core of the room. It flowed into the shelves, into the floor, into the ceiling and the door, even into the walls themselves. That is why I had it all moved, so I could be surrounded by it at all times; to absorb its power.

All except for the chronicles, of course, which can never be removed from this room. They belong here you see, they have been here for so long. They are a source of life for The Will itself; they are a vital part of the clock which makes it tick. Just to be in their presence, just to stand in this room changes people's thoughts. It makes them think differently, and no one can fight it. Think, Penelope, think of everything that you have ever loved being ripped away from you in an instant, think bad, bad things, Penelope. Think bad, bad thoughts. You want to kill me, yes, think of revenge, think of hate. Turn your thoughts to the dark.'

He walked over to the chair and placed his hand on the top of her hair, and pressed his skeletal fingers hard into her head. He clicked the fingers on his other hand and held it in the air. 'Now it begins!'

Penelope was struggling violently to try and free herself from the chair, but she didn't stand a chance, the ropes were tied tightly around her arms and legs. 'Aaaghh, let me out, let me go, I say! You'll never get away with this!'

'That's it Penelope, fight it, fight it as much as you can. That's what I need to open the window. Let your thoughts fight the very thoughts of The Will. Let its instinct take over you!'

Penelope looked up to see that there were hundreds of letters, words, numbers and symbols starting to form in the air. They were coming out from the empty shelves around the walls, and circling around the room. Above the chair, her own thoughts and memories were visibly leaving her head, flowing through Sananab's fingers and mixing with the other thoughts circling the room, the thoughts of The Will. She started to feel a pain hammering inside her head.

'Aaaghh, stop it, stop it now!' she cried.

'It's working, it's working. Do you see, Cornelius?' said Sananab eagerly.

His eyes were lit up with excitement as the thoughts and memories were glowing bright blue and white as they were spinning around the room.

Cornelius stood there watching. He had never seen anything like this before in his life, he didn't quite know what to do.

Chapter Twenty-One

Sunday 11th November, 12:17 a.m. Carotid Hill, Mount Thalamus Bay.

Mr Yanich was standing at the side of the boat, with half of the assembled army waiting behind him.

'Are the first of your min ready, Mr Chinner?' he said.

'Ready and waiting for your command, Yanich. And there's no mister, just Chinner,' said Chinner.

'Then you know what to do. Tonight we fight until the death. Min, are you ready to fight?' asked Mr Yanich, as he turned to the hundred soldiers directly behind him.

'Ready!' came the cry.

'Then we charge!' With this, Mr Yanich jumped off the boat with his spear in hand and ran up the hill towards the Security Council building. The soldiers leapt off the boat and followed him. Each brandishing their weapons, holding them above their heads as they ran. They were shouting and whooping as they went. The first attack was underway.

As soon as the first wave of attack had left the boat, the rest of the bloodthirsty bandits from the Regio-Mentalis stood waiting for their instructions. Chinner was in charge. 'Spears at the ready!' he shouted.

'Ready!' came the instant reply.

'Then attack, attack, attack!' shouted Chinner. The soldiers jumped off the boat, ran down to the foot of the hill and started to throw their spears, over the heads of the onrushing first wave, and on towards the Central Head soldiers who were defending the Security Council building at the top of the hill. Two prongs of the attack were already in place, which left only one remaining faction.

'Are your soldiers ready, Mr Quick?' said Mr White.

'Oh yes, we are ready alright. Only I have a rather uncomfortable itch that I wish to scratch before we move; I feel it will aid my performance in battle,' said Mr Quick. He took his knife out of its scabbard and pointed it at Stony Pickles.

'Ha, you do have a way with words, Mr Quick. Nevertheless, if you must kill them then you had better do it quick, we need to make our attack on the camp straight away. Ha! You had better do it quick, I said, oh the irony!' said Mr White, laughing to himself.

Stony Pickles, Raymond Curley and Ollie Gimble were standing at the rear of the boat. They each had a pocket full of sand ready and the adrenalin was pumping through their bodies.

Mr Quick and the rest of his gang slowly walked over to them; they each had their knives at the ready.

'Get ready, boys,' whispered a weary Stony Pickles to the other two. His wound was now taking its toll on him. He could only just about focus on what was directly in front of him, and his eyes were starting to shut by themselves. He was beginning to feel extremely weak.

'Now I am going to take great pleasure in killing you,' said Mr Quick. He pulled back his knife and was just about to thrust it into the chest of Stony Pickles when suddenly the shout came.

'Now, boys, now!' managed Stony.

The three friends from the Luglands immediately pulled out the handfuls of sand from each of their pockets and threw it into the eyes of the bandits standing in front of them. The bandits dropped their knives on to the deck of the boat as they tried to wipe the sand from their eyes.

'Aaaghh, its burning my eyes, I can't see!' said Mr Quick. He was jumping around, and frantically scratching his eyes.

'Right, let's do one!' shouted Stony.

They started to run towards the side of the boat. Raymond Curley picked up some of the bandits' discarded knives from the deck as he ran past them and threw them over the side into the water. They all jumped off the boat and onto the riverbank.

Mr White started to follow them with some of the bandits who were still trying to wipe the sand from their eyes.

'We can't let them get away,' he said. 'Come on, after them!'

As the three friends landed on the grass, Stony Pickles collapsed in a heap on the ground. His injury had finally caught up with him. He lay there motionless, not saying a word.

'Stony, come on we've got to run. They're gonna catch us!' said Curley.

'Yeah, Stony, we've got to run, like you said,' added Ollie.

Stony did not answer them. His two friends ran back to where he was lying. They tried to help him up, but his limp body just flopped back down to the ground below. Curley pulled back his hood. There was a mass of blood from his head wound, and it had covered the inside of his hood. His hair too was a clotted mass of red.

'Oh shit! Ollie, I don't believe it, look I think he's... No, he can't be, can he? Stony, Stony, wake up!' said Curley as he shook the body. There was no response from Stony. His eyes were closed.

'What do you mean, Curley, he can't be what?' said Ollie.

'Ollie, all that blood, I think he's...'

'Oh bloody hell, Curley! No, don't say that, what are we gonna do?' cried Ollie.

After a few seconds, Curley looked up from his friend and then looked angrily towards Mr Quick and the bandits who were still on the boat. He stood next to Ollie. 'It was him, Ollie, that bloody Quick. The other day on

213

the boat, when he grabbed Stony, and got him by the cabin. It was him, Ollie, it was him, he killed our friend.'

'Why, Curley? I mean, why? It's not fair, he never even done nothing to Mr Quick,' said Ollie.

'Well I don't know about you, Ollie, but I've have just about enough of him. And I'm going to bloody-well do something about it. Let's just see how hard he is without his knife!' said Curley angrily.

Ollie Gimble stood there, his face turned from its usual mellow appearance, to one of concentrated anger. 'Me too, Curley! He's killed my friend and my mamma says it's not good to kill folk, so I'm gonna bloody batter him, Curley! I'm gonna batter them all!' His giant fists were clenched with rage.

Mr White was the first to reach the min mountain that was Ollie Gimble. It has to be said that he wasn't exactly expecting his battle to end there and then. He was hoping to get a lot further than the edge of the riverbank, even if he was destined to die in battle. The last thing to go through his mind before Ollie's giant fist *actually* did go through his mind was, 'I do think that this chap looks rather angrier than he did a moment ago, perhaps someone ought to have a word'. His body slapped into the water as he fell.

'Right, who's next, then?' shouted Ollie to the rest of the group.

The bandits ran towards the giant figure one by one, and it was only as they got closer to him that they realised that this probably was not the greatest idea that they had ever had. It also turned out to be the last idea that they had ever had. He swatted each of them away as if they were part of a swarm of annoying flies. Their helpless bodies soared like missiles as they flew off the end of his fists, first to the left and then to the right. They were still not entirely sure what had hit them, but they assumed that it must have been something hard as they landed twenty feet away in the river.

'Go 'ed, Ollie! You show 'em, lad!' shouted Curley. He was punching the air in front of him as each of the bandits collided with one of Ollie's fists.

Mr Quick was the last of the Oesophagus Forest bandits left on the boat, the rest of them were now floating face down in the river. He was standing there looking somewhat naked without his knife. He looked down to the deck of the boat, frantically searching for a blade. There was nothing there. Curley had thrown them all over board.

The usual expression of menacing arrogance etched on the face of Zachary Quick suddenly disappeared. Firstly because he didn't have any back up and secondly because he didn't have his weapon.

'Not as hard without your knives, are you, Quick, eh?' said Curley. 'Or your friends! Well I think we're just gonna have to do this the old fashioned way, aren't we?' Curley walked back on to the boat. 'You can leave this fella to me, Ollie. This is for my mate Stony!'

Curley shot out a punch with his right hand. It connected perfectly with the face of Mr Quick. He fought back immediately and they started to trade punches. They battled on moving around the boat. The fight continued as each of them battled to try to get the upper hand. It was tough, they were very evenly matched. Nothing could separate them. Eventually they ended up in the corner of the boat where the sandbags were. Mr Quick tried to grab a handful of sand to throw into the face of Curley, returning the favour of earlier on. He missed with his throw but as he let the handful of sand go, Curley punched him square on the end of his nose and knocked him to the deck.

He lay there without moving, he was out cold.

'See! Can't fight without your knife, can you? Bloody coward,' said Curley as he turned to walk.

Mr Quick opened his eyes, still lying on the deck. He could see that stuck between two sand bags was a knife. It was one of the knives the bandits had earlier dropped. It had been kicked towards the end of the boat in the confusion.

He reached out, picked up the knife, and silently stood up on the deck.

'Curley, watch out, he's got a knife!' shouted Ollie who was watching from the bank.

Curley turned around to see Mr Quick coming at him with the knife. He had it in his hand ready to thrust. Curley quickly turned and ran towards the other end of the boat, and as he reached the side he jumped off on to the grass bank.

Mr Quick came running behind him but as he got towards the edge, his foot became caught in a rope and he tripped and flew off the side of the boat. With his foot tangled in the rope, he was somehow catapulted up into the air and across towards the bank. As he looked up, he was extremely surprised to see the face of Ollie Gimble, turned slightly to one side with his teeth gritted. He was also extremely surprised to see that directly beside the face of Ollie Gimble was the clenched fist of Ollie Gimble, moving at lightning speed towards his head.

'Aaaghh!' That was the last thing he said.

Ollie's fist cracked him so hard that he flew back towards the river. The rope that was tied around his foot snapped in two, and he went spiralling off into the water.

'That was for my mate, Stony!' said Ollie. He turned towards the rest of the mercenaries from the Regio-Mentalis still throwing spears towards the Security Council. 'Right then, form an orderly queue, and I'll deal with you one at time. Or two at a time, or three, or however many you want. My mamma says it's not good to hurt people, so I'm gonna bloomin' well batter the lot of you!'

'Blimey, Ollie, you're not seriously gonna take all of them on, are you?' said Curley.

'Yeah, Curley, I am. It's because of them that my mate Stony is killed. And that's not fair coz he never done nothing to any of them, so I'm not leaving until they're all gone! Are you with me?'

'Oh, ok then, fair enough. In for a penny, in for a pound, I suppose,' said Curley as he got ready to fight.

Ollie looked at him curiously. 'I haven't got any money though, Curley,' he said as he smacked the first soldier into the river.

'Ha, don't worry, Ollie, neither have I,' said Curley as he threw his first punch.

Sunday 11th November, 12:24 a.m. Fornix Hall, Hippocampus.

The young trialists were glued to the windows of Fornix Hall watching the battle unfolding outside. The Security Council building was not far from the hall and they could see everything played out in full view.

'Trialists, you must come away from the windows. You could be injured if any of them to go through. How many times do I have to tell you?' said Mr Pothackery. He was running up and down the hall shepherding children back to the centre of the room.

'But, Sir this is amazing,' said Henry Grip. 'I've never seen anything like this before, especially where I come from!'

'It's not amazing, Henry, it's very worrying. Not to mention extremely dangerous, now do as I say,' said Mr Pothackery.

Henry completely ignored him.

'Sir, I think they're getting closer to us now as well,' said Danny Cow. He too was standing and looking out of a window.

'Well all the more reason to come away from the window then, Danny,' said Mr Pothackery. 'Come on, I really must insist on it, trialists. To the centre of the room immediately, it's for your own safety.'

All of a sudden there was a loud banging coming from outside. Someone was trying to get into the hall. Everyone looked towards Mr Pothackery to see what they should do next.

'Don't worry, trialists. There are Security Council personnel positioned around the perimeter of this building, nobody will get inside here. That I can assure you of,' he said, confidently.

Just as he finished speaking, the door flew open and everyone gasped with fear. Leopold Schmidt came marching into the hall towards the trialists.

'So the rabble has already started its assault, Charles. I trust none of the scum have reached the camp yet?' he said.

'Oh, Mr Schmidt, Sir, what a relief. It is so good to see you,' said Mr Pothackery. 'Thank The Will you're ok, Sir, and finally here. We did everything you asked of us, to the letter.'

'Ah, so you got my note then, Charles, good. Yes, I'm ok. I'll be a lot happier when we have rounded up all of these bandits though, my friend. They'll be spending the rest of their lives in the Stomachic Sea when we're through with them. If they make it there alive, that is,' said Leopold Schmidt.

'Sir, we're so glad you're here to protect us. What do you want us to do now?' said Mr Pothackery.

The Zamindar walked over to the window and looked out towards the Security Council building. The battle was in full swing and could be seen quite clearly from the hall.

'I want you to stay here, Charles, and keep the children locked inside with you. It will be safe in here, my soldiers are outside standing guard, and nobody will get through them, believe me. I am going to go and fight, Charles; we shall put an end to this insurgence swiftly. They are no match for the Security Council,' he said confidently.

Henry was still at the window. 'Sir, I could be mistaken but if looks to me as if some of them are fighting amongst themselves, look.' He pointed down towards the riverbank.

There was a huge figure standing with his fists clenched and held up in the air, surrounded by dozens of spear-wielding bandits. There was a smaller min standing beside him, or rather hiding slightly behind him out of harm's way, and he seemed to be shouting instructions to the other one whilst punching the air. The bigger one was picking up the bandits by the throat with his left hand, throwing them gently up into the air and then punching them into the river with his right hand. The smaller min was cheering wildly every time one of the bandits splashed into the water. From as far away as the hall was from the river, the two min seemed to be having an awfully enjoyable time.

A few of the trialists ran over to the window to see. It was incredible viewing.

'Fighting amongst themselves? Yes, that doesn't surprise me,' said the Zamindar. 'Well it seems that we don't have to worry about that particular faction anymore. Well spotted, young trialist, well done indeed.'

'Thank you, Sir,' said Henry through gritted teeth.

As much as he enjoyed the praise from someone as powerful as Mr Schmidt, he was also the one responsible for sending his father away, and he wasn't about to forgive him in a hurry.

'Our trialists are the cream of the crop as usual, Mr Pothackery. I trust that they are all present and accounted for?' said the Zamindar. He began to look around to see where Monty was, he was scanning the room for his son.

'Er, yes, Sir, I think everyone is here?' said Mr Pothackery. 'We collected everyone directly from their training session. They came straight from the mountain into the hall, Sir.' He too was scanning the room for Monty, and was starting to get a little concerned that he couldn't see him.

'And, Monty, where is Monty, Charles?' said the Zamindar. 'I can't see him. Charles, where is my son?'

'Erm, well I am sure he was here a minute ago, Sir,' said Mr Pothackery anxiously.

Everybody else in the room started looking around at each other. Monty was nowhere to be seen, and their concern was mounting.

'Charles, where the hell is my son?' said the Zamindar angrily.

Mr Pothackery turned to Henry, he was now extremely worried. 'Henry is his roommate, Sir. Er, Henry, have you seen Monty? Was he in his cabin this morning?'

Henry was also looking around the room, and he couldn't see Monty either. But he quickly realised there was somebody who else who was missing too. 'Sir, where is Penelope?' he said.

Mr Pothackery looked around frantically. 'Oh my word, Monty and Penelope are both missing. And on a night like this? Oh this is terrible! What are we going to do, Sir?'

The Zamindar walked over to Mr Pothackery and looked at him straight in the eye.

'Are you telling me that you have allowed two children to go missing while there are villainous bandits baying for blood out there? And one of them is my only son!' he shouted angrily.

Mr Pothackery stood there trembling. The Zamindar's nose was inches away from his face. 'Well I'm sure they couldn't have gone far, Sir. We'll go and look for them straight away.'

'And risk more lives, Charles?' said the Zamindar.

He was interrupted by one of the trial stewards. 'Mr Pothackery, Sir, look its Monty,' he said.

Monty then came running up to the hall and in through the door. He was shouting as he ran. 'Sir, Sir, you've got to come and help. Its Sananab and Cornelius, they've got Penelope. You've got to help. You've got to come quick before it's too late!' he said.

'Monty, thank heavens you are ok,' said Mr Pothackery. 'Where have you been?'

'Sir, you've got to come now, I think she's gonna die!' shouted Monty again.

'Monty, please slow down. Now what is this about Sananab and Cornelius? Tell me what has happened, son,' said his father.

Monty was still trying to catch his breath. 'They've got Loppy in the Corpus Callosum. Sananab and Cornelius have. They've got her in some chair, tied down and she said they're going to try to transfer her. They're doing it to her now. Father, you've got to come quick!'

'What? They've got Loppy? Well I'm coming too, Monty, she's my best friend and we promised that we were going to look after each other,' said Henry.

'Transfer? That's not possible, Monty. You must be confused, son, with everything else that is going on here. No, I'm not going anywhere near Sananab and Cornelius. I've got to defend the camp, and all of these trialists. My place is here with the Security Council. I'm sure your friend is not in any danger. Sananab is the ruler of The Will. He would not do her any harm,' said the Zamindar.

'Father, I mean it!' said Monty angrily. 'Transference is possible because they've already tried it. And they've already changed The Will too because it is going to die. And he *is* harming her right now, as we speak! You are the only one who can stop him.

This is bigger than your pathetic pride for your beloved Security Council. This is about real friendship, this is about standing up for what you believe in and doing what is right. If you don't come with me and Henry right now to help our friend, then you are no father of mine. I promise you that I will never speak to you ever again.'

Leopold Schmidt looked at his son in front of him. This was probably the longest conversation he had ever had with him. He was a bad father to his son, he knew this, but he also realised that this time, perhaps, he may have been able to put things right between them.

'Ok, very well. You can fill in the details on the way.' He turned towards Mr Pothackery. 'Charles, make sure that every single trialist is kept locked inside this hall with a skeleton crew of stewards until I return. Then take every other available steward that can fight to the Security Council building and take my place with my soldiers there. It looks like they are the only remaining faction left to fight as the others seemed to have conveniently distinguished themselves already. The sooner they are captured or killed, then the sooner this battle will be over.

Monty, Henry, you had better grab yourselves a sword and a shield from the guards at the door, just in case we meet any unruly bandits along the way. Come on, we have no time to lose!'

Monty and his father, followed by Henry Grip, shot out of the hall and headed back towards Central Head.

Mr Pothackery stood in the centre of the hall. 'So, my good friends, you heard the Zamindar, which of you will join me in battle?'

There was a unanimous response from the stewards.

'Right, all but ten of you follow me! Lets finish this gentlemin, tonight we protect the honour of the trials!' said Mr Pothackery.

He marched out of the hall with the volunteers behind him. They made their way to the Security Council to join in the fight.

Chapter Twenty-Two

The Neocortex was deserted. Even at this time of night there should have been a lot more min on duty but the news of the battle had spread like wildfire and most of the Central Head-workers were at home doing their best to protect their families.

The Zamindar, with his two young companions at his side, reached the Corpus Callosum. The two guards were standing outside of the door.

'Ah, Mr Schmidt, Sir, it is very good to see you again,' said one of the guards.

'Out of my way,' said the Zamindar, as he tried to enter the room.

The two guards immediately blocked his way with their swords.

'I'm afraid I can't let you in there, Sir, Sananab's orders,' said the other guard.

'I assure you that you do not want to make an enemy of me, gentlemin,' said the Zamindar.

'Er, sorry, Sir, but we have our orders,' said the first guard.

Henry and Monty had both heard about the reputation of the Zamindar, but had never witnessed it in person until now. He grabbed each of the guards by the throat and squeezed their necks until their eyes were about to pop out of their heads. Their swords clanged on the ground as they dropped from their hands. He then smacked their heads together with a crack, and they fell to the floor unconscious.

'Now you have made an enemy of me,' he said, as he looked down at their lifeless bodies.

Henry and Monty looked at each other with surprise. They were both extremely glad that he was on their side now. The Zamindar opened the door and the three of them went inside.

Penelope was sat in the chair. She was shouting and screaming at Sananab to let her go. He still had his hand pressed onto her head. Cornelius was cowering in the corner of the room. He wasn't so sure if this was a good idea or not.

Sananab looked up to see that the Zamindar had entered the room. 'Ah, Leopold, you have returned to see our work finally complete. Look my friend, it is working like a dream as we had planned it. She is about to transfer! We can do it!'

Monty and Henry both looked up towards the ceiling. The thousands of numbers, letters and symbols were cascading through the air, whizzing around each other at great speed. The very thoughts of The Will were mixing with the thoughts and emotions emanating from Penelope's head. It was as if there was some sort of magic at play. They were real, solid enough to even touch.

'No, Sananab, it has to stop here, it's not right. We spoke about this all those years ago. We're not meant to do this, we're not meant to know!' said the Zamindar.

'But we can't stop now, it's almost complete. She has nearly transferred. Her very thoughts are leaving her mind, as we speak. You can see them, look. She is fading away, she is almost gone! All of our efforts are about to be realised, we are succeeding!' said Sananab. He had a look of sheer determination on his face. His eyes glazed over with the power of thought.

'Mr Schmidt, Sir, you've got to help Loppy. Look, she needs you!' shouted Henry.

'She is beyond help now,' said Sananab coldly.

'No! I won't see it happen again. I will not let it happen this time,' said the Zamindar. He rushed over towards the chair.

Sananab watched the Zamindar coming towards him. 'Cornelius!' he shouted.

Cornelius leapt up on to the back of the Zamindar in order to try and stop him. The Zamindar plucked him from his shoulders with one hand and threw him to the ground. Henry rushed over to him and put his sword against his neck. The Thought Apprentice was kneeling on the floor, scared out of his wits.

'Father, you've got to help her, she's dying,' cried Monty desperately.

Sananab put his two hands around Penelope's throat.

'Don't come any closer, Leopold. I could kill her with one squeeze, and you know I'll do it if I have to,' he said.

'So this is what it has all been about, hasn't it? First it was the trip to the prison, and then Cornelius overseeing the trials. As if *he* could be trusted with something as important as that. You just needed me out of the way, didn't you? So you could do it again,' said the Zamindar.

'Leopold, it is still not too late for you, we can go together, you and I. The Will is going to end, you know that now. There is no use staying here, we can rule another Will together,' said Sananab.

All the time Penelope was growing visibly weaker, the life was draining from her, as her deepest thoughts were escaping from her mind.

'I'm afraid this is where my loyalty to you ends, oh mighty Sananab. It stops here, right now. I don't care what happens to The Will. I have realised that there are more important things to me now, like family and respect,' said the Zamindar.

'Ha, I should have known,' said Sananab. 'You are weak, Leopold, weak and pathetic. You are not worthy to stand beside me anyway.

You wish to talk about family? Then let us talk about family, shall we?

These two children you have brought with you are to be the recipients of your new found respect for family? You're only son who cannot even bear to be in the same room as you. All of his life he has been a complete disappointment to you, a burden you called him. He is a social misfit, a constant embarrassment to you. He has that much respect for you, my friend, that he doesn't even speak to you.

And then, there is his companion here, the young Mr Grip. The boy whose father you sent into exile for something that he didn't even do. You manipulated the facts and conjured up the whole courtroom performance so that it would look like he had done it. You framed an innocent man, and sent him away from his family. Now you want his respect?'

Henry, who had heard all of this, suddenly spoke out. 'Well if it's true what you say about Mr Schmidt, then so be it. But I know what he did to my father, and I have accepted it. One day soon, I will find him again then it will be ok. And I always knew that he was innocent all along, it doesn't matter to me where he is for now. Mr Schmidt is trying to help my best friend, so that's ok with me. He's ten times the min that you are any day!' he said.

'Ah, your little friend has forgiven you, Leopold, isn't that nice? Do you think he will still have the same amount of forgiveness when he learns you also sent his mother away to her death, fifteen years ago?' said Sananab, angrily.

Henry suddenly relaxed his grip on Cornelius. He started to become a little more interested as Sananab continued with his speech.

'Yes, when you turned your back on her all those years ago because she didn't reciprocate your pathetic love for her, you sent her to her grave! You abandoned her, Leopold Schmidt! You let your friend fall to her death because of your own selfish gain. Shall I go on, Leopold? Do you think your little friend still has any respect for you now? After he has learned that you have destroyed his entire family?'

Henry turned towards Leopold and raised his sword.

'No!' he screamed.

'Oh, yes!' shouted Sananab. 'Do it, boy, kill him now while you can!'

Henry lowered his sword.

'No, I won't do it, but I will kill you!' he said as he turned towards Sananab.

'I'm afraid it's too late for that, my boy. Instinct is here, all around us. It is happening right now. The window is about to open and soon I shall be free from The Will. It will only be a matter of seconds before I am gone.'

'But, Sir, you said you would take me with you, I am ready to go too, Master,' said Cornelius who was still kneeling on the floor.

'Ha! You pathetic little fool. Did you honestly believe I would take you with me? You really are an idiot, boy. Your Zamindar has trained you well.

No, you are welcome to your new and respectful, idealistic, family world, Leopold Schmidt, for I am no longer in need of it!'

With this, Sananab climbed up on to the back of the chair and jumped high into the air. There was a mass of visible thoughts spiralling around directly in front of him. He wrapped his cloak around the group of letters and pulled them into his body.

As he fell towards the ground, Henry ran towards the descending figure and plunged his sword towards him. Sananab snapped his fingers together and then there was silence.

The sword made a loud clang as it dropped to the ground. It was immediately followed by the empty cape which settled gently on top of it. Sananab had vanished. All of the spiralling numbers and letters had disappeared too, ceased to be. They had all simply vanished into thin air.

Monty slowly walked over to the spot where the objects had landed. He picked up the cape to reveal the sword lying there underneath. It was clean, and free from any blood. 'He's gone,' he said.

'Yes, Monty, transferred I believe,' said his father.

'What about Loppy?' said Henry.

The three of them ran over to the chair where Penelope was. They untied the ropes and tried to sit her up. She wasn't moving, but she was still alive.

'What's the matter with her, Mr Schmidt? Is she going to be ok?' said Henry, desperately.

'She'll be ok in a couple of hours. It takes a little while for the thoughts to come back properly. She'll have a blinding headache mind,' said the lady who had just walked into the room. She quietly shut the door behind her.

Everyone turned around to see who it was.

'It can't be. Mary, is that you?' said Leopold.

'I can't say that the years have been kind to you, Leo. You could do with going on a diet, my friend,' said the lady.

'It is you, Mary! Oh my word! Will's teeth,' said Leopold. 'But what, how, I mean what?'

'It is called an exchange, Leo. You see when a person is transferred, a piece of The Will is transferred with them. It is always there, inside their head. It can never be removed, and more importantly it is constantly longing for its return. However long it takes, the part of The Will inside the head will always fight for the opportunity to get back. Back to where it belongs.

So that's what I did. I waited for fifteen years, with this tiny piece of The Will hidden inside of me. I waited until there was an opening.

Fifteen years is a long time to wait for anything, I can assure you. I passed the time by trying to learn about it all, about transference and about instinct. The window, you see, is a two way thing. What Sananab didn't realise was that it not only lets things out but it also lets things back in. In fact I passed him on the way. He didn't look very happy, as it happens, but then I suppose he never did.'

'Hang on a minute, Mr Schmidt, and I'm really sorry to interrupt here but just what the hell is going on? Who is this?' said Henry.

Leopold Schmidt walked over to Henry. He put his arm around his shoulder. 'Henry my boy, this is your mother,' he said.

Mary dropped to her knees. 'What, you mean this is my Henry?' she said almost in tears.

Henry looked up at Leopold. 'What?' he said.

'Yes, it's true, Henry,' said Leopold.

Henry ran over to his mother and they embraced each other tightly.

'Oh, Henry, I've waited so long for this moment. And look at you. You're so big and handsome too. I bet you're fighting all of the girls away, aren't you? And that is a trial uniform that you're wearing if I'm not mistaken. Oh I'm so proud of you. And your father, how is my beloved George?' she said.

'He's, er, fine. He's gone looking for you, in fact. But I don't understand?' said Henry. 'What happened? Where did you go? Sananab said that you were dead, and that Mr Schmidt turned his back on you, and that you were gone forever. I mean why did he say all of that stuff, what does it all mean?'

'Well, Henry, I'm afraid some of it is true. Mr Schmidt did turn his back on me, but I rather think that he has slightly made up for that by doing what he has done today, don't you? And I know he will do his upmost to carry on making up for it from now on too.' Mary looked at the Zamindar for a response.

'Yeah, too bloody right he will. Things are going to change around here, that's for sure,' he said as he nodded to her. He walked over to Monty and put his arm around his son.

'Fifteen years ago, I wanted knowledge. I wanted to know a lot of things, Henry, but I now realise that I wanted to know too much. I've had fifteen years to think about it and what I now realise is that I already had everything that a girl could ever wish for, a family and friends to rely on. That's what's important, Henry, and that's what makes all the difference in the end,' said Mary.

'But where have you been? Is it true that you got transferred?' said Henry.

'Yes, it is true. Sananab transferred me to another Will fifteen years ago. In fact, where I went to was very similar to here in many ways, only it wasn't called The Will, it was called The Wanda. It was ok and most of the min there were really nice but it wasn't home. I missed home so much, Henry, especially you and your father.

Mind you, they didn't really go in for all of that union nonsense like they do here, which was quite a pleasant change actually. That reminds me, how is Snap Potts doing? Still got his stupid hat on all the time?'

'Yes, Mother, he has,' laughed Henry. 'In fact speaking of the Potts family, they have been looking after me for the last few weeks, ever since Father went out looking for you. That's my best friend over there, that's Penelope Potts.'

'Oh, darling Penelope, I haven't seen her since she was a baby,' said

Mary. She got up and went over to the chair where Penelope was, she was still knocked out. 'How beautiful she looks, Maggie must be so proud. I bet Snap would be having kittens if he knew she was up here in Central Head though, wouldn't he? Come on, Leo, let's get this girl sorted out before she wakes up and finds that her mind has run off somewhere without her knowledge. We need to take her home, to where she belongs.'

'Father, what are we going to do about him?' said Monty pointing to Cornelius Crail. He was still cowering on all fours in the corner of the room.

'Ah the contemptible Mr Crail, I forgot about him, yes. That is a good question, Monty. Now what indeed shall we do with him?' said the Zamindar.

Sunday 11th November, 1:33 a.m. Carotid Hill, Mount Thalamus Bay.

The last of the Regio-Mentalis bandits to attempt to take on the might of Ollie Gimble was Chinner. He didn't exactly fancy his chances, seeing that half of the mercenaries who had attempted the same thing were now lying face down in the river, and the other half of them had long since fled.

'So you're the last one then are you, Mr Chinner?' said Ollie.

'Yeah I am, and you don't frighten me neither you big oaf,' said Chinner as he squared up to the giant.

Raymond Curley was standing on the grass next to his friend. He was feeling rather brave, but considering that Ollie had done the majority of the job without his help already, it didn't make a great deal of difference how confident he was feeling. His bravado was apparent, nonetheless.

'Ooh, I tell you what, Mr Chinner, that last person to call my mate, Ollie Gimble, a big oaf got a right good kicking, and I reckon you're next for the boot, buddy!' he said.

'Oh yeah, you do, do you?' said Chinner. 'And there's no mister, it's just Chinneeeeeeerrrrrrrrrrrr!'

That last syllable to the end of his name was still ringing out as he landed thirty feet away in the river. Ollie had indeed given him the boot. In fact it was his large right boot that had connected with a rather fleshy part of Chinner's anatomy, a part which was located directly between his legs.

'Oohh that's got to hurt that, Ollie. Ha, ha right in the goolies!' said Curley. 'Oh I tell you what, son, that was some kick that. Did you see his face? Ha, ha!'

'Yeah, but it don't make no difference does it, Curley? We've lost our mate, haven't we?' said Ollie as he turned towards their fallen friend.

They both walked over to the patch of grass where the body of Stony Pickles was laying.

Curley began to speak. 'Yeah I know, mate, but we did him proud in the end, didn't we? We showed them what we were all about. He didn't die in vain, my mate. He died with honour and dignity, and on the battlefield standing up for what he believed in. We will make it known that Stony Pickles died a true hero. He will become a testament to the good people of the Luglands. His name will be revered amongst everyone in our fair land...'

'Ah, tell him to shurrup will you, Ollie, he's giving me a bloomin' headache,' said Stony Pickles from the ground. 'I tell you what though, boys, I reckon I'll have to have at least a month off work with this head, you know? It is absolutely killing me!'

He opened his eyes.

'Stony, you're not killed!' said Ollie, in disbelief.

'Course I'm not killed, Ollie. I've got the mother of all headaches though. Jeez, you're gonna have to get me to a doctor or someone who knows what they're doing with bloody heads,' said Stony as he rubbed his head.

'But, I can't believe it, Stony. We thought you were dead,' said Curley.

'I thought I was bloomin' dead when you were going on about all that bloody hero lark. What the hell is a testament when it's at home anyway? Never bleeding heard of one of them before. I thought I'd died and gone to some bloomin poncey heaven or something. Never heard you talk like that before, Curley. What's up with you?'

'Well I don't know, it just sort of came out like, don't know where from,' said Curley.

'Well my mate's not dead anyway, so I'm happy now, Stony!' said Ollie with a huge smile on his face.

'Thanks, Ollie, you're a good mate. But I really do need to get someone to look at my head and fast, I'm not kidding, boys,' said Stony.

'Ollie, come on we'll take him up to the camp. There's bound to be somebody there who can help us,' said Curley.

'Ok, Curley,' said Ollie. He picked up Stony in his huge arms and began to carry him up the hill towards Hippocampus.

'Aw, you missed it all as well, Stony. You should have seen Ollie go! He was slapping those mental fellas into the water like no one's business. They're all gone, every single one of them,' said Curley.

'And what about Quick, what happened to him?' said Stony.

'Ah don't you worry about him, Stony. We've definitely seen that last of that horrible little weed,' said Curley. 'Ollie saw to that!'

As they reached Hippocampus, the battle for the Security Council was over. Mr Pothackery and the Security Council soldiers were standing over the bandits. The few that were left had been taken prisoner, and were kneeling down on the ground in front of them. Their hands and feet were tied together so that they couldn't escape. Most of the other bandits had either fled or been wounded elsewhere.

Mr Pothackery spotted the Lugland trio as they approached the camp. 'Hey, I do believe that is the chap who conquered the entire army single-handedly earlier on, down by the river,' he said.

'What do you mean single handedly? I helped and all you know?' said Curley, quite put out that his part had not been acknowledged.

'Sir, our friend is hurt. Can you help to make him better, Sir?' said Ollie as he got nearer.

'Oh my word, this min has lost an awful lot of blood,' said Mr Pothackery as he saw the injury to Stony. 'Quick, we must get him to the sick bay at once. Jon, can you please escort our friends to the sick bay, this min needs treatment right away. Mr Titan will know what to do.'

Curley and Ollie, with Stony in his arms, followed the steward towards the sick bay.

'Can't believe he never gave me any credit for the battle, the cheek of it!' said Curley as they walked.

'Ah shurrup, Curley, you're doing my head in now,' said Stony.

'Yeah and mine, and you never done nothing anyway,' added Ollie.

'Yeah, I bloody did!'

No sooner had they turned the corner, Leopold Schmidt suddenly came into view. He was also carrying somebody in need of the sick bay. He had Penelope Potts in his arms. He was closely followed by Mary, Henry and Monty.

'Charles, Penelope needs some rest. She is ok but she needs to get to the sick bay where she can be tended to properly. Henry and Monty will accompany her, along with Mary here. After all, she is the expert in these matters,' said Leopold.

He smiled at Mary. She winked at him in return.

'Yes, Sir, certainly,' said Mr Pothackery. He gestured to another of the stewards. 'Peter, can you take Penelope to the sick bay at once, please? Mr Titan is going to have a busy night, that's for sure.'

The steward took Penelope from the hands of Leopold Schmidt. Mary, Henry and Monty followed him to the sick bay.

The Zamindar walked across to where the captured rebels had been placed on the ground.

'Now let me see what delightful folk we have here then,' he said. 'Ah, do my eyes deceive me? Is this none other than the escaped prisoner, Mr Jeremiah Yanich? Leader of the Oesophagus Forest bandits, no less. I thought you may have been behind something like this.'

'I see you have lost none of your usual charm, Mr Schmidt,' said Mr Yanich.

'Indeed, Sir, indeed. I think we should let you have your old cell once again, Mr Yanich. Yes, would that suit you this time around? I'm sure you will remember where everything is, at least,' said the Zamindar, sarcastically.

'I will take my punishment as a gentlemin, Mr Schmidt, as that is what I am. But not before you have answered me one question.'

'And that is?'

'Just what the hell is going to happen to The Will in three years time?' asked Mr Yanich.

The Zamindar had a look of concern on his face.

'Yes, that was something that we were all rather wondering about as well Leopold,' said Mr Pothackery. 'Is it true what everyone is saying? Is The Will really going to die?'

'Well that's something that we are just going to have to worry about in the morning, isn't it Charles?' said Leopold. He turned towards his soldiers. 'Security Council, please take these prisoners to the Stomachic Sea. They won't be seeing the light of day for a long, long time.'

Leopold put his arm around Mr Pothackery. 'Now, Charles, I've decided that there are going to be one or two changes around here from now on, I feel this is perhaps a good time for me to, how shall I put it? Turn over a new leaf.'

They walked off towards Fornix Hall. The sun was beginning to rise over Mount Thalamus Bay. Leopold Schmidt started to whistle, a tune that he had not whistled for a very long time. A happy tune with happy memories.

Chapter Twenty-Three

Wednesday 14th November, 9:40 a.m. Mount Thalamus Bay, Central Head.

It was morning. Mornings were always the best time of the day for the min. Everyone looked forward to what the new day would bring to them. A new morning generally brought a fresh approach to things, but it could also have had something to do with the fact that mornings always started with breakfast.

It is said that if a min is standing anywhere in The Will, no matter where it is, at any time of day or night, there is always a sandwich no more than six feet away from them. Most min however think that this is untrue, as there would most probably be one much closer than that, normally tucked up inside their jacket pocket.

This particular morning was going to bring a distinctly fresh approach to many things, for a number of reasons. There had been a shift in Personnel. Central Head had a new ruler. A ruler who himself had his own personal reasons for bringing a fresh approach to things. He was going to make up for many years of not being very nice to people, and the process had already started. However, it would probably take an awful long time to right the wrongs of the past. Most min had long memories. Still, somehow the sky looked a little brighter.

Henry, Penelope and Monty were standing on the magnificent golden bridge which stretched across Mount Thalamus Bay. They were stood in the centre section, looking down into the blood red river below.

The busy ships of Central Head were going about their daily business, bringing passengers and cargo in and out of the bay.

'It certainly has been an eventful few weeks, hasn't it?' said Henry.

'Yeah, you could say that, Henry. Just a little bit,' said Penelope.

'I think that is an understatement, don't you?' said Monty.

'How is your headache, Loppy, still hurting?' said Henry.

'Yes, Henry, it's still hurting, but it's getting better all the time.'

'What I still don't understand is why Sananab wanted to transfer you from The Will first Loppy? If he knew how to do it, then why didn't he just go himself ages ago?' said Henry.

'Well I think it was because ages ago, Henry, he didn't know about The Will coming to an end. He always wanted to transfer eventually, yes, but he thought that he had plenty of time to do it. Discovering that The Will was going to die sort of made him get a move on I guess,' said Penelope.

'Do you really think that it's true, Penelope, about The Will dying in three years time? Do you really think it will happen?' said Monty.

'Oh I don't know, Monty. Maybe it will and maybe it won't. But I don't think that Sananab would have gone to all that trouble if it wasn't true, do you?'

'No, I suppose there is that, Penelope. And he certainly went to a lot of trouble to set it all up, didn't he?' replied Monty.

'So do you think he deliberately allowed all of that stuff to happen? Just so that he could transfer himself?' said Henry.

'Father said that Sananab knew I was in the room the day he told him about changing The Will, and he knew that I would write it all down in my diary. And on the day of the hearing, when you two scared me in the courtroom, it was his own personal guards who chased you that day, and it was them who were ordered to *let* the diary fall into the wrong hands. He did it deliberately, knowing that it would cause a diversion, and a brilliant diversion it was too. All of that just so that he could carry on with his obsession without anybody getting in his way,' said Monty.

'But that still doesn't explain why he wanted to transfer you though, does it Loppy?' said Henry. 'I mean even if he did know The Will was going to end, and he also knew how to transfer himself, then why didn't he just go? Why did he have to involve you in all of this?'

'Well, he told Cornelius he needed to transfer *me* first so that he could choose the destination, to see if he could actually *do* it. He said that when he transferred Mary all those years ago, he didn't know where she was going to end up. But that wasn't going to be nearly good enough for his own transference. He wanted to choose his path, and choose it carefully.'

'Oh,' said Henry.

'But when I spoke to Mary about it, she said that wasn't right. It couldn't have been. You see he needed *me* in order to transfer himself. He needed to use *my* thoughts against the thoughts of The Will, so that the window of opportunity could be opened for *him*. He couldn't have done it by himself, because he needed to use somebody else's thoughts to open it. Just like fifteen years ago when he transferred Mary, he used his *own* thoughts to open it then, so that she would be the one to go. But he couldn't have used his own thoughts this time because it wouldn't have worked. And he couldn't have used Cornelius's thoughts because he didn't have the gift of being able to listen to the nerves, and even if he did he would have wanted to use the power for himself anyway. It had to be someone with a thirst for knowledge, someone with the gift, but someone who didn't want to use the instinct for their own gain,' said Penelope.

'I think you're right about Cornelius, he would have definitely tried to use the power for himself,' said Henry.

'Father told me why Sananab took everything out of the Corpus Callosum and put it his office too,' said Monty. 'He said that he wanted to absorb the sheer power of everything that was in that room, but he couldn't have stayed near the chronicles because they were written by the Tri-min for one purpose and for one purpose only, for the good of The Will.

It is written in the chronicles that transference goes against the good of The Will. That's why Mary said that there was always a part of The Will which was trying to get back. It is because it was never meant to leave it in the first place. Sananab knew that because he had read it in the chronicles.'

'So what happens now then? I don't suppose everyone is just going to ignore the fact that we could all die in three years time, are they? Are we supposed to just carry on as normal?' said Henry.

'Father says that they are going to do everything in their power to get to the bottom of it and try to work out what the best thing to do about it is. After all, nobody knows if it's true or not anyway, do they? People have predicted many things in the past, and they have never come true.'

'Who would ever have predicted that you would gain your father back Monty, and you would see your mother again Henry? That is the best thing to have come out of all this, after all!'

'Yes, you're right there, Loppy,' said Henry and Monty at exactly the same time.

The three of them laughed together.

'Where is your mother now anyway, Henry?' said Monty.

'Oh she's gone to look for my father. She said that she's waited fifteen years to see him, so she doesn't mind a few more months. She'll find him eventually, she said. She also said it might take her a few months to clean up the house first anyway! What about you Monty? How are things with Mr Schmidt?'

'Oh things are good at the moment, Henry, yes. He said he wants to take me fishing?' replied Monty.

'Fishing?' said Penelope. 'Isn't that where you tie a piece of string to the end of a pole, dangle it in the river for a few hours, and then nothing ever happens?'

'Yes, I think so. I expect he thinks it will be a good chance to talk though, eh?' said Monty.

'Yes, Monty, talking is good,' said Penelope.

'Does anyone know what happened to Cornelius, by the way?' said Henry.

'Oh yeah, I forgot about him,' said Penelope.

'No, Henry, nobody has seen him since the other night. He has disappeared somewhere. Father says he will come crawling back one day though. His type always does,' said Monty.

'Yeah, his type always does,' Henry added.

The three friends looked out across the bay.

It was another busy day in Central Head. The tiny figures below were milling around the place and churning along with their daily routine. The residents of Mount Thalamus Bay were always busy doing something or another and this day was no different.

However, three of the diminutive figures below somehow didn't seem nearly as busy as the others around them. In fact they seemed to be a little lost.

One of them had a giant white bandage wrapped around his head, and was walking slightly ahead of the other two.

'I can't believe we're bloomin' lost again, Curley. You said it was here!' said Stony Pickles.

'No I never, I said it was over there where the river is,' said Raymond Curley. 'That's where you get boats, innit, on the bloomin' river, dummy! I reckon that knock on the head has affected you, you know, Stony.'

'All's I know is that I haven't had any grub for ages, and I'm a growing lad you know? My mamma says I've got to eat as much as I can to keep me strong,' said Ollie Gimble.

'Ah shurrup, Ollie!' said the other two in unison.

The three friends from the Luglands stumbled on towards the river. After they had walked a few yards further, Stony Pickles stopped near a small bush. He noticed that there was something hidden underneath it. He bent down to see what it was. He reached out his hand and picked up the mysterious object. It was a small book.

He called out to the other two who had meandered slightly ahead of him. 'Hey, boys, look what I've found, I think it's a book of some kind, see.' He waved it in the air in front of him. 'Hey, it could be valuable this, boys. I reckon there could be something in this, you know?'

Ollie and Curley spun around together. They both shouted to their friend.

'No!'

'No!'

'Ah, I suppose you're right,' said Stony. He looked at the book again, then promptly tossed it over his shoulder and ran off towards the other two. 'Hang on, boys, wait for me, eh?'

The book dropped into in a small ditch, next to the bush where it had come from. As it landed, the book fell open, with its pages facing up into the air. The early morning breeze, which flowed through the bay, gently blew across its pages as they playfully flicked back and forth.

There was a hand, awash with dust and dirt, which crept out from underneath the bush. Its thin, bony fingers were damaged with fresh cuts and bruises. Specks of blood were clearly visible on the edge of the torn black sleeve, which covered the wrist. Its wiry fingers grasped hold of the edge of the book and dragged it slowly back into the bush.

The End

Lightning Source UK Ltd.
Milton Keynes UK
UKOW03f1426070314

227749UK00001B/1/P